John Case is the [ ] d-wife
writing team of [ ] ey have
written three pre[ ] ational bestsellers together,
The Genesis Code, The First Horseman and *Trance State*.
They live in Virginia. Jim Hougan is an award-winning
investigative journalist.

Praise for John Case

"A stimulating mixture of suspense, startling and
enjoyable turns of plot, and, not least, good writing"
NORMAN MAILER

"Always intriguing . . . Case delivers a top-notch yarn
filled with fascinating details . . . delivers the thrills even
as it throws in some food for thought"
Chicago Tribune

"Entirely plausible . . . highly recommended"
Punch

"*Trance State* is full of the kind of ripples that
distinguish is a good paranoid thriller, and doesn't stint
on the enjoyable process of winding up its characters
and watching them go"
Guardian

"A glass-shattering, diesel-fueled, hard-charging thrill
ride of a read . . . [John Case is] a confident master
working at peak performance"
LORENZO CARCATERRA, author of *Sleepers*

Also by John Case

The Genesis Code
The First Horseman
Trance State

THE EIGHTH DAY

John Case

arrow books

Published by Arrow Books in 2002

1 3 5 7 9 10 8 6 4 2

First published in the United Kingdom in 2002 by Century

Arrow Books
The Random House Group Limited
20 Vauxhall Bridge Road, London, SW1V 2SA

Random House Australia (Pty) Limited
20 Alfred Street, Milsons Point, Sydney,
New South Wales 2061, Australia

Random House New Zealand Limited
18 Poland Road, Glenfield
Auckland 10, New Zealand

Random House (Pty) Limited
Endulini, 5a Jubilee Road, Parktown 2193, South Africa

The Random House Group Limited Reg. No. 954009

www.randomhouse.co.uk

A CIP catalogue record for this book
is available from the British Library

Papers used by Random House are natural, recyclable products made
from wood grown in sustainable forests. The manufacturing processes
conform to the environmental regulations of the country of origin

ISBN 0 09 941649 2

Typeset in Sabon by SX Composing DTP, Rayleigh, Essex
Printed and bound in Great Britain by
Cox & Wyman Ltd, Reading, Berkshire

For Elaine

One

It was the mailman who reported it, calling 911 half an hour before Delaney's shift was supposed to end.

The pickup was sitting in the driveway and there were lights on in the house, so the mailman thought someone must be home. But it had been days now, and still no one answered when he knocked. The mailbox was filled to overflowing. So maybe, he figured, maybe Mr. Terio had suffered a heart attack.

Delaney shook his head and swore at the mailman's timing. Brent had a play-off game at six, and it was five after five already. Helen would kill him. *(You've got to be there for him, Jack! Show a little support! What's more important – your own son or your buddies at the station?)* Well, actually . . . the truth was, he *liked* to go to his son's games. Brent was a good player – better than he had ever been – and it was fun to bask in the kid's reflected glory. When things were going well, Brent didn't really need him there. But when the kid screwed up – well, his son was one intense little guy. Took his own failure way too hard. And Helen didn't have a clue how to help the kid handle it. *(Will you stop that crying! It's just a game.)* So Delaney liked to be there – especially for a big game. But his chances of making it were fading. He and Poliakoff were all the way to hell and gone, way out by the county line where civilization turned to kudzu.

Sitting behind the wheel, Poliakoff gave Delaney a sidelong glance and chuckled. "Don't sweat it. You want to use the siren?"

Delaney shook his head.

"The guy's probably on vacation," Poliakoff insisted. "We'll take a look around – I'll write it up. No problem."

Delaney gazed out the window. The air was heavy and still, thick with gloom, the way it gets before a thunderstorm. "Maybe it'll rain," he muttered.

Poliakoff nodded. "That's the spirit," he told him. "Think positive."

The cruiser turned onto Barracks Road and, suddenly, though they were barely a mile past a subdivision of bright new town houses, there was nothing in sight but vine-strangled woods and farmland. The occasional rotting barn.

"You ever been out this way?" Poliakoff asked.

Delaney shrugged. "That's it, over there," he said, nodding at a metal sign stippled with bullet holes. PREACHERMAN LANE. "You gotta turn."

They found themselves on a narrow dirt road, flanked by weeds and at the edge of a dense wood. "Jesus," Poliakoff muttered as the cruiser crested a rise, then bottomed out with a thud before he could brake. "Since when does Fairfax County have dirt roads?"

"We still got a couple," Delaney replied, thinking the roads wouldn't be around much longer. The Washington suburbs were metastasizing in every direction and had been for twenty years. In a year or two, the farmhouse up ahead – a yellow farmhouse, suddenly visible on the left – would be gone, drowned by a rising tide of town houses, Wal-Marts, and Targets.

The mailbox was at the end of the driveway, a battered aluminum cylinder with a faded red flag nailed to the top of a four-by-four T set in concrete. A name was stenciled on the side: C. TERIO.

Next to the mailbox, three or four newspapers were jammed into a white plastic tube that bore the words THE WASHINGTON POST. A dozen other editions lay on the ground in a neatish pile, some already turning yellow.

When the mailman had reached out to 911, he'd suggested, "You should go in, take a look around the house, see what you can see."

But of course, they couldn't exactly do that. Under the circumstances, the most they could do was knock on the door, walk around the property, talk to the neighbors – not that there were any, far as Delaney could tell.

Climbing out of the cruiser, the deputies stood for a moment, watching and listening. Thunder rumbled in the south, and they could hear the distant hum of the Beltway. With a grin, Poliakoff sang in his cracking baritone, "H-e-e-ere we come to save the da-a-yyyy –"

"Let's get this over with," Delaney grumbled, setting off toward the house.

They passed an aging Toyota Tacoma at the end of the driveway, its rear end backed toward the house as if its owner had been loading or unloading something. Together the two policemen crossed the overgrown lawn to the front door.

The knocker was a fancy one – hand-hammered iron in the shape of a dragonfly. Poliakoff put his fist around it, drew back, and rapped loudly. "Hullo?"

Silence.

"Hel-lo?" Poliakoff cocked his head and listened

3

hard. When no reply came, he tried the door and, finding it locked, gave a little shrug. "Let's go around back." Together the deputies made their way around the side of the house, pausing every so often to peer through the windows.

"He left enough lights on," Delaney observed.

At the rear of the house, they passed a little garden – tomatoes and peppers, zucchini and pole beans – that might have been tidy once but was now abandoned to weeds. Nearby, a screen door led into the kitchen. Poliakoff rapped on its wooden frame four or five times. "Anyone home? Mr. Terio! You in there?"

Nothing.

Or almost nothing. The air trembled with the on-again, off-again rasp of cicadas and, in the distance, the insectoid murmur of traffic. And there was something else, something . . . Delaney cocked his head and listened hard. He could hear . . . laughter. Or not laughter, actually, but . . . a laugh *track*. After a moment, he said, "The television's on."

Poliakoff nodded.

Delaney sighed. No *way* he was going to get to Brent's baseball game. He could feel it.

Even so, there was nothing they could do, really. The doors were locked and they didn't have a warrant. There was no real evidence of a medical emergency, much less of foul play. But it *was* suspicious, and since they were already out here, they might as well take a look around. Be thorough about it.

Poliakoff walked back to where the newspapers were piled up, squatted, and sorted through them. The oldest was dated July 19 – more than two weeks ago.

A few feet away, Delaney checked out the truck in the driveway. On the front seat he found a faded and sun-curled receipt for a cash purchase at Home Depot. It, too, was dated July 19 and listed ten bags of Sakrete, 130 cinder blocks, a mortaring tool, and a plastic tub.

"A real do-it-yourselfer," he remarked, showing the receipt to Poliakoff, then reaching into the cruiser to retrieve his notebook.

"I'll check around the other side of the house," Poliakoff told him.

Delaney nodded and leaned back against the cruiser, going through the motions of making notes. Not that there was much to put down.

August 3
C. Terio
2602 Preacherman Lane
Oldest paper—July 19
Home Depot receipt, same date

He looked at his watch and noted the time: 5:29. The whole thing was a waste of time, no matter how you looked at it. Delaney had responded to a couple of hundred calls like this during his ten years with the department, and nine times out of ten the missing person was senile or off on a bender. Once in a while, they turned up dead, sprawled on the bathroom floor or sitting in the BarcaLounger. This kind of thing wasn't really *police work*. It was more like a janitorial service.

"Hey."

Delaney looked up. Poliakoff was calling to him from the other side of the house. Tossing the notebook onto the front seat of the cruiser, he glanced at the sky – there was a curtain of rain off to the south, which gave him more hope that Brent's game would be rained

5

out – and headed off in the direction of his partner.

As it happened, there was an outside entrance to the basement – a set of angled metal doors that opened directly onto a short flight of concrete steps, leading down. Poliakoff was standing on the steps, the doors at attention on either side of him, like rusted wings. "Whaddya think? We take a look?"

Delaney frowned and inclined his head toward one of the doors. "That the way you found them?"

Poliakoff nodded. "Yeah. Wide open."

Delaney shrugged. "Could be a burglary, I guess – but let's make it quick." He was thinking, *Dear God, don't let there be a stiff down there, or we'll be here all night.*

Poliakoff ducked his head, calling out Terio's name as he descended the steps, Delaney right behind him.

The basement was utilitarian – a long rectangular room with a seven-foot ceiling, cinder-block walls, and a cement floor. A single fluorescent light buzzed and flickered over a dusty tool bench in a corner of the room. A moth beat its wings against the fixture.

Delaney glanced around. Nervously. He didn't like basements. He'd been afraid of them ever since he'd been a kid, though nothing had ever really happened to him in one. They just creeped him out. And this place, with its cheap shelves crowded with cans of paint, boxes of nails and screws, and tools, it was like every basement he'd ever seen: ordinary and evil, all at once.

Poliakoff wrinkled his nose.

"You smell something?" Delaney asked, his eyes searching the cellar.

"Yeah, I think so," his partner said. "Sort of."

On a shelf beneath the tool bench Delaney noticed a red plastic container marked: MOWER FUEL. "It's probably gas," he told his partner.

Poliakoff shook his head. "Unh-unh."

Delaney shrugged. "Whatever," he said, "there's no one here." Turning to leave, he started for the steps but stopped when he realized that Poliakoff wasn't following him. "Whatcha got?" he asked, looking back to his partner, who was holding a Maglite at shoulder height, its powerful beam funneling into the farthest corner of the room.

"I'm not sure," Poliakoff muttered, crossing the basement to where the flashlight's beam splashed against the far wall. "It's weird."

Delaney looked at the wall and realized Poliakoff was right: it *was* weird. At the north end of the basement, a corner was partitioned off by what looked like a pair of hastily built cinder-block walls. At right angles to each other, the walls were each about four feet across and went floor-to-ceiling, creating a sort of concrete closet, a closet without a door. "What *is* that?" Delaney asked.

Poliakoff shook his head and moved closer.

The closet – or whatever it was – was amateurishly made. Blobs of mortar bulged between the cinder blocks, which were stacked in a half-assed way that wasn't quite plumb. The deputies stared at the construction. Finally, Poliakoff said, "It's like . . . it's like a little jackleg *room*!"

Delaney nodded, then ran a hand through his thick brown hair. "It's probably what he did with the Home Depot stuff. He must have –"

"You smell it now?" Poliakoff asked.

Delaney sniffed. Even though he'd been a smoker most of his life, there was no mistaking the stink in the air. He'd spent two years in a Graves Registration unit at Dover Air Force Base and, if nothing else, he knew what death smelled like.

"Could be a rat," Poliakoff suggested. "They get in the walls. . . ."

Delaney shook his head. His heart was beating harder now, the adrenaline coursing through his chest. He took a deep breath and examined the construction more closely.

The sloppiest part was closest to the ceiling – where the top row of cinder blocks lay crookedly upon the lower course, mortar dripping from the joints. Delaney picked off a piece and crushed it between his thumb and forefinger.

"You don't think this guy . . . ?" Poliakoff let the sentence trail away as Delaney crossed the basement to the workbench and came back with a hammer and a screwdriver. "Maybe we'd better call this in."

Delaney nodded. "I know," he said, and began to chip away at the mortar, using the screwdriver as a chisel, sending a little spray of grit into the air. Poliakoff fretted about "disturbing the scene," but his partner was in the grip of something, his heart almost racing. "We're the investigating officers," he muttered. "So I'm investigating."

It only took a minute, and then the cinder block was more or less free of its binding. Hitting it one more time with the hammer, Delaney broke the block loose. Then he laid his tools on the floor and, reaching up, wiggled the block back and forth.

As it came free, a stench rose up, so pungent that Delaney could almost taste it – as if he'd touched the tip of his tongue to the place in his gum where a rotten tooth had just been extracted.

"Gimme a hand," he ordered, and with Poliakoff's

help he removed the block from the wall and set it on the floor. By now, there was no doubt in either man's mind about what waited behind the wall, but they still couldn't see – the opening was too high. Taking up the hammer and screwdriver, Delaney went to work on a second cinder block, attacking it with a kind of desperation – even as he held his breath. Soon this second cinder block was free, so that there was now a window into the little room, just above Delaney's head.

Poliakoff was doing his best to keep his stomach still as Delaney looked around for something to stand on. He saw a straight-backed chair near the basement doors and dragged it over. Delaney climbed up on it and took the Maglite from his belt. Then he cast its beam through the window he'd created – and fell silent. From somewhere above, the laugh track surged.

"So what is it?" Poliakoff demanded. "What –"

Delaney swayed. "I'm gonna be sick," he said. And he was.

The medical examiner arrived about forty minutes later, accompanied by a homicide detective, three deputies, a forensics technician, and the meat wagon. An aging Ichabod Crane, the ME stood about six-two and 140 pounds. Judging by the deeply jaundiced tint to his fingers, Delaney figured he'd been chain-smoking since birth.

The storm hit a few minutes later, riding a strobe of lightning and volleys of thunder. Sheets of rain began to fall as one of the deputies erected a brace of lights in front of what everyone was now calling the tomb. Nearby, a second deputy dusted for prints while a third recorded the scene with a camera, its flash mimicking the lightning outside. Finally, the ME suggested that the tomb should be partially dismantled, so that he could examine the body.

It was, after all, a murder scene – or that, at least, was the presumption. Unless and until the ME determined otherwise, suicides and accidental deaths were treated by the police as homicides.

"What a corker," the ME muttered.

Delaney nodded somberly and handed the detective a list that he and Poliakoff had made, enumerating the surfaces that each of them had touched: the doors to the house, front and back; the newspaper and mailbox; the door to the truck; and one of the windows on the side of the house. Hammer and screw-driver, the cinder blocks and light switch. The receipt from Home Depot.

"What kinda sick son of a bitch would do something like this?" Delaney wondered, as much to himself as anyone else.

The ME lit a cigarette and threw him a look. "What do you mean?"

Delaney frowned. "What do I mean? I mean . . . what do you *think* I mean? They buried him alive, for chrissake!"

"Who did?"

Delaney's frown deepened. Was the ME an idiot? "How do I know? Whoever *did* it. All I'm sayin' is –"

"He probably did it himself."

Delaney stared at the man, uncomprehending.

The detective chimed in. "Look at the mortar," he said, nodding toward the cinder block. "The tailings are all on the *in*side. So's the tub. And the trowel. Bags of Sakrete."

"You're saying he built it *himself*?" Delaney asked.

"Looks like it."

Delaney cast his eyes toward the tomb, which was almost open now. The deceased was sitting on the floor with his back to the wall, legs splayed, eyes wide. "*No*. Why would anyone do that?" Delaney asked. He didn't believe it. Even the trowel, lying on the floor at the dead man's feet, didn't prove a thing. Who's to say there wasn't a second trowel, a second tub, another bag of Sakrete?

The ME didn't answer him at first. Instead, he told the deputy that enough cinder block had been removed. When the deputy stepped aside, the ME inched into the little room, crouched, and snapped on a pair of surgical gloves. Then he began to search the dead man's pockets. "People kill themselves for dozens of reasons," he mused. "Sometimes, there's a lot of self-hatred." Extracting a wallet from the pocket of the dead man, he flipped it open and peered at the man's driver's license. "Terio. *T* as in *Tom*, -*e-r-i-o*. Who's taking notes?"

One of the deputies said that he was.

"First name: Christian; middle name: Anthony. D-O-B: six-eleven-fifty-three." The ME placed the wallet in a transparent plastic Baggie, sighed, and shone a penlight in the dead man's eyes. "Had a case two years ago," he said. "Guy decapitated himself – cut off his own head!"

"Bullshit!" Poliakoff exclaimed, coming down the stairs. "How you gonna do that?"

"Well," the ME told them, "the way *he* did it, he tied a rope around a tree and looped the other end around his neck. Then he got in his car and floored it. Had a Camaro, so it came off pretty clean."

"But . . . *why*?" Delaney wondered.

11

The ME shook his head and continued to examine the body. "Depression."

Poliakoff guffawed – "*I'll* say!" – and Delaney, disgusted, walked outside, into the rain. It only took him a second to reach his cruiser and get in, but that was enough time to get soaked. Sitting there, with the rain clobbering the roof, he studied the water pearling on the windshield and tried not to think about the basement.

But that was impossible. What he'd seen had rattled him. He had a touch of claustrophobia himself – maybe more than a touch – and the idea of sitting in the dark, waiting to die in that jackleg crypt, was the stuff of nightmares.

And if the ME was right about it being a suicide, then – the idea skittered through Delaney's head like an insect scurrying from a drain – that made it even worse.

Because this guy, Terio, had obviously changed his mind. Delaney was sure of it. The first thing he'd seen in the flashlight's beam was the dead man's hands – or what was left of them. The fingers were stumps, the nails worn away, the torn flesh crusty with blood.

So he'd been trying to get out, Delaney figured. Alone in the dark, he'd tried to claw his way through the stone.

Two

The car – Caleigh's sensible Saturn – was well built, Danny thought. Here they were, five miles out of Nag's Head, cruising back to Washington at sixty-two miles per hour, and you couldn't even hear the road beneath the tires. In fact, you couldn't hear *anything*. And that, of course, was precisely the point. Riding in the passenger's seat with his eyes on the flat Carolina landscape, Danny was the target of an unmistakable Meaningful Silence.

Which was completely unfair. They'd had a great time in the rental cottage. Just the two of them, a block from the beach. They'd ridden his Boogie board, splashed in the surf, basked in the sun. They'd danced till two A.M. two nights out of five. There had been candlelit dinners, thirty-six holes of miniature golf, and long walks on the beach at sunset. Now it was time to go home, and the silence coming off his girlfriend was like a cold front sweeping down from Canada.

He hadn't proposed.

After all the sunsets and inspired sex, he *still* hadn't proposed. And it was getting to her, he could tell. Because they'd been together for *three years* and, though they were still crazy about each other, he just couldn't do it. *The problem*, Danny told himself, *is that I'm too marginal – and she's too centered*. To put it another way, Caleigh was one year out of B-school and pulling down eighty grand a year, while he was four years out of the Art Institute and pulling down eighty bucks a day.

A portfolio management intern at the John Galt Fund, Caleigh was a born workaholic who logged sixty-hour weeks without complaint. Even on vacation, she'd been up at seven every day to snag one of the four *Wall Street Journal*s at the town's only newsstand. She'd checked her e-mail twice a day at the local library and had been caught, repeatedly, watching MSNBC with the sound turned off.

For Caleigh, making money was an art and a game, as absorbing and nuanced as the ballet must be to a professional dancer. Not so for Danny, who liked to kid that he was "beyond money – an *artiste*."

Which was at least half-true – the beyond money part, that is. Most of what little money he made came from moonlighting – not from art. He worked part-time at a gallery, which gave him "exposure" but didn't pay a whole lot more than minimum wage. The real bucks came from the twenty-five dollars an hour he made freelancing for Fellner Associates, a big investigative firm in the District. The investigative work was easy, if uninteresting: for the most part, he collected filings at the SEC, culled records at the courthouse, and interviewed third-tier sources in connection with mergers and acquisitions and litigation of various kinds. As near as Danny could tell, Fellner Associates was almost always on the wrong side – a circumstance in which the firm took pride. Because, of course, "the wrong side" was where the money was, and that was where Fellner Associates liked to put down roots.

Still, his freelance work more or less paid the bills,

though there were lots of things that Danny craved but couldn't afford – not least of which was a nonlinear video-editing suite that would enable him to make the kind of art that, for now, he could only dream of.

The system he wanted cost twenty thousand dollars – about twenty times as much as he had in his savings account. Which pretty much put it out of reach. He'd never save that much working for Fellner, and as for his art, that wasn't moving at all. *Not at all, at all,* as Caleigh would say. In point of fact, he hadn't sold any of his work in months – not since a Latino bank in Mount Pleasant bought a bronze that he'd made: *Forest and Threes.*

He leaned back, closed his eyes, and rested his head against the jittering window. Caleigh had the radio tuned to NPR's *Morning Edition* – one of those whimsical first-person narratives that she liked and he didn't. He tuned it out, thinking, *If a three fell in the forest, would anyone hear it?*

Caleigh must have seen him smile, because she broke the Meaningful Silence to ask, "So . . . what are you thinking about?"

He shook his head slowly, pretending to be half-asleep. *What am I thinking about? I'm thinking about not selling anything, about not having money, about not getting married. I'm thinking about all the* knots *in my life.*

"Danny?"

His eyelids fluttered. She could be relentless. "Wha?"

"What are you *thinking* about?"

The truth was, he was contemplating the mystery of how he and Caleigh, who had almost nothing in common, were nevertheless made for each other.

15

Something had ignited when they met, and Danny believed the flame would never go out. When they were separated, even for just a few days, Danny began to languish, a shipwrecked man. It was the same for Caleigh, or so she said. They were magic together. Each of them lit up in the presence of the other. Despite their entirely different career tracks and backgrounds, they were so attuned that half of the time they could read each other's minds. *Same brain,* they'd say when one spoke aloud the thought of the other.

Of *course* they'd get married, someday when he felt a little more grounded, when he was getting somewhere, when he was at least making some kind of money. *Maybe I'll have to get a* real *job,* he thought, *if something doesn't break for me soon.*

"Danny?" Caleigh said again. "The mind police want a report from your brain."

He opened his eyes. Blinked. "I've got a sunburn."

"Poor baby!"

"And I'm all gritty from the sand."

"Awww . . ."

"And I was thinking . . . maybe I'm too old to be a 'Danny.' Maybe it's time I became a 'Daniel.' "

She thought about it. Frowned. "No. I don't think so."

"I'll be twenty-six tomorrow."

"So? You're having a birthday. That doesn't mean you have to change your name."

He shifted in the seat. "Let's not talk about me," he said, taking Caleigh's hand in his and bringing it to his mouth. Kissing her fingers, which tasted like salt. "Let's talk about you."

Caleigh giggled. "What about me?"

"I bet you can't wait to get home. Short GE. Buy a ton of pork bellies. Put some calls –"

"You don't 'put calls,' " she told him.

"Well, whatever. . . ."

She sighed and clicked off the radio. "I know you think it's boring –"

"But I don't," he said. "I think business is probably more interesting than art – I mean, as *a scene*."

Caleigh giggled. "You're just saying that because you have to go to Jake's opening and suck up to all the gallery owners."

He winced but was relieved the cold front seemed to have passed. "Wanna come?"

She shook her head and sent a sloe-eyed smile in his direction. "Well . . ."

"So you'd rather wash your hair, watch *Wall Street Week in Review* –"

"I didn't say that."

"No, you didn't say it, but . . ."

She laughed. "Same brain."

Danny groaned. "Maybe I'll stay home and wash *my* hair – it's got enough sand in it."

Caleigh shook her head. "You can't!"

" 'Can't' what?"

"Bail on Jake. And I can't, either. He's counting on us. And, anyway, it won't be that bad."

"Yes, it will," he told her, and let his head fall against the window with a soft *thunk*.

The opening was at the Petrus Gallery in Georgetown.

A single room with high ceilings, batteries of track lights, and rosy brick walls, the gallery was in a part of the city that Danny had always found interesting – and even mysterious. This was K Street, Down Under. Half a mile to the east, the street morphed into a canyon of glassy high-rises, housing law firms and NGOs like the Pan American Health Organization. But here, in what used to be a ghetto of freed slaves, it ran for half a dozen blocks beside the Potomac River – and *under* the elevated Whitehurst Freeway.

From the standpoint of "urban planning," this stretch of K Street was a disaster. And for Danny, the opening wasn't any better.

If he heard the words "coolest July on record" one more time, he swore he'd take off – even if that meant thinning an already emaciated "crowd." There were only a couple of dozen people, and none of them seemed remotely interested in the monster canvases that hung from the walls. Judging by the accumulating empties in the recycling bins, the gallery's clientele were there for the free booze, not the paintings.

A voice to his left insisted that "they didn't even *start* to keep records until 1918, so it's really only the coolest since *then*."

That's it, Danny told himself. *We're outta here.* Caleigh, trapped in a conversation with Jake's earnest mom, had been throwing him *let's go* glances for fifteen minutes. He'd already done his best with the various luminaries in attendance – the *Post*'s critic, the writer from *Flash Art*. There was no reason to stay and he was halfway to Caleigh's side when a whispery voice cooed in his ear, "Is that *you*, Danny Cray?"

Lavinia. No one knew exactly how old Lavinia was, but there were photos of her with JFK and Andy Warhol, Peggy Guggenheim and Lou Reed. The doyenne of the D.C. arts scene, she ran the Neon Gallery in Foggy Bottom and the Kunstblitz in Berlin.

"It is," he said as he and Lavinia came together for a ritual embrace. "At least, I think so." He rubbed his hand back over his short spiky hair.

She burbled, as if what he'd said was somehow witty, and eyed him through her heavily mascaraed lashes in a way that was almost flirtatious. Caleigh, spotting him with Lavinia, raised her eyebrows and volleyed an encouraging smile. "Well, I *hope* it's you," Lavinia said, "because you're the man I've been looking for." She held out her empty wineglass. "Plonk, please – *white* . . . then there's something I want to talk to you about."

They went out to the little garden behind the gallery so that Lavinia could have a cigarette. The air was so leaden and oppressively humid that the smoke didn't seem to rise but hung in the air like ground fog. He did his best to pump her for a reaction to Jake's show (because, of course, Jake would ask), but she dismissed the subject with a shake of her famous blond mane. "Not my cup of tea," she told him.

"Why not? He's good!"

She shook her head dismissively. "No, he's not 'good.' His palette's muddy and he's derivative. But look," she said, changing the subject. "That's not what I want to talk about. I want to talk about . . ." She pushed him in the chest with one red-enameled finger. "You!"

It took about a minute, and then he was floating. She told him that she'd seen a sculpture of his at the Banco Salvador in Adams-Morgan and that she'd been very impressed. So much so that she'd sought out his other work. She'd seen some lithographs that he'd loaned to a restaurateur in Georgetown, a painting the Cafritzes had bought and which was hanging in their music room, and an installation that he'd done for the Torpedo Factory in Alexandria. "I loved it."

"Which?" he asked.

"It! Them! All of it!"

"That's great. Really!"

But that wasn't the point. The point was: A "window" had opened up in the exhibition schedule at Neon. "Actually," she confided, "it's more like a skylight: two weeks in October. You'd open Friday, October fifth." Was he interested?

"Well . . ."

"You'd install on the Wednesday and Thursday, the third and fourth." A thought occurred to her. "You *do* have enough work . . . ?"

He nodded without thinking. "Sure, but – what happened? I mean . . ."

She made a tsking sound and cast her eyes to the heavens. "One of my 'projects,' " she confided. "Young, bright . . . and thoroughly bipolar. I don't see him getting out of bed before Christmas, and I can't wait for that – I'm running a business, not a clinic." She paused, a look of bemusement on her face. "So?"

He hesitated for the better part of a second, shrugged unconvincingly, and said, "Yeah – sure!"

"Wonderful!"

After that, he had to stay because, somehow, it didn't seem right to leave before Lavinia did.

A minute later, Caleigh materialized at his side, with Jake and Jake's mom in tow. "Wasn't that Lavinia Trevor?" she asked, excited. "What did she *want*?"

Danny didn't want to say anything with Jake right there. The Neon was a much bigger deal than the Petrus. He shrugged. "Someone to fetch her some wine and keep her company while she had a smoke."

20

"She say anything?" Jake asked. "About the show? What did she think?"

Danny shrugged again. "Sorry. All she talked about was a friend of hers who's bipolar."

Caleigh peeked at her watch. Mondays she had to get up at five-thirty in order to read the early papers and write her on-line column before the market opened for the week. Danny squeezed her hand. "I think you should head home. I'll catch a ride with someone." Caleigh smiled. She knew something was up with Lavinia.

It was half an hour after Caleigh's departure that Lavinia finally left, tossing Danny a conspiratorial little wave as she made her exit. At this point, Danny decided he'd better stay to the end. Jake was half in the bag and in no shape to drive.

On the way home, Jake was looking for reassurance. "That sucked," he said, swigging from a half-empty bottle of merlot.

"It was fine," Danny told him.

"Really?" Jake asked, skepticism and hope vying in his voice.

"Absolutely! It was a home run."

His friend made a grumbling sound and looked out the window. "Nothing sold."

"That's not the point," Danny told him, although it sort of was. "First you show – then you sell. It takes a while."

"You think?"

"Yeah."

Jake cocked his head and regarded Danny with suspicion. "What are *you* so happy about?"

"Me?" Danny scoffed. "I'm not happy. I'm depressed!"

His friend thought about that for a moment, then nodded to himself and closed his eyes. "Good," he said, and, almost immediately, began to snore.

Maybe it was a self-fulfilling prophecy, but after he dropped off Jake, Danny's elation began to fade. The truth was, he had a few pieces that were good to go, but they weren't enough. He'd have to round up everything he'd sold, along with pieces he'd left in the care of friends. And the installation at the Torpedo Factory – the one Lavinia liked so much – was beginning to look like one of a kind. It was a mixed-media piece, and he no longer had any way of putting together the intricate video effects that kind of work demanded. The editing suite he'd used at the Artists Co-op was no longer available, its owner having reclaimed the system to go into business making "video memorials" of dead pets (a lucrative trade, by all accounts).

And there was another problem: the most interesting of his sculptures, and the pièce de résistance of any foreseeable show, was *Babel On II*. This was a mind-boggling construction that consisted of more than eight thousand transparent Legos put together in such a way as to create a nearly invisible city – at the center of which was a six-inch high three-dimensional hologram of Walter Mondale praying over Kurt Cobain's funeral bier. The hologrammatic image was wonderful and haunting, as delicate and ephemeral as its subjects' fade-to-black celebrity. The only problem was: How was he going to get the piece to the Neon Gallery without destroying it?

No big deal, he thought. *I've got two months to figure it out.*

Since he was driving Jake's VW, parking was easy;

finding a space for his own car, a huge and rusting '76 Oldsmobile, was always a challenge in Adams-Morgan.

When he bounded up the two flights of stairs to tell Caleigh about Lavinia's offer, she was even more excited than he was. "I knew it!" she beamed, throwing her arms around him. She broke out a bottle of Mumm's from the refrigerator ("it was supposed to be for your birthday, but we can always get another").

Danny was feeling no pain when the phone rang, just after midnight. Caleigh answered it, then handed the receiver to him with a questioning look. "Jude Belzer," she said.

He shook his head. It wasn't a name he knew. Nor did he recognize the voice, which had a peculiar accent: half English and half something else that he couldn't identify.

"Mr. Cray?"

"Danny."

"As you like. I'm sorry to call you so late, but –"

"No problem," Danny told him.

"I'm a lawyer."

"Okay."

"A mutual friend suggested I get in touch."

"And who was that?" Danny asked.

"One of your many fans at Fellner Associates," the lawyer explained. "Look, I'm just in from Milan and I'm off to San Francisco tomorrow. Would it be possible – is there any *way* – you could meet me in the morning? I know it's short notice, but –"

"I don't know. . . ."

"I have a proposal that I think will interest you. We could meet at the Admirals Club at Reagan National."

Danny winced. He'd lived in the D.C. area most of

his life. The airport would always be just plain National to him.

"Danny?"

"Yeah, I'm here."

"I was thinking . . . ten-ish?"

Danny wasn't sure what to say. The Neon exhibition was going to be huge, but it wouldn't be easy. He had a lot of work to do to make it happen. Then again, the grand that he had in the bank wasn't going to last. And he couldn't – he *wouldn't* – live off Caleigh.

The silence must have dragged, because Belzer prodded him a second time. "Danny?"

"Yeah, sure – ten would be fine."

"The Admirals Club?"

"Right. At National."

It wasn't until he hung up that Danny realized they hadn't bothered to establish a way of recognizing each other. But, somehow, he could tell that wouldn't be a problem. There was something in Belzer's voice, a tone more than an accent, that made Danny think the lawyer already knew what he looked like. And maybe a lot more.

Three

He looked . . . decent.

That was Danny's conclusion as he stood in front of the mirror with a towel around his waist, dripping from the shower. Regular features, blue eyes, clear skin. Kinda tall, thin, and, for someone who didn't "work out," in pretty good shape. Though, actually . . . he played soccer on the Mall twice a week and went running with Caleigh in Rock Creek Park on the (admittedly *rare*) occasions when he got up as early as she did. So he wasn't exactly a couch potato.

All in all, he thought that he looked okay, though maybe a little too edgy for a first meeting, especially with a lawyer. His hair, for instance. Short, brown, and spiky, it had blond highlights at the tips (thanks to Caleigh, who'd obviously been deprived of dolls as a child). Maybe if he slapped a little gel on his hair and combed it straight back (Pat Riley style), it would look okay – just sort of sun-streaked.

He ran a brush through his hair, cocked his head, and considered the result in the mirror: not bad, except that he looked like a pirate. A young and affable pirate but a buccaneer nonetheless – which might not be appropriate for a business meeting.

It was the tattoo that did it. And the piercings.

The tattoo was a black silhouette, tribal and abstract, that curled up and around his right shoulder.

The piercings consisted of three gold rings in the helix of his left ear and a fourth through his right eyebrow – the result of a lost bet.

But it didn't matter, really. The tattoo would disappear beneath his shirt, and the piercings only took a second to remove. When this was done, he was his mother's son again – a nice young man with no apparent edges.

Walking into the bedroom, he opened the closet door and took out the clothes that he kept for occasions like this: the Zegna suit and tie that Caleigh had pounced on at Glad Rags (an up-scale consignment boutique), the Cole-Haan loafers (leftover from graduation), the oh-so-cool windowpane shirt from Joseph Abboud. It was a dark and businesslike ensemble, funereal or gangsterlike, depending on your point of view. And it made him smile, because the beautiful suit and gleaming shoes were like a disguise.

He drew the line at an attaché case, though. Instead, he carried a leather "envelope" that held a yellow legal pad and the Mark Cross fountain pen that his father had given him in a moment of wishful thinking and largesse.

Riding the Metro out to the airport, he read the *Washington Post* – or, more accurately, *Doonesbury*, Style, and the sports page. Then he was there, amid the throng surging in and out of Terminal B. Finding a security guard, he asked the way to the American Airlines lounge and was directed to the third floor at the south end of the terminal. There, on the wall beside a wooden door, was a brass plaque that read: ADMIRALS CLUB.

A buzzer beside the door gave admittance to a large

and airy room with a wall of plate glass at the far end. The attendant at the reception desk asked Danny to sign in as a guest, then nodded toward a corner of the room that overlooked one of the airport's busiest runways.

Jude Belzer was sitting in a wing chair that might as well have been a leather throne, watching Danny as he made his way past a flotilla of empty easy chairs and couches. Nearby, three men in business suits sat nibbling honey-roasted peanuts and sipping Coca-Colas. Although they didn't talk among themselves, they were obviously together – a phalanx of well-dressed pawns guarding their king's perimeter.

To Danny, they seemed like Xerox copies of one another: each of them was thirty-something and squarely built, with thick black hair cut close to the scalp. They'd be difficult to tell apart, he thought, except for the guy in the middle, whose right eyebrow was cleft in two – so that he almost seemed to have three.

Belzer shared the same palette as his bodyguards (or whatever they were). Everything about him was dark, from the suit that he wore to his pitch-black hair and wraparound shades. He removed these as Danny approached, revealing fathomless brown eyes. When he got up to shake hands, Danny noticed, first, the silver-handled cane he leaned on, the gold blob of a Rolex, and the leather boot encasing a deformity of some kind.

"Danny Cray."

"Jude Belzer."

Rangy and athletic-looking, Belzer had a powerful grip and was handsome enough that he flustered the young woman who materialized to ask if they'd like something to drink. The lawyer had the presence of a movie star, and Danny could see the wheels turning behind the waitress's eyes as she tried to place him in her firmament of celebrity. Blushing and stuttering, too eager to please, she finally dashed off to fill their order: coffee for Danny, Pellegrino for Belzer.

Belzer put his sunglasses back on, apologizing as he did so. "My eyes are sensitive to glare," he said in a regretful tone.

"So," Danny said, settling into an easy chair. "Here we are."

"Yesssss." With a smile, Belzer leaned forward and, without any introduction at all, quietly explained why the two of them were there. "I'd like to retain you for a little damage control."

" 'Retain' me?"

Belzer's hands fell open, like a book. "A bit of freelance investigation. You do that, don't you?"

Danny nodded. "Sure."

"Well then . . ." A flash of teeth. "I have a client – a businessman in Italy – Zerevan Zebek. . . ." The lawyer paused, as if waiting for a reaction. When none came, he resumed talking. "For some time now, Mr. Zebek has been the target of . . . I'm not sure what to call it . . . *a campaign* to destroy his reputation."

A sympathetic frown settled on Danny's face as the waitress arrived with their drinks. "When did it start?" he asked.

"A few months ago," Belzer replied. "One of the Florentine papers – *La Repubblica* – began to publish certain rumors. . . ."

"About?"

"Mr. Zebek's businesses. Our first reaction –"

"And what did they say?" Danny asked. Unused to

interruption, Belzer frowned. "I mean – I was wondering about the allegations," Danny explained.

The lawyer shook his head, closed his eyes, and made an impatient gesture with his hand, as if he were waving good-bye to someone he didn't care about. "What difference does it make? There's nothing to them."

Danny sat back in his chair, sipped his coffee, and let the silence between them grow – which wasn't easy. The lawyer's body language expressed an attitude somewhere between annoyance and contempt.

Finally, Belzer relented with a sigh. "Okay, they say he's in bed with the Mafia – that he's an arms dealer . . . a polluter, and a cheat. *They say* he's the devil incarnate."

Danny grinned. "Whereas . . . in fact . . . ?"

Belzer shrugged. "He's a venture capitalist. Secretive? Of course. But that goes with the territory, doesn't it? We're talking about someone who's invested hundreds of millions of dollars in a string of small companies, some of which have done very, very well – and may do even better. We're talking about cutting-edge science – robotics and MEMS – not Telepizza."

Danny wouldn't know MEMS from Reese's Pieces, but he understood what Belzer was driving at. Over the last year and a half, he'd done enough work for Fellner Associates to know that the high-tech universe was a cutthroat one in which billions came and went like tropical storms. The lawyer obviously believed that his client was being smeared by a competitor. "So why doesn't he sue?" he asked.

Belzer took a drink of water and leaned forward with a wolfish grin. "Well, that's the point, isn't it? I mean, that's why we're here."

"Ah."

The older man sat back. "We know who some of the people involved are – tabloid hacks and others. But there's no point in going after *them*. We want to trace the stories to the source – find out who's behind them."

Danny thought about that. It might be something he could do.

"One of the people *we know* was involved," Belzer continued, "was an American."

"Ah . . ."

"A man named Terio."

"And how can we be sure of that?" Danny asked.

Belzer regarded him coolly. "Maybe this isn't something you need to know." When the younger man looked doubtful, the lawyer shrugged. "Mr. Terio was overheard talking to a reporter."

" 'Overheard'?"

Belzer nodded.

"You mean like . . . he was sitting at the next table, or . . . you bugged him?"

Belzer's face tightened in mock indignation. "I've never bugged anyone in my life," he protested. Then he paused and added, "We have people for that." The remark made Danny smile. But he must have looked worried, too, because the lawyer hurried to reassure him: "It was in another country, Mr. Cray. The laws are different."

Danny nodded thoughtfully. "So what is it you'd like me to do?"

"Well, if we could get a look at Mr. Terio's papers . . ."

"His 'papers,' " Danny repeated. "What kind of 'papers'?"

Belzer shrugged. "Whatever there is. And if we could find out who he was talking to, or who *else* he was talking to, that would be even better."

Suddenly we're in the past tense, Danny thought. " 'Was'?"

Belzer nodded. "Mr. Terio passed away."

Danny blinked.

The lawyer shifted in his chair. "It was in the news."

Danny gave him an apologetic look. "I just got back in town," he said. "My girlfriend and I were in North Carolina, so –"

"It was in the papers," Belzer told him. He twirled a finger in the air. "TV. Radio."

Danny thought about that. "So this guy was, what – prominent? I mean, to get in the papers –"

Belzer shook his head. "No," he admitted. "He wasn't actually 'prominent.' He was a college professor. It was more the way he died than who he was."

Danny took another sip of coffee and leaned forward. "The *way* he died?"

Belzer watched a 737 land on the runway behind the window. After a moment, he said, "Mr. Terio immured himself."

Danny wasn't sure that he'd heard right. A couple of seconds ticked by. "Excuse me?"

Belzer turned back to him. "I said he *immured* himself."

It's a language thing, Danny supposed. *This guy's English is perfect, but it's English-as-a-second-language perfect, so maybe he doesn't mean what he thinks he means.* "When you say 'immured,' you mean like . . . like in that Edgar Allan Poe story?"

Belzer nodded. "Except, in Mr. Terio's case, it was a do-it-yourself activity."

The younger man sat where he was and said nothing for a while. Then his businessman imposture dissolved and he sank back in his seat with a chuckle of incredulity. "I'm sorry, man, but ... 'do-it-yourself'?"

Belzer inclined his head in confirmation. "He buried himself alive."

Danny heard himself say, *"What!?"*

Belzer nodded.

"But ... how do you even *do* that?" Danny asked.

The lawyer shook his head in bafflement. Then he frowned and tried to explain: "According to the police, he went to something called the 'Home Depot' and bought what he needed. Then he built this little room from the inside out."

Danny couldn't believe it. The idea blew him away. "But why? Why would anyone ever *do* that? There are guns for that. Bridges! Pills!"

Belzer shook his head, almost wistfully. "Obviously, he was crazy."

No shit, Danny thought. "Of *course* he was crazy, but ... what I'm getting at is: What made him do it? Even crazy people have *reasons* for what they do. They're just *crazy* reasons."

Belzer made a gesture that conveyed a mix of helplessness and indifference. "I'm sure you're right."

Danny nodded, then ran a hand through his hair. Finally, he made an effort to get down to business. "Okay, so Mr. Terio's kind of a mystery. But why me? I mean, I can understand why you want to find out about this campaign against your client, but – why not go to Fellner Associates?" Before the lawyer could answer, Danny plunged on. "Don't get me wrong – I'm flattered. It's just that ... They're the A-team. I'm just one guy. I don't have anything *like* their resources."

It wasn't something that he wanted to say, but it was so obvious that it couldn't be avoided. He was a part-time PI who didn't even have a license – whereas Fellner Associates had a dozen offices in half a dozen countries and 120 staffers, including a former deputy director of the CIA. It also had subscriptions to a hundred esoteric databases and a Rolodex packed with the names and telephone numbers of experts on everything from "questioned documents" to data forensics. So *Why me?* was by no means a bad question.

"Actually," Belzer confided, "you've worked for Mr. Zebek before."

Danny looked surprised. "I have?"

The lawyer nodded. "You were . . . I think they call it a 'subcontractor.' "

"A 'sub'."

"Exactly. You helped with a matter that Fellner was handling for Mr. Zebek's holding company."

Danny shook his head. "Remind me."

"Sistemi di Pavone."

Danny thought about it. He'd done lots of work for Fellner, but at such a low level that he sometimes wasn't even told the client's name. *Sistemi di Pavone* didn't ring a bell, but it seemed impolite to say so. "Ri-iight."

"Mr. Zebek has rather a lot of – what should I say? – 'work-type work' with Fellner. Due diligence, for the most part, some mergers and acquisitions. But the Terio issue is different. It's a personal attack." Belzer paused to be certain Danny got the point, and then went on. "So there's no need to involve Fellner. What

33

we'd like to do is isolate the Terio investigation from our other work – while still keeping everything . . . in-house, so to speak."

Danny nodded his understanding. He could see where it might make sense. Then he shifted in his seat and leaned forward. He should raise the question of fees – which was a little bit tricky. Fellner paid him twenty-five dollars an hour but billed him out at double that. So maybe he should ask for thirty-five. Or even fifty (if he could do it with a straight face).

An announcement came over the public-address system, and Belzer glanced at his watch.

"When does your plane leave?" Danny asked.

Belzer's chin lifted slightly. "When I tell it to," he said.

It took a moment for this to sink in, and, when it did, Danny heard himself say, "Well, I can probably help, but . . . maybe you could be a little more specific about what you're after."

"Christian Terio," Belzer insisted, looking a bit annoyed. "It's as simple as that. Who *was* he? What was he up to?"

"You said he was a professor."

"He was in the Philosophy and Religious Studies Department at George Mason University," Belzer explained. "It's hard to understand why anyone in that position would want to malign Mr. Zebek. So we'd like to find out a little more about his friends and colleagues – the people he was close to, his correspondents, if any. It may be that someone was using him as an intermediary, or that he was being paid to do what he did."

"Which was . . . ?"

"Smear my client."

"Would it be possible to see the stories?" Danny asked. "It might help."

Belzer thought about it. "Do you read Italian?"

Danny looked regretful.

Belzer shrugged. "Well, perhaps we could have them translated for you, though actually . . . I'm not sure they'd be all that helpful." He paused and shifted gears. "We're *particularly* interested in any files you can obtain – paper, computer, whatever. There might be items of interest – connections to Mr. Zebek – that *we'd* recognize but you would not."

"Things that would be meaningful to your client."

Belzer let his hands fall open like the pages of a book. "Exactly. The more raw data we get, the better. Apart from that, we'd like you to investigate Mr. Terio as if we were in a hostile takeover situation."

"So . . . you want me to profile him."

"Exactly. And with as much detail as possible."

"An assets search?"

The lawyer nodded. "Keeping in mind that Terio was a professor and not a Nigerian dictator – yes. An assets search might tell us who was paying him."

Danny cleared his throat. "I don't see a problem with any of that," he said, "though I'll need to know what sort of budget you have."

The lawyer made a dismissive gesture. "The budget is . . . open. We'll pay whatever expenses you have – and your rates, which are . . . what? A hundred dollars an hour?"

Danny tried to keep a straight face. Here he was, trying to find the chutzpah to jack up his rates to thirty-five or forty bucks an hour, when Belzer *volunteers* a hundred! He took a deep breath. "That's fine," he managed.

Belzer grinned. "I know you're an artist, Mr. Cray –"

"Dan."

"– and that you're still getting established. I don't mind helping you with that, so long as the client's interests are served."

"Of course."

"And I do hear great things about you."

"You *do*?" This seemed so unlikely that Danny couldn't suppress a nervous laugh.

"I do," Belzer insisted. "I saw a piece of yours at Les Yeux de Monde – brushed aluminum – very nice. And I understand you had something at the Torpedo Factory. I didn't see it, but I did read that you took a first-in-show."

Danny was flattered and a bit unnerved. Obviously Belzer himself knew something about investigation.

"Maybe, when this is done," Belzer went on, "I could take a look at your . . . *oeuvre*."

"Actually, I'm having a show," Danny told him. "In October – at the Neon Gallery."

"Fantastic. I don't buy a lot of art, but I do have a few pieces, so who knows?" And with that, Belzer handed him an envelope bearing the logo of the Admirals Club. "Your retainer," he explained. "There's five thousand to start – against your time and expenses. If you'll keep an accounting, we'll supplement this as needed."

It was Danny's first retainer. Usually he had to wait as long as two months for Fellner to process his hours and expenses. Having so much cash all at once, and up front, was startling. "So –"

"Just do whatever it takes," Belzer said. Then, getting to his feet with the help of his silver-handled

36

cane, he removed a business card from inside his jacket. The card was embossed with a telephone number – and nothing else.

"My cell phone," Belzer explained. "Call me when you have something." Then he turned and, with a little wave over his shoulder, stabbed his cane into the thickly carpeted floor and walked out.

Danny just stood there, card in hand, thinking, *A hundred dollars an hour eight hours a day five days a week – what happened to the guys with the honey-roasted peanuts?*

He looked around. They were gone.

Four grand a week, sixteen grand a month . . . It wasn't until he was back on the Metro that he let the thing that was bothering him actually come to the surface: *What kind of lawyer has bodyguards?*

Four

It was a dream, and he knew it was a dream even as he dreamed it. Still . . .

He was standing on a cliff at the edge of the ocean, tingling with vertigo. He was holding Belzer's business card, but it was impossible to read. No matter how hard he focused, the numbers softened and blurred, then changed into letters that changed into *other* letters even as they began to form.

The telephone beside the bed was ringing, pulling him up from sleep. He didn't want to answer it. He wanted to read the card. It was important to read the card. But his hand obeyed a reflex of its own and reached out, fumbling, for the phone. Half-asleep, he dragged the receiver to his ear.

"Happy Birthday, Son!" His father's booming voice.

Danny mumbled an incoherent reply and propped himself up on an elbow, blinking.

"I tried to get him to wait," his mother chimed in, "but you know what he's like."

"Hi, Mom. Dad." He yawned and rubbed his eyes. They were calling from the cottage in Maine, the summer place his grandfather had built.

"It's seven-thirty," his father said in a mixture of mock surprise and feigned innocence. "*Everybody's* up at seven-thirty! It's the way of the world!"

"Happy Birthday, Danny boy," his mother cooed. "And I'm sorry we woke you."

"You snooze, you lose," his father announced.

Danny chuckled. "It's okay. I was having a bad dream anyway."

"I think your father should learn to respect your hours," his mother insisted. "Artists operate in a different time frame than the rest of us. *I* understand that."

A snort from his father.

"I mean it, Frank!" As usual, his parents were not so much talking to him as bickering *around* him in their good-natured way. Their affection for each other was bedrock for him. He was the youngest of the three Cray boys and by far the most easygoing. Unlike Kevin and Sean, Danny enjoyed his father's ribbing and usually gave back as good as he got.

"What kind of dream?" his father asked. "The recurring nightmare of being thirty years old –"

"Hey!"

"– and no job?"

"I'm only twenty-six!"

The old man let out a whoop of delight.

"*Frank!* It's his birthday."

"Excuse me. *Twenty-six* years old," his father mused. "Finest education money could buy . . ."

"Frank."

Leaving the bed, Danny dragged the telephone cord around the corner and tramped into the kitchen. "Actually," he said, "I've got some good news: I'm having a show. In October. At the Neon Gallery."

"Really," his father replied, suddenly serious.

"It's kind of a big deal," Danny confided as he filled the electric kettle with water.

"Oh, Danny!"

He made coffee while his mother gushed about what a genius he was and how everybody knew it was "only a matter of time . . ." Finally, his father couldn't stand it anymore and changed the subject, booming in a thick, improbable brogue, "We're goin' back to the auld sod, we are – me and your mum!"

"You're doing what?"

"Goin' home, Son – twelve days and eleven nights, Dublin, Waterford, Kerry, and Cork. It's certain to be grand."

Danny laughed. *The auld sod.* To the best of his knowledge, no one in his family had been to Ireland in a hundred years.

Before she'd gone to work, Caleigh had prepared a birthday breakfast for him, and Danny sat down to it while his parents rattled on about the trip. Like Danny, Caleigh was – most of the time – a vegetarian, though they ate dairy products and, on rare occasions, fish. They told themselves it was for the omega-3 oils. On a Saran-wrapped plate, smoked salmon and cream cheese were flanked by rings of onion sliced so thin as to be translucent. A poppy-seed bagel waited in the toaster. Reaching over, he pushed the lever down and watched the coils flare to orange.

Nearby, a birthday card was propped against the salt- and pepper shakers. On the front of its heavy cream stock a teddy bear sat with a birthday cake before him, getting ready to blow out the candles. Opening the card, Danny found a handwritten message that read: *Happy, Hap-py Birthday, Ba-a-by.* C.

Then the kettle began to boil and he poured a stream of water over the coffee grounds, listening patiently to his father's monologue about Caleigh. (*How did he get from Dublin to Caleigh?* Danny wondered.)

"She's a great girl," his father was saying, "and one of these days she's going to wake up and realize she's been living with a cad –"

"A 'cad'?! What century are we in, Dad?"

A grunt from his father. "Hey," he said, "we got a present for you – but your mother didn't send it on time."

A whimper from Mom. "I was hoping you might come up, even if it's just for a weekend. Your dad's thinking of buying a new boat – so he could use your advice."

His father whistled. "You'll like this one, kiddo! Got some zip."

"Too much zip, if you ask me!" his mom exclaimed. "Anyway, honey, I'm sure you've got things to do. But Happy Birthday!"

"Thanks."

The toaster popped.

"Love you love you love you."

"Love you, too."

By ten o'clock, Danny had been sitting at the kitchen table with his laptop, on-line for nearly an hour. The first place he'd gone was to the George Mason University Web site, where he found what looked like all of Terio's numbers: address and phone, e-mail, and fax. The Philosophy and Religious Studies Department had its own Web page, with biographical notes on each of its fac-ulty members. According to the site, Terio had earned his undergraduate degree at Georgetown in 1978. Twelve years later, he'd received his doctorate from Johns Hopkins University. (*What took him so*

41

long? Danny wondered.) From Johns Hopkins, he'd gone on to teach at Boston University before coming to George Mason. In the last decade, he'd published a dozen articles in peer-reviewed journals, as well as a 1995 book titled *The Radiant Tomb: Hermitage and Ecstasy in Early Christianity.*

According to Amazon, the book was out of print, so Danny went to Alibris.com, where he found a used edition for twenty-eight dollars and change. After ordering the book and paying for Next Day delivery, he clicked his way to the *Washington Post*'s Web site, where he knew he could download any stories they'd run about Terio and his death. Much to his irritation, the site was down and there was no way to know when it would be up again – probably in a few minutes but maybe not for hours.

Using paper filters and a plastic cone, he made another cup of coffee, and tried again. Nothing.

With a sigh, he rocked back in his chair and considered the alternatives. He didn't know anyone at the *Post* well enough to ask for a favor, but there were lots of people he did know who had access to Nexis – the supernaturally expensive database whose electronic archive stored the full text of thousands of newspapers and magazines. Fellner had a sub-scription that he could use, but . . . no. Belzer wanted to keep them out of it, and that was fine by Danny. He'd do things the old-fashioned way – at the library.

Grabbing a notebook, he took the fire stairs down to the lobby, where he checked the mail and, finding none, descended the front steps to the sidewalk. His apartment building was a somewhat down-at-the-heels three-story building on Mintwood Place, about one hundred feet from Columbia Road, itself the site of an ongoing carnival.

He considered driving but decided against moving the Brown Bomber from its current resting place. Not only did the Olds demand a supersized parking space, but because it still had Virginia tags he couldn't park for longer than two hours in the many spots restricted to D.C. residents. Besides, the air conditioner didn't work and the starter was sketchy and parking anywhere but in a lot was always a hassle. He'd take the bus. Boom boxes throbbed to a salsa sound, while homeless men stood in the street, directing cars into parking places (whether they wanted them or not). Kids on skateboards wove in and out of the pedestrian traffic. Near the corner, a well-dressed white woman stood by the curb, arguing with an implacable black cop who was ticketing her Jaguar.

"But why shouldn't I park there?" she demanded. "You haven't given me a reason! Just because the meter's broken – that doesn't mean the *space* is defunct."

This made Danny grin. He'd never heard anyone use the word *defunct* before – not in conversation and not in Adams-Morgan, where half the residents weren't what you'd call completely *fluent*.

His shirt was already beginning to stick to him as he waited for the bus outside the bank – waited until it occurred to him that his expenses were being covered. And not just expenses: at a hundred bucks an hour, he wouldn't be doing his client any favor by taking the bus.

So he hailed the first cab he saw and, five minutes later, got out in front of the Cleveland Park library on Connecticut Avenue. Most of the time, he avoided libraries. Microfiche was a nightmare to handle, and microfilm wasn't any better. As often as not, he couldn't find what he was looking for at the library and, when he did, the machines spit out gray-on-gray copies that curled in his hand. He hated it.

Fortunately, Terio's death was recent enough that the newspapers he was looking for were still on the shelves. Not that there was much in any of them.

The *Post* carried an obituary with a photograph at the top. Danny studied the picture for a long moment, but there was nothing to be learned from it. Terio was a nice-looking man in his late thirties, with a soft smile and a salt-and-pepper beard. The obit itself was brief, summing up Terio's life in a chain of bland sentences that ended with the words "left no survivors." Still, the story wasn't entirely without interest. According to the *Post*, Terio had been a Jesuit priest for six years prior to renouncing his vows and becoming a teacher. (*So that's why it took him so long,* Danny thought.)

The *Washington Times* covered the story as news, rather than as an obituary. It reported the circumstances of the body's discovery, including the names of the concerned mailman and the Fairfax County sheriff's deputies who'd actually found the body. The *Times* quoted the medical examiner, who attributed the death to dehydration occurring between July thirteenth and fourteenth.

There wasn't much else in the newspapers, so Danny searched through the *Readers' Guide to Periodical Literature*, looking for articles the professor had written. There were quite a few, and Danny listed each of them in his notebook, compiling a bibliography of sorts. (If nothing else, it would help him to pad out his report if he came up empty in other areas.) Looking over the titles, he saw that the most recent efforts were "Syncretism in Western Kurdistan" and "Uzelyurt: 'Vatican of the Yezidis.' "

Danny considered himself well read, but Kurdistan wasn't a country he knew. And as for the Yezidis, well, forget it. The encyclopedia straightened him out on Kurdistan:

> *a traditional region, an extensive plateau and mountain area inhabited mainly by Kurds, including large parts of what are now eastern Turkey, northern Iraq, and northwestern Iran (also smaller parts of northern Syria and Armenia).*

To Danny's mind, the locale conjured up a vortex of political psychopathology, but that was it. He didn't really know much about the area. Just the usual things: dictators and dust. Handicrafts and torture.

Turning to another volume of the encyclopedia, he found a single reference to Yezidi, which it defined as "a syncretic religion in the Near East."

And that was it for the library. Going out to Connecticut Avenue, he bought a slice of pizza at Vace's Italian grocery, then flagged down a cab to take him to the Fairfax campus of George Mason University. As it turned out, the driver was new to the country. A former Liberian diplomat, he needed a lot of help just to find Virginia, but Danny got him there, directing him to the Key Bridge, then out 66 past the Beltway.

Set on a suburban campus fifteen miles from Washington, Mason was a state school with a growing reputation and a rapidly expanding student body. Danny knew where it was. A couple of months earlier, he'd taken Caleigh to a Dave Matthews concert at the nearby Nissan Pavilion.

Walking up a low hill toward the Visitors Center, wondering if the cabdriver would ever find the way back to the District, Danny asked himself whether or not he was padding his hours. After all, what did he really expect to find? Probably nothing when you got right down to it. But visiting the school was one of those stones that couldn't be left unturned – or he'd look like an idiot in the client's eyes. *(You mean, you didn't even go out to where he worked?)*

So he found his way to the Visitors Center, where a muscular young woman gave him a brochure with a map on its back. "You want Robinson," she said. "Religious Studies are on the second floor."

On his way to "Robinson," he thought about a pretext he could use. Something simple. Undramatic. Like . . . *Hi, I'm a friend of the family – thought I'd check out Chris's office, see how hard it's going to be to move things.* Or, better: *I loaned him a book a few weeks ago – I was hoping maybe I could see if it's on his desk.*

It was a lie, of course, but only a small one – and besides, pretexts went with the territory. You couldn't work as a PI without them.

In this case, though, a pretext proved unnecessary. The department secretary – a jowly woman in a floral dress – explained that the late professor didn't *have* an office.

"You mean: he doesn't have one *any longer?*" Danny said.

The corners of her mouth turned up in a patient smile. "Sort of," she said. "I mean, of course he *had* an office, but . . . we're just growing so fast! When

Professor Terio went on sabbatical, we had to give his space to Dr. Morris – who was visiting from Oxford."

"Oh," Danny said, disappointed.

"Professor Terio was supposed to get it back," the secretary explained. "Dr. Morris returned to England months ago, but . . . for some reason, Professor T. just took his time about moving back in. Not that there was any hurry – and, obviously, he had things on his mind – but . . ." She shook her gray curls and squeezed her eyes shut.

"I'm sorry," Danny told her.

"We weren't friends or anything. It's just . . . well, it was just so *awful*. Every time I think of him in there . . ." She shuddered and squeezed her eyes closed again.

After a moment, Danny asked, "How long was he on sabbatical?"

The secretary shook her head. "The usual. A year. He was doing research. Someone said he was in the Near East, in Ankara or some such place. And then I think he was in Rome."

"Well . . . do you know when he came back?"

"Oh, it was a couple of months ago," the secretary said. "He was supposed to resume teaching in the fall. So we've had to cancel both his classes. Luckily, they weren't requirements."

"What do you think made him do it?" Danny asked.

She shook her head. "No idea. I'd have thought he'd be the last person to commit . . . to do what he did. He was very religious. Though I suppose, from a religious standpoint, he didn't actually kill himself. He just . . . created the conditions to . . ." Another shudder.

"You think he was religious?" Danny asked. "I thought he renounced the priesthood."

"Oh, he lost his vocation, all right, but not his faith." She sighed and cocked her head to the side. "Who did you say you were?"

"Danny Cray."

"And you're . . . a friend?"

Danny shook his head. "I'm with the law firm handling Dr. Terio's estate," he told her, wondering even as he spoke, *Where did that come from?* "We want to make sure that the will we have is the most recent one."

The explanation seemed to satisfy her. The wrinkles in her brow flattened out, and her smile reappeared.

"I was wondering," Danny went on. "Do you think any of his colleagues are around?"

The secretary gave him a wry look. "Now? You've got to be kidding. It's intersession! There's no one here but us slaves. If you come back in a couple of weeks . . ."

He said that he would and left carrying a course catalog listing the faculty and classes that were scheduled for the fall. Leafing through the catalog as he walked back to the Student Union, he saw that Terio had been set to teach a class in Islamic mysticism and a graduate seminar in something called the *Black Writing*.

Hungry now (it was almost three), he went to the cafeteria and called Red Top Cab from his cell phone. Then he wolfed down a Gardenburger and strolled outside. It was another five minutes (which Danny calculated was worth about $8.33) before the cab came. He told the driver to take him to the Fairfax County Courthouse.

There he hoped to find the professor's last will and testament. At a minimum, it would identify the executor of the estate, someone who would know what had happened to Terio's papers. Since there were no survivors, the executor would presumably be in control of the professor's effects.

The courthouse was a reasonably well organized and efficient place that Danny had visited a number of times before. Even so it took him nearly an hour to get his hands on the will, and when he did it proved to be a disappointment. Dated five years earlier, the document bequeathed Terio's estate to "the priests and nuns of the orphanage that nurtured me" – the Catholic Home Bureau in Brooklyn, New York. The law firm that had drawn up the will was listed as its executor.

Informed that it was five o'clock and that the courthouse was closing, Danny wrote down what little information there was and joined the rush-hour tide flowing toward the nearest Metro stop. Half an hour later, as the train rocked past Arlington Cemetery, his thoughts of Terio were interrupted by the sudden recollection that it was his birthday – and the happy realization that he'd just made seven hundred bucks.

Thank you, Jeezus!

Five

And thank you, too, for this grand armful of girl, Danny thought as he and Caleigh made their way down Columbia Road. She was a South Dakota girl, right out of Pierre – which, as she liked to remind people, was not pronounced in the French way but in the clipped, no-nonsense accent of the Dakotas: *It's "Peer,"* she'd insist, *just "Peer."*

Danny had gone home with her for Christmas the year before, and it struck him as a stripped-down kind of place, plain, bare, and hard. The land was like a hardwood floor, flat and beige, stretching toward the horizon, its temperatures sinking into the imaginary numbers. *Ten below. Twenty below. How low can it go? How low can you stand?* And her family . . . She was the baby and the only female of eight kids, each of her seven brothers huge, hearty, rawboned. It was difficult to figure how generations of sodbusters and tractor salesmen could have produced a child as delicate, luminous, and beautiful as the woman on his arm. Not that Caleigh would agree with his assessment. "I'm okay, I guess" was about as far as she'd ever admit to being a beauty.

But the Latino men on the corner of Eighteenth and Columbia Road knew better. As the couple walked past, one of the Latinos turned his eyes to heaven and muttered a kind of prayer while his friend made a show

50

of looking thunderstruck. Staggering slightly, he clapped a third guy on the back and exclaimed, *"Chica sabrosa, chavo!"* And then the three of them burst into laughter.

They stopped in front of the pet store window for Caleigh's "critter fix." She was crazy about animals – their apartment building's strict no-pet policy was the bane of her existence. Every Sunday, she pored over the real-estate listings, looking for a "pet-friendly" place. She dragged Danny to them, but the rental market was so tight that the apartments on offer were, without exception, "the real dogs" – as he put it.

By now Caleigh and the pet store owner, Magda, were good friends. Tonight, as usual, he and Caleigh had to go inside the store so a puppy (this time an "otter hound") could be picked up and cooed over.

Five minutes later, they arrived at their favorite Italian restaurant, I Matti, where the maître d' greeted them with a theatrical *"Buona sera!"* Clasping Caleigh's hands in his own, Marco asked, as he always did, if Danny was treating her right. And when she admitted that he was, the maître d's stern look dissolved into a smile and he ushered the two of them to a primo table overlooking the street.

When he'd gone, Danny murmured that "the guy's in love with you – you know that, don't you?"

Caleigh rolled her eyes and waved it off. "That's just Marco. He's like that with everybody."

"Right! And that's why we get this table – you and me and, if he's lucky, the mayor. I don't think so."

"Well . . ." She shrugged.

When they'd ordered, she said, "Tell me about the case."

" 'The case'?"

She blushed. "Yeah! That's what it is, isn't it? You're on a 'case.' Just like Nero Wolfe."

Danny frowned. "Nero Wolfe was a fat guy. And old! And he never left his apartment."

"Well," she said, "except for that."

He shrugged. "It's going okay, I guess. Lucrative, anyway."

Soon a plate of bruschetta pomodoro arrived with glasses of Greco di Tufo, and he told her about his disappointing visit to George Mason University. "So, after that, I went to the courthouse."

"What for?"

"The guy's will."

"But what's the point? I mean, I'm sure a will might be interesting, but –" A bite of bruschetta fractured into little cubes of oily tomato. "Yikes," she muttered, and pushed them into a mound on her plate. "I might not be up to the challenge of pasta," she confided.

It had been a decade since she'd come east from Pierre, and Danny could still hear the Plains in the flat vowels of her voice, just as he could see the Sioux blood in the high cheekbones of her face. She was as polished as a pearl and as hip as anybody, but even Swarthmore, Harvard, and Washington hadn't been able to obliterate the farm girl in her. She knew not just how to drive a tractor but how to repair its engine.

His own bruschetta exploded when he took a bite, and Caleigh giggled. "We may not be ready for dining in public," she decided. "So anyway, what about this will?"

"I think the guy was an orphan," he told her.

"Really? Why?"

"Because he left everything to this charity in New

York. Otherwise, the courthouse was kind of a bust. The will was five years old, and there wasn't anything in it about his papers. No 'directed disposition of personal items' – nothing."

"What about his executor?" she asked.

Danny shook his head. "It's just a law firm – the one that drew up the will."

"So . . ." Caleigh winced. "He didn't have any friends? Relatives?"

"Not that I can see."

"That's terrible!"

Which was just like her, Danny mused – feeling sorry for somebody she'd never even heard of. And a *dead* somebody at that.

"Then what happens to his papers?" she asked.

"I don't know."

"But they might let you have them, right?"

Danny frowned. "Mmnnn . . . maybe not."

"Why not?"

"Because there are lawyers involved and lawyers are funny about 'papers' and . . . technically, they belong to the beneficiary."

"You mean, this charity –"

"The Catholic Home Bureau in Brooklyn. It's an orphanage. I checked."

"But they might let you look at them, right?"

Danny nodded slowly. "Yeah . . . they might. Or maybe not."

Caleigh risked another bite of bruschetta. Finally, she said, "So, actually . . . you're not really getting anywhere."

Danny made a helpless gesture. "I'm getting a hundred bucks an hour – which is *some* kind of somewhere. I mean, when you think of it, the worst thing that could happen is – I solve the case. Right away. Then where would I be?"

An hour later, they were back in the apartment, high on each other's company.

"And now, for a truly slammin' dessert," Caleigh promised, her blue eyes lighting up as she headed for the bedroom. Danny watched her go, her hips shifting in a liquid saunter. *It's the wine,* he thought. *Two glasses and her inhibitions disappear.* The truth was, for someone as straitlaced as Caleigh, she had a libido that just wouldn't quit. "In another century," she'd once kidded him, "I would have been 'tormented by the yearnings of my body.' But that was then." *And this,* Danny thought, *this is now* – as she leaned out through the doorway to the bedroom and threw him a look. "Don't go 'way."

He wouldn't. But while he was waiting, he jotted down a note on a Post-it and clapped it to the refrigerator door: *Call lawyer re estate.* Then he snuck in a quick call to an information broker in Daytona Beach, requesting an expedited list of Terio's phone calls in the month before he died. "Not just the numbers," Danny said. "Names, too." He was reciting his Visa number and expiration date when Caleigh sashayed into the living room wearing a pair of see-through black harem pajamas.

"Whoa!" he exclaimed, sparking a laugh from Caleigh as he made a show of fumbling the phone as he tried to hang it up. "Can I get you something?"

"Like what?" Caleigh asked.

"I dunno. Me?"

In the morning, she was long gone by the time he came out of the shower.

Wrapping a towel around his waist, he made a cup of coffee, then telephoned Alfred Dunkirk, the lawyer handling Terio's estate. Although Belzer hadn't said anything about suing Terio's estate, it seemed prudent to take a low profile with the late professor's lawyer.

"I saw the story about Mr. Terio's death," Danny told him, "and the obituary in the *Post*."

"Yes?"

"I was wondering about the house. . . ."

"Excuse me?" The lawyer seemed genuinely baffled.

"I was wondering when it might come up for sale."

Dunkirk made no attempt to disguise his repugnance at Danny's opportunism, but neither did he blow him off – not entirely. "Call Spencer Realty," he suggested. "They're handling it."

And so he did. "Al Dunkirk said I should give you a call," he told the Realtor. "He said you were handling the Terio property."

"That's right," the woman replied. "We are."

"Well, I'd be very interested in seeing it."

"Oh, well . . . that's *great* – although I should tell you, it's a little premature. I won't really have the listing until next week."

"Oh." Danny made his disappointment obvious.

And the real-estate agent rushed to reassure him. "Oh, I can show you the house!" she promised. "I just can't sell it to you. Not yet! But if you're really interested – we could look at it this morning."

It didn't seem like a good idea to arrive at Adele Slivinski's office in the Bomber – it was a car that tended to make people skeptical of the driver. So he took a taxi. A forty-year-old with a helmet of stiff blond hair and a button nose that didn't seem to go with the rest of her face, Adele was an ebullient woman with a white Mercedes and a vanity plate that read: HOMEY.

"I like your plates," Danny remarked as they pulled away from the curb, heading toward Route 50 West.

"I wanted HOMES or even HOMZ, but they were taken. So I had to settle for HOMEY, but . . ."

"What?"

"Well, it's sometimes misunderstood."

Danny chuckled.

The real-estate agent kept up a steady patter about mortgage rates and lenders, new homes versus older ones, as the Mercedes forged westward, passing huge tracts of expensive town houses, until, quite suddenly, they were in the country.

"Isn't it fab?" she asked as they turned onto a washboarded road. "It's one of the last corners of Fairfax that isn't developed to within an inch of its life."

From the outside, the house had a slightly down-at-the-heels look, but from a buyer's point of view there was nothing obviously wrong with it. On the contrary, it was a comfortable-looking house in good repair, with copper gutters and a towering oak that shaded its roof from the afternoon sun. The inside was neat as a pin, with bloodred Oriental carpets sprawling across the living-room floor. Hand-colored nineteenth-century engravings hung from the walls in simple wooden frames: desert landscapes, crowded caravan-saries, and scenes from the souks.

Nice stuff, Danny thought, *and the real thing, too – not something you'd pick up at K-Mart.*

The furniture was worn but comfortable, with simple wooden pieces and overstuffed couches and chairs. Following Adele as she opened and closed doors to empty closets and a tired-looking bathroom, they came into the kitchen – which Adele declared "serviceable. But if it were me," she said, "I'd retire these harvest-gold appliances. I mean, really!" Then she led him past "the laundry room" and "a nice big pantry – that's a good feature," hesitating, finally, before a scuffed white door. "And this is the study," she sighed. "I really do apologize for the state it's in – you're getting a preview here, so I hope you'll understand: I haven't had a chance to tidy it up yet." Opening the door, she stepped aside and let Danny enter ahead of her.

He expected to find a mess, but it was actually quite tidy – just a little small and full of stuff. Some black filing cabinets and crowded bookshelves. A wooden desk with a flat-screen monitor amid piles of paper and stacks of books, some quite old – and everything covered with dust. Beneath the desk: a Dell Dimension computer. A map of eastern Turkey on one wall, a map of the Vatican on another.

For the first time, Danny felt that he was getting somewhere.

"It's a little musty," Adele said.

"No, it's a nice room," Danny assured her, pausing to study the contents of one of the bookshelves.

Not unexpectedly, most of the books were academic titles that concerned various aspects of religion. Slim volumes described the lives and works of medieval saints and mystics, while other and thicker tomes cogitated on an array of esoteric subjects, with works ranging from *Elizabethan Jews* to books in Arabic and Italian whose subject matter Danny was unable to fathom from the titles.

57

Adele wrinkled her nose. "Of course it's a lot more spacious than it *looks* because of the clutter," she said. "And the built-in shelves are a nice feature."

Danny nodded. "Yeah," he said, "they're good to have."

"One of the things I love about this place is the traffic flow, the way everything sort of *swooshes* from one room to another. That's because of the floor plan – it's so open!"

Danny was nodding, but he wasn't listening. His attention had strayed to a single shelf, directly behind the professor's desk. What struck him about it was the look of the books that it held – for the most part, they were bright and new, unlike those on the other shelves. His eyes flickered over the titles:

*Lipid Tubules and the Paradigm of Molecular
    Engineering
The Hermetic Apocalypse
Protein-Based Computers
The Magical Writings of Thomas Vaughn
Nanotechnology and the Quantum Corral*

"It's a terrific room if you have a book collection," Adele confided. "All that *shelf space*."

Danny continued to nod. "You read a lot, Adele?"

"Actually," she said, "I do. I'm reading Margaret Atwood's new book . . ."

Danny made interested sounds as he removed a volume from the shelf and let it fall open in his hand. He read the first sentence he saw: "Nanotechnology is the art and science of building complex, practical devices with atomic precision." *Hunh,* he thought, considering the words. *Thinka that.*

58

But he didn't, really. What he thought about, instead, was that this was a very strange shelf of books and that few of them had much to do with Terio's own expertise. Nor, in fact, did they seem to have much to do with one other. Terio was a religious scholar, and this stuff was all about . . . what? Magic and technology? Alchemy and molecular biology? It was as if Terio had been a schizophrenic, with one foot in the Middle Ages and the other in the year 3000.

A tiny sneeze burst from the realtor, a little chime of noise. *Chw!*

"Bless you."

She smiled in a half-embarrassed way and turned to leave. But when he didn't follow her, she hesitated in the doorway. "You like this room, don't you?"

"Actually," he said, "I was wondering about the computer." He made a brief inclusive gesture. "What happens to it when the house is sold?"

"Oh, it will be auctioned off at an estate sale," she told him, fishing a Kleenex out of her purse and dabbing at her nose. "I think Laws' is going to handle it."

"And the filing cabinets?" Danny asked, idly opening a drawer and glancing inside.

"As I said –"

Legal-size. Alphabetized. Neat little labels.

" 'Everything must go!' " she exclaimed in a cheery voice.

"Right."

She turned on her heel, and he had to follow her.

They toured the upstairs bedrooms and took a peek at the attic, which was virtually empty. Then they returned to the ground floor and went outside. As Adele relocked the doors, she asked, "What do you think?"

Danny smiled his approval. "It's really nice, but . . . what about the basement?" Might as well be thorough.

The real-estate agent gave him a bright smile. "If you'd like," she said, and led him around to the back. Kneeling to work the combination lock on the basement doors, she looked up in sudden concern. "You're not superstitious, I hope."

Danny gave her a puzzled look and shook his head.

"Mr. Terio . . . passed away . . . in the basement," she explained.

"Really!"

"It was in the newspapers," she confided. "Suicide."

Danny winced.

"Some people are nervous about that kind of thing," she told him. Then the lock came open, and Danny stooped to help her with the doors, which opened with a shriek of rusted metal. The realtor took the lead, descending the steps with exaggerated care, then snapped on an overhead light that flickered weakly. "I should really change that bulb," she muttered. And she was right. The basement was gloomy and colorless. "Anyway, this is it. You can see it's a nice *space*! Lots of room for shelves – or you could finish it and put in a pool table. Are you married?"

Danny shook his head. "Not yet," he mumbled, and took a few steps into the long rectangular room. Slowly his eyes adjusted to the artificial twilight, and he found himself staring at the ruined construction in which the previous owner had ended his days.

"The workbench is a good one," Adele gushed, hoping to distract his gaze. "Solid as a rock and – I haven't asked, but I'm sure it conveys."

Danny nodded without really listening. He wanted to examine the construction (or what was left of it),

60

but something held him back. An arc of adrenaline sparked through his chest, and suddenly the room seemed terribly stuffy. For a moment, it was almost as if he couldn't breathe.

Then the real-estate agent turned on her heel and began to mount the steps to the outside. "Well, that's about it," she chirped.

Danny was relieved to follow her out to where the Mercedes was parked. On the way, they passed an open trash container, and he saw that it was half-full.

"Oh, lord!" Adele exclaimed. "Do you think the service will pick it up if I call them?"

"Probably." He flipped the lid closed and pulled it along behind him. The container had wheels and a handle, but dragging it over the gravel and out to the curb was tough going.

Returning to the real-estate office, Adele used her cell phone to call a taxi. Then she gave him a sheaf of information about the house, with her card stapled to the outside folder. Finally, she offered Danny her hand and a bright smile. "Think it over," she told him, "and let me know if you have any questions."

It took him nearly an hour to get back to the apartment, but when he arrived he found a UPS Next Day Air package sitting outside his door. It was the book that he'd ordered from Alibris, and he carried it inside with him. Tossing the package onto the desk, he found a fax waiting for him on the floor, where the machine had ejected it.

It was from the information broker in Daytona. The first page was an invoice for "Business services: $425.15." The fifteen cents made him wonder, but the second page had what he was looking for: a list of long-distance calls that Terio had placed in the last month of his life. The list included the time, date, and duration of each call, along with the subscriber's name.

It was a short list, though Danny saw that there had been a flurry of contacts the day before Terio died – and that all the calls went to one of three places: Oslo, Istanbul, or Palo Alto.

This unlikely juxtaposition gave him pause. Palo Alto and Istanbul were like Helen Keller and Sly Stallone. Throw Oslo into the mix, and you added . . . Uncle Scrooge. What could they possibly have in common?

He looked at the names. In Istanbul, the subscribers were identified as Remy Barzan and the Agence France Presse. The Palo Alto calls went to someone named Jason Patel. And the calls to Oslo were to a number belonging to Ole Gunnar Rolvaag at the Oslo Institute. None of the names meant anything to Danny, but Turkey had come up before – and recently. He looked out the window, trying to remember. And, after a moment, he did. It was the secretary at George Mason. She told him that Terio had been on sabbatical until a couple of months ago. And that he had spent the time "in Ankara or some such place." And Rome.

So the calls had something to do with his studies, Danny decided. That much seemed obvious, because Palo Alto meant Stanford University and Istanbul – well, Istanbul was probably where Terio had been doing his research. The stuff about Islamic mysticism and the Dark Writing (or whatever the hell it was).

Then, again: the Agence France Presse was a news agency, and if Terio was spreading lies about Belzer's client, the AFP was certainly capable of disseminating them. So maybe that was a lead, after all.

As for Oslo . . .

It occurred to him that maybe he ought to call one or more of the numbers and see what he could find out. But no. Most of the time, Danny knew, you only got one kick at the dog. Better to wait and see what he could learn. And in the meantime, he could think about a pretext for calling.

Besides, he thought, *Belzer might want to weigh in on that.* In fact, he ought to call Belzer. Report in. Tell him what he'd found out.

But not yet. The first thing he should do is call the estate agent, a guy named Howie Culpepper at Laws' Auctions. His phone number was in the brochure that Adele had given him, and he answered on the first ring.

"Culpeppah!" The auctioneer had a good-old-boy accent and a stuttery laugh. When Danny asked him if he could buy the computer and the filing cabinets from the Terio estate, the older man fired off a laugh that morphed into a long curve of regret. "Sorry, pod'nah – wish I *could*. But I cain't! I just *cain't*! No way I can break up a lot before the liquidation date."

"You're sure?"

"Damn sure! 'Gainst *all* the rules."

" 'Cause I really need a computer and some filing cabinets," Danny told him. "And I thought – you know, *used*, they'd be cheaper than buying them at Staples."

"Yeah, well – you'd probably get quite a deal, but . . . you're just gonna have to wait."

"Till when? When's the auction?"

Culpepper mumbled into the receiver, and Danny could hear him turning the pages in a ledger of some kind. Finally, he said, "Here we go . . . October first.

63

High noon – out in Manassas! You want, I can send you a list of what we'll have – and a map to the site. That he'p you out?"

Danny said that it did and gave the man his address. Then he hung up and glanced at his watch. It was almost twelve-thirty – which meant that it was nine-thirty in San Francisco. A good time to call, but . . . he was scheduled to work. In fact, he was supposed to be at the gallery from one to five, and the last thing he wanted to be was late. Even if it was only ten minutes, the guy who ran the place – a neurotic Brit named Ian – would sink into a passive-aggressive pout that could last all afternoon. Not that he'd say anything. He'd just simmer with unhappiness until the atmosphere turned toxic.

Still, there was time, if he was quick.

Taking Belzer's business card from his wallet, he dialed the telephone number that was the card's only content. Then he listened as a phone began to ring. When the lawyer answered, the clarity was astounding. It wasn't as if he was in the next room; it was as if he was in Danny's head.

"*Ciao.*"

"Hi, it's . . . Dan Cray."

"Ah. *Dan.* Goooood."

"I thought I'd check in. Got a couple of things to report."

"Already?" Belzer said approvingly. "You *are* quick."

Danny told him about the list of toll calls he'd obtained from "a source in Florida. Terio made a few phone calls just before he, uhhh, locked himself up in the basement. You want me to follow up?"

"How do you mean?"

"These people he called – I could try to interview them."

"Noooo," Belzer replied. "I don't think you need to do that, Dan. If you'll fax me the list, I'll take it from here." The lawyer gave him a number with a San Francisco area code.

"I'll send it as soon as we finish talking."

"Perfect," Belzer said.

"So I went out to his house," Danny told him.

"Whose?"

"Terio's. It's a farmhouse."

"I see."

"There's a computer – which could be interesting – and some filing cabinets."

"Is there anything in them?"

"As a matter of fact, yes. They looked like they were full. I didn't get a chance to read anything, but if you're interested, it's all going to be auctioned off October first."

"That's months from now!" the lawyer complained.

"I know."

"Well, can't we make some sort of . . . preemptive bid?"

"I don't think so," Danny replied. "I talked to the auctioneer, and –"

Belzer muttered something Danny didn't understand. Finally, he asked, "Is that it, then?"

"For now? Yeah, that's pretty much it," Danny told him.

"*Bene* – so far, so good. Just keep me informed, and I'm sure we'll get to the bottom of it. Ciao!" And with that, the lawyer hung up.

Danny put on his black chinos and the chartreuse Tommy Bahama shirt that Caleigh had given him for

Christmas. Standing before the mirror in the bath, he inserted the gold rings through the top of his left ear. Then he slammed some gel into his hair, stirred it up with his fingers, and hit the stairs.

To save time, he drove the Bomber to the gallery – even though Ian didn't like him to park it in the Wexler's lot. *It's the size of a goddamned aircraft carrier, Danny; it takes up two spaces. And it looks like hell.* Which was true. The paint job had begun its life as a metallic bronze, but over the years the color had faded to a matte brown. The plastic dashboard was cracked, the front seats were sprung, and the rearview mirror was held in place by globs of stickum dispensed by Caleigh's glue gun. The car got twelve miles to the gallon (on the highway) and required two quarts of oil a week.

It was, in a word, totally incorrect – environmentally, aesthetically, and automotively. Even so, Danny liked it. A gift from his grandfather (who'd nursed it into its senior years only to be told by Danny's grandmother that she would no longer ride in it), the car came without any monthly payments. And it had *that sound*. Turn on the key, and it roared – really *roared* – to life.

Of course, it was about as easy to park as a tractor-trailer, but if he could find a space, he'd gotten pretty good at it. He seemed to have an intuitive grasp of volume and dimension, so that he could whip into tight parking spaces with no obvious effort – sometimes turning Caleigh's knees to water.

Swinging into the little lot behind the gallery, Danny left the Bomber next to Ian's Z-3 Roadster. The effect was similar to parking a double-wide on Rodeo Drive – and Danny had to admit it gave him some pleasure.

Inside, he found Ian standing next to a fifty-ish woman, his chin propped on the back of his fist, the fist supported by an elbow resting on his other hand. The two of them were gazing at a busy little watercolor of a duck pond streaked with rain. Finally, Ian threw up his hands and muttered something about "circular composition."

Time did not fly.

Danny spent about half an hour in the showroom helping a woman in a white linen suit find a painting that would "pick up" the vermilion in a swatch of upholstery material that she had with her. Ian couldn't believe it, rolling his eyes as the woman held up the fabric to one artwork after another, including a Rauschenberg lithograph that went for five figures. After that, he spent the remainder of the afternoon crating up recent sales, filling out shipping forms – and feeling conflicted. Here he was, making nine bucks an hour, when he could be making ten times as much sleuthing for Belzer. But he knew better than to quit his "day job." The PI business was unpredictable, and with him working solo like this, his lone client could put an end to the investigation whenever he pleased. And besides, Danny told himself, he didn't want to stiff Ian, even if Ian wasn't his favorite person (or even, for that matter, his favorite gallery owner).

At five o'clock, Danny helped Ian lock up and joined the commuting masses on a very slow drive out to Fairfax County. It took him an hour and forty-two minutes, but he eventually arrived at Chris Terio's farmhouse. There, he got out of the car and, feeling like a criminal, went to retrieve the garbage bags from their container. Briefly it occurred to him that there might be a way into the house and, once inside, he could take a long, slow look at the late professor's files. But no. It was one thing to pick up the guy's garbage and quite another to go into the man's house and paw through his files. As long as the bags were out by the curb, anyone who wanted them could take them. They were public property.

So it wasn't like he was breaking-and-entering. On the contrary, though Danny himself had never done it before, Dumpster diving wasn't that unusual. Every investigative firm had someone in its Rolodex who did the work.

To his dismay, he saw that the bags were lying in a couple of inches of water. Fortunately, neither was torn. He dragged the bags across the lawn to the Bomber, opened the trunk, and tossed them inside. Then he drove back to Adams-Morgan, accompanied by a faint whiff of rotting fruit.

In the morning, he picked up a jar of Vicks VapoRub at the local CVS, then crossed the street to Martin's Hardware. There he bought a couple of plastic tarps, a package of rubber gloves, and a "state-of-the-art" air freshener called Ozium. Finally, he carried his purchases the two blocks to where the Bomber was parked and drove to his studio.

This was on the third floor of what had once been a department store at the corner of Florida and Tenth Street, Northeast. Looted and firebombed in the wake of Martin Luther King's assassination, the building had become a moldering pile of brick, festooned with graffiti. A fringe of trash and broken glass glittered against the old store's foundation, which was itself a backdrop for countless petty drug dealers and dozing drunks.

As mean as the building was, the studio itself was filled with light and remarkably spacious. Not to mention dirt cheap. Though the first floor had been bricked up for twenty years, each of the other tiers was girded round by floor-to-ceiling windows that looked out across the ghetto toward the suburbs.

Danny's "atelier" (as Caleigh jokingly referred to it) was in the building's northwest corner, a rectangular space with ten-foot ceilings and a row of floor-to-ceiling windows along both of its exterior walls.

The northwest corner of the room served as Danny's "office," with an old steel desk facing a threadbare couch and a worn leather chair. Nearby, a beat-up TV rested on a recycled filing cabinet, while a few feet away an electric kettle stood on a counter next to a small sink.

It was the industrial equivalent of the "clean, well-lighted place" that Hemingway had once described, though it was anything but "crisp." The hardwood floors were spattered with paint, as if Jackson Pollock had suffered a seizure with a brush in each of his hands. In one corner of the room, a welding rig stood before a tangled mass of rebar whose sculptural intent Danny could no longer recall (if, indeed, he ever really knew). Across the room, a soapstone bust of J. Edgar Hoover, an artifact of Danny's college days, gazed fixedly at the world beyond the windows. Elsewhere, half a dozen canvases leaned against the wall beside the door, which looked as if the DEA had kicked it in – and not just once. Most of the canvases had been painted years before when Danny was just out of college and living on Mallorca with a beautiful (if schizy) Dutch mime.

As he entered the studio with Terio's garbage and

the things he'd bought at Martin's, it occurred to Danny that he really ought to make an inventory of the pieces that he had and those that he'd loaned to friends. Then he'd know where he stood when it came time to organize the Neon show.

Dropping the garbage bags on the floor, he snapped on the TV (the radio was on the fritz) and glanced around the room. What was there? What did he actually have that he could show? Some wire sculptures, a couple of collages, a nascent "installation" whose focal point was a mordant white outline on the floor. At first glance, it seemed to be the taped silhouette of a homicide victim. But closer inspection revealed something else or, rather, two things: a bulge in the shoulders that might have been wings or the beginning of wings, and a carefully painted hand at the end of an outflung arm. The effect of the wings and the hand was ambiguous and disquieting, precisely because one couldn't be sure if they were coming or going. Were they remains – or portents? Was the figure fallen – or emerging? Even Danny didn't know.

It had taken him most of a week to get the silhouette (and the hand) just right, and now he wanted to buy one of those turning red lights that police cars have. With the lights flickering over the outline and Handel's *Messiah* in the background, the installation would be unsettling. And maybe more.

Then there was *Babel On II*.

Standing in a pool of sunlight in the center of the room, Danny's most recent work was eerie and yet undeniably beautiful – a see-through city with a mysterious hologram at its heart. In daylight, the floating image looked even more like the apparition he'd intended: washed-out and faded, the hologram was hallucinatory, startling.

He threw open the windows, stretched the tarps out on the floor, and applied a dab of Vicks VapoRub to each nostril, hoping it would mask the sour smell emanating from the bags of garbage. That done, he dumped one of the sacks onto the tarp and pulled on a pair of disposable gloves.

The trash was anything but fresh, but it wasn't as bad as he'd feared. It looked as if Terio had been a vegetarian. At least there wasn't any meat in the bags, so there weren't any maggots, either. But there *were* fruit flies, a cloud of them that rose up, dancing in the air above the tarp.

Using the handle of a broom, he stirred the trash around, separating it so he could see if there was any medical waste. For all Danny knew, Terio could have been a junkie, a diabetic, or a hemophiliac. But there were no needles or bandages or anything else with blood. What there was, was a lot of packaging: an empty box of Cheerios, an egg carton, some yogurt containers, and a wad of corn husks, black with mildew. There were coffee grounds and Melitta filters, some crushed Coca-Cola cans, and half a dozen Dasani water bottles. A crumpled shoe box that had once held a pair of Nike Predators (size 10½) – and lots of old newspapers. *Not a recycler,* Danny thought.

More substantively, he found some notes with hand-writing on them, Post-its with telephone numbers, reminders and short lists *(butter leeks yogurt bread)*, envelopes and bills, junk mail, catalogs, and credit card receipts. Danny set the paperwork aside to be examined later – the priority being to get the trash back into the bags and onto the street before the smell could take up residence.

Meanwhile, he noticed that the television was tuned to Caleigh country, MSNBC, where a couple of analysts were yakking about "basis points" and an upcoming meeting of the Fed. For Caleigh, MSNBC was more entertaining than a U2 concert. In the apartment, it seemed like the channel was always on, with his girlfriend mesmerized by the ebb and flow of valuations, the hubris of the dot-coms, the moving-average of the Dow.

The first time he'd realized that her interest in finance was as much an avocation as a job, he'd reacted with suspicion – as if he'd learned a dark secret. It seemed to Danny that Caleigh's interest must be symptomatic of some deeper flaw – specifically, greed – and that this flaw did not bode well for a future with an artist. But, very quickly, he'd come to understand that while her fascination with finance had a lot to do with money, it had nothing to do with consumption. She was not a shopper. For Caleigh, the equity markets were a kind of track meet in which she was called upon to perform feats of insight and analysis. The money itself was just a measure of performance, the financial equivalent of a stopwatch.

Danny understood all this, but he didn't share her enthusiasm – not for the market and not for the channels that covered it. To him, MSNBC was a kind of visual Novacain, with talking heads droning on and on above an inscrutable scroll of red and green symbols. He would have changed the channel, but his hands were filthy. At least it was company of sorts, and it had the advantage of being easy to ignore.

Soon he was finished with the first bag, his "finds"

pushed to one side of the tarp. Rebagging the rest of the trash, he pulled the red drawstring tight and set that bag aside. Then he dumped the second bag onto the tarp and, crouching, began to sort through the mess, glancing up from time to time at the TV.

The numbers on the tube were mostly green – which was good, because it meant that Caleigh would come home in a good mood. It occurred to him that it might be fun to create something involving Wall Street. Maybe he could put together an installation using a ticker of some kind. Get it to undulate, rather than scroll. Or not just undulate. Why not put it on the forehead of a guy in a pinstriped suit? And not just any guy – the Man in a Bowler-Hat, of Magritte's famous painting.

Or maybe not. It was kind of literal.

Before long, he was almost done with the second bag of trash and idly wondering about the scroll. Would he have to get permission from Dow Jones to use it? Or could he just videotape it, and then play with it – *on his new video-editing suite*.

Not that he had one. Not yet. So far he'd racked up fourteen hours on Belzer's payroll – which was fourteen hundred bucks. That was a lot of money in a very short time, but it was still just a drop in the bucket. He needed twenty grand – fifteen, if he could get it wholesale.

The idea gave him pause – literally. There was no need to rush through what he was doing. In fact, why not take his time? Be thorough. With a sigh, he looked up at the TV and saw that one of the network's correspondents was doing a stand-up outside a *Blade Runner*–like fortress. *What is that place?* Danny wondered as the correspondent told how Silicon Valley denizens were shocked in the wake of a CTO's murder.

Danny didn't know, or even care, what a "CTO" was, but the story piqued his interest because murder wasn't the kind of story that you saw on MSNBC.

The correspondent was standing next to a sign that read VSS, hair flying, squinting into the sun. "– in the foothills, and I have to say that people here are really unnerved, and not just because the company is known to be seeking investment and this is the kind of thing that tends to make lenders skittish. According to police, Mr. Patel was found early this morning in an extremely remote area of the Mojave Desert, an area so out-of-the-way that it is rarely visited, even by campers and hikers. Authorities consider it something of a miracle that the victim – who was tied to a Joshua tree with fiber-optic wire and apparently tortured – was discovered at all, let alone so quickly."

Patel?

The camera shifted to the studio, where an attractive Asian woman asked, "What about the company where Mr. Patel worked? Have they issued a statement?"

"Not yet, Pam."

Danny found himself gaping at the screen, a loopy half grin on his lips. *No way! It's a different guy – gotta be!*

Still staring at the tube, Danny watched as a middle-aged man in a dark suit emerged from the building – only to be buttonholed by the correspondent. The man, with a froth of red hair and a skittery look in his eyes, obviously wanted to bolt – but the camera held him like a deer in headlights.

"Did you know the victim?"

There must be a zillion Patels, Danny told himself. *Bob, Ravi, Omar –*

"Everyone knew Jason." Whoa! *Jason!* "We're not that big a firm. Now, if you'll excuse me –"

"He was the chief technology officer at VSS, isn't that right?" the correspondent asked.

"Yes," the man replied, eyes swinging left and right, as if he was looking for the exits.

"Can you tell us what he was working on?"

"No." And with that, the interviewee strode out of the frame.

Fuckin' hell, Danny thought. *Does Belzer know about this?* Maybe he should call him. Or maybe not. The likelihood of multiple Jason Patels in California seemed small but not impossible. Before he called Belzer with the news (if it was news), he should find out if the dead man's telephone number was the same one that Chris Terio had called.

Not that Danny doubted for a second that it *was* the same guy. *It had to be.* Two people, crazy-dead. One tortured, the other entombed. Maybe the phone calls were a coincidence, but Danny didn't think so. No matter what anyone said, "a cigar" was almost never just a cigar.

But first things first.

Turning away from the TV, he got back to work on the trash, retrieving a schedule for George Mason's soccer team, a take-out menu from a Chinese restaurant, and appeals from Greenpeace and the Paralyzed Veterans Association. Finally, he stirred the broom handle through the mess one last time, then swept it into a Hefty bag and tied it shut.

The tarp was slick with vegetative slime. He thought about cleaning it but decided it would be more discreet to get rid of it in the Dumpster. So he jammed the tarp and the plastic gloves into a third garbage bag and carried the three of them down the fire stairs, into the basement, and outside.

Returning, he sniffed the air, and retrieved the can of Ozium. Waving it as if it were a conductor's wand, he sat down on the floor and began to sort through the bits of paper that he'd collected.

For the most part, they weren't of much interest. A couple of offers for credit cards, some familiar catalogs, and perforated receipts for payments that Terio had made to Virginia Power, AOL, Sprint, and DirecTV. A reminder from the Fairfax County Library that *Engines of Creation* was overdue.

Then he saw it. A FedEx receipt, damp from the garbage and dated July 19. This was the same day that Terio had made his telephone calls to Jason Patel and the guy in Turkey and the same date mentioned in the *Washington Post* story – the one on the Home Depot receipt for the do-it-yourself tomb. Danny sat up straight and studied the receipt:

Recipient: Piero Inzaghi, S.J.

The address was blurry with dampness, the ink feathering out, but he brought it into focus with a squint:

Via della Scrofa
N. 42A
Roma, Italia

This guy, Inzaghi, must be a priest – a Jesuit, in fact, judging by the initials after his name. Maybe an old friend, Danny thought, someone from Terio's own days as a priest. Danny's eyes drifted to the space

76

beneath the recipient's address, where Customs information was recorded:

Total Packages: 1
Total Weight: 7.8 lbs
Commodity Description: IBM Thinkpad (used)
Total Value for Customs: $900

Jeez Louise, Danny thought. *This is going to make Belzer happy! This is gonna –*
Fuck me.

It was, he suddenly realized, the end of the investigation. There wasn't much of anything left for him to do. The client didn't want him to interview any of the obvious sources (Rolvaag, Barzan, or Patel). And the estate auction would happen on its own in two months. Maybe Belzer would ask him to attend and bid, but even if he did, that was a couple of hours of work and nothing more. As for the laptop, it was sitting in Italy. And the client was *from* Italy. So that was that. Obviously, Belzer would take it from here.

End of story.

The End.

Six

Only it wasn't. The End, that is.

He still had a report to write and a couple of loose ends to tie up. Sitting down at his desk in the studio, he went on-line to the FedEx tracking Web site and typed in the waybill numbers to see if Terio's computer had arrived in Rome. It had.

The next thing to do was make sure that the Jason Patel who'd been killed in California was the same one that Terio had called.

There were a couple of ways to do that, Danny thought. For instance: he could call the number he'd been given by the data broker in Daytona and see who answered. But no. If it *was* the same Jason Patel, either no one would answer or the police would pick up – in which case things might get complicated.

A safer course of action, and the one he took, was to run a credit check on the Jason Patel whose telephone number he had. This wasn't entirely legal, of course. The dissemination of credit reports was supposedly restricted to a handful of requesters: landlords and employers could get them, and so could insurance companies, collection agencies, and businesses that grant credit to consumers. But aside from those, and aside from the person whose credit history it was, that was about it – in theory, anyway.

As a practical matter, it was really just a question of establishing a dummy account with one of the credit-reporting agencies. Fellner Associates had a number of such accounts, using bland names like Franklin Realty, First Manassas Investments, and Harriman's Department Stores. On occasion, Danny had run credit checks for one investigation or another, so it only took him a minute or two to find the password that he needed in one of his old notebooks.

He went to the Experian Web site and entered what little information he had – in essence, Patel's first and last names and the phone number that he'd gotten from Florida. Then he clicked on one of the boxes on the screen, indicating that all he needed was the report's "top line." This would give him Patel's most recent address and current employer but no financial information – which was fine. Danny didn't need to know how much Patel was making or whether he paid his bills on time. He just wanted to know if the guy had been tortured to death.

After plugging in the data, Danny hit the RETURN key, sat back, and watched. After a bit, the screen shivered and the information appeared: Patel's name, address, and telephone number. Then the words:

Very Small Systems, Inc.
Chief Technology Officer

Christ, he thought. *It is the same guy.*

His first instinct was to call Belzer. But it was still early in the morning in San Francisco – so he decided to wait. In fact, he tried to put the whole thing out of his mind.

Removing a small notebook from the top drawer of his desk, he leafed through its pages until he found what he was looking for – a list of sculptures and paintings, lithographs, and other works, pieces in galleries and loaned out to friends. There were fifteen of them, total, of which he still liked nine or ten. Taken together with what he had in the studio and with the pieces in his own apartment, he might be able to put together twenty works that would be worth showing.

Crossing the room to the bank of windows on the far wall, he gazed out across the tops of trees, without really seeing them. In his mind's eye, he was taking a virtual tour of the Neon Gallery, hanging the show. The gallery consisted of two large rooms, with very high ceilings, and a smaller room on the second floor. Most of his work would fit nicely in one of the larger rooms, with maybe some spillover onto the second floor. But there was no way he could furnish the entire gallery – not with what he had.

So maybe it's a good thing Belzer's over with. I gotta get rolling.

For a second he remembered Lavinia's cool glance of assessment, her bloodred lips and businesslike tone: "You *do* have enough work . . . ?"

Today was – what? – August tenth. The show was October fifth. That gave him almost two months. But of course he still had to put in twenty hours a week for Ian. Unless he quit. For a moment he considered that. It might make sense. The show was a lot more important than anything he did at the gallery. On the other hand, he had exactly what – a grand? – in the bank. Plus whatever he got from Belzer. *Not enough.* And he'd have extra expenses, mounting the show.

Which meant that if he quit working for Ian, he'd have to survive on the kindness of . . . Caleigh. Not something he wanted to do.

What he really needed was video equipment. There was just so much he could do with it. But that wasn't likely to happen. He'd worked about twenty-five hours for Belzer – not enough, even, to earn out his advance. He still had a report to write, and there was an outside chance that Belzer would want him to go to the estate sale to bid on the filing cabinets. So maybe he'd rack up thirty hours all together. About half of what he'd need just to make the down payment on a good system.

Frustrated, he picked up a pair of wire snips and began to rework a mobile that he'd put aside the week before. It was a delicate piece, which he'd fabricated from strands of heavy-gauge copper wire, crimped and bent into a painterly simulacrum of Albert Einstein. Suspended from the ceiling by a nylon thread, the mobile turned slowly on its axis, looking for all the world as if it had been sketched in the air. It was an interesting experiment and Danny was proud of it, but if it was going to work it would have to work from every angle. No matter which way the mobile turned or where one stood in the room, it should be obvious – immediately obvious – that this was a representation of Einstein.

And it wasn't there yet. From the back, it looked more like Jerry Garcia. Using the snips and a pair of pliers, he twisted the wire this way and that, adding a line of metal here and removing one there. Soon he was lost in the moment, aware of nothing but his hands and the wire in his hands – the image, the shape, the surprise.

He worked for nearly an hour, until – quite suddenly – he looked up and realized where he was. The transition he went through was as profound and instantaneous as that a swimmer feels when he breaks the surface of the water, moving from one atmosphere to another. He stepped back, cocked his head, and considered the mobile. Then he walked around it. *Not bad,* he decided. *Less Jerry. More Albert.*

But he was going to be late if he didn't hurry. He had to be at the gallery at one, and it was already a quarter to. Even so, he paused long enough to gaze unhappily on *Babel On II*. It was the best thing he'd ever done. He had to have it for the show. But he still had to figure out how the hell he was going to move it and keep it in one piece.

He spent the rest of the afternoon working at the gallery. Caleigh called. ("It's for you," Ian grouched.) She told him she had to work late. Also, she'd have to bail on their weekend plans. Tomorrow, she was heading to Seattle – some kind of meltdown at headquarters.

After Jake stopped by to borrow twenty bucks, Ian cut loose with a tight-assed little speech about "personal phone calls and visitors to the workplace." Danny listened patiently, idly toying with the rings in his ear and secretly feeling sorry for the guy – who couldn't even look him in the eye. It was embarrassing. The man was almost hyperventilating.

"Okay," Danny said when Ian seemed to be done. "Take it easy."

That just set him off again. "Take it *easy*?" Ian wheezed. "I might take it easy if . . ." And so on.

Danny tuned out, but when Ian finally wound down he couldn't keep his mouth shut. "Remember," he said, "you only pay me nine bucks an hour."

If Ian hadn't already worn himself out venting, Danny thought, he might have gone nova.

After work, he stopped at Mixtec for a plate of rice and beans, which he washed down with a couple of bottles of Negra Modelo. Then he went back to the apartment, wrote up his report, and, using the Quick Books program, logged in the expenses he'd incurred and the hours he'd worked. When he was done, he called Belzer to tell him about the FedEx receipt he'd found in Terio's garbage.

"That's very good work," Belzer remarked. "Very smart!"

"Thanks."

"And he sent the computer to Rome?"

"Right," Danny said, "to a priest named Inzaghi."

" 'Inzaghi' . . . and how do you know he's a priest?"

"Because there's an 'S.J.' after his name." When the lawyer didn't react, Danny added, "Society of Jesus. It means he's a Jesuit."

"I know what it means," Belzer replied. "I was just thinking . . . *Roma*."

"Nice town," Danny joked. "If you need someone to look up the good father . . . I'm available."

To his surprise, the suggestion was greeted by a long silence. Finally, Belzer said, "I thought you didn't speak Italian."

Danny laughed. "I don't. I mean, I can order pasta. 'Penne penne penne. Vino.' " He paused. "That would be three orders of penne and, ummm – some wine."

Belzer chuckled. "Let me think about it," he suggested. "I'll get back to you in the morning."

Rii-ight, Danny thought. *I'll wait by the phone.*

He was smearing marmalade on a piece of toast when the phone rang. To his astonishment, it was Belzer. "I was thinking," the lawyer said. "It might be an advantage."

"What might?" Danny asked.

"Being an American. Being *so* American. And not having the language."

Danny frowned. Was he serious? "I don't get it. Why would *that* help? I couldn't even ask him about the computer. Which is what we're talking about, right? The priest – the computer?"

"Exactly. But what if you had some good ID – and telephone backup? You could tell the priest you're a detective – a police detective – and that you're investigating Mr. Terio's death."

The suggestion was so unexpected, and such a non-starter, that even though he was alone in the apartment, Danny mimed a look of shock. *You gotta be kidding,* he thought as the silence between them grew.

After a while, Belzer cued him: "Dan?"

"Yes . . ."

"I was saying that" –

"It's just . . . not the sort of thing I do," Danny told him.

"Oh, but it is," Belzer replied. "It's exactly the sort of thing you do. Didn't you pretend to be in the market for a house when you called the real-estate agent?"

"Yeah, sure, but that's a lot different from impersonating a police officer. One's a white lie; the other's a felony."

"Not in Italy," Belzer said. "A Fairfax County sheriff's deputy has no authority whatsoever in Rome, so impersonating one would be more like an eccentricity than a crime. It's not like you'd be pretending to judicial authority – because you wouldn't have any . . . not *really*." Belzer paused and then went on. "And let's not lose sight of what we're doing here: Zerevan Zebek is being smeared from one end of Europe to the other – and it's costing him millions. He can afford that, I'll admit. He's a very wealthy man. But he's not the only one getting hurt. When a company like Sistemi di Pavone takes a hit, a lot of people suffer. Suppliers lose money; people lose jobs. There's a snowball effect."

"I understand, but –"

"A little subterfuge isn't the end of the world. It's not as if I'm asking you to do something illegal."

"I know, but –"

"You could give it a try," Belzer suggested.

"You mean –"

"Go over there. See what the comfort level is."

Danny thought about it. Thought: *Roma!* Thought: *No more Ian!* Then he heard himself say, "And if I do?"

"You'd be very well paid."

"And what is it you'd want me to do?"

"Talk to the priest. See if you can get the computer back."

A skeptical look settled on Danny's face. *And how am I gonna do that?*

"I'll give you ten thousand dollars," Belzer went on. "That's in addition to your hourly rate and expenses. Maybe the priest will sell you the computer.

If he does, fine – you can keep whatever's left. I don't care how you handle it, actually. What I'm hoping is that you'll use your imagination to come up with a pretext that works for everyone. And if, in the end, you're unsuccessful – well, you'll have been well paid for your time."

Danny wasn't sure what to say. The idea of pretending to be a cop made him nervous. Even if it wasn't illegal, it was sleazy. Like Dumpster diving. That was legal, too, but you wouldn't want to put it on your résumé. *And that's not all. . . .* He'd seen a follow-up story on the "desert crucifixion" the night before. Watched a woman in a red suit standing in front of a monster Joshua tree, her eyes crinkling against the desert sun. She was talking about how Patel's body had been pierced by dozens of cholla cactus spines. *I'm told that these are so sharp and strong, John, that if you kick a cholla even with the thickest leather boots, the spines go right through.* Even so, he hadn't bled to death. *Preliminary indications are that Mr. Patel died of dehydration.*

Just like Terio, Danny thought. It was another coincidence and, like the first, it made him nervous. As did Belzer himself. The guy was way slick, even for a lawyer. And a little bent, too. Otherwise, he wouldn't suggest this stuff about pretending to be a cop.

On the other hand . . . there was ten thousand dollars out there. Maybe he could just *buy* the computer from the priest. He might not even want the thing. The Vatican probably had a boatload of computers already. In fact, they were probably *swimming* in computers.

He'd offer, say . . . two or three grand – leaving Danny with . . . seven or eight grand. And even if the

86

holy father didn't want to sell the goddamn thing, Danny would still be racking up eight hundred dollars a day just for going to see him.

"As I said, we'd take care of the expenses," Belzer reminded him.

"Uh-huh." Danny had been to Italy once before – right out of college, the backpacking thing with Jake. Even with them "picnicking" on bread and cheese and sleeping in hostels, the country had been almost supernaturally expensive – so much so that they hadn't even gotten to Rome. They'd kicked around Florence for three or four days, spending as much money as they'd budgeted for two weeks. They couldn't keep it up, hopped a bus down to the Boot, found a boat to Corfu. Missed the Vatican and so much else. Maybe it was time he saw Rome. . . .

And how long was the flight anyway? Seven or eight hours? Call it ten hours, door-to-door – Adams-Morgan to the Spanish Steps. If you thought about it like that, he'd make a grand just for making the trip.

What are you thinking about!? A man's dead. You put his name out there, and now he's dead. And all you can think about is your hours. You're turning into a sleazebag, he told himself. A voice in his head replied, *To be fair –*

Danny shook his head. It was magical thinking, putting himself at the center of the universe, taking the credit and blame for everything that happened, when in fact he knew practically nothing about Jason Patel – whose death probably didn't have anything to do with Belzer's client, Zerevan Zebek.

"You still there?" Belzer asked.

"Huh? Yeah! Absolutely. And, uhh, sure – I'll be glad to do it." *Sleaze.*

"Excellent! I'm delighted."

"Well, I can't promise anything."

"Of course not. You can only do your best – that's all anyone can ask." A little pause. "How soon do you think you could go?"

The sooner the better, Danny thought. With all the work he had to do for the Neon show . . . "Actually, the best time would be . . . pretty much right away."

"Tomorrow night?"

"Tomorrow night would be fine."

"I'll have a car pick you up – there's an eight o'clock flight out of Dulles. I'll make sure the driver has everything you'll need, tickets, ID –"

"What ID?"

"The tickets will be in your name, of course, so you'll need your passport. But what I mean is the other ID. I suppose it would be – what? Fairfax County. Police or sheriff – whatever they have." When Danny didn't react, Belzer added, "As we discussed . . . "

"Well, maybe that won't be necessary," Danny suggested, a hopeful tone in his voice.

"If you can think of another pretext – one that's just as good, one that works – I don't have any problem with that. But just in case you can't . . . "

Danny let out a breath. "Okay."

"Then it's settled. *Buon viaggio, Danielo!*"

Caleigh was thrilled for him and made a big show of wanting to go with him. But that was impossible, and they both knew it. In the end, they toasted his good luck with a bottle of Old Vine red. "Tell me what you want," he said. "I have to get you something, at least. Whatever you want!"

"A T-shirt would be nice," she said, her face a mask of innocence. "If you can find something with the Colosseum on it, that would be great. I'm so tired of jewelry."

The next evening, Danny was standing at the window, waiting for his ride, when a jet-black stretch Mercedes pulled up outside and double-parked. *Rich bastard,* Danny thought, wondering when his own ride would show up. A minute went by, and then another. Finally, he saw the driver of the Mercedes climb out from behind the wheel and walk slowly up to the front door of Danny's apartment building. Even then, it wasn't until the doorbell rang that Danny realized the limo was there for him.

A stocky man in his forties, the driver was right out of *GQ*, resplendent in a dark suit, wing tips, and a black fedora. Wresting the duffle bag from Danny's hand, he trotted back to the car and held open the door to the backseat. "For you," he said, nodding at a leather attaché case on the backseat. Trying to look casual, and not quite managing it, Danny struggled to suppress the grin that held his mouth in a kind of rictus. "Thanks!" he said, sliding into the backseat as if it were home plate.

Thunnnk.

The car was virtually soundproof. Just behind them, the driver of a sanitation truck leaned on his horn, impatient to go by. Danny sensed that the horn was a loud one, but even so, he could barely hear it. And the limo driver couldn't have cared less. Taking his time, the driver stowed Danny's duffle in the trunk, walked around to the side of the car, got in, and fastened his seat belt. Then he adjusted his hat, carefully checked the results in the rearview mirror, and smiled. "Now vee go," he said in an accent that Danny couldn't quite place.

Central Europe, maybe.

As the limo moved forward, Danny eyed the accoutrements around him. There was a small television, half a dozen magazines, and a split of champagne nestled in a silver bucket of crushed ice. A blood-red rose stood at attention in a cut-glass vase, coloring the air with its fragrance. Reaching over his shoulder, Danny switched on the reading light, which cut through the gloom imposed by the limousine's tinted windows.

It was all very impressive, slightly embarrassing – and fun. But what made him blink was the sheaf of magazines he found in front of him. *Art in America. Daruma. Bomb. Asian Art.* Clearly they'd been chosen with Danny – and only Danny – in mind.

As flattering as that was, he felt a twinge of apprehension as he opened the attaché case on the seat beside him. Inside he found a portable cell phone, its instruction manual, and a short note. *This will help us stay in touch,* the note read. *American cells don't work in Europe, and hotel phones aren't secure. Suggest you use this, as needed. B.* Danny glanced at the manual, which explained (in six languages) that the phone was a digital unit with embedded encryption based upon the GSM standard common in Europe.

In addition to the cell phone, the attaché case contained a leather portfolio. In this Danny found his tickets and itinerary, with a confirmation number for a suite – *a suite!* – at the Hotel d'Inghilterra. Clipped to the itinerary was a business card for "Paulina Pastorini, Translations," and an envelope containing the phony ID that Belzer had promised. This consisted of a small stack of expensive-looking business cards and a laminated ID. Both the cards and the ID were embossed with a small gold shield. To his surprise, Danny saw that the ID bore his picture (*Where did they get that?* he wondered), and the name *Frank Muller (Det.)*.

There was even a badge – a glob of metal with wings and a number: 665. Seeing it made him acutely nervous. What if he was stopped going through the metal detector at the airport? How would he explain the fact that he was carrying phony ID – and police ID at that? *Be cool,* he told himself. No one was going to look at the badge or the ID. And even if they did, it wasn't illegal to have it. He'd just put it in his duffle bag and check it.

It took about forty minutes to get to Dulles. Danny took out the tickets to check the airline and the departure time – and saw with a shock that he was flying first-class. Instead of making him happy, this only increased his anxiety. The limo, the suite at the hotel, first-class tickets. *What am I getting into?* he wondered.

The agent at the counter bathed him in a radiant smile as she processed his ticket and attached a PRIORITY/FIRST CLASS tag to his Army-Surplus bag. Before long, he was reclining in what amounted to a leather armchair, sipping a glass of champagne, gazing out the window as the city of Washington dwindled away under the wings. He was in pig heaven – or he would have been, if it wasn't for that badge in his duffle bag.

The badge was wrong. The badge made him nervous. There was something about playing a cop that was . . . well, not what the good guys did. And that raised a question, a very interesting question, a question so fundamental that he didn't even want to think about it.

What if I'm on the wrong side?

Seven

There was a crowd at the gate beyond Customs, where half a dozen drivers stood in a kind of receiving line, waiting to be found by their passengers. Danny's driver turned out to be a square little man with bushy black eyebrows and a hand-lettered sign that read:

CRAY

SISTEMI DI PAVONE

Seeing Danny react to the sign, the driver came forward with a smile. "Signore Cray?"

"*Si.*"

"*Benvenuti!*" Taking the duffle bag from Danny's hand, he led the two of them on a brisk walk through the terminal. "*Parle Italiano?*" he called over his shoulder.

"No."

The driver's shoulders rose and fell. "*Non importa.* I go Hotel d'Inghilterra, okay?"

"*Si.*"

"*Molto bene.*"

Coming out of the terminal, Danny was staggered by a wall of heat, noise, and diesel fumes. As excited as he was to be in Rome, he hadn't been able to sleep on the plane, and the jet lag he felt was like Karo syrup in his veins. Then the driver was standing in front of him, holding open the rear door to a shiny new Alfa Romeo, illegally parked in a taxi zone. A few feet away, a policeman in an elaborate uniform nodded deferentially to the driver, who exchanged a little salute with him. Soon they were on their way.

It seemed to Danny that the industrial suburbs of Rome were like the outskirts of any big city. Weed-ridden and trash-strewn fields separated factories, office buildings, and car dealerships that were uniformly modern, ugly, and dull. Except for the wall of oleander bushes that divided the highway, he might have been anywhere, anywhere hot. The sun was a smear of glare in the colorless sky.

Then – had he dozed? – they were in the city itself, and the ruined grandeur of it all suddenly surrounded him, magnificent and impossible to ignore. The driver followed the Tiber as it wound past a huge castle, then crossed the river into a vast and confusing square. Scattering a cluster of nuns, the Alfa glided through a towering stone gateway that took them into a sprawling and tree-shaded park. Surprised by the leafy quiet, Danny leaned forward in his seat and asked, "What *is* this? *Dove?*"

"*E la Villa Borghese,*" the driver replied in an incredulous tone. "*Naturalmente.*"

They were out of the park almost as quickly as they'd entered it. Now they were on a busy thorough-fare, bumper-to-fender with Fiats and Vespas and thronged with shoppers. Antiquarian showrooms and designer boutiques stood side by side: Missoni, Zegna, Gucci, Bulgari. It was as if he'd wandered into an advertising supplement for an in-flight magazine. Then the traffic slowed to a crawl as the driver nosed the Alfa through the crowds, growling at pedestrians and

94

fellow drivers alike. To Danny's surprise, the man never once hit the horn but contented himself with a litany of mumbled expletives.

The mob began to dwindle; the Alfa turned up a cobbled street and moments later rolled to a stop at the edge of a faded red carpet. Danny heard the trunk spring open as the driver jumped from the car, calling to the bellman. In an instant, the door was held open for him, and he stepped out at the entrance to an old-fashioned hotel – an ochre pile of stone whose facade bore the name ALBERGO D'INGHILTERRA.

Danny checked in. The desk clerk took his passport. The driver disappeared. And a geriatric bellhop showed him to his room.

This was, as promised, a suite – adjoining rooms that looked as if they'd been designed for *Masterpiece Theater*. Velvet drapes guarded the windows, quenching the light and muffling the sounds from outside. In the center of the larger room, a welcoming bouquet rested on a round mahogany table, the flowers' sweet scent vying with the pungent aroma of furniture wax.

The adjoining room had much the same feel. At once funky and luxe, it was dominated by a massive sleigh bed that carried the weight of an impossibly thick mattress. An avalanche of feather pillows was piled high against the headboard, atop a thin down comforter. Testing the mattress, Danny keeled backward on the bed – just for a second, he told himself, just to catch his breath – and felt his eyes close.

Late afternoon.

Waking with a start, and with the unreasonable sense that he was somehow *late*, Danny fairly vaulted out of bed. He padded across the Oriental rug toward the shower and stepped inside the marble enclosure. A torrent of water leached the jet lag from his bones.

Suddenly, he was hungry and excited to be in Rome. Dressing quickly, he clambered down the stairs to the lobby and out onto Bocca di Leone. Without much caring which way he went, he wandered with the crowds until he found himself climbing the Spanish Steps. Losing himself in the streets at the top of the stairs, he wandered through a labyrinth of side streets. He emerged twenty minutes later on the Via Veneto, having no idea where he was in relation to his hotel.

Dropping into a chair at a sidewalk table outside the Cafe de Paris, he ordered a mozzarella and tomato sandwich *("si, si, si – a Caprese, signore"),* a bottle of Pellegrino water, and a Campari-soda. Then he sat back and watched the parade.

It was an elegant and stylish crowd of passersby. The women were uniformly thin and beautifully dressed – as, indeed, were most of the men. Everyone seemed to smoke, and no one wore a fanny pack. Except the tourists. Half of them appeared to be Americans who'd "supersized" one too many meals. As for Danny himself, okay, he wasn't fat, and he wore his good shoes – the Cole-Haan loafers. But apart from that, he felt almost dowdy among the Italians, dressed as he was in khakis from the Gap and a polo shirt from nowhere in particular.

There were two ways he could go, he thought. Either he could get to work right away (like the good boy that he was) or he could do what came more naturally – which was to spend a couple of hours in the cafés, reading the *Herald Tribune* and savoring *la dolce vita.*

A tough call, but virtue prevailed. Paying the bill with his Visa card, he crossed the street to an ATM at the Banco Ambrosiano. He coaxed half a million lire from the machine, then caught a taxi back to his hotel.

He collapsed into a wing chair next to the window and sat with the phone in his hand, silently rehearsing the short speech that he'd devised on the flight from Washington. Satisfied that he had it down, he punched in the number from the FedEx receipt, pressed SEND, and waited. Momentarily the phone began to squawk at the other end of the line. Danny leaned forward with his elbows on his knees, concentrating. Finally, a recorded voice came on the line: "*Ciao! Avete raggiunto Inzaghi. Non posso ora venire al telefono . . .*"

The only words he recognized were *Ciao, Inzaghi,* and *telefono,* but he got the point. The priest was out. He'd call him again in the morning.

There wasn't much else for Danny to do, really. Father Inzaghi was the only reason he was in Rome. If the priest was out of town or if he refused to meet with Danny, well . . . in that case, Belzer's client would have spent a lot of money for not much at all. Which was *his* problem, Danny thought. *There's nothing I can do about that.* If Belzer wanted to keep him in the Inghilterra for a day, a week, or a month, making the same phone call every couple of hours, that was up to him – and it was fine by Danny.

Taking a bottle of Peroni from the minibar, Danny dropped into a chair and switched on the television with the remote. Soon he was immersed in the end-to-end drama of a UEFA Cup match, blissfully uncaring that it had been played months earlier. Somewhere in the second half, the phone rang, and he answered it with a distracted "Yeh?"

"Mr. Cray?" It was a woman's voice, but deep and lightly accented.

He pressed the MUTE button on the remote. "This is Danny Cray."

"It's Paulina Pastorini – your interpreter. I think Signore Belzer told you that I'd be in touch?"

"Ri-ight!"

"Well, first let me welcome you to Rome –"

"Thanks –"

"– and ask if I can be of any assistance. Do you have everything you need?"

"I think so," Danny told her, "but . . . I'm trying to reach someone –"

"Yes?"

"Yes. And I'm having a little difficulty. He's a priest. And I guess he works at the Vatican."

"Yes?"

"Well, I have his phone number, but all I get is an answering machine. And, of course, it's in Italian, so . . ."

A soft chuckle – very sexy. "If you'd like . . . I could call him for you. See if he speaks English."

Danny thought about it for a moment and frowned. "It's kind of complicated," he said.

"I understand. Our friend explained it to me. But this is not a problem. I'll simply say that I'm helping you arrange things."

"Well –"

"It's 'Detective Muller,' yes?"

"Yes."

"Then I will call him in the morning," the interpreter announced. "First thing."

"Great." He tried to keep the unhappiness out of his voice, but he knew that he wasn't entirely successful. It bothered him that the interpreter knew about "Detective Muller" – though, of course, she had a need to know.

"I'll simply make an appointment," she said. "*With* me if he doesn't speak English – *without* me if he does. Is that okay?"

"Fine."

"So that's what I'll do. And what about you? Tomorrow . . . you're free?"

"As a bird," Danny told her.

"I am sorry?"

"I said I'm free as a bird."

That laugh again, a floating trill. "Of course. You have to excuse me, but – we don't have that idiom in Italy. And it's just as well, because in Roma most of the birds are pigeons – and it's very hard to think of them as 'free.' They are just – what is the word? – *homeless.*"

It was his turn to laugh, and he did.

After she'd hung up, he opened another Peroni and telephoned the States to get his messages.

The first was from Jake, calling to report that he'd actually sold a painting. *Gimme a call, dude! I'm buyin'!*

The second message was from Caleigh, phoning home from the Coast to let him know her number at the Oyster Point Inn. *I loves ya, Danny boy! Ciao!*

Then Mom: *Just checking in. Thought I'd remind you we're off to Ireland Tuesday. Kevin knows how to reach us if you need to get in touch.* And then, almost conspiratorially: *Why don't you sneak up here with Caleigh, while we're gone? I'll leave the keys in the usual place. Captain is staying with Mr. Hutchins.*

And finally: *Dan? Hi, it's Adele Slivinski at Remax. And I'm afraid I've got some bad news. I don't know how serious you were about the Terio property, but unless you wanted it for a teardown* . . . Big sigh. *It's gone. There was a fire last night and now* . . . *well, now there's nothing. But I wanted you to know that I've got another listing in the same area, and I think you'll love it.* And then she signed off, leaving a cascade of numbers.

So much for Terio's files, Danny thought, and tossed the phone onto the couch. Getting to his feet, he wandered over to the window, parted the curtains, and gazed down at the street below. *This is beginning to get scary,* he thought. *First Terio – then Patel and now the house. That's a lot of violence. Though the house could have been vandalism. In fact, it probably* was *vandalism. Old house – no one living in it. Weird stories about a "basement tomb." It was probably kids from the town houses down the road.*

It was a reassuring scenario, and he wanted to believe it. He could imagine the kids getting buzzed, jumping in the old man's car, trucking over to Terio's house. *Goths. It was probably some Goths – saw the house on TV, heard the spooky stories – figured they'd star in a horror flick of their own. So they broke in, partied down, maybe some candles and* . . . *a fire broke out. Who knows what happened?*

He fell asleep around ten, sitting in front of the TV, watching CNN with his feet up on the coffee table. In the middle of the night, a flying squad of American drunks woke him from a bad dream as they staggered down the street beneath his window, bellowing, "Rubber Ducky, you're the one!"

He didn't remember the dream at all – just that it scared him. And he didn't remember undressing, either, or getting into bed, but he must have. Because he was very much between the sheets when the sun came pouring through the windows at just after six in the morning.

It was still too early to do anything, so he went out in search of a *Herald Tribune*, thinking there might be a story about Jason Patel. Most of the shops were still closed, but he found a newsstand on the Via del Corso. Buying a copy of the paper, he carried it with him to a café in the Piazza Colonna.

There he stood by the counter for a long moment, watching how things were done. First you paid the cashier for what you wanted. She relayed the order to one of the countermen, and then you went to pick it up.

The joint was hoppin' with tradesmen and shop girls, businessmen on the way to work, and a couple of Italian soldiers with – literally – feathers in their caps. A trio of men in dirty blue coveralls – they must have just come off shift – were playing cards in the corner, drinking coffee with shots of brandy. Everyone was smiling and high-spirited. The sun was blazing. It was all so different from Washington – it revved him up. If he could get this interview with Inzaghi set up, he could take the afternoon off and check out the Sistine Chapel. Go for a walk in the Villa Borghese, buy a present for Caleigh . . .

When his cappuccino was ready, he climbed onto a stool at a copper-topped counter and searched the newspaper for a story about Patel. But there was nothing. And why should there be? It was just another murder in America. There must be a dozen every single day.

And house fires. Lots of *them*, too.

The sun poured through the windows of the café, emblazoning the pall of cigarette smoke that hung in the air. *The truth is,* Danny thought, *I'd like to be done with this thing.* Rome or no Rome, the business with Belzer was making him nervous. There was too much bad news – too much *violence* on the periphery of it all. And as much as he was enjoying it, the assignment itself was entirely too swank, too good to be true.

Danny finished the second of the little crescent rolls and slid off the stool. *Just do it,* he told himself. *Get it over with. It's no big deal. Just put the question to the priest, who will tell you either yes or no: you can have the computer, or you can't. Either way, then you can fly home and get back to work – your real work.*

It was almost seven-thirty when he got to the Inghilterra. The interpreter was waiting for him in the lobby and came up to him as he stood at the desk, asking for his key.

"Mr. Cray? It's Paulina."

He wasn't sure what he thought she'd look like – a woman in her forties maybe, bookish, gracious, reading glasses. But the woman in front of him was something else entirely: a dark beauty, thirty at the outside, with the kind of high-gloss glamour that costs real money. She was wearing a low-cut lettuce-green linen suit with a very short skirt and brown alligator heels.

"Hi." It was the best he could do.

Her smile was dazzling as she looked up at him through thick lashes, flirting. "I thought you'd be older," she told him.

"I thought *you'd* be older."

That musical slide of a laugh. "Well. Anyway, sorry

102

to just ... *materialize* ... like this. Shall we get coffee?"

She didn't wait for an answer but turned on her heel and headed for the hotel's bar/café. Danny padded after her like a dog, wary and excited all at once, eyes locked on the seesaw of her hemline. The skirt was so short it was barely decent, and when she perched on a stool and crossed her legs Danny felt as if he'd lost the power of speech.

Happily, a waiter appeared out of nowhere, rescuing Danny from the need to make conversation. The interpreter lifted her eyes toward him. "Cappuccino?"

Danny nodded. With an effort, he added, "Sure."

When the waiter left, she said, "I'm sorry to just *appear* like this. But you didn't answer your telephone. And I hate voice mail, so ..." She shrugged, a small gesture that called attention to the long swoop of her neck and the delicate lines of her clavicles. "I thought, *I'll just leave him a note.* And then" – a truly dazzling smile – "there you were!"

"Hunh!" Danny replied, incredulous at how stupid he sounded, even to himself. *Get a grip.* "And, uhh ... what would the note be about?"

That trill of a laugh. "Father *Inzaghi*, of course. I thought it best to call him first thing – before he wandered off for the day. ..." She pushed her hands out and stirred the air. "I don't know, praying or something. I realized I had no idea what priests *do* all day. I mean, where do they go? Well! Now I know."

"So you got him!"

"Yes!"

"And what does Father Inzaghi do all day?"

"He is in the Vatican Library – slaving away."

"On what?"

"He is . . . what do they say? He is *digitizing* the incunabula."

"No kidding," Danny said.

She nodded brightly.

"And the incunabula is . . . what?" Danny asked.

"Oh, good," Paulina replied. "I was afraid you knew what they were, because I didn't – I had to ask. And if you knew and I didn't, that would have been bad, because – well, words are my business." She leaned toward him, seemingly oblivious to the effect her cleavage had on him. He tried not to look, but it was about as easy as defying gravity. In a glance, his eyes flew past the tan line to the café au lait that lay beyond it. The shadow and press of her nipples . . .

"The incunabula," she said, eyes twinkling. "I think it's a little spooky, no? But no – they're just books printed before 1500. This priest, Inzaghi, is an expert. In books or computers – one or the other. I think perhaps both. But he's been working so long in the archives, they call him 'Rex Topo.' "

Danny gave her a quizzical look. "Rex Topo?"

Her eyes flashed. "He is King of the Mice! That is what they call the priests who work with the books. Mice! And this one – he is their king." She uncoiled from the stool and got to her feet. "If you'll excuse me for a minute." With a smile, she swayed out of sight, her body a magnet drawing looks from every corner of the room.

The waiter arrived a moment later. With the speed and panache of a blackjack dealer, he dealt out two porcelain cups half-full of coffee, a small white pitcher with foamed milk, and a pewter-and-glass setup that held four kinds of sugar.

Danny took a sip of the delicious coffee and listened

to the rise and fall of the conversations around him. Another sip and then a pause in the noise – a sudden caesura that caused him to raise his eyes. And there she was, making her way toward him, her purse bouncing provocatively against her thigh. It was hard not to stare.

"Where was I?" she asked, setting her purse on the counter and raising herself onto a stool.

"You were talking about mice."

"That's right!" She took a sip of coffee, set the cup down, and turned serious. "As I said, I spoke to Inzaghi this morning. And I told him what you wanted to see him about – in a general way. I said it was a police matter, concerning Professor Terio."

Danny nodded. "And he said . . . ?"

"You're having lunch this afternoon. I made reservations at a super little trattoria in the Via dei Cartari. I think if you give him a good meal, a little wine – maybe a lot of wine – he might be helpful."

"And what about *you*? Will you be there?"

She shook her head. "His English is excellent. Fluent, even. He studied in Scotland. You'll do better without me."

"Oh, I doubt *that*," he told her, and instantly regretted it. *Why not just wink at her, while you're at it?*

Her eyes twinkled.

He felt like a pig. Even though he hadn't done anything *(yet)*, even though he hadn't so much as laid a hand on the woman, his betrayal of Caleigh was a fait accompli, a done deal, if only in his imagination.

"Well," Paulina said, her dark eyes merry, "thank you. But I think it will be better if it's just the two of you."

Danny gave a regretful shrug. Reaching for the little pitcher of milk on the counter, he added a bit to his coffee and stirred. As he did, his eye was caught by her purse, which was lying on the counter. A silky pouch the color of new broccoli, it had a drawstring closure that gaped open. And inside he glimpsed the white papery cylinder of a Tampax and, next to it, the dark-blue cylinder of a gun barrel.

His eyes jerked away and then snapped back for another peek. He'd heard it said that guns don't look real when you see them – they look like toys. This one was small enough to be a toy, but there was no confusing it with one. The gun in her purse was dense with reality and easily concealed. A belly gun. *Maybe it's normal,* Danny thought. *Maybe, in Rome, a woman like Paulina needs some protection. Maybe, in Rome, all the good-looking women are packing.*

"Well," she was saying, "I'll write down the name of the restaurant, shall I? I made the reservation for twelve-thirty." And with that, she extracted a pen from her purse and scrawled an address on a scalloped paper coaster.

"How long will it take me to get there?" Danny asked, taking the coaster from her.

She wrinkled up her face in a charming way and rocked from side to side. "Twenty minutes, if you walk." The high-wattage smile. "More if you take a taxi." Then she glanced at her watch, raised her hand toward the waiter, and pantomimed writing on the air.

"I'll get that," Danny said.

"Good, because I really have to go," she said, standing up and smoothing her skirt. "If you need anything, you'll call me, yes?"

"Yes." He got to his feet.

Then she leaned toward him, her hair brushing his face. He caught a heady rush of expensive perfume as she kissed him, first on one cheek, then the other. Unlike the air kisses he was used to at the gallery, she made actual contact – and lingered on the second kiss. Her lips relaxed, and he could feel her breath on his cheek. Then she pulled back, holding his shoulders in her outstretched hands. "Oh, no," she giggled, "I got lipstick on you." She dabbed at his cheek with a napkin until, satisfied, she dropped it on the counter. *"Buona fortuna!"*

And then, before he could manage a word, she was gone.

The "little trattoria" wasn't the homey place that Danny had imagined. It did not have checkered tablecloths or bottles of Chianti wrapped in raffia. It was, instead, an essay in sophisticated minimalism, with navy-blue walls and tables draped in white gauze. Danny identified himself to the maître d', who showed him to a table near the window, where a round little man in his fifties was sitting. Seeing Danny approach, the man got to his feet.

"Investigatore!" he said, with a deferential nod. "It's a pleasure." They shook hands.

The man was wearing a dark-blue suit that had seen better days. The cuffs had a sheen that spoke of long wear, as did the pinholes in one of the sleeves – evidence, Danny thought, of moths in the Vatican. The only indication of his companion's ordination was a tiny gold cross, affixed to the lapel under his chin.

A waiter appeared with menus and asked about drinks. It wasn't something Danny ever did – drink at lunch – but he nevertheless suggested a bottle of wine and proposed that Inzaghi choose it. The priest was only too happy to comply. Donning a pair of reading glasses, he studied the wine list with a skeptical air, then snapped it shut and handed it back to the waiter. A brief exchange ensued, and then the waiter turned on his heel to fetch the bottle in question.

Inzaghi sat back in his seat, polishing his reading glasses as he studied his luncheon companion. "You're very young," he decided.

Danny shrugged.

"For a detective, I mean."

Danny nodded.

"Well, you must be very smart."

Danny resisted a second shrug but didn't know quite what to say. So he nodded, thinking, *This isn't going well.*

But the priest didn't seem to notice. "I was shocked," he said, "to hear that Christian died." He shook his head. "I found out about it when I couldn't reach him. I sent one e-mail after another. I telephoned, and . . . nothing. So I called the university. And they told me. A suicide!" He shook his head, as if to clear it.

"So you were surprised?" Danny asked.

"Surprised? Of course. I'm not saying he didn't have problems, worries. But you must understand: This was a man in love with life! A man with a great sense of humor. Although . . ." The priest leaned closer and, in a confidential tone, added, "His jokes were terrible."

Danny smiled. "How so?"

Inzaghi gave him an exasperated look. "Perhaps it's the language problem. My English is –"

"Excellent!"

"No, no. It's just adequate. And Chris, he was

always making . . . puns. Terrible puns, I think, but then . . . maybe I don't understand because of the language."

Danny nodded politely.

"Example!" the priest declared. "I ask you: what is so funny about 'heigh-ho the Terio'?"

Danny chuckled. "Not much." It was some nursery rhyme, he thought, although he couldn't remember which one.

"That's what I think," the priest remarked. "It's just not funny. But every time he said it, he couldn't help himself. 'Heigh-ho the Terio!' And he'd laugh!" The priest shook his head.

"You wouldn't think it would come up that often."

Inzaghi nodded with a rueful grin. "But it did, for Christian. It was his – how do you call it? – his 'reminder question,' in case he forgot a password," he explained. Then the grin faded, and the priest looked morose. "I let him down."

Danny looked puzzled. "Why do you say that?"

Father Inzaghi shrugged. "Because he was a friend!" The priest heaved an exasperated sigh. "I should have been more sensitive to his feelings. I should have noticed something! But . . . I had no idea." He cast a hopeful glance at Danny, looking for commiseration.

"I think most people feel that way," Danny told him, "whenever someone dies . . . like that. Even if it's an accident, they think, *If only I'd been with him, he'd still be here.* But usually, there's really nothing anyone can do about it. Nothing anyone *could have done* about it."

The waiter arrived with a bottle of Barbaresco, uncorked it with a flourish, and waited for Inzaghi to pronounce it good. When the priest nodded his approval, the waiter filled their glasses and took their orders. After he'd left, Inzaghi leaned forward and with an embarrassed look said, "I wonder, Detective . . ."

"Yes?"

"I wonder if, perhaps . . . I could see your credentials?"

The question took Danny by surprise, though of course it shouldn't have. A rush of adrenaline flashed through his chest, and a nervous smile lifted the corners of his mouth. A telephone pretext was one thing, but lying was something else – and this, whatever this was, was even worse. Impersonating a cop. What was he thinking? "No problem," he said, and, reaching inside his coat, retrieved the ID that Belzer had made for him. Then he handed it to the priest, who gave him an apologetic look.

"It's just that you're so young," he said. "I was expecting an older man." Inzaghi barely glanced at the ID, then handed it back, embarrassed. "I'm sorry."

Danny shook his head. "It's good to be cautious – you never know."

"Indeed," the priest replied.

"So . . . did they tell you how it happened?"

"No." Inzaghi gave him a curious look and shook his head. "What difference would it make?"

"Well, it's one of the reasons I'm here. It was a very unusual 'suicide.' "

The priest frowned. "And why is that?"

Danny described the circumstances under which Terio had been found, watching the priest's face as the shock registered, the initial distress giving way to a wash of repugnance. When he was done, Inzaghi took a long sip of wine, then dabbed at his mouth with a napkin. "My *god*! That's grotesque. I mean – oh!"

110

Danny gave him a hapless look.

"Although!" Inzaghi raised a forefinger for emphasis. "Although!" he repeated, shaking his finger as if he were Fidel. "It's not unheard of."

Danny blinked. "No?"

Solemnly the priest shook his head.

"Well, it's the first *I* ever heard of it. Mostly, people jump – or maybe they shoot themselves," Danny insisted. "Or else they take pills or something."

"Yes, of course, you're right. But in the context of the faith – in the context of *Christianity* – this sort of thing has a long history."

"It does?" Danny looked puzzled. His religious upbringing had been minimal. Anything was possible, of course, but if people were running around walling themselves up for Jesus, you'd have thought he'd have heard about it. "A long history?"

The priest took a long sip of wine, then topped off his glass and savored its color against the light from a nearby window. "The world," he announced, "is the enemy of salvation. And always has been. It's the battleground for the soul, the place where the flesh meets the devil. Withdraw from the world, and the devil can't touch you." Another sip, and he leaned closer. "They were called 'anchorites' – from the Latin, *anachoreo,* meaning 'I withdraw.' The earliest ones went into the desert and lived in caves. The strangest were the stylites, who spent their lives on tops of pillars."

"Pillars?"

"Classical ruins," the priest explained.

"And they spent their *lives* there?! Sitting on a pillar?"

The priest nodded. "Most of their lives," he

111

confirmed. "Later – in the medieval era – they were . . . entombed. In the walls of the churches. The north walls."

"Entombed," Danny repeated.

"I think this is the word. It means *per seppellire vivo*. Buried alive. It's the right word, no?"

Danny nodded. "Yeah," he said, "it's the right word."

"I thought so, but sometimes my English . . . it goes away. In any case, these anchorites were put into small cells – *anchorets* – behind the altar. The anchorets had little windows – *slits*, you call them – so the holy men could watch the mass and receive food. But, once inside, they never left. There weren't any *doors*."

Danny was dumbfounded. He imagined what it must have been like – not from the point of view of the anchorite, who was obviously mad, but from the point of view of those who'd come to church to pray. The eyes in the walls. He shivered.

Inzaghi chuckled. "It wasn't just men," the priest told him. "There were anchoresses, as well. And like the men, once they were walled in, once they became 'prisoners of faith,' they were 'dead to the world.' Officially – and in fact. They didn't exist, except to be fed."

"Jeezus," Danny muttered.

"You should read Chris's book," the priest told him. "It's a bit academic, a little slow, but well worth it – especially the chapter on what he calls 'the reluctant anchorites.' "

Danny frowned. "And who were *they*?"

"Well," Inzaghi said, "*they* were anchorites who didn't *want* to be anchorites. Men and women –

112

infants and children – who were walled up against their will."

The waiter arrived with their salads, gave each of them a triple twist from a pepper grinder, and withdrew with a soft "Prego."

"These anchorites who didn't want to be anchorites –" Danny began.

"You really should read Chris's book. Do you have it?"

Danny nodded. *"The Radiant Tomb*. Yeah, I brought it with me."

"It's all in there," Inzaghi told him.

"I'll look at it tonight."

The priest shrugged. "You know," he said, leaning forward and speaking in a confidential way, "I must say I'm not at all clear why it is you're here, Detective. I mean if Chris committed suicide . . . ?"

"Well, that's just it," Danny replied. "We're not entirely sure it *was* a suicide."

A soft "aaaahhhh" escaped from the priest's lips. Wordlessly he laid his fork upon the table, placed his hands in his lap, and looked directly at Danny.

"It's possible," the American said, "that Mr. Terio's death was a homicide."

The priest nodded slowly. "That would make more sense," he decided.

It was Danny's turn to look surprised. "It would?"

Inzaghi continued to nod. "Chris was upset when he left Rome. He was worried. Maybe a little more than worried. Maybe *frightened*."

All of a sudden, Danny was obliged to play detective for real. "And why was that?"

"Something happened to him."

"In Rome?"

113

"No," the priest told him. "In eastern Turkey."

That figures, Danny thought. Terio had spent a part of his sabbatical there, and even after he'd returned to the States, he'd made phone calls to Istanbul, so . . . "What was he doing there?"

Inzaghi spread his hands in a hapless gesture. "Research."

"On what?"

"A new book. *Avatars of Syncretism.*" The priest smiled. "He wasn't so good with titles."

Danny frowned. He *almost* knew what the words meant. Five or six years earlier, they'd gone in one ear and out the other in a Western civ course that he'd taken during his sophomore year in college. Let's see: *avatar.* He frowned.

Inzaghi saw his puzzlement and took pity on him. "Christian was studying the founders of certain religions in the Near East, religions that embraced elements of other religions."

"Like . . . ?"

"Mani and Zoroaster," the priest replied. "Baha'Allah and Sheik Adi."

The first three names were vaguely familiar, as if they'd been part of a multiple-choice question in that same sophomore year. They connected to three obscure religions: Manicheism, Zoroastrianism, Baha'i. But Sheik Adi meant nothing to him – which was fine. A sheriff's detective wouldn't know any of this stuff. So he said, "Hunh!," sipped his wine, and forked a bit of arugula into his mouth.

Once again, Father Inzaghi came to the rescue. "They were all founders of religious sects in the Middle East."

"That's what I figured."

"So you've heard of them?"

It was Danny's turn to shrug. "Most of them."

"But not Sheik Adi."

Danny nodded.

"I thought so," Inzaghi said. "The Yezidis are not so well known."

" 'Yezidis'?"

"Sheik Adi. He was the Yezidis' man."

Danny rolled his eyes, finding the not-so-bright detective's role disturbingly easy to play.

"It's a Kurdish tribe," the priest explained. "A sub–ethnic group."

Danny nodded glumly. *Kurds,* he thought. *Now we got Kurds.* The truth was, he didn't know any of this stuff – not really. Like the Kurds. All he knew about the Kurds was that they were in Turkey or Iraq (or maybe Iran). And persecuted! That was it. One fact, maybe two, and he was tapped out on the entire subject of the Kurdish people.

"Sheik Adi was their prophet," Inzaghi added, and, taking up his fork, impaled a sheaf of greens.

"Whose prophet?"

"The Yezidis', " the priest replied. "Chris went over there to study the *Black Writing*." Inzaghi smiled. "It's their *Bible*," he added. "Their sacred text."

Danny sat back as the waiter returned with their main courses – a delicious-looking steak for Inzaghi and for himself linguini dusted with flecks of black truffle. He was wondering how to maneuver the conversation around to the computer. Idly he asked, "So why do they call it the Black Writing?"

Inzaghi chewed thoughtfully on a forkful of steak, considering the question. Then he said, "Who knows? I'm not sure why the Yezidis do *anything* the way they

115

do. I mean, we're talking about people who pray to the Peacock Angel!"

Danny looked skeptical. "They worship peacocks?"

"Satan," the priest said.

Danny chuckled. "Sorry, Father, but . . . how do you get from peacocks to Satan?"

Inzaghi smiled in a way that was not meant to be patronizing, but . . . "They're a symbol of the devil."

"Peacocks?"

"Yes."

Danny thought about it. "So you're saying these Kurdish guys . . . they worship the devil?"

"Exactly. Not all Kurds, not at all. Most Kurds are Muslims."

"Just these – what? – Yezidis."

"Exactly. The Yezidis venerate Satan."

Danny stared. "You're kidding me."

The priest shook his head and chewed his steak.

"You mean, like . . . *Satan* Satan?"

Inzaghi nodded and went on to explain that although they were once more numerous, the Yezidis now numbered about a million. "They've been persecuted for a very long time," the priest explained. "You can imagine. They've suffered terribly – first as Kurds and then as Yezidis. It's a real double whammy."

Danny shrugged. "Yeah, well, you worship the devil, you're gonna get *criticized*."

Inzaghi laughed. "It's not what you're thinking," he told him. "They're not sacrificing children or riding around on brooms. They've made a conscious decision to venerate Satan because the *Black Writing* tells them that on the eighth day God grew weary of the world and gave it over to the devil. To them, the

116

devil is not evil; he's the Tawus, sort of the chief angel."

"Like Lucifer."

"Like Lucifer without the fall, yes."

"That's interesting," Danny said, "but . . . getting back to Terio . . . you said he was upset, that something happened in Turkey."

The priest shifted in his chair, as if he'd been suddenly discomfited. "Right."

"So? What happened?"

Inzaghi took a deep breath. "According to Chris?"

"Yeah."

"Well, Chris said – I know it sounds ridiculous, but . . . he *said* he'd seen the devil."

The Brits have a word for it, a word Ian used every chance he got: *gobsmacked*. And that's what Danny was. For a long moment Danny didn't know quite what to say. Finally, it occurred to him. "*What?*"

"I said, 'He *said* . . . he'd seen the devil.' " A nervous laugh.

"Get out!"

The priest shook his head.

Danny didn't know whether to laugh or cry. He might be a Catholic boy, but religion had never been much of an issue in his family. While some part of him held out the possibility that there might be a God, he came from a long line of lapsed Catholics – virtual agnostics. Except for a couple of spinster aunts who were devout, the role of the Church in the lives of the Cray clan was to supply a framework for rites of passage. Crays might get married in the Church, and they might baptize their kids there (his own baptismal certificate was in a manila envelope in the bottom drawer of his mother's rolltop desk). The Church might oversee their funerals and help bury them. Some might even go to mass more or less regularly, especially when they got older – although his parents hadn't reached this point yet. But no one in his family (except the aunts) was religious; no one actually believed in the *devil*.

Evil was real, he knew that, but it was not incarnate. The devil was like . . . the Tooth Fairy.

"So what did he look like?" Danny asked at last. "Horns, tail, what?"

The priest shook his head, looking slightly embarrassed. "Chris didn't say. Just that he was riding in a Bentley."

"The devil."

"Right."

"And this was where?" Danny asked.

"Somewhere in eastern Turkey." Inzaghi leaned forward with a sly grin and added, "You'd think the devil would have a Rolls, wouldn't you?"

Danny gave an uncertain chuckle. What was he supposed to say to that? What would *a cop* say? Was the priest *testing* him or *kidding* him? "Weird," he said.

"I agree."

As the waiter cleared their plates, Danny decided it was time to cut to the chase. Producing the FedEx receipt that he'd fished out of Terio's trash, he asked Inzaghi if he could take a look at the professor's computer. "We're hoping there may be something on it. Something that might help in the investigation."

The priest frowned, and Danny thought, *Uh-oh*. "I'm afraid I don't *have* it," Inzaghi told him. "Not actually."

"Why not?" Danny asked.

"Because it's still in Customs." According to the priest, an import tax of more than a million lire – about five hundred dollars – had yet to be paid. Until the tax was discharged, the machine would remain in the Cargo Terminal at Leonardo da Vinci Airport. "You know how it is," Inzaghi told him. "I've asked for the funds, but it could take months. And the truth is, it will be nice to have a laptop, but I don't actually *need* it. There are other computers I can use."

"Then why did he send it to you?"

Inzaghi chuckled. "It was just a present. I always wanted a laptop, and Chris – he was always complaining about its weight. I remember him joking that 'a portable computer' was an oxymoron."

Danny laughed. "So it was a hand-me-down –"

"Exactly!" the priest replied. "Only not so cheap, as it turned out. If he'd sent it to my office – in the Vatican – I'd have it by now. But he sent it to my flat in the Via della Scrofa. That's in Rome, and so we must pay Caesar."

Danny thought for a moment, then leaned forward, elbows on the table. "What if I get it for you?" he asked. "I can expense it through the sheriff's department. And after I've had a look at it, I'll make sure you get it back right away."

The priest pursed his lips, sat back, and thought it over. After a moment, he inclined his head in a consent, as if to say, *It's a deal.* Then he reached into his pocket and produced a beautifully made business card, which he presented to Danny. "The number at the top is my apartment in the Casa Clera. I'm usually there at night. But you can always get me on the mobile – except when I'm in church. I shut it off when I'm there."

119

"Terrific," Danny said. He scrawled his cell-phone number on the back of one of Frank Muller's business cards and handed it to the priest.

"I'll give you a letter for Customs," Inzaghi promised. "And a copy of the manifest. You shouldn't have any problems at the airport."

"That's very kind," Danny told him.

"Not at all," the priest replied. "One good turn deserves another."

Eight

They walked to the Vatican from the restaurant, with Danny following Inzaghi through a maze of ancient streets so narrow that even on a summer afternoon twilight reigned. Occasionally they'd turn a corner and find themselves in a piazza drenched in sunshine. A moment later, they'd round another corner, and the light would fade from gold to silver.

They crossed the Tiber on a pedestrian bridge just west of the hulking Castel Sant' Angelo. The bridge was an open-air marketplace of sorts, where olive-skinned Arabs and listless Africans were selling everything from hashish, umbrellas, and caricatures to battery-driven tin soldiers that crawled on their bellies with rifles cradled in their arms.

It was hot on the Via della Conciliazione, a broad boulevard that funneled tourists and tour buses directly into St. Peter's Square, where a sea of folding chairs was set out in anticipation of a papal appearance. Inzaghi escorted Danny past a gatepost manned by Swiss Guards, then down an ancient byway that opened onto a vast courtyard – the Cortile della Pigne. Surrounded and defined by an arcade of umber buildings, the courtyard was divided into quadrants by cobbled walks and greens with a roaring fountain at their center. At the far end of the yard, to Danny's delight, was a gigantic pinecone – it looked to be about

121

eight feet tall and made of marble – resting on a magnificently carved capital.

"Where did *that* come from?" Danny asked.

Inzaghi shrugged. "A gift," he said. "Or looted."

Passing through the arcades, they entered a building that was almost as modern on the inside as it was ancient without. Inzaghi signed in for the both of them at a small reception desk, then led Danny to an escalator. Descending one flight and then another, they soon found themselves in a sort of mezzanine, a brightly lit glassed-in waiting room. Behind the glass was a subterranean warehouse of books and manuscripts, standing, leaning, and piled on miles of shelves. Nearby a small sign identified the place as the ARCHIVIO SEGRETO.

"There was a huge renovation – a rebuilding, really – about ten years ago," Inzaghi told him. "There wasn't enough space for the manuscripts. So now we have this! Forty-three kilometers of cheap metal shelves. You could run a marathon on them." The priest smiled. "If you'll give me a minute, I'll get the paperwork."

Danny was left in the company of an elderly nun who sat behind an antique desk, paying him no mind. She was speaking quietly into a telephone headset, her eyes locked on a Silicon Graphics monitor as her right hand clicked away at a mouse.

Eventually Inzaghi returned with a thick envelope. "Sorry to be so long," he said, "but I've given you a copy of the manifest, as well as a letter authorizing you to collect the computer for me. I don't know that a letter is actually necessary, but –" A laugh. " – we *are* in Italy, and more paper is always better."

"Thanks."

"And you'll let me know what you learn?"

"Absolutely," Danny promised. It was all going great, he thought. The hardest part of the job, the part that he'd dreaded – lying to a priest about being a cop – was more or less over. And it hadn't been all that bad. On the contrary, it had gone so well that this generous man had actually written him *a letter*.

"I wonder, how long do you think you'll need it?" Inzaghi asked.

The American hesitated. He couldn't imagine Belzer keeping the computer for long. Then again, what did *he* know? If the files were encrypted, it could take a while. On the other hand, once they'd copied the files the computer would be superfluous. "Not too long," Danny promised, "unless we get lucky. If we find something, if there's *evidence* . . ." He let the sentence fade and made a gesture with his hands. "It could be a while," he confessed.

Inzaghi nodded. "I understand. Well, you have my number – and I have yours."

"Right."

"But I think – maybe you shouldn't try today."

"Try what?" Danny asked.

"The airport," Inzaghi replied. Then he tapped the watch on his wrist. "It's three now, and with the traffic . . . you'll never make it."

"Customs is open till five," Danny told him. "I checked."

Inzaghi nodded. "Of course. But that means they'll be gone by four." With a chuckle, the priest guided him to the escalator, where he waved good-bye with a smile so genuine that Danny, rising slowly from the library's depths, was haunted by it all the way back to the Inghilterra. The man's kindness was depressing.

But the afternoon was not. The sun was shining, and

Rome was *happening*. Taking the elevator to his room, Danny retrieved *The Radiant Tomb* from his suitcase. The book had arrived from Alibris a couple of days before, and he hadn't even opened it. Now, he saw that it was a thin volume, with a photo of Terio on the dust jacket – the same photo the *Washington Post* had published above his obituary. Tucking the book under his arm, Danny took the elevator downstairs, went out, and hailed a cab.

"Villa Borghese," he directed, and, feeling adventurous, added, "*per favore*."

The ride was a short one and, as he suspected, the park turned out to be the perfect place to read on a summer afternoon. Huge plane trees shaded the lawns and benches. Lovers strolled. Children played. Gelato vendors wheeled their carts along the paths. Danny bought a small cup of pistachio ice cream, sat down, and began to read.

The first half of *The Radiant Tomb* was devoted to the early anchorites. In telling their stories, Terio argued that Saint Anthony of Egypt and those who came after him were largely responsible for the emergence of monasticism in the West. This was so, Terio argued, because religious hermits invariably attracted a following. Ironically, the more profound their retreat – the farther they got into the desert – the more likely they were to come out the other side with a retinue. And a good thing, too: it was the monastic orders that preserved the written word during the Dark Ages – and, in so doing, saved Western civilization from ignorance and obscurity.

This was all interesting, but what really got Danny's attention was a chapter near the end of the book. Addressing the subject of "reluctant anchorites," Terio wrote about a ballad or folk song that was said to be more than a thousand years old. Titled "The Walled-Up Wife," the song was well known from Bombay to Bucharest. There were, Terio wrote, more than seven hundred versions of the ditty in various languages and dialects.

In the Yugoslavian variant, a woman is immured in the walls of a fortress. In Turkey, it's a caravansary. In Persia, a bridge. And always for "good luck" or, in the case of bridges, to placate the river gods who were angered by such crossings.

The most poignant of the songs, to Danny's reckoning, was Transylvanian. In that variation, a group of masons labor mightily, far from home, to build a monastery – only to have their work undone by night. "Spirits" are said to be at fault, and the men are distraught: will they never return home? Thinking about the problem, the head mason hears a voice, which tells him that the river's spirits can be placated only by the sacrifice of a woman. Specifically, the first woman who comes to the site must be immured in the foundation of the bridge. Relieved that a solution has been found, the mason recounts the tale to his colleagues, and it's agreed: the first woman to come to the site will be buried alive. The next morning, they anxiously watch the road, and soon a woman can be seen approaching from a great distance. As she draws closer, the mason's excitement turns to horror as he realizes that the woman is his young wife, come from far away, carrying flowers, food, and wine. The mason begs God to make her turn around, to go back the way she came, but she doesn't. And so she's cemented into the wall, even as the mason dies of grief.

In discussing the song, Terio acknowledged that

there were as many interpretations of its meaning as there were variations in its lyrics. To some postmodern analysts, the song was "a deadly metaphor for married life" (in which a woman was said to be "figuratively immured in marriage to protect her virtue"). Another commentary claimed that the song represented "the symbolic immurement of the Serbs" by Muslim invaders.

For Terio, however, the song was meant to be taken literally. In his view, "The Walled-Up Wife" was neither more nor less than oral history – the popular account of a historical custom by which women and children were burned alive to ensure the success of major construction projects. As evidence of the practice, Terio cited the immurement of a woman, said to be a virgin, in a wall of Germany's Nieder Manderscheid castle. A second example was the Bridge Gate in Bremen: when demolished in the Nineteenth Century, the structure was found to have concealed a child's skeleton in its foundation. Further evidence had been uncovered in the course of renovations to English churches and French cathedrals. Terio noted in passing that some scholars thought the nursery rhyme "London Bridge" referred to the practice. Unbidden, the song popped into Danny's mind:

London Bridge is falling down,
Falling down, falling down.
London Bridge is falling down,
My fair lady.
Take the keys and lock her up,
lock her up, lock her up.
Take the keys and lock her up,
My fair lady

The jingle didn't make sense, when you thought of it. What keys? Lock who up? Was that the sense of it – lock up some fair lady to keep the bridge from falling down? Jesus. It gave him the creeps.

All in all, it was chilling stuff, dryly told but fascinating. So much so, in fact, that when Danny finally closed the book, he was surprised to find that it was now evening. Unnoticed, the lights in the park had flickered on and the afternoon's long shadows had dissolved into a more generalized darkness.

Getting to his feet, he set out in the direction of a distant glow, a haze of light that he hoped was the Piazza del Popolo. Not that it mattered. He was lost in thought and might just as well be lost in fact. At some point or other, he'd find a cab and the cab would take him to his hotel, where he'd have a quiet dinner and turn in. Meanwhile, he trudged through the park past statues of Third World poets and revolutionaries, *The Radiant Tomb* clasped in his hands behind his back. For the first time Danny wondered if Chris Terio *had* committed suicide. *What if he was a "reluctant" anchorite? Who would do something like that? Bury someone alive?*

He shook off that train of thought, but the one that followed was no improvement. If it was suicide and Terio actually sealed himself in there, *what was he thinking?* Danny wondered. *What was he thinking when he put the last block in place?*

It was hot in the morning, the air gritty against his skin, as Danny stood at the reception desk in the Customs office at Leonardo da Vinci Airport, waiting for a stamp. Behind the counter, an elegant young man pecked away at an antique typewriter, a cigarette

127

smoldering in the corner of his mouth. A Customs agent, the man was amazingly intent, as if the keyboard was a mystery of huge proportions. Occasionally he took a slow-motion slap at the carriage return, squinted through the smoke, and resumed pecking. Finally, he paused and, ever so slowly, reread what he'd typed.

"*Va bene,*" he proclaimed, and, twirling the platen, ejected the page. Getting to his feet, he pushed the paper across the counter at Danny. "You sign."

Danny complied again, and the Customs agent stamped and countersigned the paper. Then he pointed to a number (it was 1,483,000) and said, "Now, you pay." Danny complied, counting out the bills from a wad that he'd gotten from the bank that same morning. The agent sorted the bills and put them away in a drawer beneath the counter. Then he locked the drawer, muttered something that Danny didn't quite get, and disappeared into a back room. A minute later, he returned with a package in his arms, presenting it as if it were a crown resting on a cushion.

"*Grazie!*"

"*Prego!*"

On his way back to the Inghilterra, Danny sat in the rear of the cab with the computer beside him in its box. His intention was to FedEx it to Belzer within the hour, but it occurred to him that shipping the computer without copying its contents would be a mistake. FedEx didn't lose much – but shit happened, and if it happened this time, it could cost Danny a whole lot of money. Better to copy the files onto a floppy, so that he'd have a backup just in case.

At Danny's direction, the cabbie stopped at a chic little office-supply store on the Via del Corso. Leaving the car parked on the sidewalk and the driver reading a soccer tabloid, Danny went inside and bought a box of floppies and some mailing labels. Then it was back to the hotel and up to his room, where he sat down on the bed and, using a letter opener, carefully slit the seals on the package.

Just as he'd hoped, the Thinkpad was in a black cordura case, with all of its accessories, including an external floppy drive and the adapters needed to accommodate Italian plugs. It only took a minute to get everything up and running. He went immediately into the root directory.

He found a dozen directories containing text files. The rest were system files and applications that he absolutely didn't need. So he re-created the same directories on a floppy and copied the text files to it. Finally, he slid the floppy into one of the Inghilterra's envelopes, wrote *Terio* on the front, and shoved it into his duffle bag. Then he repacked the Thinkpad in its case and put it back in the cardboard box.

It was time to call Belzer. Time to get paid.

The lawyer's telephone number was on his business card, and Danny dialed it, using the cell phone that Belzer had given him. The connection was pristine, a dead silence interrupted by a distant electronic warble. Then: *"Prego."*

"Uhh . . . I'm trying to reach Mr. Belzer?"

The voice warmed up. "Daniel! My friend! How are you enjoying the Eternal City?"

"It's a knockout. I'm blown away."

"Wonderful! And you have news for me?"

"I have good news for you," Danny replied.

"So! You've seen the priest, then."

"Even better – I have the computer."

"What?! That's terrific!"

"Yeah, well – how do I get it to you?" Cray asked, pen in hand. "I was thinking I could FedEx it. . . ."

Belzer chuckled. "Well, yes, I suppose you could. But why don't we save a little money?"

"Okay . . . how do I –"

"Instead of FedEx, why don't you take the elevator?"

"What?" Danny thought he'd misunderstood.

"I said you can bring it up to me on the elevator. I'm on the third floor."

Danny blinked. Wondered: *Is this a joke?* Decided that it wasn't. Asked himself: *What's he doing here – how long has he been here?* Somehow, the idea that Belzer was staying in the same hotel at the same time – without Danny knowing it – bothered him. It gave him a claustrophobic feeling. *Then again: why shouldn't he be here? Maybe this is the hotel he always uses, that's why he put me here. Maybe he's got business in Rome.* Not that it mattered. It just made Danny's job that much easier. "Which room?" he asked.

Belzer's chuckle. Then: "All of them."

"The whole floor?"

Danny could almost hear the lawyer shrug. "It's a security measure," Belzer explained. "Anyway, it gives me privacy, and, besides, it's only a few rooms."

"Only a few rooms"? At five hundred bucks a night? "I'll be right up," Danny promised.

The elevator took him to the third floor, where it was immediately apparent that this was indeed Belzer's domain. As soon as the doors opened, a square man in a black business suit got to his feet from a straight-backed chair and stepped toward the

130

elevator. His eyes swept over Danny, then he cocked his head deferentially and gestured down the hall to where two other men were standing.

Danny followed the gesture and found the lawyer waiting for him in an old-fashioned library with walnut wainscoting.

"Dan!" Belzer exclaimed as he came around from an antique wooden desk to shake hands. Once again he wore a dark well-cut suit and glasses with gray lenses – not quite sunglasses but dark enough to make it hard to see his eyes. "I can't tell you how pleased I am. Really!" Taking the younger man by the arm, Belzer led him to an oval table that stood beneath a mullioned window, overlooking the street. "Is this it?" he asked, taking the package from Danny's arms.

"Yeah, that's it," Danny replied. Then he took a seat in a leather armchair and watched as Belzer examined the package. Finding it opened, the lawyer looked inquiringly in Danny's direction.

"I wanted to be sure it was all there," Danny told him.

Belzer nodded and took a seat at the table. As he did, a waiter came into the room with a tray and poured each of them a glass of ice water. "Drink?" Belzer asked, his manicured hand making a circular gesture in the air.

"No, thanks, I –"

"Cigar? Coffee?"

Danny shook his head. "No, really – I'm all set."

Dismissing the waiter as if he were a fly hanging in the air between them, Belzer pulled the Thinkpad out of its package. Placing it on the table between them, he raised the monitor and slid the ON button forward. It took about a minute for the fanfare to sound, and then, as Danny watched, the lawyer's fingers began to tap on the keyboard.

He couldn't tell exactly what Belzer was doing – the screen was facing the other way – but Danny guessed that the lawyer was searching through Terio's directories, looking for something in particular. Or maybe not. Maybe he was fishing.

Five minutes went by, and then ten. Occasionally Belzer would pause to read or reread an item of interest. Danny didn't pay much attention, just sat where he was, toting up the hours in his head and trying to recall exactly what it was that Belzer said when they made their deal about the computer. *I'll give you ten thousand dollars . . . in addition to your hourly rate . . . Maybe the priest will sell you the computer. If he does . . . you can keep whatever's left.*

Something like that.

Danny took a sip of water and calculated. One-point-five-million lire was about six hundred and seventy-five dollars. That's what he'd paid Customs for the computer. The question was: Was that an "expense"? Or did it come under the "beg, borrow, or steal" proviso? *Don't be greedy,* he told himself. *You'll be lucky if this guy even pays you for the hours that he owes. It's too easy. For ten grand, someone should have taken a shot at me or something.* Not an expense, then. A cost of doing business. Which left . . . about nine thousand dollars. Unless Belzer kept the computer, in which case he'd have to buy the priest a Thinkpad. (Make that a *used* Thinkpad.) Which was . . . what? A grand? This *was* Italy. Maybe two.

Anyway . . . worst-case scenario: If Belzer kept the

Thinkpad, Danny would still come out of the deal with seventy-five hundred bucks – plus his hours. Which were at fifty-eight and counting. All together he'd probably make about fifteen grand. Enough for the video suite – or enough, at least, so that Danny could probably borrow the difference from the folks.

Belzer puttered with the computer for another five minutes. Once or twice, Danny started to say something – should he stay, or should he go? – but the lawyer quieted him, softly patting the air with his right hand, even as his eyes stayed glued to the screen.

Finally, he opened an attaché case that was sitting on the floor beside the table and retrieved a CD. Inserting the CD in a drive at the base of the computer, he slid the bay closed and began to type. Soon the hard drive started to grind, a rhythmic, pulsing noise that seemed entirely out of place in the nineteenth-century room. Maybe he was copying stuff; Danny wasn't sure. Then, after nearly a minute, the machine fell silent. Belzer shut it off and closed the screen. "I'm *very* happy with you," he said, bathing Danny in a broad grin.

Danny almost blushed. "Thanks."

Belzer shook his head. Took his sunglasses off, held them in one hand. The lawyer did this every now and then, and Danny had come to recognize it as a gesture used to emphasize important points. A gesture of inclusion. "No. The thanks are mine. If you hadn't found that FedEx receipt – *in the garbage*, no less . . ."

Danny acknowledged the compliment with a modest shrug.

"I've been thinking," Belzer said. "You're an interesting young man: smart, fast, creative – and from what I can tell, you don't have any holdback at all. That's rare."

The praise made Danny uncomfortable. He practically winced but managed, instead, to look Belzer in the eye. For the first time, Danny noticed that the lawyer's eyes were the color and texture of mud. "Thanks," he said.

"Well . . . I've been thinking . . . it might be a good idea to put this on a more regular footing."

Danny gave him a puzzled look. "What do you mean?"

"I mean: I want you to come to work for me – full-time."

Danny didn't give it a second thought. "Thanks," he said, "but – I don't think so. This is . . . just a kind of sideline for me." He paused, gearing up to launch into a speech about art and how important it was to him, when the lawyer interrupted him.

"Hear me out," he said. "I was thinking we'd convert your hourly rate to a salary. You'd have to travel, but we'd make it first-class – so I don't think you'd be suffering too much."

Danny thought about it. The truth was: He *liked* to travel – especially first-class (which he had now done exactly once). "And where would I be traveling *to*?" he asked.

Belzer shrugged. "The client has a lot of interests. London, Moscow, Tokyo . . . LA. It's hard to say. I see you as a kind of fireman. A troubleshooter. Something comes up – you get on a plane, check it out, and report back. To me. I think you'd find it interesting, even if it was only for a year or two." Now Belzer put the glasses back on, leaned back in the chair, as if to give Danny some room to think about it.

And he did. It was impossible not to do the math: One hundred dollars an hour at forty hours a week for fifty-two weeks was . . . what? *Two hundred grand a year?* Not bad for a twenty-six-year-old artist. It would blow Caleigh *away*. Then again, and on the other hand, he wouldn't be an artist, he'd be working for *this* guy, and –

Belzer was looking at him.

"Sorry?" Danny asked.

"I said you don't have to decide this instant. Think it over for a couple of days – and give me your answer over the weekend."

"The weekend?"

"We can talk about it in Siena. I'd like you to come up for the Palio."

The Palio, Danny thought. "What's a Palio?"

Belzer frowned. "You're kidding me."

Danny shook his head.

The lawyer smiled and leaned forward. Resting his elbows on the table, he made a steeple with his fingers and began to explain. "It's the oldest and most spectacular horse race in the world. They run it twice a year in the Campo – which is one of the most beautiful piazzas in Italy, a really *big* piazza that's shaped like a seashell. Each of the *contrade* has a horse in the race, so –"

"What's a *contrade*?" Danny asked.

"Contrada," Belzer corrected. "One of the old neighborhoods in Siena." Then he laughed. "It's very *West Side Story* – very *Romeo and Juliet*. Montagues and Capulets – and me." He laughed again. "Anyway . . . it starts with a cannon. Fifty thousand people jammed together into the Campo, shoulder-to-shoulder, horses circling. The jockeys ride bareback."

"Sounds amazing."

Belzer removed the glasses again and leaned toward him. "It's glorious. Italy *stops*. It's like a national heart attack during the time it takes to run the race. For an artist like you . . . it's what life is all about. Crowds, blood, speed." Belzer's muddy eyes held him with their gaze, a faint smile on his full lips.

Danny thought about it. *That's what life's all about?* Probably not. Anyway, what he really wanted to do was get paid, catch the next plane back to the States, fall in bed with Caleigh. Then, again . . .

"While you're there, you can meet Zebek – he *wants* to meet with you – and we'll cut you a check on the spot. Have it waiting for you, when you arrive."

Danny wasn't sure what to say.

The lawyer chuckled. "It's just a day or two," he promised. "And we'll continue to pay your hourly fee and expenses."

"It isn't that," Danny told him. "I've got a show coming up. . . ."

Behind the glasses Belzer looked disappointed, and Danny realized that he must seem ungrateful. The lawyer was being extremely generous, and – suddenly an awful thought occurred. If he didn't go to get the check, how long would it be before it was sent to him? And when it was sent – *if* it was sent – would it all be there? Or would Belzer have second thoughts about his generosity? And what about Zebek? It would be interesting to meet someone that rich, that powerful. Maybe he collected art. Maybe – "Okay," Danny decided. "Why not? It's not like I get to Italy every day."

"Wonderful," Belzer replied. "I'll look for you at eight tomorrow evening. For dinner, alfresco, right in the Campo. It's a special night, the one before the race."

"And how do I find you?"

Belzer shrugged. "Go to the Campo and look for the Palazzo di Pavone in the Logge della Mercanzia. The tables will be set out below. You'll see the flags."

Danny searched his pockets for a pen.

"You don't need to write it down," Belzer told him. "Everyone knows where it is. Look for a long balcony with peacocks shitting all over it. It's the only one on the Campo." He laughed and missed the startled look in Danny's eyes.

Peacocks? What was it Inzaghi had said? Something about a "Peacock Angel." "You mean, he's got peacocks – right in town?"

Belzer laughed. "Why not? They're better than any watchdog – and Zebek couldn't resist."

"Resist what?"

"The palazzo. It's sixteenth-century, and when it came on the market – well, you can imagine; it was just so appropriate."

Danny frowned, not understanding.

Belzer smiled. "I forget. You don't speak Italian." He thought for a moment, then explained. "Each of the *contrade* has a symbol. Usually it's an animal, but not always." He paused. "Anyway," he said, "one of them is *il pavone* – the Peacock. So, naturally, if you have a business called *Sistemi di Pavone* and it's head-quartered in Siena . . . well, acquiring the *Palazzo di Pavone* was a no-brainer. I think it's called 'branding.'" With a shrug, Belzer planted his cane on the floor and leveraged himself to his feet.

"What about the computer?" Danny asked, standing up.

The lawyer glanced indifferently at the laptop. "What about it?"

"I told the priest I'd try to get it back to him."

"Then get it back to him," the lawyer said. He glanced at his Rolex. "I nearly forgot." From his jacket pocket he extracted a brown envelope and handed it to the American.

"What's this?"

"Your ticket on the *rapido* to Siena. It leaves the Termini at ten thirty-two. That's in the morning. And there's a voucher for the Villa Scacciapensieri." He looked regretful. "It's a nice hotel, but maybe not as central as you'd like. Still, with the Palio . . . we're lucky you're not in a tent. The city's packed."

Danny dismissed the inconvenience with a mumble, and the two of them shook hands.

"Until tomorrow, then."

"At eight," Belzer reminded. "And then, the next day, you can watch the race with us from the balcony. It's really something, and everyone agrees – the view is to die for."

Danny took his time over breakfast the next morning, sitting at a table in the Inghilterra's somnolent dining room. There was a lot to think about, and fragments of an old rock song ran through his head:

Should I stay,
Or should I go?

On the one hand: He had a life. And, obviously, the right thing to do was go back to that life and work his ass off; he could buy the video suite that he needed and . . . who knows? Maybe he'd sell a couple of pieces.

That was all an artist could ever really ask for – to make enough money to keep working. If he someday hit it big, that would be great. But it was *the work* that mattered. Not the money.

"More coffee, Signore Cray?"

Danny looked up. Nodded. "Please."

The waiter refilled Danny's cup, inclined his head, and withdrew.

On the other hand . . . he could bag the truth-and-beauty biz and go over to the dark side – not forever, of course, but long enough to savor a world of private jets and swank hotels with Belgian chocolates on the pillows. That's what Belzer was offering him – a chance to "live large."

Which was tempting. But the temptation – and it was obviously as much a question of temptation as "opportunity" – raised questions. For instance: that business about "the dark side." In his (admittedly limited) experience, it was seldom the rich who fought the good fight. This was simply a fact of life.

And this thing with Belzer, he had no way of knowing who was right and wrong – or even what the issues were, really. The question was: Did he really *care* whose side he was on? He thought he did, but in the face of Belzer's offer he was beginning to worry that whatever virtue he had owed less to integrity than to a lack of options. Maybe he wasn't the good guy that he'd always imagined – just a bad guy waiting for a chance to get started.

Danny sipped his coffee. Admired the creamy porcelain cup. The thing was: This business with Terio and Belzer – it was *unlucky* somehow. He could feel it. The peacocks, the violence, it was all so weird. It made him want to cross himself, which was –

Jesus, Danny thought, *I'm losing it.* Impatient with his conscience, he signed for the check and went up to his room.

Retrieving Terio's laptop from under the bed, Danny sat down on the sofa and turned it on. *Maybe there's something on it that will help me decide. Something about Terio or Zebek –*

But there wasn't.

What there was, was nothing.

Zero. Zip. Niente.

Danny stared. The monitor was a wall of white-hot pixels. For a second, he thought it must be broken – but no, it had worked for Belzer. Just yesterday. He shut it off and turned it on again. Same thing.

He sat for what seemed like a long while on the edge of the sofa, with the computer in his lap. He remembered Belzer sitting across from him in the library, studying the monitor. After a while, the lawyer had put a CD in the drive – so he could copy the files. Or so Danny thought. One of the drives had started to grind. And now . . .

Suddenly he understood. Belzer hadn't been copying the files. He'd reformatted the hard disk, and overwritten it with DiscWipe or some other program. That's what the CD was for.

Danny felt blindsided. And when he thought about it, the meaning of what Belzer had done began to expand. For the first time, he knew for sure which side he was on – the *wrong* side. Destroying the files put a whole new spin on Belzer and on "the investigation" he'd commissioned. This wasn't an investigation – it was a cover-up. It wasn't about Terio spreading false information, because then Belzer would have *copied* the files before giving the computer back to Danny.

140

They were evidence of what Terio had done. Instead the lawyer had wiped them out.

So now Danny knew. He wasn't a good guy *or* a bad guy. He was a just another dupe, a stooge. The lawyer wasn't paying Danny for his smarts – Fellner Associates was *smart*. Belzer was paying him for his naïveté. Because Fellner would have seen through Belzer's scheme. With all the resources of the firm, the first thing they would have done was run a Nexis search on the smears against Zebek. Then they'd have had the results translated. And if it turned out that there weren't any hits, they'd have realized that the client was lying to them – and they would have walked away from the case.

Which left Danny flushed with anger. He was an easygoing guy, for the most part, but he had an Irish temper – and when it went off it was a good idea to get out of the way. His mother worried about it. *You're like a broken hammer, Danny! You fly off the handle, and I don't think you care who gets hit.*

Actually, he did. He cared very much. Right now, he wanted to hit Belzer – and no one else would do. But hitting Belzer wasn't an option. Not really. So he set the computer aside, fell back on the couch, and stared at the ceiling. *Now what?* Danny wondered.

The answer came back in an instant: *Get paid.*

Confronting Belzer would accomplish nothing. The thing to do was play along, collect the money that he was owed, and walk away on good terms: *Thanks for the offer, Mr. Belzer – it's been wayyyy interesting – but I've got an exhibition to put together. Ciao!*

And, in the meantime, he'd fuck him. He'd restore the files to the computer, using the backup that he'd made. Belzer didn't know about the backup – and there was no way he'd ever find out. The priest would get whatever there was to get, whatever it was that Terio had *wanted* him to get – if there *was* anything. Maybe the computer was not some kind of message in a bottle. Maybe – as Inzaghi thought – Terio simply sent the Thinkpad as a gift to his friend and that was it. In which case the priest could repeat Belzer's actions and strip all of Terio's files off the machine.

But there must have been something on the computer, or Belzer wouldn't have wiped the disk. That was another thing Danny didn't know, why Belzer wanted the files erased. Didn't know. Didn't *want* to know. Danny Cray would deliver the Thinkpad – files restored – to the priest. And feel a whole lot better about the whole thing. After that – let the wind take it.

It wasn't quite that easy. Belzer had reformatted the hard disk, destroying not only Terio's text files but the Windows operating system as well. The first task, then, was to restore the operating system – something Danny had never done or ever wanted to do. Obviously, he needed a geek – but where to find one?

As it happened, one of the advantages of staying in a great hotel is the great concierge who comes with it. Giorgio's job was to take care of his guests – to get them whatever they wanted. Tickets, reservations, information, introductions – whatever, whenever, however. After explaining the problem to the con-cierge, Danny returned to his rooms, leaving the elderly Giorgio to work the phones. Which he did, and successfully. After an hour or so, a young man came to the door with a battered CD jewel box. Inside was a pirated copy of the Windows 98 operating system.

It didn't take the kid long to install it – a little more than half an hour. When the job was done, Danny gave him the equivalent of one hundred dollars and showed him to the door. Then he sat down with the laptop and, one by one, restored the text files that Belzer had deleted. The process took about two minutes and, when the job was done, he telephoned Inzaghi.

"That was fast," the priest said, not bothering to hide his surprise. "I thought you'd want to keep it for days."

"There was nothing on it we were looking for," Danny explained. "So! How do I get it to you? I'm leaving tomorrow. I guess I could FedEx it."

Inzaghi hesitated. "That's okay, but – where are you off to? Back to the States?"

"Actually, I'm going to Siena."

"For the Palio! Of course! A beautiful city – I envy you. Don't miss the cathedral. Even after St. Peter's, it's spectacular!"

"I'll make a point of it."

The priest paused, as if a thought had just occurred to him. "And how are you traveling?"

"Looks like I'm taking the train."

"Well, in that case," Inzaghi exclaimed, "I'm going to Frascati in the morning – I could meet you at the Termini."

"You're certain?"

"Absolutely. There's an information board in the main concourse. It's massive – you can't miss it. When's your train?"

"Ten thirty-two."

"Then I'll see you at, say, nine forty-five. Just . . ."

"What?" Danny asked.

"Watch out for the children," the priest told him.

"What children?"

"The gypsy children. They're adorable, but they'll pick you clean."

Nine

Crowds and dust and noise.

Danny and the priest were sitting on straight-backed chairs in the Termini Cafe, just inside the entrance to the train station. Inzaghi was across the table from him, with the strap of the Thinkpad's case looped around his arm – a precaution against the child-thieves who trawled the station in search of open purses and unattended luggage. He took a tentative sip of espresso and winced. "Not so good."

Danny nodded, not really listening. He was in a kind of future-oriented reverie, only remotely aware of the man across from him and the hubbub of the station. He'd surged past this meeting, the trip to Siena, the Palio, and whatever thanks-but-no-thanks discussion he was going to have with Belzer. He was thousands of miles away, spending money on video equipment at a store in Lower Manhattan.

"Any petrol station in the provinces can do better than this, Detective," Inzaghi was saying. "I'm ashamed to be Italian."

Danny shrugged. *Detective*. The word brought him back to the present, back to Italy. He looked up at the priest. "Listen," he said. "There's something I ought to tell you."

Inzaghi frowned. Obviously the detective hadn't heard a word he'd said. "Yes?"

"It's that . . . well, I'm not actually a detective. I'm . . . an investigator."

Inzaghi nodded. So what?

"A *private* investigator," Danny added.

The priest's eyes flickered, suddenly curious.

"I don't work for Fairfax County," Danny elaborated.

"But . . ." Now Inzaghi was really confused. His hands fluttered, then settled back down. "Your identification – I saw it. Fairfax County." He frowned. "*Virginia*. And then – you brought me this." He tapped the computer with the back of his hand.

Danny nodded. "I know, but . . . my name's Danny Cray. And I'm really an artist, a sculptor. This investigative work, it's just a way to pay the bills. Sometimes there are pretexts, and . . . I'm sorry."

Inzaghi looked surprised, but there wasn't any anger in him. After a moment, he asked, "So who hired you?"

It was an obvious question, and it was equally obvious that Danny didn't want to answer it. But he did. He told Inzaghi about Belzer and Zebek. And then, when he was done, he rolled a forefinger in the air beside his head. "It was *Ka-ching, ka-ching*. All I could hear was the cash register. Next thing I know, Belzer has me in his web and I'm 'Detective Muller.' "

Inzaghi leaned back in his chair, frowned, drummed his fingers on the little table. "It's like the gypsies. Using children."

"How's that?"

"The way they exploit innocence."

Embarrassed, Danny looked down at his hands. "I knew what I was doing. It was a lot of money. So I wouldn't say I was all that 'innocent.' "

The priest smiled. "I wasn't talking about you. I was talking about me."

Danny's embarrassment deepened. After a moment, he pushed back his chair. "Well," he said, starting to get up.

The priest laid a hand on his arm. "I'm not upset. The important thing is, you've told the truth – and I have the computer. Don't worry about it."

Danny relaxed. Sat back in his chair. "Thanks," he said, a little uncertainly. Inzaghi was giving him the benefit of the doubt, and he wasn't sure that he deserved it.

The priest pressed his hands together. "Though, actually," he said, "maybe you *should* worry about it."

Danny looked at him.

Inzaghi leaned forward. "I mean, you should be careful," he said.

Danny shrugged. "I'm going home soon –"

"No. You're going to Siena soon. Home is later." He hesitated. "What I'm saying is: Be careful in Siena."

"All right."

"Let me ask you something," Inzaghi said. "This Zebek – how much do you know about him?"

"Not much."

"That's what I thought," the priest told him. "I think he must be a very private person. Because you could read all the major newspapers and you wouldn't see his name in a year. Except in passing, maybe, and on lists."

"What 'lists'?"

"The richest. The most powerful. The most this, the most that. He's always right up there: Agnelli, Berlusconi, Zebek. And this man – he's not even Italian."

"He's not?"

The priest shook his head. "He's a Turk – though he's lived in Italy for many, many years."

Danny wasn't sure where the conversation was going, and his face showed it.

Inzaghi saw his uncertainty. "The point is: There was no smear campaign against Zerevan Zebek."

"You're sure?"

The priest nodded. "Absolutely. There's almost nothing published about him – in Italy or anywhere else. I remember a picture in *Oggi*. A party in Milan. Gucci, or an AIDS ball. The lists. That's about it."

Danny looked skeptical. "If he's so rich, you'd think –"

"He's famously litigious. Which might explain a lot. Of course, so might other things."

"Such as what?" Danny did not want to be curious – he wanted to be done with this business – but he couldn't help himself.

The priest pursed his lips. "Perhaps he's connected to the Mafia."

Danny blanched.

"Or worse," the priest said.

"Worse? What could be worse?"

Inzaghi made a gesture. "He's Turkish. Almost anything is possible."

"What do you mean?" Danny asked.

"I mean . . . the country is run by the army and by certain clans. Together they own banks and poppy fields, munitions factories and trucking companies. On one level, it's all quite respectable – with Western corporations as their partners. But I think if you go deeper, you'll come across arrangements with

148

Lebanese militias on both sides of what used to be called 'the Green Line.' Bulgarian gangs. Political factions in Armenia and Iraq, in Iran and Syria. There's a lot of smuggling. By comparison, our Mafia is a provincial institution."

"How do you know all that?"

"I read *Le Monde*."

"And you think Zebek –"

The priest shook his head. "I don't know anything about Zebek – except how much I *don't* know. Mr. Zebek is a mystery. But so are you."

Danny raised his hands as if to fend off an accusation. "Not anymore I'm not."

"Oh, but you are. I still don't know why you were paid to get the computer."

"Belzer wanted to erase the files," Danny told him. "And he *did* erase the files."

The priest's face sagged with disappointment. "When Chris told me that he was making me a gift of the laptop, he said he'd left some of his preliminary work on the machine for me to read. I thought maybe I could do something for him. You know, perhaps some posthumous publication of his recent work, his research for the book. Now I guess not; I –"

"Don't worry," Danny interrupted. "I made a backup, a floppy – Belzer didn't know about it. I put the files back for you. So whatever *was* there . . ." He shrugged.

The corners of Inzaghi's mouth lifted for a moment and then flat-lined. "That was very kind of you. But now I'm sure of it. You shouldn't go to Siena."

Danny rolled his eyes. "It's payday, Padre. I am definitely on that train."

*

149

And so he was. Arriving in the city in the early afternoon, Danny found himself unprepared for the beauty of Tuscany's crown jewel. The city was an urban gem inset in a golden landscape, with farms and olive groves surrounding a collage of palaces and towers draped across three softly rolling hills.

He found a taxi – a battered Fiat – outside the railway terminus and sat back as the driver embarked on a hair-raising drive along a narrow road that wound its way through the hills, corkscrewing higher and higher. Girded by ancient stone walls, Siena strobed in and out of view as the taxi climbed through the hills in the shimmering heat of summer.

"You come for the Palio, no?" The driver was a short dark man with a bright silk scarf around his neck – an improbable accessory that looked strange against his faded polo shirt and gray pants. The scarf itself was magenta and green, and Danny saw that a gold dragon peeked from its folds.

"Yeah, right!" Danny said, raising his voice above the straining engine. "The Palio!"

The driver pinched the point of the scarf's fabric and pulled it out, away from him. "Drago," he announced, looking into the cracked rearview mirror to see if Danny understood.

Danny acknowledged the display by tugging lightly at the collar of his shirt and declaring his own allegiance: "USA."

The driver laughed, then swung the wheel to the right and back to the left, as a black Renault sent the taxi sliding onto the gravel shoulder. A string of curses followed as the cabbie turned in his seat, punishing the offending car with a stare.

Then it was Danny's turn to swear as an oncoming

truck bore down upon them from around a curve. Reluctantly the driver returned his gaze to the road and applied the brakes.

"In English, the Dragon," the driver said. Slowly the car returned to its excessive speed as the driver continued the conversation in a nonchalant tone. "We going to win, I think. I'm seeing the horse." He removed a hand from the steering wheel and kissed the bouquet of his fingers. He removed his other hand from the wheel and made an expansive gesture. "This horse, he's a good mover."

Danny willed the man's hands back to the steering wheel. His relief when they careened into the pebble courtyard of the hotel translated itself into a big tip, despite the fact that the ride had included, as was normal in Italy, two near-death experiences. It was an integral part of Danny's system of superstition that generous tips kept disaster at bay.

The hotel stood on a hillside above an olive grove in one of the most romantic settings he'd ever seen. Checking in, he found that, once again, a suite had been reserved for him. It was off to itself in a quiet courtyard whose walls were plastered with climbing roses. Bees swayed in the air, drowsing, and then shot off into the sun. Birds sang. Water burbled. Terra-cotta pots stood everywhere, spilling flowers and trailing vines. Clinging to everything was the scent of roses and lavender.

Danny's own rooms were pleasantly cool and cheerfully decorated, with beamed ceilings of dark wood, a corner fireplace, and a marble bathroom. He thought about heading into town – Siena was a city he was itching to explore – but decided to have a drink on the terrace first.

151

He was halfway through his second Campari-soda, eyes resting on the olive groves below, when Paulina Pastorini sashayed into view. Seeing him, she gave a little wave and crossed the terrace with a lacquered walk so sensual it might easily have been designated a road hazard.

She was wearing a tangerine halter-top dress and white sandals with high heels, her eyes hidden behind a pair of expensive sunglasses. With her café-au-lait skin and chestnut hair the effect was heart-stopping. A voice in the back of his head insisted that he was not happy to see her there, that it would be better to be alone, that she was an accident waiting to happen. But it didn't work. Not for a second. The woman was a thrill.

"Ah, *there* you are," she said, with a flash of teeth. She tossed back her gleaming hair. "May I join you?" she asked, and, without waiting for an answer, pulled out a chair and sat down.

The waiter appeared out of nowhere. "Signorina?"

She fired away in Italian. The waiter nodded and withdrew. With a soft smile, she lowered her chin and looked at Danny over the tops of her sunglasses.

Bambi eyes, he thought.

"Have you been very, very good?" she asked.

Danny shifted in his seat. Searched desperately for something witty to say: "I guess."

She laughed.

"Are you here for the Palio?" he asked.

She shook her head. "I'm here for *you*," she told him. Paused. "To show you around Siena, translate – whatever you need." Her elegant shoulders lifted in a shrug.

A moment later, the waiter returned with a bottle of

Pinot Grigio and two glasses. Angling the bottle toward Paulina, he awaited her approval. When she nodded in assent, he opened the bottle expertly and poured her a small amount. When she tasted the wine and smacked her lips in comic delight, the waiter laughed. And so did Danny.

It was all very leisurely, entirely in keeping with the somnolent glory of the afternoon. *This is what it's like to be rich,* Danny thought. *This is what you write when you write your own ticket: P-a-u-l-i-n-a.*

When the wine was almost gone, they summoned Paulina's car – a white Lancia – and drove down the hill toward town. She was a good driver, a hundred times better than the cabbie, easing the car through one gear after another, turn after turn. Danny found himself looking at her legs and pulled his eyes away.

"I'm told you're an artist," she said.

He nodded.

"Signore Belzer says you're good. A real Picasso!"

Danny chuckled. "Rii-ight – that's me. 'A real Picasso!'"

"That's what he *said*," she told him. "I'm just reporting. Anyway, I thought we'd see some art. I can show you things that will knock your eyes off."

He didn't know what she meant for a moment. Then he understood. " 'Your socks,' " he told her.

"Excuse me?"

" 'Your socks.' It's your socks that get knocked off – not your eyes."

She glanced at him. "Really? Not your eyes? Your *socks*?" Her laugh was pure magic, but there was something in it that made him think she'd deliberately muddled the idiom – that she was being "cute" for him. "Why does that make sense?" she asked. "I,

153

myself, don't wear socks. Fortunately, you do. So maybe we can knock them off."

In between masterpieces – the famous frescoes of Good and Bad Government in the Palazzo Publico, the cathedral with its baptistry and Donatello's reliefs, an exquisitely inlaid marble pavement – she told him about the Palio.

"Siena – it's not such a big town, you know? Maybe sixty thousand people in seventeen *contrade*." She looked at him. "You know what a *contrada* is?"

He nodded. "It's like a neighborhood."

She looked impressed. "That's amazing," she told him. "Americans almost never know." She paused, then continued. "Well, then you know that each of the *contrade* has its own borders within the city – its own chapel, museum, and social club, its own patron saint, flag, and totem."

"Like the Dragon."

"Yes, like *Drago*. There is a Panther, too, and a Wolf, but it isn't all what you would expect. I mean, I know you have these . . . *symbols* in the States for your sports teams, but they are for the most part . . . mmmmm . . . ferocious creatures. Powerful. Fast. Violent. But here it isn't like that." A musical giggle. "Not at all."

"Why not? What do you mean?"

"Well, there's a Goose, a Snail and a Wave, a Forest. Even a Caterpillar." She giggled again, and it occurred to him that she was feeling the wine. "And not even a pretty one, like the fellow in *Alice in Wonderland*. No stripes or fanciful whiskers. Just a green tomato worm."

"Get out of here."

She admonished him, tapped his bicep with one

154

perfectly manicured finger. "You'll see. Anyway, the loyalty to the neighborhood is a lifelong thing. Once a Snail, always a Snail – and the same goes for the others. You can marry outside your *contrada*, but you never give up your allegiance."

"What about you?" Danny asked.

"Me?"

"Yeah, what *contrada* are you?"

That giggle again. Then, "Mmmmn . . . how do you say? Uptown." She laughed. And he did, too.

After checking out some early Michelangelos in the Piccolomini Chapel, they returned outside to find the city in shadow, the sun a pink glow in the western hills. "Let's go to the Campo," Paulina suggested, and, taking Danny by the hand, led him through a maze of passageways and little streets.

"We're in Onda territory," Paulina confided. "The Wave. You see?"

Indeed. Onda flags hung from every balcony, rippling bars of white and royal blue, the colors alternating, one on top of the other. The motif was everywhere, emblazoned on planters, painted on doors, carved into the very foundation stones of the buildings around them. Ahead of them, a streetlight flickered on, and Danny laughed when he saw that the fixture was in the shape of a fish – a stylized fish dancing on stylized waves.

"Do you know," Paulina asked, "that sociologists come from all over the world to study the *contrada* system? It's true! They say, long ago, the *contrade* were ancient tribes. And these tribes, they are like big families. Everyone is a cousin, you know? So they take care of each other. But outside the *contrada*? Always,

155

they fight. Now, I think, these rivalries are what hold the city together."

They walked through a small square where children with Palio scarves were playing soccer with a red rubber ball.

"What about the race itself?" he asked.

"It's twice a year," she told him. "The same dates, no matter if it's the weekend. July second and August sixteenth. And not all the *contrade* compete in both. There is only room for eleven. So, in July it's the six who didn't run in August the year before – plus another five they pick by drawing lots. Then, in August, it's the six who didn't compete in July, plus a second drawing for the other five places."

"So it's what? A pageant? Or an honest-to-god race?"

"It's not just for show, that's for sure. Horses die. Sometimes jockeys. Even the occasional spectator."

"You're kidding."

She shook her head. "Oh, no. The *contrade* take it very seriously. This has been happening for a thousand years. It's a whole week of festivities, yes, that's true. A spectacle. You'll see – tonight is the final evening before the battle, so it's always the most extravagant. Anyway, there are days and nights of medieval pageantry, singing and flag throwing – this part is all quite civilized. Then, when the cannon starts the race . . . well, it's as *brutal* as it is corrupt. You'll see tomorrow. Three times around the Campo, bareback, with fifty thousand people in the middle of it all, roaring as the horses fly past. It only lasts a minute and a half."

"Why do you say it's corrupt?"

She shrugged. "It's part of the competition.

156

Anything goes. Everything's allowed. Most of the jockeys come from the Maremma, and they're good with the whip – though they use it mostly on each other instead of the horses. Some of the horses are drugged, and every year it seems like one or two of them are killed in the San Martino turn – which is padded but impossible nevertheless." She paused and then went on. "And, of course, the whole thing is fixed. It's always fixed, although the fix doesn't always work because the race is so chaotic. One jockey is paid to lose – a second is paid to get in the way of a third. Still, it's up to the horses in the end – because they don't need a rider to win."

"What?"

She shook her head. "It's not the Kentucky Derby. Half the jockeys are knocked off or thrown off in the turns. It's the horse who finishes first that wins. So, in the end, the rider doesn't really matter."

"Who won in July?"

She frowned. "Not Pavone." She thought for a moment. "Istrice, I think."

"Let me guess," he said. "The Ostrich?"

She smiled, shook her head. "The Porcupine."

They turned right, walked down a very narrow street, and Paulina restrained him with a hand on his arm to point out that the flags and decorative features had changed. The flags were now turquoise and gold, and visible everywhere was the insignia of the Peacock, its tail feathers fanned out. "We're in Pavone territory now," she said. "It's one of the central *contrade*."

A moment later she pressed a finger to her lips. "Shhhh," she said. "Listen."

He cocked his head and then heard it: a vast subdued hum of human conversation, with the sharper counterpoint of cutlery, the chink of plates and glasses. Behind the hum, faint melodies rose and fell. He heard the thin blare of trumpets.

"Magic, isn't it?" Paulina asked.

They resumed walking. Paulina stumbled and grabbed his arm, leaned into him. The hot air carried her scent and he noticed the faint gleam of perspiration on her face, the damp tendrils of hair on her brow. Turning a corner, they stepped through the arch of a narrow arcade and, in an instant, were inundated by a waterfall of noise.

The Campo.

Ringed with mansions older than America, the piazza was paved in the city's distinctive brown stone – the "burnt sienna" of a million palettes. At the moment, the entire piazza was the site of a vast alfresco banquet. Perspiring waiters rushed back and forth, carrying trays of pasta, fish, and game to a couple hundred of fifty-foot-long banquet tables packed with thousands of festive Sienese. Peculiar and beautiful flags were everywhere, standing on every table, hanging from every balcony.

Ancient songs hung in the air, and the sound of trumpets rose and fell. Taking a step backward, Danny noticed for the first time that he was standing on a makeshift racetrack. Squares of inverted turf had been laid down around the perimeter of the Campo, covering its time-worn stones.

Paulina led him to an area reserved for the Pavone *contrada*, where hundreds of people were feasting at a score of tables, each of which was covered in gold cloth. Pennants and scarves and peacock feathers made it clear whose turf it was. Paulina gestured to an umber palace that rose up in the darkness behind the tables.

158

"The Palazzo di Pavone," she said. "We'll be there tomorrow. It's a fantastic view."

Danny gazed up at the long and sinuous balconies, where peacocks strolled amid a forest of potted palms. "What about tonight?" he asked. "I thought I was supposed to see Belzer."

She pouted in apology. "I spoke with him earlier. He's late getting in, but he didn't want you to miss all the fun. He said he'd see you tomorrow." Seeing Danny's disappointment, Paulina tilted her head and pursed her full lips into an even more exaggerated pout. "I'm not good-enough company?"

"It's not –"

She took his hand and pulled him. "Come on. We're at table three."

Though he hadn't given a thought to dinner, he realized that he was hungry – and it was a good thing, because the food came at him in waves. There seemed to be an endless number of courses, each paired to its own wine. Everything was delicious, and the energy in the Campo was nothing less than electrifying. As the banquet progressed, a fanfare of trumpets sounded. Conversation dwindled, a hush fell over the crowd, then a roar of applause shot into the air as a parade of men and women in medieval garb came into the square through one of its arched entrances. In measured steps they advanced along a wide path that lay between the tables. A burst of shouting and singing celebrated the arrival of each *contrada*'s contingent, bearing huge banners to the center of the square, where a makeshift stage stood ringed with torches. When the Pavone contingent reached the middle of the Campo, a sea of banqueters around Danny stood as one and began to sing, slowly waving little flags emblazoned with peacocks. Confetti flew from the balconies behind them, a blizzard of gold and azure that painted the crowd in glitter.

It was too noisy to engage in conversation with anyone but immediate tablemates – and the only one Danny could talk to was Paulina. No one else seemed to speak English. She translated for him, and although this was so awkward it hardly seemed worthwhile, when she left to visit friends at other tables he felt abandoned. All he could do with his tablemates was return their friendly smiles and lift his glass when they said things like *Buona fortuna* and *Victoria a Pavone!* – which they did quite often. By the time they got to the coffee and *vin santo*, and then to the *grappa*, it was after eleven.

He wanted to make his excuses, but at the moment Paulina was thirty feet away, at the head of the table, talking animatedly to an elegant gray-haired man. She glanced up, caught Danny's eye, volleyed a smile.

Danny tapped his watch, gave her a nonchalant wave, and stood up. The Campo swayed. *Whoa . . . "Grazie tutto,"* he called out, *"grazie mille!"* His Italian was really quite good, he decided. *"Arrivederci, mon amici!"* His tablemates laughed and raised their glasses.

"Danny," Paulina said, arriving at his side and entwining her arm in his. "I didn't know you spoke Italian!"

"Neither did I," he mumbled.

"But where are you going?"

"Hotel." He began shaking hands with people at the table.

"Already? But it's not even midnight."

He looked at her. "I'm a little . . . tired."

160

She giggled. "I think you're a little . . . drunk."

He thought about it for a moment. "That's possible," he replied, nodding with exaggerated seriousness.

"Well, all right," she said, taking a last sip of her *vin santo*. "Let's go!"

Danny shook his head. "I'll get a taxi."

"Don't be silly. I'm supposed to be looking after you. And, anyway, you'll never get a taxi tonight. It's impossible."

They walked back to where the car was parked. Danny was concentrating on the cobblestones, which required a bit of navigation, while Paulina wobbled along on her high heels, stumbling into him once or twice, laughing, whispering, touching his arm, talking. Her reckless giggle floated above them.

Then they were in the Lancia, roaring up the hill toward the hotel. Paulina put a CD into the player and Thelonious Monk spilled over them. Danny was thinking what a beautiful night it was, thinking what a beautiful girl she was, when her hand grazed his thigh. He didn't think it was an accident.

He was doing his best to be faithful, he really was, but it wasn't easy. Still, he was determined to get it right, because Caleigh was the one – he was sure of it. And she'd walk if he cheated on her, because fidelity meant *everything* to her. She'd made that clear from the start.

A few drops of rain spattered onto the windshield, not enough for Paulina to turn on the wipers. The drops clung to the glass like liquid jewels, lit up by the glow of oncoming headlights. Paulina was talking about the last time she'd visited the States – how everything was supersized. "Houses, cars, Happy Meals. Everything!"

Danny nodded in agreement and forced his eyes away from her legs. By then, he'd memorized them as thoroughly as his ABCs.

"What about you?" she asked.

"What about me what?"

"Are you supersized, too?"

His jaw dropped. *I've really had too much to drink,* he thought. Because she couldn't mean what he thought she meant. It had to be an English-as-a-second-language thing. "No," he said, "I'm a little taller than average, that's all."

She laughed, and her hand brushed his thigh again as she downshifted through a curve.

She'd never know, Danny told himself, thinking of Caleigh. She was thousands of miles away, and the women's paths would never cross, not in a million years. His eyes dropped to Paulina's knees and to the creamy flesh above them.

Whatcha gonna do, boy?
Whatcha gonna do?

He laughed to himself and looked away.

"Why do you laugh?" Paulina asked.

Danny shook his head. "I was thinking of an album I used to listen to."

"Which one?"

"*Bat out of Hell.*"

She looked puzzled. "I don't know it," she said.

He shrugged. "It's not important." For a moment he considered telling her about the album and, in particular, the song from which the lines came: "Paradise by the Dashboard Light." *Better not,* he thought.

162

The thing was: It didn't really matter if Caleigh never knew. That wasn't the point. The point was not to cheat, not to lie. He'd been faithful to her for almost a year, now, and it was better this way. Secrets poisoned a relationship, and other women were like land mines – you never knew when one of them was going to go off.

Her hand rested lightly on his knee. *Maybe I'm too drunk to know right from wrong,* he hoped.

Suddenly the hotel loomed before them as the Lancia thundered into the Scacciapensieri's courtyard. Killing the engine, she unfolded her legs and climbed from the car. Then she tossed the keys to the bellman and, taking Danny's arm, put her head against his shoulder. Together they walked into the lobby and took the elevator to the third floor.

Stepping into the corridor, she hesitated. His room was to the right and hers to the left. "Well," she said, her perfect almond eyes searching his own.

"G'night," he muttered. "Thanks. It was really great." Leaning down, he gave her a peck on the cheek and headed toward his room. He felt relieved and disappointed at the same time. Standing before the door to 302, he fumbled with the key and cursed the wave of virtue that had broken over him. A voice in the back of his head – a sort of counterconscience – shouted: *What are you doing? What are you thinking? She's gorgeous – you're drunk. Caleigh's six time zones away! She's not even in the same day you are! Go for it!*

But no. He was being good. The key turned in the lock, and the night's temptation was behind him. Going into the bathroom, he undressed slowly, washed, and brushed his teeth. He didn't think he'd

163

had that much to drink, but the wine had really gone to his head. Tapping a couple of Advil from a bottle, he swallowed them with a glass of water, hoping they'd soften any hangover he might have in the morning. Then he flicked off the light and headed for bed.

And there she was – *in* the bed, with her hair fanned out across the pillow and a teasing smile on her lips.

Jesus Christ, he thought, standing in the middle of the room in his boxer shorts. *Now what?* Without intending to, he found himself moving to the side of the bed, as if he were on one of those moving sidewalks at the airport. He didn't know what to say.

She stretched, and her breasts heaved. "I'm not quite done looking after you," she purred, and patted the bed beside her.

It's too much, he thought. *I can't do this. There's only so much –*

Wordlessly she drew back the sheets, and he saw in a glance that turned into a stare that she was completely undressed. The look in his eyes brought a smile to her lips. "What are you waiting for, Picasso? Dive in."

Ten

Lying in bed with his eyes closed, Danny drifted in and out of sleep, increasingly conscious of the sunlight filling the room around him. Sightless, his field of vision was a blank page – empty, bright, and glowing. Which was fine with him. That was just the way he liked it. He didn't want to get up. He wanted to stay where he was, in the never-never land just this side of dreaming. But no. He had to get up. He had things to do and music to face. Bravely then, because he knew that he had a hangover, he opened his eyes and, quick as a gunshot, slammed them shut against the flashbulb of morning.

Lay there, thinking, *Ohhh, man* . . .

Furtively he moved his arm in an arc across the sheets and breathed a sigh of relief when his hand found nothing but fabric and air. With a low groan he forced his eyes open for the second time, sat up, and swung his legs from the bed. *You're scum,* he told himself.

For what seemed like a long while, he sat where he was with the sun on his back, staring at his bare feet, thinking dully about the night before. Lorenzetti's frescoes, Donatello's reliefs, Paulina's . . . everything.

"Ohh, Jesus," he muttered, remembering something he'd said, a line he'd delivered late at night. Not that a line had been necessary. Images of Siena flickered through his mind: the tables in the Campo, Paulina being funny and beautiful, the platters of food, blue and gold glitter sifting down from the sky. What was it she'd said? *What are you waiting for, Picasso? . . .*

God, he felt awful – and sitting there, he examined the parameters of his hangover. There was a percussive throb at the base of his skull and a jittery feeling behind his eyes. A sense of pressure throughout his head, too, as if his brain were slightly too big for his skull. But all in all, he could tell that it wasn't such a bad hangover. He hadn't had *that* much to drink – didn't have *that* much of an excuse. Still, he didn't feel *well*. Getting slowly to his feet, he slumped into the bathroom, turned on the tap, cupped his hands, and pressed the water against his cheeks and eyes. He simultaneously gasped at the cold and sighed with relief. Looking up, he saw a crimson imprint on the mirror. A kiss.

And there, against the chrome-plated toothbrush holder, a note on hotel stationery – addressed to *Danielissimo*:

Working at Sistema (borrr-ing). Back at two or so to give you a lift into town. B. wants you at the palazzo by two-thirty. Mmmmmm . . . what a notte di amore! I'll never forget – and don't you. Love and kisses (and you know where the kisses go)!
    P.

Jesus, Danny thought, crumpling the note. A "notte di amore."

He tried not to think about it, but it was impossible. Even as he tested the temperature of the shower, images of the night before flashed through his mind. Paulina this way and that, the way she tasted, the soft

166

incline of her belly, the rise and fall of her breasts. As he stepped into the shower, it occurred to him that it was something of an understatement to say that he'd gone to bed with her. In reality, he'd reveled in her like a dog rolling on the lawn.

It wasn't his best moment.

Turning his face to the showerhead, he let the water wash her off and gradually felt his hangover ease. When the room was thick with steam and he'd begun to feel human again, he stepped out of the glass-enclosed shower and dried off with a terry-cloth towel as thick as his wrist.

That done, he took a facecloth to the mirror and did his best to eradicate Paulina's kiss but succeeded only in reducing it to a pink smear. Giving up on the mirror, he ran a brush through his hair and pulled on some clothes. His eyes were bloodshot. He was going to need some shades.

Finally, he took the stairs down to the terrace, where he attempted to jump-start the day with a double espresso, chased by a tall glass of freshly squeezed orange juice.

It worked. Sort of.

It was almost noon. The sun was blazing, stabbing at his eyes. The clerk at the front desk told him where he could find sunglasses and told the bellhop to get him a cab. As Danny turned to leave, the clerk handed him his passport.

"Grazie."

The cab took him to the outskirts of town, where he bought a pair of Maui Jims. Then he returned to the hotel. Going up to his room to pack his duffle bag, he hesitated over what to do with the floppy – the one with Terio's files. He didn't need it anymore. His work for Belzer was over, and Inzaghi had the files. Still, he was curious, and it wouldn't hurt to take a peek when he got back to the States. So he jammed the floppy into his bag and zipped it closed.

Returning to the lobby, he asked the concierge about train connections between Siena and Rome. Alas, he was told, the trains were infrequent. Siena was only a branch off the main line. A bus would be better.

"The thing is: I've got a nine-fifteen flight."

"But you're staying for the Palio?" the concierge asked.

"Absolutely."

"Then I think your connection will be difficult. The race starts at four, so the only possibility is the five forty-eight to Chiusi. From there, you could catch the six forty-five to Rome. That will put you in the city by . . ." – his hand rotated one way, then the other – ". . . eight, or a little after. Then a taxi to the airport – another half hour. I don't know. . . ." He looked skeptical and disappointed, all at once.

Danny nodded. "It's tight, but I've got a first-class ticket, so –"

"In that case," the concierge said, "it's possible. But still difficult. I think, perhaps a taxi." He screwed up his face. "Although it's such a busy weekend, it might not be possible."

"And how much would that cost?" Danny wondered, thinking if it was a District cab it would be thousands.

"To Rome?" The concierge shrugged. "Maybe two hundred dollars."

Danny told the concierge to arrange it, figuring he could expense the cost because, after all, if he didn't make the plane, he'd have to get a hotel. The concierge promised to try, although that was *all* he could promise. The *signore* had to understand that the Palio was only twice a year. "The number of people is three times as many, but the taxis – they are the same, you understand?"

Danny said he did, and the concierge promised to do his best. Then Danny went to the front desk and checked out, leaving his bag with the clerk so that, when he returned from town, all he had to do was grab it and go.

He sat in the lobby and waited for Paulina, although the truth was he would have preferred not to see her, to simply take a taxi. At two-twenty, he wondered how long he should wait. Belzer was a busy guy, and Danny certainly didn't want to be late. If she didn't show up in five minutes –

Before he could finish the thought, the cell phone went off – emitting an urgent and quavery tone. He flipped it open and pressed it to his ear, thinking it must be Paulina.

Someone barked his name. "Daniel?!" A man's voice.

"Yeah . . . who is this?"

"Inzaghi! Can you hear me?"

"Big-time."

"What?!"

"I said I can hear you. You don't have to shout."

"Where are you?" the priest demanded, making little or no effort to modulate his voice – whose amplitude betrayed a sense of urgency.

"Siena. On the way to the Palio. I told you."

"Don't go. It's not safe for you."

"What?"

"Come back to Rome. We have to *talk*."

" 'Talk'? About what?"

"Listen. I've been up all night with the files," the priest said, "and –"

"What files?"

"Terio's files, what do you think? The ones on the computer. And it's terrible! You can't imagine what he's up to, this Zebek!"

"What do you mean?" Danny asked. Before Inzaghi could answer, Paulina came rushing into the lobby, wearing a tiny black suit, a big white hat, and huge sunglasses. Danny glanced at his watch. Two-thirty. "Hang on a minute," he said. And got to his feet.

"Sorry I'm late," Paulina told him, holding on to her hat with one hand. "You ready? I changed the appointment to three, but we have to hurry."

Danny acknowledged this with a nod, then spoke into the phone again. "I've got to go. Let me call you back in a couple of hours, okay?"

"No, Danny, it's not 'okay.' I think you should –"

Paulina pointed urgently to her watch as she looked at him.

"Listen, I'm really sorry, but . . . I have to go," Danny said into the phone. "I'll get back to you as soon as I can." And then, over the priest's protests, he ended the call and followed the hurrying Paulina out to the car.

The cell phone rang again, but when he heard the priest's voice, Danny pretended it was a bad connection. "I can't hear you," he said over Inzaghi's protests. "Sorry, Father. You're breaking up."

"Persistent," Paulina said as she got into the Lancia.

As a precaution, once he was in the car's passenger seat Danny turned the telephone off. He was curious about what the priest had to say, but right now what he wanted above all was to see Belzer, get paid, and hustle back to Leonardo da Vinci in time to catch his plane. Anyway, he certainly couldn't have a conversation with Inzaghi about Terio's files in front of Paulina. Better to call the priest when he was on his way to Rome.

"Do you have a hangover?" he asked Paulina as they bounced down toward the city.

"Ooooof – what do you think? I'm dying." She laughed, but it sounded a little subdued.

Soon they arrived at the city wall. A red-and-white-painted barricade – manned by a uniformed policeman – blocked the big archway. Paulina pulled into an area of striped pavement off to the right. She got out of the car but left the motor running.

"No cars at all permitted into the *centro* today," she said. "I'll drop you here. Just head downhill. All roads lead to the Campo and you know where to go once you're there. At the palazzo, just go to the gate – it's beneath the long balcony we sat under last night. They'll have your name on a list." She glanced at her watch. "You don't have to run, but you can't . . . window-shop, okay?"

"But what about you?"

"Ah – no." She shrugged. "I'm off to Torino, where I have some work to do. Translating. A bit of a rush job. And anyway, I've seen the Palio many times."

"Well – thanks for everything."

She took her hat off, sailed it into the backseat, tossed her hair, leaned forward, and, before he could stop her, kissed him full on the lips. "Ciao then, Danny. Maybe I'll see you again. It was fun, wasn't it?"

*

171

When he reached the Campo, Danny waded through the surging crowd in search of Zebek's palazzo. Scanning the walls of the ancient square, he spotted the blue-and-gold flags flying from a long and curving balcony. Making his way toward the flags, he saw that the tables previously ringing the perimeter of the square were gone. Thick pads were suspended from some of the walls of the buildings that enclosed the plaza. By the time he arrived at the open iron gates – with peacocks figured into the wrought metal – it was nearly three o'clock.

Beyond the gates, in a shaded courtyard studded with Palio flags, a muscular security guard stood beside a trickling fountain. He wore what would turn out to be a sort of uniform worn by all the "help" at the party: black slacks and Doc Martens and an expensive black T-shirt with *pavone* emblazoned on the chest. The *o* in *pavone* was the turquoise-and-gold eye of a peacock's feather. The guard asked Danny his name and consulted a printed list. Satisfied, he then whispered into a cell phone and told the American to wait. Soon a curvaceous young woman appeared, wearing a gold miniskirt and a blue halter top that ended just above her navel. "Hi-iii," she cooed in an accent that sounded vaguely German. "I'm Veroushka."

"Danny," he managed.

"I know." Leaning into him, she entwined her arm with his own and said, "I'm supposed to look after you, okay?"

What was he supposed to say? "Great." Together they ascended a stone staircase, heading toward laughter and a piano, with Danny thinking, *I know this woman, but . . . how? You'd think I'd remember.*

How do you forget someone like that? She was gorgeous. At the top of the stairs, he turned to her. "How do I know you?"

She giggled. "I don't know."

And then it hit him: she was one of the girls in the Victoria's Secret catalog. Caleigh got a new one every month, and Veroushka was on every other page.

A moment later, they were in the midst of what must have been the most cosmopolitan party in Europe. A Scandinavian chanteuse sat by herself at a massive black Steinway, singing "When Did You Leave Heaven?" in a sweetly plaintive voice, while NATO generals and white-robed sheiks mingled with a blond duo Veroushka told him were the transgendered heirs to a German industrial fortune. Danny recognized a couple of people from magazines and television. Veroushka identified others. There were bankers and businessmen, writers and politicians. She squeezed his arm and nodded toward a young man who was sitting by himself, reading a comic book. "Rivaldo," she confided.

Plucking a glass of champagne from a passing waiter's tray, Veroushka took Danny by the hand and led him out to the balcony, where they gazed across the throbbing Campo. Below them, child-drummers in medieval costume strutted past while another contingent threw flags in the air. "Where are the horses?" Danny asked.

His escort giggled. "In church," she told him, "getting blessed." Seeing his skepticism, she snuggled against his arm and laughed. "*Really!*"

"They take them to the church?"

"Chapel – every *contrada* has one. Then they bring the horses here and put them into the starting gate."

173

She gestured to the right. "It's over there. They bring them only a few minutes before the race and then they seal off the Campo until it's over." She sipped her champagne. "If you're betting, you should put your money on Pavone."

"Is there a lot of betting?"

She hiccuped, giggled, then nodded solemnly. "Ohhh, *yes.*" Danny smiled and continued to make small talk, but he didn't really feel like it. Everyone at the party seemed to be rich and famous – except himself. And yet here he was, with this lingerie queen on his arm, handicapping the Palio. *What's wrong with this picture?* he wondered. And the answer came back, *You're out of your league, kiddo. You've been out of your league for a long time.*

Not that he was unattractive. Women liked him, and he was undeniably young, clean, and symmetrical. Also, he was a pretty good listener and knew how to dance. So he did just fine. But, until very recently it had not been his experience that beautiful women latched onto him like limpets. Maybe that happened to Brad Pitt and George Clooney but not to Danny Cray. Except . . . lately. Which suggested one of two things: Either he'd suddenly come into his own as the world's most eligible bachelor – or Belzer wanted him really bad.

"So where's our friend?" he asked.

Veroushka gave him a puzzled look.

"Belzer," he hinted.

She looked blank.

"Zebek's lawyer?" he reminded.

She shook her head. "I think our host has many lawyers. But I don't think they come to his parties."

He was about to ask her what she meant when one

of the guards – a bodybuilder by the look of him – touched him on the shoulder. "*Scusi* – Signore Zebek, he asks to see you now."

With a hapless shrug in the direction of his escort (or perk or whatever she was), Danny followed the security guard up a marble staircase, then down a long hallway to a large and gloomy library, where Belzer waited for him in a leather wing chair behind an ornately carved desk. A study for *The Flaying of Marsyas* hung from the wall at his back, illuminated by a single beam of light. Danny guessed that the drawing was an original – one of the last Titian ever made. Belzer gestured to a chair, and Danny settled in.

"Is it just us then?"

Belzer nodded.

Danny looked disappointed. "I've never met a billionaire before. I was hoping to meet Mr. Zebek."

The lawyer's lips curled in an ironic grin. "You are. You have."

It took a moment for this to register. Self-consciously – because he didn't quite get it – Danny glanced over his shoulder. Saw the muscular security guard standing by the door. No one else. Just Belzer, himself, and the guard. And then it hit him. "You're kidding," he said, and laughed aloud.

Belzer's eyebrows lifted, and he pursed his lips. "The investigator, at last!" he remarked.

Danny let the sarcasm slide but couldn't hide his puzzlement. "I don't get it. I mean, what's the point? Why would you do that?"

Belzer – Zebek – shrugged. "I like to stay in the background – especially when I'm in someone's face." Reaching into the top drawer of the desk, he removed a thick envelope and tossed it to Danny.

"Per diem, bonus, and expenses. You'd better count it."

Danny shook his head, thrilled by the weight of the envelope. "That's okay. I'm sure –"

"Count it."

Embarrassed, Danny opened the envelope and removed a wad of hundred-dollar bills. One by one, he went through the stack until he'd counted to 164.

"Is that about right?" Zebek asked.

Danny nodded. "Yeah, it's –"

"Now give it back."

Danny gave him a blank look. "What?"

Zebek held out his hand and waggled his fingers. Reflexively Danny gave him the money. "I hate getting fucked," Zebek confessed.

The words hung there, so unexpected that Danny thought that he'd misheard. Or hoped that he had. But no. Zebek put the cash back in the drawer and closed it.

"What are you doing?" Danny asked.

Zebek ignored the question. Leaned forward and asked one of his own. "You're a lot like Bruco, you know that?"

" 'Bruco'?"

"The Tomato Worm. He's my nemesis at the moment."

Danny blinked. It was beginning to look as if he wasn't going to be paid, and the unhappiness he felt was a lot like vertigo. "What are we talking about?"

"The Palio," Zebek replied. "There are favorites, you know, just like the Kentucky Derby. This time, the smart money is on two horses – the Peacock and the Worm. *Pavone o Bruco.*" His right hand rotated with uncertainty. "*Bruco o Pavone.* I made Bruco an offer, but . . . who knows? The rider's local. Most of the jockeys come from the Maremma, so they're very professional. Easy to deal with. This kid . . . I think he wants to be a hero with the girls." He shook his head. "Not smart."

Danny frowned. The billionaire was beginning to piss him off. "Is this supposed to be a parable?"

Zebek chuckled. "Yes. But it doesn't matter. It's more fun this way. The other riders will take care of Bruco. That's what they're paid for."

Danny nodded, his mind racing. *He thinks he's been screwed – and he has. But he doesn't have any way of knowing it. Not for a fact. So this – this business – it's just a test. A bluff. Hang in there.*

"So, I guess you're not coming to work for me," Zebek continued, moving from one subject to the next (or maybe not).

For Danny, it was as if a lightbulb had gone off. *So that's what this is all about,* he thought. *He's used to getting whatever he wants, so anyone who says no is suddenly the enemy.* "Listen," Danny began. "The offer was tremendous, but –"

Zebek shut him up with a snort of derision. The billionaire removed his shades, his eyes held Danny's, and the silence deepened.

A question occurred to Danny. "How did you know I decided not to take the job?"

Zebek punched a button on a console at the edge of his desk. Immediately Inzaghi's voice filled the room.

Come back to Rome. We have to talk.

Danny's heart lurched as he heard his own voice reply, *"Talk"? About what?*

Listen, the priest said. *I've been up all night with the files, and –*

What files?

Terio's files, what do you think? The ones on the computer. And it's terrible! You can't imagine what he's up to, this Zebek!

As the conversation went on, Danny sank lower and lower into his chair, thinking, *Not good, not good. . . .* Finally, the recording came to an end. Zebek snapped off the machine.

"How did you do that?" Danny asked. "I thought cell phones were encrypted over here. The GSM standard, or whatever they call it."

Zebek smirked. "You're right. They are. But if you clone the smart card, you've got a second phone that acts like an extension." He paused to let the idea sink in. "Now let me ask *you* a question," he went on. "What did you *do* exactly? Did you copy the files for him? Did you put them back on the computer?"

Danny looked away.

Zebek looked mournful. "And now this crazy priest – he calls you 'Daniel'?"

The American shrugged.

Zebek shook his head in disbelief, milking the moment. "Didn't you even bother to use the ID that I gave you?"

Danny took a deep breath and looked him in the eye. "Yeah," he said, "I used it." He paused, and changed the subject. "Do you bug everyone who works for you?"

Zebek acted as if it was a cheap shot. He grimaced and said, "Just the new boys." Then he paused, and his eyes narrowed. "You know, *Daniel*, before you fuck with someone, you really ought to think about who you're pissing off." He cocked his head and added, "Do you even know what I *do*?"

178

The American shook his head, trying to get past the vitriol in the billionaire's voice. He was feeling a little panicky and had to remind himself that what was happening was just a dressing-down. It wasn't the first time he'd been reamed out. All he needed to do was keep cool – and make sure he got paid.

"I asked if you know what I do," Zebek repeated.

"Venture capital," Danny replied.

Zebek pursed his lips. "Well, I'm a little more focused than that. Mostly, we're invested in start-ups working on protein folding and MEMS – cutting-edge stuff. You'd be amazed at the applications. Like this." His finger tapped a black metal box that was connected by a cable to the console on his desk.

Despite himself, Danny was curious. "What's it for?"

"It's a prototype ... for building personality engines."

Danny frowned. After a bit, he said, "What?"

"Well, let's see ... you know what a doppelganger is, don't you?"

"Yeah. It's someone's double. You see your own, you're supposed to die."

Zebek smiled. "That's what they say, but ... it's just a superstition. The doppelgangers I'm talking about – the doppelgangers we *make* – are virtual. At least, they are for now." The conversational tone of his voice was irritating, a patronizing lecture from a patient adult to a slow child. It made Danny's temper fizz, especially because he still wasn't sure what the billionaire was talking about.

"It's like this," Zebek went on, his voice even more confiding. "If you give us a minute of audio and video

– home movies will do – we can use them to make a template."

"To do what?" Danny asked.

"The template looks a lot like a credit card," Zebek said, ignoring the question. "But it's encoded with an algorithm that's derived from a person's movements and expressions. The result is what we call 'a personality engine.' If I plug one of the cards into a box like this, we can use it to animate any image or voice that I'm able to broadcast or project. All I need is a picture. Or a tape." Zebek paused, obviously pleased with himself. "We've got patents pending in the States. We're doing Beta tests now. It's a year or so off, but you can imagine the impact it's going to have on the film industry. We'll be able to make new pictures with dead actors, using their old roles to create the templates. And that's just showbiz. Once we get into politics, it becomes even more interesting."

"It's still just movies," Danny told him.

"Is it? I wonder. What if we apply the principle to biology?" Zebek paused to let the idea sink in and then continued. "Cloning, for instance. We can replicate the biological identity of an individual – but not the personality. For now, that's left to chance. So even if we make a genetic duplicate, it's still only a copy – and it *behaves* differently. As soon as it moves, we know it's not the real thing. But if we can bring together a person's genetic inheritance with the personality engines that we're creating in the labs, we can build doppelgangers that are perfect in every way."

Danny didn't believe a word of it. And even more to the point, he didn't really care. What he wanted was: to get paid. "Good luck," he said.

Zebek drew back at the sarcasm. "You're skeptical."

Danny shrugged.

"I'll show you what I mean," the billionaire promised. Removing a plastic card from the top drawer of his desk, he slotted it into the black box and flipped a toggle switch on its side. A green LED light clicked on. "I made this from a tape," he said. "It's just the voice, but . . . you'll see what I mean." Connecting his cell phone to the console, Zebek gave Danny a set of earphones and told him to put them on. Then he motioned the security guard to stand behind his guest. *"Gaetano, se dice niente, l'uccide."* Turning back to Danny, he explained that "if you open your mouth, my friend here is going to break your neck." Seeing the American's surprise, he added, "I'm not kidding. He's done it before, and he doesn't mind at all."

With a grin, Zebek punched a number into the cell phone and sat back.

Donning the headphones, Danny heard a telephone ringing over and over again. Finally, a voice answered.

"Prego?"

Hearing Inzaghi's voice, Danny began to get up, then sank back in his seat when he felt the weight of a hand on the back of his neck. It was a big hand, but there was almost no weight to it.

Zebek began to speak, talking into the microphone. "It's Danny, Father —"

Danny gasped. The voice was his own – accent, pitch, and timbre, it was him to a tee. And it scared him. He could feel the hair on the back of his neck.

Through the earphones he heard Inzaghi heave a sigh of relief. "I was worried about you! Where are you?"

181

"Siena," Zebek replied.

"Get out of there! I mean it, Danny – you have no idea what this is all about. And for God's sake don't meet with these people. It's dangerous."

"Don't worry about it," Zebek insisted. "I'm coming to Rome tonight – we can talk then. These cell phones – I don't trust them."

As he listened to the conversation, it was all Danny could do to stay in his chair. Zebek's voice was so indisputably his own that it seemed almost as if his soul had been stolen.

"I'm sure you're right about the phone," the priest was saying. "I didn't think. When will you get here?"

"Nine or ten," Zebek continued in Danny's voice. "Can we meet at your place? I haven't got a reservation yet."

"Of course – but it's not so easy getting here," Inzaghi replied. "Do you have a pen?"

Danny couldn't take it any longer. He had to warn Inzaghi. But the bodyguard must have sensed his urgency, because his hand tightened on Danny's shoulder. Leaning over, he lifted the spongy pad of one of the earphones and whispered, "No."

Danny fell back in the chair as Zebek repeated Inzaghi's directions to his rooms in the Vatican-owned Casa Clera. Then they were done. Good-byes were exchanged and the connection broken. Zebek turned his muddy eyes to Danny and smiled.

"Now what?" Danny asked, feeling as far from home as he had ever felt.

The billionaire shook his head in a way that suggested regret as much as uncertainty. Then he stabbed the floor with his silver-topped cane and pushed himself to his feet. "What am I going to do with you, Danny? You're a real disposal problem, you know that?"

The American frowned. Within a day, he'd gone from golden boy to hazardous waste. *How soon they forget. . . .*

Zebek made a show of thinking about the problem, pacing back and forth in front of the bookshelves. "On the one hand, I suppose we could break your neck, say you took a fall –"

Danny couldn't believe it. "Isn't that kind of strict – I mean, just for making a backup disk?"

Zebek chuckled.

"I'm not kidding," Danny said. "You said it yourself: I don't know what's going on. And you talk about *killing* me? I just want to get paid. What's going on?"

Zebek dismissed the question with a wave of his hand. "There really isn't time to go into it. So I'll put it this way: You fucked up – The End."

Danny took a deep breath and leaned forward. "There are a lot of people out there," he muttered, appalled to hear the reediness in his voice. It occurred to him that maybe he ought to launch himself at Zebek, knock something over, create a ruckus, start yelling.

"On the other hand," Zebek said, raising a finger as if to make a point, "that wouldn't be much fun." Suddenly a grin snapped into place, and the billionaire stopped pacing. "You know what?"

Danny shook his head, muscles tensing. If Zebek looked up – if he raised his eyes to the security guard – Danny would come across the desk like a load of birdshot.

"You're on your own," Zebek decided. "It will be

183

more fun this way. Like the race with Bruco, a real contest."

The American blinked. "What?"

"I'll give you five minutes. After that, you're fair game."

Danny glanced at the guard behind him, then back to Zebek. "You're insane. I mean, really: you're *out there*. I mean, clinically. Am I right?"

Zebek nodded. "Probably." Checked his watch. "Four and a half minutes." He looked up and cocked his head. "Still here?" A smirk of incredulity from the billionaire.

Danny came out of the chair with a low curse and headed for the door, half expecting to be stopped and ready to swing on anyone who reached for him.

"I'll watch from the balcony!" Zebek called out.

Bursting into the corridor, Danny brushed past a coterie of NATO generals, ran to the staircase, and descended the steps two at a time. The party was in full swing, the air alight with laughter and music, the chatter and clatter of a hundred people having a good time. But not him. He hit the courtyard at a run, only to stand by the door while one of the security guards spoke quietly into a cell phone. Finally, the guard yanked open the door and nodded deferentially. "*Ciao.*"

Then he was on a dirt track, about ten yards from a makeshift fence of red-and-white-striped barricades. Behind the barricades were fifty thousand Italians – and tourists – jammed shoulder-to-shoulder in an area about the size of a city block. The noise was deafening, the air bright and stifling. A policeman stormed up to him, then grabbed him by the arm and, gesturing dramatically, led him away from the track and pushed him toward the packed mob. Squeezing between the barricades, Danny merged with the crowd, hoping it would convey invisibility.

His instinct was to run and to keep on running, to put as much distance as possible between himself and Zebek. But the density of the mob was such that even walking was a challenge. The best he could do was sidle between one person and another, making his way a step at a time. It was like moving apologetically through quicksand. *"Scusi, scusi –"*

Suddenly the crowd surged and he found himself swept up in a kind of human current, with no more control over his own direction than a leaf on a river. He was a part of the mob, and it was all he could do to remain on his feet.

He'd never been in a throng like this – not even in Times Square on New Year's Eve. The square was more densely packed than a rock concert, more crowded than the Metro at rush hour. The whole piazza was a holding pen, enervated by the heat, suffused with noise, spiced with the pungent scents of sweat, garlic, and horseshit. Mixed with the adrenaline roaring through his heart, the scene left him breathless. Bodies pressed against him from every side. An elbow jabbed him in the ribs; a belt buckle dug at his spine. Realignments were constant, as tides of people were carried away by unseen forces. *Contrada* gangs joined hands above the crowd in a hopeless effort to stay together while plunging this way and that, laughing and giggling. Flags floated in the air. Songs broke out. People shouted to one another in a dozen languages and dialects. Somewhere someone was thumping a drum, while off to the right a ceremony of some kind was taking place. A fanfare of trumpets went up, and the crowd roared its approval. Rising to his tiptoes, Danny saw a dozen horses being led to the starting gate.

So far, so good, he thought. He was a needle in a haystack, and it would take a miracle for Zebek's goons to find him. Giving himself up to the crowd, he let himself be carried along until he arrived at the heart of the Campo. This was the eye of the storm, a relatively calm place where people sat cross-legged on the paving stones, worn out by the heat, the noise, and the long wait for the race to begin.

It was, of course, the very worst place to watch the race. Even at six-one, Danny had to lean forward on the balls of his feet just to scan the crowd. Anyone shorter would see nothing but the backs of other people's heads – except for the children and some girls who perched on the shoulders of their fathers and boy-friends.

Not that Danny was interested in the race. Lifting his eyes to the buildings around the square, he searched the balconies until he found Zebek. The billionaire was standing beside a peacock, looking directly at Danny through a pair of opera glasses, speaking calmly into a cell phone.

Their eyes met (Zebek had the shades off), and a shock of recognition went through Danny. The Campo was a trap, a killing floor where every exit was blocked and nothing would be simpler than to die. Tracked by Zebek from the moment he'd left the palazzo, Danny was a murder waiting to happen. It was as simple as that. Amid the drumming and singing, the cheering and laughter, few would notice an American sinking to the ground with a knife in his back.

Seeing Zebek, Danny suddenly understood what the

billionaire was doing with the cell phone. He was hunting him down by remote control, sending telemetry to the thugs who'd been sent to kill him.

By now, the head start was long gone (if it had ever been real) and Danny was fair game. Glancing wildly around, he searched in vain for the man who was hunting him, then lowered his head and plunged deeper into the crowd. As if on cue, a cannon went off like a clap of thunder. A dozen horses broke from the gate in a surge of color, the mob roared, and the Campo became a trampoline, with thousands jumping up and down in place. Nearby, a blonde punched the air with her fist, shouting, "Oca Oca Oca!" from her perch on her boyfriend's shoulders, digging her heels into his ribs.

Danny moved to his left, staying as low as he could, heading for the gate farthest from the Palazzo di Pavone. With a little luck, he might still lose himself in the crowd. The idea that anyone could follow him in this casserole of humanity was ridiculous – or so it seemed until he saw something that made him freeze in his tracks.

A few feet away, a peacock feather winked at him from the background of a black T-shirt. Looking up, his eyes locked with Gaetano's. Another step, and he'd have walked into his arms. For a long moment, the two of them remained where they were, a still-life amid the frenzied crowd. Zebek's thug had a cell phone in his left hand and a shank in his right.

It was Danny's soccer instincts that saved him. Without thinking, he dropped his right shoulder, threw a head fake, and didn't so much juke as *dive* to the left. Gaetano moved in the same instant but went the wrong way, lunging upward with such force that if

187

he'd connected, Danny's colon would have been lying in a loop on the ground.

Finding a seam, Danny plunged through the crowd in a crouch, his head below his shoulders, invisible to the balconies around the square. The mob was crazy now, roaring louder than ever as the horses drove toward the finish line, galloping under a dozen whips. And then it was over, as quickly as it had begun. The crowd held its breath – and sagged, its roar dwindling to a disappointed murmur that soon gave way to a woman's screams and a chorus of angry shouts.

He cut someone, Danny thought. *When he lunged at me, he must have cut someone.*

"*E Pavone,*" a man complained. "*Pavone vince.*"

The woman's screams became louder and more hysterical.

Danny shuffled toward the gate. He hoped that Zebek had lost him, but there was no way to know if he had. And it was impossible to stay in a crouch. The Palio-goers were in the grip of their own centrifugal forces, flooding the half-dozen exits leading out of the square. Like everyone else, Danny moved in slow-mo, inching forward with tiny steps.

An ancient arch loomed about twenty yards ahead of him, and he was sure that once he reached it he'd be home free. If nothing else, he could break into a run. But then he sensed, as much as saw, a commotion to his left and, turning, glimpsed Gaetano, fighting his way through the crowd in a desperate effort to get at his prey.

A chorus of complaints rose up in the killer's wake, then turned to shock as Gaetano grabbed a woman by the face and shoved her out of the way. A man who might have been her husband reacted in anger, then crumpled to his knees when a head butt shattered the bridge of his nose. Children screamed, someone threw a punch, and the crowd swayed in panic. Beside Danny, a dark-haired woman with carefully drawn eyebrows began to whimper with fear.

He knew how she felt. Only ten feet from the exit, the crowd was now so tightly packed that a stampede seemed likely. If it happened, the crowd would become an avalanche of meat and they'd all be trampled. Danny was getting ready for it, unconsciously holding his breath, when the ground seemed to lurch. Then the mob surged and he popped through the archway like a champagne cork flying across the room.

It was a Palio version of the Big Bang, with the crowd exploding from the Campo in every direction, the distance between people growing like the distance between stars. Danny's shuffle turned into a trot, the trot to a run. Taking the path of least resistance, he set off on a broken-field sprint down an ancient street hung with flags. Left, right, left, up an alley, and down an arcade, he ran until he could run no more. Finally, drained of air and adrenaline, he leaned against a shop window and gasped for breath. He had no idea where he was, other than downhill from the Campo.

A dark-haired woman in a lavender skirt turned the corner, walking hand in hand with a little girl in overalls. Seeing Danny breathing hard and thinking him drunk, she veered to the other side of the street, while the little girl pushed herself into her mother's skirt, pulling its lavender fabric around her.

In a coffee bar across the street, a dozen men stood watching a replay of the race on TV. His breath restored, Danny began to walk, following the street downhill, trying to figure out where he was, where he should go, and what he should do. *The first thing,* he thought, *is . . . call Inzaghi.* He had the priest's phone number on a scrap of paper in his wallet and he still had the cell phone Zebek had given him.

Though he knew the billionaire could monitor his calls, it didn't make any difference where Inzaghi was concerned. Zebek was already trying to kill them both, so warning the priest was a kind of freebie. They could only kill each of them once, after all.

The phone rang four times; then the answering machine picked up. Danny waited for the tone and left a message that was borderline coherent: *Forget our meeting. You gotta get out. He knows about the files. Check your machine. I'll call back every couple of hours.* It was something like that, but with lots of exclamation points.

Next up: he had to get his bag from the hotel. It had his tickets and everything else except his passport. (He had that on him.) Then he'd catch a cab to another town, where Zebek wouldn't be looking for him. Then the train to Rome, a hotel, and a flight out in the morning. Once he got home, he'd sort things out. Take a look at the floppy with Terio's files on it. Get the FBI involved. *Whatever it takes.*

But first, the bag. He couldn't go back to the hotel. Zebek would almost certainly have the place watched. But he could call the hotel and ask the concierge to send a taxi to him with his bag.

Stopping at a café on a side street in the Dragon *contrada,* Danny ordered a double espresso and searched through his wallet for the hotel's card. Finding it, he asked the *barista* if could use the house phone. Then he dialed the Scacciapensieri and asked for the concierge.

"I was hoping you could send a taxi for me," Danny said.

"If you like, signore –"

"And I'll need my duffle bag," Danny reminded him. "They're holding it at the front desk."

The concierge chuckled. "I think we have a confusion! Signore Zebek's staff – they collect your bag a few minutes ago. But this is okay, because they're still here. They wait for you outside. So I think, maybe you don't need a taxi. Do you want to talk to one of them?"

Eleven

He hitched a ride with a trio of Brits who were "on holiday" from a candy factory in Liverpool and, like him, didn't have a place to stay in Siena. But they did have a car – a rented VW Golf – and, unlike Danny, they were much too drunk to drive.

He met them on the way out of town, where they were drinking cans of lager by the roadside while fumbling with a jack in a slapstick effort to change a flat tire. "Oy!" one of them shouted, raising the jack in the air. "Mate! Can ya tell us what *the fuck* we're supposed to do with this?"

It was a newfangled scissors jack that Danny did, in fact, know how to use. Soon the tire was changed, and so grateful were his new friends that they thrust a can of Holstein's into his hands and offered to take him wherever he might be going – so long as he drove.

They decided upon San Gimignano, about twenty miles away. One of Italy's most famous hill towns, its skyline was pierced by an array of improbable and faintly sinister watchtowers that, seen against the sun, suggested a child's drawing of Lower Manhattan.

Danny left "the lads" at a small pensione and went looking for a taxi that would take him to Rome. No dice. One after another, San Gimignano's cabdrivers gave him a sorrowful look or laughed in his face. It wasn't so much the drive to Rome, they explained. It was the return trip. They wouldn't get back until morning. A wad of cash might have worked, but he didn't have one.

He had better luck at the bus terminal, where he learned that he could catch an express to Florence in half an hour. There he'd have a fifteen-minute wait, after which there would be another express to Rome. Or maybe in Firenze he could get a cab. He bought a ticket to Florence, crossed the street to a café, and ordered a bottle of Peroni. Then he pulled out the cell phone and started to call Inzaghi.

This time, he didn't wait for the answering machine to come on. After the third ring, he hung up. There just wasn't any point in leaving the same message that he'd left before. And, besides, the cell phone was beginning to worry him.

Could it be used to track him?

He remembered a news story that he'd read about a woman who had been carjacked. Imprisoned in the trunk of the car with her cell phone, she'd dialed 911 and kept the line open to the police. The cops tracked the call from one cell tower to another. Before long, they realized the woman must be heading south on Route 29 (or whichever road it was). Eventually, they set up a roadblock and rescued her.

The newspapers said the police had "triangulated" the call, but that wasn't accurate. The woman's car had been traveling through a rural area, so its signal was never within reach of more than a single tower. As a result, all the police could tell was which "cell" she was in and how far she was from the tower at its center.

If the carjackers had been in the city, where cell towers were numerous, the cops might have triangulated the call by measuring the time it took for the signal to arrive at three different locations. Then they could have located the woman to within a few feet.

Could Zebek do that? Danny stared at the phone in his hand. Probably not, he decided. Even if the billionaire was wired into the cops or the local phone company, Danny had no intention of keeping the line open or of staying in one place. So he ought to be okay, unless . . .

Unless the phone was more advanced than its American counterparts – which seemed likely. Zebek made a point of being on the cutting edge of just about everything. Which meant that the phone might well be equipped with "enhanced 911," an Orwellian "safety feature" federally mandated for all American cell phones by 2005. Embedded with geo-positioning devices, the new phones would broadcast signals establishing their whereabouts to within fifty meters.

Screw it, Danny thought. Finishing his drink, he dropped the cell phone in a trash can on the way out and returned to the bus station. An hour later he was in Florence, and twenty minutes after that he was on a second bus to Rome. This time, he had a seat at the front, where he was given a close, and in fact unavoidable, view of the day's video selection.

It was a Disney movie – *The Incredible Journey* – and it began to play as soon as the bus pulled out of its bay.

Grimly Danny watched as two lost dogs and their fussy little pal, the cat, made their way through a dangerous world to rejoin their human family. For upwards of two hours the lovable fur balls skirted disaster, weaving in and out of one tough spot after another, all the while speaking Italian.

Danny knew the movie had been made with kinder-gartners in mind, but he found himself completely caught up in the tale. Maybe it had something to do with the fact that, like him, the wandering pets were in danger and desperate to find their way home. Or maybe it was deeper than it seemed – a pet-centric retelling of *The Odyssey*. He hoped so, because otherwise he'd have to admit that he had the emotional maturity of the average five-year-old.

That would have been Ian's theory.

Ian was merciless where Danny's predilection for popular culture was concerned. "It's one thing to be 'open'," he'd once remarked, "but it's another to be a Dumpster with the lid up." This because Danny played pickup basketball, listened to the Cowboy Junkies, and thought Krazy Kat was more interesting than Andy Warhol.

It was an aspect of Danny that Caleigh found charming. He could be happy at the Kennedy Center listening to Verdi, but he'd be just as content at a *Survivor* party.

Caleigh. Thinking of Caleigh reminded him of Paulina, and Paulina reminded him of the trouble he was in – here, there, and everywhere. A soft groan fell from his lips, prompting the woman in the seat next to him to nod and smile vigorously at the television. *"Si,"* she whispered, *"e cosi triste."* Her eyes were wet, he saw, and, what was worse, so were his own.

As the bus rolled through the twilight, he stared at his reflection in the window and began making deals between himself and God. These were complicated bargains that bound marriage and fidelity to his continued survival. Not that he believed in God. Not really. Then again – not that he didn't. Some immutable Catholic-boy core must have survived his childhood, because he found himself thinking that if he could save Inzaghi that ought to count for something. After all, the man was a priest.

Zebek's face floated into his mind, the rich man's dark eyes boring into him, his cane punching the air: *You know,* Daniel, *before you fuck with someone, you really ought to think about who you're pissing off.* Danny thought of Chris Terio in his little tomb, of Jason Patel crucified in the desert, of Terio's house reduced to ashes. Where Zebek was concerned, it was pretty much his way or the die-way.

He thought back to what the billionaire had said on the phone, when he'd been speaking in Danny's voice. He'd told the priest that he'd get to Rome by nine or ten – an hour or two before Danny himself could arrive. Zebek knew that Danny was listening to the conversation, so he must also have known that Danny would try to warn the priest. Either Danny would call Inzaghi or, if that didn't work, he'd go to the priest's apartment.

It occurred to him that this might be what Zebek was counting on – a backup plan, in case Danny escaped the thugs in the Campo. A way of killing two birds with one stone. If so, Danny wasn't going to let it happen. When he got to Inzaghi's, he'd create a ruckus – set off fire alarms, get the cops involved, whatever it took. He was determined to warn the priest. One way or another, he had to try.

Like Shadow.

On the inescapable little blue screen before him, Shadow the dog was giving it his all. He and his pals were trapped in a railyard, having narrowly escaped the wheels of a passing freight train, only to have fallen through some rotten planks, landing in a deep pit. The cat and the younger dog had managed to clamber up its slippery sides, but Shadow was too old – and too weakened by his adventures. "Jump, Shadow! Jump!" pleaded Sassy the cat.

"I can't believe I'm watching this," Danny muttered to himself. "A guy's trying to kill me, and I'm practically in tears because some actor-mutt falls into a hole."

Speaking in a world-weary baritone, Shadow ordered the other critters to *"continuare senza de mi."* Danny knew what the old dog was saying and knew, also, that the Disney organization was not about to let this lovable *cane* expire in some industrial pit. Nevertheless, when the bus finally pulled into the terminal in Rome and Shadow came bounding out of nowhere into the arms of his young owner Danny's heart slammed against his chest.

"Ecco!" the conductor announced. The mechanized door wheezed open and disgorged its passengers into the hot Roman night. The concrete apron where the buses pulled in was crowded with people waiting to greet friends and family while travelers edged their way onto the buses. Arriving passengers stood in bunches around men in caps, who dragged their luggage from the compartments under the buses. Loudspeakers boomed unintelligibly.

Danny followed the crowd into the bus terminal and out into the street. Unruly clusters of people waited for taxis at what seemed like random points beside the road. Nothing resembling a line – or a system in lieu of a line – seemed to exist. After ten minutes of losing ground, Danny lunged past a well-dressed woman in red, who gestured mightily and complained noisily as he slid into the backseat of a white taxi. When the driver spoke to him in Italian, Danny gave him the business card with Inzaghi's address on it.

The driver glanced at it, then rolled down his window and cursed at the woman in red, who'd had the effrontery to slap the car's fender. Then he chuckled. *"Andiamo,"* he said, and the cab jerked away from the curb.

There were no thoroughfares in Central Rome, as far as Danny could tell. The trip to Via della Scrofa took twenty minutes and involved at least as many turns – and they still weren't there. Raindrops spattered the window. The pavement gleamed. Neon pooled on the street, just like it did in a Michael Mann movie – or in a Hiroshige print.

Even this late and in the rain, Rome was wide open, the streets crowded. The cafés, bars, and gelato stands were packed, the corners clotted with people looking for an opportunity to cross the street in the rain. The driver tapped his horn once or twice to clear jaywalkers out of the way, but his touch was so light that Danny realized that he'd hardly heard a horn in Rome. It must be illegal, he decided. Otherwise the Italians would be leaning on it all the time.

They were not, from what he could tell, a diffident people.

On one corner, Danny watched a young couple jump out of the way. They laughed – the man's arm around the woman's shoulder. She had a cone of gelato and Danny watched her take a tiny bite, then round her mouth into an O of delight. There was something about her that reminded him of Caleigh and something about the moment that stung him. *What was he doing in Rome?* Everything he loved was in Washington. What was he thinking, coming here?

The driver drummed his fingers on the dash. *"Merda,"* he muttered, then turned to Danny and fired off a question.

"Sorry," Cray said, a helpless look on his face.

"No capiche?" The driver sat back in his seat and sighed. A Vespa whined past, only inches away, as the driver reached for a small book and began turning its pages. Finally, he shut off the meter, got out, and jerked open the door to the backseat.

"Camminata," he said. "You walk now."

"I *what?*"

"Is no far. *Accidenti.*"

Danny saw what he meant. Traffic was at a standstill. Climbing out of the backseat, he paid the fare on the meter and added a couple of thousand lire. "Which way?" he asked, looking this way and that.

The driver sighed and held out his hand, palm down. Keeping his fingers and thumbs aligned, he gestured left and right. *"A destra, sinistra, a destra.* Is shoo-shoo-shoo, okay?"

Danny nodded, not sure if it was or it wasn't okay. The driver gave him a you-can-do-it smile and a little pat on the shoulder. "Ciao!" he said, and slid behind the wheel.

Danny did as he'd been told. Not the shoo-shoo-shoo part (whatever that was), but the right-left-right. The turns took him deeper and deeper into a working-class neighborhood that seemed to be the site of an intractable traffic jam. People stood on tiptoe in the street beside their cars, doors open, craning to see what was up ahead.

Danny kept walking until he saw a placard affixed

199

to the second floor of a corner building: VIA DELLA SCROFA. It was a big street, lined with shops, but it wasn't a straight street, as it would have been in Washington or New York. After a block or so, it veered off sharply to the left, following some invisible demographic of its own.

"*Che cosa e questo?*" a silver-haired man asked Danny. All he could do was shrug. He passed an art gallery, a shoe repair shop, the window of an antiquarian bookstore. Then he turned a corner and the reason for the backup became apparent. Red and blue lights fluttered against the walls of the old buildings, casting puddles of light on the wet pavement. In the center of the street, crowds pressed up against a fragile wall of candy-striped barricades. All around, people craned to see what lay behind them.

"*Che cosa e?*"

"*Che e esso?*"

"Alastair?" a woman asked in a plummy accent. "Was there a crash?"

"Dunno, mollycoddles. Can't quite see."

Danny's stomach tightened as he glanced back at the wall above the antiquarian bookstore. The number, he saw, was close to Inzaghi's own.

Alastair turned to the man beside him and put the question to him in fluent Italian.

Danny shrugged.

"Well?" the woman demanded.

"*He* doesn't know, either," her husband replied.

Then the crowd parted as yet another police car klaxoned its way toward the barricades. People were beginning to lose patience. A wall of horns rose up around them.

"I'll just have a word with the *poliziotto*, shall I? See

200

if we can wiggle by or if they're going to make us detour. You'd better go back to the car."

"This could take forever," the woman complained.

"Not to worry," Alastair assured her, and shouldered his way into the crowd.

Danny didn't know what to do. Filled with dread, he found that he couldn't move. Finally, Alastair reemerged, and Danny put out a hand to stop him. "Was there an accident?"

The Englishman regarded the American with mild surprise, then shook his silver head. "Jumper," he said. "One of the padres. Launched himself from Casa Clera." Seeing Danny's sudden unhappiness and mistaking it for irritation, Alastair leaned in and muttered, "No thought for others, of course."

Danny wanted to bolt, but the barricades drew him forward, bringing him closer and closer to the scene. There were two police cars that he could see, an ambulance, and a couple of cops trying to keep the voyeurs at bay. Behind the barricades, a photographer went about his business, his flash pulsing on and off like heat lightning.

Pushing his way to the front, Danny was finally able to see. Dressed in a blue shirt and dark pants, Inzaghi lay on the pavement, dead still. He was on his side with his arm flung out, his right hand bent all the way back at the wrist. One leg was twisted beneath the other, as if the knee had been anchored in a vise and the leg rotated 180 degrees. The photographer's flash went off again and again in a weird imitation of a fashion shoot. In the cold light of the camera's flare, Danny saw that the priest's head was no longer symmetrical. The left side was grotesquely flattened and oozing.

Danny himself was nearly as still as the priest,

unable to tear his eyes from the halo of blood around Inzaghi's head. *Everyone's gonna think it's a suicide,* Danny thought. Inzaghi's friends and family, the people who loved him – their grief would be deepened by a sense of guilt, a feeling that they hadn't been there when he'd needed them.

A gurney bumped over the cobblestones, pushed by a paramedic. Part of the barricade was pulled back to admit him, and a second man arrived with a body bag. After a brief conversation with a plainclothes detective, the paramedics donned surgical gloves and gently lifted the priest's body into the bag. Then they zipped it shut.

The crowd began to melt away. A sigh went up and, one by one, people began to wander off. Behind the barricades, Danny saw a figure that seemed familiar. A big guy, scanning the crowd, looking for someone. *Gaetano?* Danny couldn't be sure, but it was a real possibility. Zebek would have guessed that he'd come here. The wonder was that they hadn't been patient and simply waited for him in the apartment. Or maybe they had – and Inzaghi had forced their hand. Maybe –

Maybe I should think about this somewhere else, Danny thought, and, turning, began to walk away. It took all of his nerve not to look back. Once or twice, he idled in front of a store window, seeming to window-shop, while in reality studying the reflection of the street behind him. The rain was falling lighter now, the drizzle turned to mist. And then it was gone entirely and the heat seemed to suck the moisture right out of the air.

He couldn't tell if he was being followed. There were too many people on the street, and the truth was, he didn't know who to look for – Gaetano, certainly, but the Big Guy wasn't Zebek's only retainer.

Turning a corner, he quickened his pace until he heard a roar, then passed beneath an arch into a large square. An artist, he knew in an instant where he was. Bernini's Fountain of the Four Rivers was a torrent in the heart of the plaza – which meant that he was in the Piazza Navona.

Late as it was, the place was filled with people. And it was a real marketplace. He strode past a clutch of caricaturists who worked at the perimeter of the square, taking advantage of the light from the street lamps. There were tables of souvenirs and people selling roses and scarves and God knew what else, their wares covered by protective sheets of plastic. He passed a knot of teenage boys teasing a knot of teenage girls, then found himself in the midst of some battery-driven cats. These were being flogged by an African man who seemed to take enormous joy in the cats' activities. With green and glowing eyes, the robots teetered from paw to paw, spitting out tiny meows.

Walking over to the fountain, Danny scooped some water into his palm and dribbled it over the back of his neck. *What now?* His eyes rested on the titanic statuary, floodlit in the water and surrounded by a nimbus of swirling gnats. *Now what?*

He felt stranded, as much in time as place. Until he'd seen Inzaghi's body – the crushed head and gouts of blood – his own predicament had been more theoretical than real. He'd read reports of Terio's death, seen coverage of Patel's murder, and listened to Zebek say that he was going to kill Inzaghi. But now, everything was different. There was blood on the floor. Had he wanted to, he could have put his finger – hell, he could have put his whole hand – in the priest's wounds.

Seeing an empty table at a café across the square, he wandered over to it and sat down. All around him, the air was alive with chatter, glasses clinking and Vespas roaring on a nearby street. He ordered a beer from a passing waiter and tried to remember the last time he'd eaten. That morning, he thought, or the night before. Not that it mattered.

A few feet away, an Oriental woman was going from table to table in an effort to unload a basket of small bronze cherubs. To hoots and howls she demonstrated the cherub's secret: when she pressed the back of its head, a beam of red light shot out from the little guy's penis. At any other time, Danny might have been amused by the sight or by the irony of its taking place in the shadow of Bernini's masterpiece. But the color of the light was so close to what he'd seen on the pavement of the Via della Scrofa that the whole pantomime struck him as sinister and obscene.

It occurred to him that maybe he should go to the American embassy and ask for help. But what could the embassy do? They'd just send him to the police – and what could he say to *them*? That Zebek had sent his goons to kill a priest? Danny could imagine the reaction. The detective would point out the obvious – that Zebek was an important man. He'd cross his arms, cock his head, and fix Danny with a skeptical stare: *What evidence do you have?*

Well . . . none, actually . . . just . . . I guess it's my word against his.

And Signore Zebek's motive?

He was after some computer files.

Aha! And what was in these files?

204

I don't know.

I see. . . .

Maybe if he'd still had the diskette of Terio's files, going to the police would have been a real option. He didn't know what was on the files – he'd probably *never* know now – but whatever it was, it was evidence of something important. Important enough to get Inzaghi killed. But, of course, the diskette was in his duffle bag, and his duffle bag, left at the hotel desk in Siena, had been picked up by Zebek's men. So he had nothing. Nothing but his story. And that seemed a little thin.

And what if the police asked about Danny's own relation to the priest? They'd probably find out that he'd pretended to be a cop. That would get their attention, all right, but not in a way that Danny would like. And if Danny should then invoke the mur-ders of Terio and Patel, what then? Either the cops would throw up their hands (jurisdiction meant something, after all) or they'd lock him up – though whether in jail or an asylum was anyone's guess.

So the cops were out.

Which left Plan B. Flaps up. Danny goes home. This was what he longed to do: go home to Caleigh and his work at the studio. Unfortunately, going home was no more viable an option than going to the police. Because Zebek would *expect* that. He'd *look* for Danny at home, was probably *waiting* for him at home. Still . . . he would be on his own turf. And whatever happened would happen in English. So at least he'd understand what was going on.

Then again, the home-field advantage hadn't been a lot of help to Chris Terio or Jason Patel. And then there was Caleigh. If he went home now, he'd put her directly in the line of fire, if she wasn't there already. The possibility made him sit up in his chair. How much did Zebek know about him – really *know*? Danny thought about it for while and concluded: *A lot.* He knew about the first-in-show at the Torpedo Factory, and he'd seen the brushed aluminum sculpture at Les Yeux de Monde. So he probably knew about Caleigh, too. And maybe a lot more.

He had to get to a phone.

Sliding a ten-thousand-lire note under the empty bottle of Peroni, Danny got to his feet and went out in search of one. It took him a while to figure out how to use the pay phone. When he got through, the connection was remarkably clean. But all he heard was his own voice. *Hi, you've reached Caleigh and Dan. We can't come to the phone just now. . . .*

It was just past midnight in Rome, which made it six P.M. in D.C. – so there was no telling where she could be. Still at work. On the Metro. Coming up the stairs to the apartment. He tried her at the office and got voice mail once again. But this time it was *her* voice and the sound of it sent him into a spin of longing. He began to leave a message, saying he was in trouble, *real* trouble, but it was the kind of trouble that was hard to explain. He was about to tell her maybe she ought to stay a couple of days with her friend Michelle or with Magda –

But no. A message like that would accomplish nothing. It would only scare her . . . for him. She'd stay where she was and wait for him to call back. So what he said was: "Hey, babe. Sorry I missed you. It's kinda crazy over here, but . . . I'll try again tomorrow. Just don't forget to, uhh, lock the doors, okay?"

Now what? The truth was, he was too tired to think.

He needed a hotel. Most of them in the area around the Piazza Navona seemed to have three or four stars next to their names, and he needed something cheaper. No stars would be ideal. A meteorite or a crescent moon would be fine, thanks.

Before long, he found himself in the small and bustling Piazza di Rotonda, where a fat American was raving in a Long Island accent, "I'm talkin' about the *Pantheon*! D'you have any idea what that *means*?" His companions' replies were muted with embarrassment. "I'm talkin' Julius fuckin' Caesar. Romans! Walking around in togas. Can you believe it? Right where I'm standin' – two thousand years ago!"

There were half a dozen hotels on the square, one of which was the Abruzze, a two-star establishment directly across from the brooding cupcake of the Pantheon. Danny filled out a registration card and, at the clerk's suggestion, paid in cash.

"No bagaglio?"

You didn't have to speak Italian to know what he meant. "The airline lost it," Danny explained.

The clerk rolled his eyes toward the ceiling and chuckled sadly. Then he grabbed a key from the mailboxes behind him and led Danny up the stairs to the second floor, where he opened the door to a small room with high ceilings. *"Caldo,"* the clerk remarked as he went to the windows and threw open the shutters.

A soft breeze pushed at the curtains. The clerk smiled and nodded encouragingly. Then he smiled some more. Tired as he was, it took a while for Danny to understand what the guy was getting at. Finally, the light dawned and, fumbling in his pockets for change, he gave the clerk a dollar bill.

207

"*Grazie, e buona notte,*" the man said, and, with a deferential nod, let himself out.

Alone at last, Danny sat down on the bed, fell back, and closed his eyes. Beyond the windows, a saxophone moaned sweetly. A fountain splashed. Italian, French, and English rose and fell amid bursts of laughter. What was it the guy was playing? He didn't remember the name of the song – and then he did. "My Funny Valentine."

He didn't know whether to laugh or cry.

And he didn't remember falling asleep, either, but then, who ever did? One moment he was lying on the bed, and the next . . .

He felt the sun on his face and heard the first strains of what soon became an industrial symphony of garbage trucks and motor scooters. Blinking awake, he glanced at his watch and saw that it was just after six in the morning.

He ought to sleep a little more, he thought. But no. He needed to talk with Caleigh, and the sooner he called the better. There was a six-hour time difference between Washington and Rome, which made it just after midnight in the States – so he knew she'd be home.

His room didn't have a phone, so he pulled on his clothes and went out looking for one. She answered on the second ring, her voice thick with sleep and kind of subdued – as if she missed him. The tentative "Hello?" really got to him and, for a second, he thought about proposing to her, there and then, but decided against it. A proposal wasn't something you phoned in.

"Hey, babe. . . ." The connection was so clear that when she said nothing in reply the silence crackled. "Uhhh, Caleigh?"

"Fuck you." And she was gone.

For a second, he thought he must have the wrong number. But that was wishful thinking. Of course, it was her. *Not good,* he thought. *And not what I need right now – not at all.*

He redialed. This time he got their voice mail, which meant one of two things. Either she was talking to someone else (not likely) or her phone was off the hook (very likely). When he heard the beep, he said, "Listen, Caleigh, I'm in a little trouble over here, so . . ." *So what?* "I'm at the Abruzze Hotel in Rome. Call me." He dug the hotel's card out of his pocket and left the number.

Then he stood there for most of a minute, thinking about the tone in her voice. Angry, hurt, angry – more one than the other, but he couldn't tell which. Not from two words. It puzzled him, and not just that: it pissed him off. He had enough to worry about without Caleigh going off the deep end because he hadn't called every night. What was her problem, anyway?

Though it was late in the States and he knew that he'd be waking people up, he didn't want to wait until mid-afternoon to call. So he telephoned Preston, who wasn't in, and Jake, who was. Unfortunately, he was also stoned and hadn't seen Caleigh since the show at the Petrus.

"Where are you calling from?"

"Rome."

A pause. *"Italy?"*

"Yeah."

A moment's silence. "What are you doing in Italy? You on . . . vacation?"

"No. I'm working. Though, mostly, I'm trying not to get killed."

Jake laughed. "My man! Magnum PI!"

"I'm serious!"

"Of course you're serious. But that's what you do. You get in harm's way. Just like an aircraft carrier, except . . ." He thought for a moment: "Smaller."

"What are you smoking?" Danny asked.

"What do you *think* I'm smoking?" Jake replied. "I'm an artist."

After a minute or two of this, Danny asked him for Michelle Peroff's telephone number. She was Caleigh's best friend, and the four of them had double-dated once or twice. If anyone knew what was happening with Caleigh, Michelle would.

And so she did.

"You're amazing," Michelle said when he got her on the phone.

"I am?" The way she said it, "amazing" did not sound like a compliment.

"You're such a dickhead! How *could* you?"

"How could I *what*?"

"Send her that thing."

"What thing?"

"That . . . attachment."

He didn't have a clue as to what she was talking about. "What 'attachment'?"

"The video clip – in your e-mail? As in 'download now.' Well, she did."

Danny shook his head, as if to clear it. Then he took a deep breath and exhaled. "Listen Michelle –"

"You must be sick or something!"

"I didn't send her anything," Danny told her. "I don't even have a computer with me. What kind of video clip?"

"*You* know."

She was beginning to irritate him. "No, Michelle, I really don't. That's why I'm asking. What are you talking about?!"

"I'm talking about you and your little friend."

"My 'friend'? What friend?"

"How should I know? She's your friend! What were you, *bragging* or something?"

He didn't know what to say.

"Did you think it would make Caleigh jealous –"

"No –"

"Because it didn't. It just . . . lost her for you. How drunk *were* you, anyway?"

"I don't know," Danny confessed. "I mean, I'm not sure what we're talking about."

Michelle scoffed. "No?" She paused. "Look, I used to think you were a nice guy, but . . . don't call me again, okay?" And with that she broke the connection.

He stood where he was for what seemed like a long time, reprising the conversation in his head, trying to make sense of it. He had a sinking feeling that, somehow, Michelle was talking about Paulina. Because, when you thought about it, Paulina was the only thing she *could* be talking about. What was it she'd said? Something about his "little friend." *That's what women call other women,* Danny thought, *when the other women are . . . the Other Woman.* But an e-mail attachment? How could that be? There would have to have been a camera in the room, and . . . Could Zebek do that? Danny thought about it and decided, *Yeah. If he could fix the Palio, he could bribe a couple of maids to put a camera in the room.*

Which would explain Danny's sudden, and really rather astounding, popularity with the opposite sex. Turns out: He wasn't irresistible, after all. Just a sucker. What was it Paulina said? *Are you supersized, too?* He shook his head.

Muttering to himself, he stumbled back toward the hotel, stripped his clothes off, and headed for the shower, which turned out to be more of a drizzle than a downpour, more tepid than hot. Even so, he stood beneath the showerhead for ten minutes, thinking and soaking. It wasn't like he really had any kind of brainstorm, but he had to do *something*. So he dried off in a hurry, pulled on some clothes, and took the stairs down to the lobby two at a time. He remembered an Internet café that he'd seen the night before, and headed in its direction. It was only a couple of blocks away, just off the Via del Corso. As he walked, he thought about what he was going to do.

The cops were out, and so was going home. Which left . . . Plan C. Find out what's going on – or enough, at least, so that when he *did* go to the police they'd have to listen to him. Unfortunately, the only real leads that he had were the handful of phone calls that Terio made just before he went incommunicado. A couple to Palo Alto, a couple to Istanbul, one to Oslo.

Palo Alto was a dead end (literally), but the guy in Istanbul might still be around. Danny thought hard, trying to remember his name. *Remy Something. Then a B. Balzac, maybe. Remy Balzac. Something like that.* And the Agence France Presse. Terio had called them, too. Which might or might not be helpful, depending on how many people they had in the Istanbul bureau. Two or three? Ten or twenty? The only way to find out was to call and ask.

Turning a corner, he found himself outside the café he'd remembered. Tucked away in a baroque building of no particular distinction, the coffee house was one of those hard-edged high-tech places with lots of plastic and primary colors. Ordering a double *macchiatto,* Danny paid an attendant for an hour on the Internet and sat down in an Aeron Chair at one of a dozen computers. Then he logged onto Yahoo and, out of habit, checked his e-mail. The only message of interest was from Lavinia, who reported that *Flash Art* had promised to be at the opening, and how were things coming anyway?

Everything's hunky-dory, he typed, happy that he did not have to explain his whereabouts. *Working like crazy!* Then he clicked SEND and sat back to think.

Caleigh . . .

What could he say? That he was sorry? That he'd been drunk? That he'd never do it again? With a soft groan, he leaned forward and clicked on the COMPOSE button. A new window opened, and he entered her address. Below that, he typed:

Caleigh – Luv

Then he sat back and watched the cursor blink. A minute went by; then a second minute, and a third. Finally, an idea occurred to him. Sitting up, he leaned over the keyboard and began to type:

You can't believe your eyes. I know it sounds crazy, but please – just read what I have to say.

He paused for a moment, rereading the words on the screen. *This is bad,* he told himself. *But losing her would be worse. I wouldn't lie to her if I didn't love her.*

I'm in a situation.

Without getting into a lot of details, I'm tangled up with this high-tech psycho-billionaire who's got this technology that lets him make films "starring" anyone he wants in any role. Using old film clips as templates, he can create – I'm not making this up – he can create "a virtual actor" by making what he calls "a personality engine." In other words, he could remake Stars Wars *with Humphrey Bogart – or me – as Luke Skywalker.*

And not just Star Wars. *He could also remake* Deep Throat *and, judging by what Michelle says, he has.*

*She says you got an e-mail, supposedly from me, with a video "attachment." I swear to God, *I didn't send it.* Why would I? I mean, how stoned would I have to be? (Think about it: could anyone even *get* that high?)*

But I don't blame you if you think I'm lying. Seeing is believing. I know that. Only it shouldn't be – not anymore.

*Which brings me to the next point. This guy, Zebek, can do the same thing with voices that he can with images. So don't take any calls from "me." Because I'm telling you right now, they won't be *from* me. They'll be from him.*

Don't believe anything that comes from me until I'm standing in front of you. And remember, no matter what happens, I love you. Always have. Always will.

D.

P.S. Delete this.

There was one other e-mail that he needed to send.

Mamadou Boisseau was a twenty-four-year-old intern at Fellner Associates. A graduate of Sidwell Friends and Rensselaer Polytechnic, he had grown up in Washington, the son of an Ivoirian diplomat and his American wife. With a major in management information systems, Dew was intensely idiosyncratic. A sci-fi nut who'd learned to play the bagpipes (and played them well), he was a database maven whose office was dominated by a huge poster for *The Matrix*. Danny liked Dew a lot and was sure that he could be trusted. The fact that his Honda was plastered with sun-bleached bumper stickers urging people to kill their television sets and *Question Authority* suggested to Danny that Dew was not the kind of guy who'd go to the boss if someone asked him for a favor.

Dew –
I've got a big problem with one of our clients. Which is that he's trying to kill me. (And no, that's not a joke.) I was doing some work on the side, and now . . . well, it hasn't worked out so great.

Anyway: I will owe you big-time – and by that I mean I will put up those track lights you were talking about, stretch canvas, reframe your Matrix *poster, whatever! – if you'll check out a couple of companies for me. (And the guy who owns them.)*

The first is Sistemi di Pavone, S.A. It's headquartered in Siena (Italy). The second is Very Small Systems, Inc., in Palo Alto. Both companies are owned by a guy named Zerevan Zebek (aka Jude Belzer).

I'll take anything you can get, but basically I need to know what they do. Neither company is publicly traded (as far as I can tell), but Zebek must have

215

some kind of credit facility. I'm interested in their
finances, the kind of R & D they're doing – and
whatever you can find out about the work we're
doing for them at Fellner. Also, anything you learn
about Jason Patel – a Very Small Systems exec who
was murdered in California – would be helpful.

When the e-mail was on its way, Danny wandered
out to the Via del Corso. Traffic was bumper-to-
bumper but moving fast in a thick haze of ozone and
carbon monoxide. Walking past the Rinascente
department store, Danny went inside to buy a change
of clothes. Twenty minutes later, he came out with a
shopping bag containing a couple of polo shirts, some
socks and underwear, and a pair of khakis. Heading
back toward the Piazza di Rotonda, he bought a
backpack from a street vendor and stuffed it with his
new clothes.

The day was heating up.

Pausing at the entrance to a travel agency, he studied
the peculiar display in the window. It consisted of a
totem pole covered with colored squares of paper, each
of which was emblazoned with bargain fares and
package tours to faraway places. Tenerife, Prague,
Majorca, Bangkok, Orlando, and – *hello* – Istanbul
was on sale for 350,000 lire. How much was that,
anyway? Danny did the calculation in his head and
came up with something less than two hundred dollars.
Which surprised him. But why not? It wasn't all that
far, really – not from Rome, anyway.

A few minutes later, he found himself in the shadow
of the Pantheon. Barbaric and immense, the prehistoric
structure seemed as if it were radiating time itself.
Danny could feel the hours coming off the stone, like

216

heat rising from an asphalt road in the dead of summer. Drawn to its massive doors, he climbed its worn steps and, almost tentatively, stepped inside.

The walls of the building were in perpetual shadow, but the structure's heart was bright with sunlight, streaming through a circular hole, or oculus, in the ceiling far overhead. Seeing the building's interior for the first time, Danny was stunned by the grandeur of the setting and, for a moment, forgot his cares.

Then, as he wandered more deeply into the building, a cloud came between the oculus and the sun, eclipsing the ancient temple and casting a gray pall over everyone inside. Danny's steps slowed, then stopped, as a feeling of dread spiked through his heart.

Now the great dome seemed like a bell jar haunted by ghosts. Tourists milled in the deepening twilight, whispering among themselves. Slowly, and with enormous apprehension, Danny raised his eyes to the ceiling, half expecting to find Zerevan Zebek gazing down through the oculus as if it were a crystal ball.

I'm losing it, Danny thought. *Got the heebie-jeebies, bad.* The phrase made him smile to himself, and as he did the darkness eased as suddenly as it had come. A shaft of sunlight pierced the roof, illuminating a fresco. A glimpse of angels and sunbeams lightened his heart.

Walking back outside, he was crossing the square toward the Abruzze when he saw them, coming out of the hotel. Two guys, big in the shoulders and impeccably dressed. Dark suits and sunglasses. They didn't look like tourists. More like professional wrestlers who'd just had a makeover.

Danny stepped into the shade of a café umbrella. The men were standing on the sidewalk outside the hotel, looking around. Then, one of them took off his sunglasses. Even at a distance, Danny recognized the Brow. He was one of the guys in the Admirals Club who'd been eating honey-roasted peanuts while Danny met with "Belzer." His was the asymmetrical face with the worm of scar tissue snaking through one eyebrow.

But how had they found him? How did they know where to look? Had they followed him the night before from the Casa Clera, when he'd gone to warn Inzaghi? Maybe. But if so, why not grab him then and there?

Turning, he began to walk away, distancing himself from the scene. Every instinct he had told him to run, but running would attract attention and that could get him killed. So he walked, putting one foot in front of the other, oblivious to where he was going – so long as he got there in one piece.

It wasn't until he'd crossed the Tiber that he began to relax, and by then he was starting to wonder if he'd been seeing things. Walking into a bar on the Via della Renella, he ordered a Campari-soda and, using the bar phone, called the Abruzze. When the desk clerk answered, Danny asked if he had any messages.

"Si, Signore Cray! Two gentlemen come to see you."

"At the hotel?"

"They ask to wait in your room, but this –" A pause. "– this I do not allow."

"So they're –"

"Outside. I think they have coffee."

Danny hung up the phone, finished his drink, and tossed a few thousand lire on the bar. Then he went out to the street and began to walk. How did they find him? They didn't follow him from the Casa Clera, because then he would have been toast last night. They couldn't have gone to every hotel in Rome, asking if he was a guest. Yet somehow they had found out where he was staying. But how? He hadn't made a reservation. And he'd used cash, not plastic. Which left, what?

His call to Caleigh. But there'd been no time to get a call log like the one he got from the information broker for Terio's phone. There was a time lag for that kind of thing; it was forty-eight hours at a minimum before calls posted up.

It took him a while to figure it out, but eventually he did. There was no other way. They must have hacked the voice-mailbox on the phone.

This wasn't something that Danny himself had ever done, but he knew enough about this *kind* of thing to know that it was possible. Most answering machines and voice mail services worked the same way. To access messages from another phone, you called the number and waited for the outgoing message to play. Once it did, you pressed a key – usually the asterisk or pound sign – on the touch-tone pad. Then you entered an access-code that was two to four digits long, depending on the service and equipment. Half the time, people used a default number (like 1234) that was easy to remember. And, of course, just as easy to guess. Not that you would ever bother guessing. For fifty bucks, you could buy a tone-dialer on the Internet and download a shareware program that would run through all the possibilities for you.

Which was another way of saying that he'd made it easy for them. What were his words? His exact words? *I'm at the Abruzze Hotel in Rome. Call me.* He'd even left the number.

Way to go, Sherlock.

He had to get out of here. Because as dumb as it was to leave a message like that, it would be an even bigger

219

mistake to assume that he had Zebek figured out, that he knew how the billionaire's goons had found him. He was probably right, but if he was wrong, they'd find him again. And if they did, he had a hunch he could kiss his ass good-bye.

Twelve

So he kissed Rome good-bye instead.

Getting out of town wasn't the hardest decision he'd ever made. It was just a question of Istanbul or Oslo – and Istanbul made more sense. Norway would have been cooler, but Terio had worked in Turkey, so Turkey was where Danny went.

The four-ten flight landed just in time for a bloodred sunset. Passing through Turkish Customs, he could feel the tension slide from his body, and he heaved a sigh of relief.

Kemal Atatürk International Airport was sterile, modern, and efficient. Danny used his ATM card to get two hundred dollars in cash from a machine and was astonished to receive nearly a quarter of a *billion* Turkish lire. Examining the money, he saw that all of the crisp new bills looked alike, though their colors were different. Staring at them, he realized that until he memorized the colors he would have to count the zeros on each bill whenever he paid for anything.

A rank of taxis waited outside the terminal and Danny went up to the window of the first one that he saw. "How much to Cankurtaran?" he asked, naming a neighborhood that he'd read about in the in-flight magazine. The Blue Mosque was nearby, and so was Aya Sofia, one of the oldest and grandest churches in

Christendom. It was a tourist area, anyway. He figured he'd blend in.

"Ten million," the driver told him.

Danny laughed. "No problem."

The traffic into town was heavy, but the driver had a way around it. Every mile or so, he'd abandon the road, swerving onto the tram tracks that ran beside it. This allowed him to surge from twenty to sixty miles an hour, passing hundreds of cars and trucks – until the single headlight of a trolley would sparkle in the distance and rapidly swell. At that point, the driver would swerve back onto the road, but only until the trolley passed. Then it was back to the tracks and playing "chicken."

"Is this, uh, legal?" Danny asked.

"Oh no," the driver said cheerfully. "It's big trouble if they catch me. Two people killed this way last month."

Danny sat back and looked for a seat belt. There wasn't one, but it didn't really bother him. Though the ride was way too exciting, he was pretty sure that he wasn't meant to die in a traffic accident. Not now. Not under these circumstances. That would be like a piano falling on someone who was dying of cancer. It just didn't happen. The terminally ill were immune to fatal accidents, and Danny realized that was how he saw himself – as "terminally ill."

Anyone who had a case of Zerevan Zebek didn't need to worry about seat belts.

Meanwhile, the city slid by outside the window, a jumble of ancient and modern buildings, massive apartment blocks, mosques, and markets. Up ahead, a trolley's white headlight bore down upon them, and the driver swerved from the tracks onto the road.

Suddenly they were cruising along the waterfront on a highway named for President Kennedy. Beyond the cab's smudged window, dozens of freighters rode at anchor, their decks alight, glittering on the coal-black Sea of Marmara.

It was a stunning sight, but Danny found it depressing. It was exactly the kind of thing that you wanted to see, that you really *needed* to see, with someone you loved. Someone like Caleigh, whose last words to him were what?

Oh, yeah. Now, I remember. "Fuck you."

The Asian Shore Guesthouse was an antique wooden structure that the Turkish Automobile Society had renovated ten years earlier. Around the corner from the Cankurtaran railway station, it sat on the side of a hill, overlooking the Golden Horn. It had ten rooms and a roof garden where drinks were served.

The rooms weren't bad, a little down-at-heels but clean and spacious. The view, however, was heart-stopping, with half of Istanbul laid out beneath the windows. With the lights off and the foghorns sounding, it was one of the most romantic rooms Danny had ever been in. And at twenty-three million a night, it was a steal: about fifteen dollars.

It didn't take him long to settle in, since his only luggage was the nylon backpack that he'd bought in Rome. He took a quick shower, changed his clothes, and went out to look for something to eat. Though it was after ten, there were still plenty of restaurants open. He settled on a smoky little joint two blocks from the hotel, where he wolfed down skewers of vegetable kebab, served up with rice and a spicy

223

eggplant salad. On the way back to his room, four different guys tried to sell him rugs.

And the incredible thing was: *He almost bought one.*

Back at the hotel, he asked the young desk clerk, whose name tag read HASAN, if he had a telephone directory.

The desk clerk shook his head. "They haven't printed a new one for years," he said. "What name do you want? I can get it from Information."

"Barzan," Danny told him. "Remy Barzan."

Hasan picked up the phone, dialed a number, and spoke briefly with an operator. Turning to Danny, he switched from Turkish to English without missing a beat. "You want the number?"

"And the address," Danny said.

Hasan muttered something in Turkish, waited a moment, then scribbled on a scratch pad. When he was done, he hung up the phone and tore off the top page of the pad. "It's in Beyo˘glu," he said. "Near the big Catholic church."

Danny thanked him and asked if he could have a wake-up call in the morning.

Hasan smiled. "You don't need."

"Yeah, I do," Danny told him. "I'm –"

"Trust me! You don't be needing this."

Danny gave him a look. "Trust *me*: I do be needing it."

The desk clerk laughed. "What time?"

"Eight would be good."

"I'll make sure you're up. No problem."

He *said* it was no problem, but Danny could tell the request went in one ear and out the other. The guy didn't even write it down – just smiled at him. *Must be a Turkish thing,* Danny thought, and trudged up the

224

stairs to his room. There he dialed the number the clerk had given him and listened to the phone ring in Beyoˇglu on the other side of town. He wasn't sure what he was going to say, but the main thing was to set up a meeting – and soon. Except: Barzan wasn't in. All Danny got was an answering machine with a message in Turkish. And after what happened in Rome, he wasn't about to leave a message. Replacing the receiver in its cradle, he stripped off his clothes and fell back on the bed, exhausted.

The call to prayer – the *insanely amplified* call to prayer – blew him out of bed at dawn. This wasn't a "Let us now pray" kind of thing but an ululating wail that went on and on, beseeching, reminding, cajoling, whining. To Danny's ears, it sounded as if the muezzin was seated on a hot stove surrounded by amplifiers. This was a sound level that would have worked for Metallica in Yankee Stadium. When it finally stopped, Danny was wide awake and staring.

Taking the stairs down to the lobby, where a dozen neatly set tables were waiting, he breakfasted on bread and olives, cheese, and tomatoes washed down with fresh orange juice and hot black coffee. Just as he was finishing, Hasan appeared in the doorway with a sly smile.

"Well!" he exclaimed. "You're up early."

Danny laughed. "Yeah, I thought I heard something outside."

"We're a very spiritual people."

"I'm sure you are."

"You need a driver?" Hasan asked. "I can get you a good one, cheap."

Danny shook his head. "I don't think so," he

replied. "I feel like walking. But maybe you could help me with directions, though. I'm looking for the Agence France Presse."

"No problem." Turning on his heel, the young Turk left the breakfast room and returned a minute later with the address. "It's in Taksim," he said. "A long walk, but you can always get a cab. I think, best way: go down to the docks, where the ferryboats leave. This is Eminönü. Go left at the water toward the Galata Bridge, and cross over to the other side of the Golden Horn. Then you walk uphill toward the Tower and keep going. This address – it's near there."

"What tower?"

"Galata Tower. Round, stone, seventy meters high, maybe seven hundred years old. You don't miss it. Once you're there, it's better you ask somebody – because the street . . . it's not like the States." He wrote the address on a slip of paper, extended it toward Danny, and hesitated. "Maybe you should take a taxi," he decided.

"I'll find it," Danny told him, taking the note.

In fact, he was looking forward to exploring this city, which, on first impression, seemed like a hybrid of San Francisco and Tangiers.

He found his way down to the water without any trouble and made his way over to Eminönü, which was as crowded as Grand Central Station. Boats came and went from the docks, heading for destinations near and far, on both sides of the Bosphorus. A river of pedestrian traffic flowed through a haze of smoke boiling from little boats, rocking at the quay, where vendors sold grilled fish and rounds of bread encrusted with sesame seeds. There were almost no women to be seen – just a mob of lookalike men with short black hair and thick mustaches. Danny maneuvered his way through the crowd to the Galata Bridge, where he joined a stream of men going to work or heading home.

Traffic on the water was almost as dense as that on the land. Rusting freighters plowed the waves beside glittering cruise ships, sailboats, and tankers. Arab music – dissonant and hysterical – came at him from every direction. Seagulls dipped and soared. Sunlight twinkled on the waves. The sky was implacably blue. The whole scene suggested a painting by Childe Hassam on dope.

Once Danny reached the other side of the bridge, the road began to climb, leading him up a narrow street packed with hole-in-the-wall shops selling an improbable mix of satellite dishes, cable boxes, and descramblers. At the base of the Galata Tower, he drank a Turkish coffee in a small café and showed the waiter the slip of paper that Hasan had given him.

The Agence France Presse office was on the third floor of a plain brick building off a thronged pedestrian mall known as Istikal Caddessi. A scholarly-looking fat man with square-rimmed eyeglasses and strands of hair combed over a bald spot answered Danny's knock. Behind him Danny saw a couple of old wooden desks, piled high with newspapers, books, and reports. A tangle of wires networked the computers to a quartet of telephones, a fax machine, and a printer. In the back of the room, a woman worked on a laptop while she talked animatedly into her cell phone.

"Oui?" The man in the doorway regarded him curiously. Obviously, they didn't get many visitors.

"Do you speak English?" Danny asked.

In reply, the man made a seesawing gesture with his right hand. *"Un peu."*

"I'm looking for . . ." Danny hesitated. The fact that Chris Terio had called both Remy Barzan's apartment and the AFP did not mean that Barzan worked for the AFP. He might or might not. Maybe Terio knew more than one person in Istanbul. Still . . .

"Yes?" The man in the doorway looked impatient.

"I'm looking for Remy Barzan."

A frown accompanied a definite change in the man's mood. He crossed his arms in front of his chest. "He's not here."

"But you know him, right?"

"Of course."

"So . . . he's a reporter for you?"

"He covers Kurdish affairs." The man angled his head, as if to get a better look at Danny. He frowned, as if he didn't like what he saw. "What do you want with him?"

Danny hesitated. Good question. But a truthful answer was impossible. Where would he begin? "I was told to look him up if I got to Istanbul, so . . . here I am. Do you know when he'll be back?"

"No. We haven't seen him for a while. To tell you the truth, we don't even know if he's *coming* back." Danny's disappointment was so immediate and obvious that the man's attitude softened. "You tried his flat?"

"No one answers."

The man nodded. "Donata!" he called over his shoulder. "This man's looking for Remy!"

Donata kept the cell phone to her ear but rolled her eyes in sympathy. She fashioned a big shrug and turned her back. The older man made a hapless gesture that

228

was meant to end the conversation, but Danny was reluctant to leave. Barzan was just about the only lead he had, so he stood where he was, thinking, *Now what?* Norway?

The woman at the back of the office closed her cell phone and came toward them. She was heavyset and masculine-looking, with a frizz of reddish hair and a lot of makeup. "Donata," she announced, offering a pudgy hand.

"Danny Cray."

"You're wanting to see Remy?"

"Right."

"And it's important?"

Danny glanced at the older man and shrugged. "Yeah," he admitted, "it's pretty important."

The older man snorted. "I thought you were just 'looking him up.' "

"Believe me," Danny said, "it's a long story. I was told to look him up – but it *is* important."

Donata pressed her mouth into a line. Thought about it. And came to a decision. "I think: maybe he's in the east."

" 'The east,' " Danny repeated, as if it were a street address.

"He specializes in Kurdish matters," Donata continued. "So he's often in Diyarbakir. But if you're thinking of going there, I wouldn't. It's dangerous."

"Oh."

The man peered at Danny, seemed to realize he didn't have a clue. With a glance at Donata, as if to get permission, the man spoke. "There are terrorists. Kurdish separatists. So the military is there in big numbers. Lots of excesses. Lots of trouble. Good for a journalist. Bad for tourism."

Donata sighed. "I don't know what we're going to do if Remy doesn't come back. When he started, I thought he was just amusing himself. A rich boy, writing the occasional color piece. But he's actually very good. A serious journalist." She shook her head. "He'll be difficult to replace."

"You talk as if you don't expect him to return," Danny said.

The two exchanged looks and seemed to come to some agreement. "I don't see the harm in telling you," Donata said. "Remy, he disappears" – she looked up at the ceiling as if it had a calendar imprinted on it –"a little more than a week ago. On the day we don't see him, his car –" She clapped her hands together and said, "Boom! It's nothing left."

"But he wasn't *in* it?" Danny's heart danced in his chest.

The man shook his head. "He let his housekeeper borrow the car. She was a college student."

Danny's heart sank. Was he responsible? Probably. He'd given the list of Terio's phone calls to Zebek. "So who – ?"

The man expelled a puff of air. "Who knows? With the Kurds, it's like . . ." He paused, trying to think of the right phrase. After a moment, he turned to the woman. *"Qu'est-que-c'est 'un panier de crabes'?"*

" 'A basket of crabs,' " Donata replied. She turned to Danny. "You have this expression in English?"

Danny shook his head.

"Well," the man told him, "it's very bad. And very complicated. Maybe Remy writes something someone doesn't like. The PKK. The military. A faction within a faction. Who knows? The result is the same. He's gone."

Donata said, "Remy did call, after the car bomb, to say that he would not be available for a while." She turned toward the man. "How did he put it?"

A bittersweet smile played on the man's lips. He mumbled something in French, then cocked his head, obviously translating. "He says he has to keep his head down." He ducked his own head by way of illustration. "You see?"

Danny nodded.

"So we know he is all right, for the moment," Donata said. "I think maybe he's just gone home. His people – they live there. And they're close. Like a fist," she added.

"You mean the Yezidis," Danny said.

Donata looked surprised. "Exactly."

"And where is that?" Danny asked. "His home."

"Uzelyurt," the man replied.

Danny blinked.

Donata laughed. "You don't know Uzelyurt?"

He shook his head.

"Well, it's about as far east as you can go and still be in Turkey," she told him.

"And you think he might be there?" Danny asked.

She pursed her lips. "I think, yes. It's where he's *from*. His family is there – old, powerful." She shrugged. "So maybe that's where he goes." She frowned. "*Probably* that's where he goes. But he could be in Paris. He lived there for many years." She thought about it. "To be honest, he could be anywhere."

"But if it was important – *really important* – where would you look for him?"

Donata looked at her colleague and shrugged. "I'd start in the east."

"I mean, this place you mentioned – Oozleyurd – what's it near?"

The older man snorted derisively, spelled out the name of the town, then patted the few strands of hair on his head, as if to make sure they were still there. "It's near nothing," he said. "It's in the middle of nowhere."

On the way back to the Asian Shore, Danny's sense of progress began to erode. Unless he was willing to set off for the "middle of nowhere" on the off chance that Remy Barzan might be there and might have something useful to say, he'd reached a dead end. Then again, he *was* already in Turkey, so maybe it was a matter of "in for a penny, in for a pound."

When he asked if Hasan could show him the location of Uzelyurt, the kid pulled out a battered motor club map of the Turkish republic. He smoothed out the creases, consulted the printed guide, then drew one finger down from P and another across from 12. The fingers met at a dot about an inch to the right of a place called Diyarbakir.

Hasan frowned. "You want to go *there*?" he asked. The idea seemed to cause him pain.

Danny shrugged. "I don't know. Is it hard to get to?"

"It's a long flight – but there's nothing there. Checkpoints. Curfew. It's dangerous. Why would you go?"

Danny ignored the question. "When you say it's dangerous –"

"It's a civil war. This city, Diyarbakir, it's all Kurds. The newspapers say the war is over, the army wins. But this is only during the day. At night, it's criminals. Terrorists."

232

Danny thought about this for a moment and asked, "But if I had to go – if it was business – how would I do it?"

"You mean, to Uzelyurt?"

Danny nodded.

Hasan considered. "Well, you'd have to fly to Diyarbakir, then . . . I don't know. Maybe a bus. Or a taxi, if you can get one." Seeing his guest consider the possibility, Hasan repeated his objection. "But I am telling you: There is nothing. No business, even. No tourist sight. Steppe only." Then the desk clerk sharpened his gaze. "You go to Topkapi?"

Danny shook his head.

"Aya Sofia?"

"Not yet."

"Blue Mosque?"

"No."

Hasan refolded the map. Then he twisted his face into a sad and disapproving look. "You don't go to Aya Sofia – which is builded in the *sixth* century and is right here next to the hotel, a UNESCO treasure of the world – you don't go there, but you go to *Uzelyurt*?"

"It's just an idea," Danny told him with a smile. "And I *will* check out Topkapi and the rest. But, first, I think I'll have a drink. Is the roof garden open?"

"Of course," Hasan replied, and gestured graciously toward the stairs.

Climbing to the third floor, Danny stepped out onto the roof, where half a dozen tables sat beneath big umbrellas overlooking the great, tumbling waterscape that was Istanbul. Taking a table, he asked the waiter for a glass of sweetened apple tea. As Danny sat down, it occurred to him that this was the most foreign place that he had ever been – and, under the circumstances, the loneliest.

A small group of backpackers sat nearby in the shade of a green umbrella. In flat midwestern accents punctuated with laughter, they talked about Lebanese hash, the best clubs in Bodrum, and the cheapest pensions in Ephesus. Danny envied their camaraderie and the feeling of immunity that came off them like warmth from an oven.

His tea was delicious. Gazing out at the ships on the Golden Horn, he had an overwhelming urge to call Caleigh but found the gumption to resist it. Seeing a copy of the *International Herald Tribune* abandoned on a nearby table, he reached for it and signaled the waiter for a second glass of tea. Then he sat back in his seat and opened the paper to the sports section. He was thinking that he'd read for a while, then walk over to the Aya Sofia. Afterward he'd go to a travel agency and buy a ticket to Diyarbakir for the next day. But as he sat there, sipping his tea and reading about Barry Bonds's home-run spree, an argument broke out in the lobby, two floors below.

Soon the argument became a shouting match. The backpackers fell silent, exchanging glances and giggles, while Danny strained to hear what was being said. But the argument ended before he could understand a word. There was a clipped shout and a cry of pain, followed by the thud of feet pounding up the stairs to the second floor. Then . . . silence, ending in a sudden crash that Danny knew – he just *knew* – was the door to his room, splintering. Getting to his feet, he looked wildly around but saw in an instant that there was nowhere to hide and nowhere to run. The only way off the roof was to take the stairs or jump – which was suicide, either way.

"Vaff!"
"Dove e lui?!"
"Porco mondo!"

Danny didn't know what the words meant, but they were unmistakably Italian, and he was pretty sure they were coming from his room or just outside it. His eyes scanned the rooftop for something he could use as a weapon, but he saw nothing that would help. One of the backpackers had a walking stick, but a club wasn't going to cut it. Not with these guys. At a minimum, he'd need a chain saw or a Glock. Both would be better.

Walking quickly to the edge of the roof, he judged the distance to a chestnut tree outside the hotel. If he got up to speed and launched himself, he could probably make it – though whether he'd be able to hang on or not was a separate question. Not that it mattered. The roof was edged by a low wall, about six inches high, making a flat-out run impossible. What began as a long jump became a broad jump in the end – and an impossible one at that.

Then they were there – not on the roof but standing in the street, outside the hotel. Pausing in the shade of the chestnut tree, the Brow and his friend seemed uncertain about which way to go or what to do. To his horror, Danny saw they were standing next to a menu stand advertising the roof garden's delights. If they noticed it, the Italians would undoubtedly want to check it out.

But they didn't notice.

The Brow removed a cell phone from his pocket, flipped it open, and punched in a number. While he waited for the phone to ring, he raised his eyes to the hotel's upper floors and slowly scanned the windows, left to right. Then someone must have answered, because the Brow shook off his stillness in an instant. Suddenly animated, he spun around on the ball of his foot and, leaning into the phone, began an urgent conversation that lasted no more than twenty seconds. Then he shoved the phone back in his pocket and headed off with his friend in the direction of the Blue Mosque.

Danny exhaled. *Jesus Christ,* he thought, *it's like Butch Cassidy or something. Who* are *these guys?*

Taking the stairs to the second floor, he saw at a glance that the door to his room was hanging off its hinges. Going down to the lobby, he found Hasan sitting on the floor with his back against the front desk and a bloody handkerchief pressed to his nose. Behind him, a frightened housekeeper pleaded with someone on the telephone.

The desk clerk looked up. "I think they saw you come in."

"Who?" Danny asked.

"The Italians. They ask for your room. I don't want to tell them, but . . ." He winced in pain.

"It's okay."

Hasan regarded him over the top of his handkerchief. "You were up on the roof?"

Danny nodded.

The desk clerk chuckled, but it cost him, and he winced. "He hit me."

"I can see that."

Hasan cast his eyes toward the ceiling, tilting his head back in an effort to stop the bleeding. "I think it's broken."

Danny nodded. "I know. Listen, Hasan –" He wanted to thank him.

The desk clerk gestured toward the room where Danny had breakfasted that morning. "You can go out the back way, through the garden. There's an alley behind the gate." As Danny turned to leave, he added, "But I have to ask . . ."

Danny paused and looked back. "What's that?"

"The minibar. Did you use it?"

The alley took him out to a leafy street of carpet shops, cafés, and small hotels. There were really only two ways to go, he saw. He could walk uphill in the direction of the Aya Sofia's massive dome, or he could follow the same street down to the highway that ran along the water's edge. If he was lucky, he might find a cab that would take him to the airport.

If he was lucky . . . Danny considered the possibility. If he was *lucky* he wouldn't be looking over his shoulder on a street called Yeni Sarachane Sok.

He headed uphill past the ancient church and caught a glimpse of Topkapi Palace off to his right. Then a little park with a forlorn zoo, followed by a couple of blocks of cheap "pansiyons," some kebab shops and stores, then downhill toward the docks at Eminönü.

Turning a corner, he came upon the Basilica Internet Cafe & Laundromat and stopped inside to see if Mamadou had come up with anything. Ordering a cup of coffee, he sat down at one of the computers and logged onto Yahoo. Nearby, a grizzled old man sat beside a washing machine, reading a battered Penguin paperback, while a young woman stood a few feet away, folding polo shirts and underwear.

There wasn't much in the way of mail. Most of it was spam, promising to get him out of debt or offering to hook him up with "the horniest chixxx on the

237

Web!!!" There was a string of bad jokes forwarded by his brother Kev and, finally, what he was looking for:

Sender *Mamdou3@fellner.com*
Subject *Your Big Problem*

Zebek's trying to KILL you? You gotta be kidding! He's one of Fellner's best clients. I think we billed him close to half a million last year. What did you *do* to him, anyway?

Assuming this isn't a joke, has it occurred to you that you might want to call the cops? Because I don't see how a credit report's gonna help. But if that's what you want . . . I'll get on it. Meantime, I looked at a couple of databases, and what I got was this:

Zerevan Khalil Zebek: Born: June 6, 1966. Azizi, Turkish Republic. Baccalaureate degree (Business Economics and Management) Università di Ca'Foscari, Venice, Italy, 1987. MBA Massachusetts Institute of Technology, 1989. Residence: Palazzo di Pavone, Siena, Italy. Director, Zebek Holdings, Plc (Liechtenstein); CEO, Sistemi di Pavone, S.A. (Siena). No criminal record in the U.S. or Italy.

Very Small Systems, Inc.: subsidiary of Sistemi di Pavone. Sistemi controlled by bearer shares, which are probably parked with the Liechtenstein holding company. (No way to know.)

Kroll did a report on VSS about a year ago, but I couldn't get it. Some Japanese zaibatsu (is there any other kind?) made an offer for it – but nothing happened. Which was surprising, because this is a company with serious cash-flow problems.

(A note from Rappaport, Reich & Green sez VSS had a $32.4 million credit facility – this was in February – no revenue, and a burn rate of $4 million *a month.* So, obviously, they're going to need an angel – and soon.)

Company's about as secretive as you can get – and you can get real secretive when you don't have any clients, revenue, or product. Near as I can tell, it's all R & D – for now, anyway.

As you've probably guessed, I'm taking this stuff directly off the Web – so if you think I don't know what I'm talking about, you're right. But it sounds to me like you might be in the middle of an industrial espionage problem.

Which brings me back to my first suggestion: the PO-lice. Maybe you should call 'em.

Gotta run. Luv ya, man!

Dew

P.S. Nothing new on Patel. He was the CTO at VSS. Well thought of in the Valley. Cops think his murder was "a gay thing" (whatever that means). But all of that was in the papers. Watch this space, and I'll try to do better next week.

He saw them on the way out of the Laundromat, walking on the other side of the street. The Brow was leaning into his cell phone, talking hard, while his buddy – a squarely built man with long hair and sunglasses – marched at his side.

Danny didn't know if they'd spotted him. He didn't think so, but he sure as hell wasn't going to wait around to find out. Falling in with a tourist posse en route to one of the city's sights, he kept his head low and his eyes on the ground, desperate to disappear. This was not, he realized, a rational way to act. It was basically what an ostrich would do. But he had the gut feeling that if he kept the Italians in view – if he kept checking to see if they'd seen him – they would somehow feel the weight of his eyes. And then they'd know that he was near.

This was, of course, insane. He knew that. But it didn't matter.

As it happened, the tourists' destination was only twenty yards up the street from the café-Laundromat that Danny had just left. One of the yellow signs that mark tourist attractions in Istanbul identified this particular one as the Basilica Cistern. Danny saw the words in passing as he and the tour group filtered into a low and unimpressive building with a ticket office just inside the front door. A few feet away, a turnstile stood at the head of a dark and narrow staircase leading . . . down.

Danny's pulse went into overdrive as he worked up the nerve to look behind him. Buying a ticket, he glanced over his shoulder and was relieved to see . . . no one in particular. Just tourists. Like him. Not Gaetano. Not the long-haired thug. And not the Brow.

Heaving a sigh of relief, he paid and went through the turnstile, trailing a troop of older Brits led by a red-haired woman. She held a walking stick topped with a droopy bouquet of fake flowers that she hoisted into the air from time to time. Danny thought this must be so that her charges could find her should they become separated, but they seemed to stay as close to her as a kindergarten class.

As nervous as he was, as worried as he was, he was curious as well. To his mind, a cistern was a holding tank for rainwater. That a hole in the ground should be a tourist attraction seemed unlikely. And then he looked up and saw where he was – in an underground cathedral that was half lagoon. There was nothing primitive or crude about this space. It was both grand and fantastic, at least three stories high, with a vaulted ceiling upheld by a forest of massive stone columns. The bases of the columns stood in a lake of black water that appeared to be one or two feet deep. The lake was as long and wide as a racetrack, its darkness pierced by floodlights, creating a chiaroscuro effect.

Classical music played.

"Here we are," the redheaded woman said, standing on one of the wooden walkways that crisscrossed the underground lake. "Cool, isn't it?" Murmurs of agreement rose up from the group. "You see, water came to Constantinople by way of an aqueduct from a source about seventeen kilometers away. And because the city had to endure *quite* long sieges, an extensive system of cisterns was built to store water. In this, as in the other cisterns, the water could have come all the way up to the roof, if necessary. Isn't it something?"

"Oh, look, *fish*!" exclaimed a woman with tight gray curls. Everyone craned to see a flotilla of carp sliding between the columns.

"It's believed to have been built by our old friend

241

Constantine," the guide continued. "And until it burned down in 425, a basilica stood above it, which is how this particular cistern came by its name. If you'll follow me . . ."

They stopped at the Wishing Pool, where half the people in the crowd (including Danny) dutifully tossed some change at the water. Watching the coins sashay toward the bottom, he could see how they shrank in size. It was deeper than he thought – a few feet, maybe five. He wished . . . that he'd get out of here in one piece . . . and that Caleigh would forgive him.

"This way. . . ." The tour guide gave Danny a sidelong glance that seemed to say, *Don't freeload*. But he didn't have much choice. The walkways were narrow, and the tour was a one-way loop that led everyone to the same exit. Still, he let a gap develop between himself and the last of the Brits.

At the end of the lighted area, they reached a walkway that went around a pair of columns before heading off toward the exit. Danny could see a pair of marble heads splashed with light. The heads were massive and inverted, with each of them supporting a huge column. Beyond them was a black void. The tour guide explained that only a small part of the cistern was illuminated and accessible by walkway. Most of it lay in darkness.

"These are heads of Medusa," the guide told them. Danny looked closer and saw that the curly heads of hair were, in fact, tangles of snakes. But the effect was subtle – not a writhing mass of serpents but a few curls that only upon inspection turned out to be reptiles. Nor were the Medusas monstrous. Rather, they were big, sightless, innocent-looking heads, with broad, cherubic features. "Justinian rebuilt and restored the cistern in 535," the woman told them, "and it's thought that these Medusas were taken from pagan temples in Lebanon – as, indeed, were many of the columns. Justinian was a great recycler!" This earned her a few appreciative chuckles. "Well," she said crisply, "that's it then. We'll make our way up to the exit. Tiffins, everyone! Tiffins!"

An enthusiastic murmur rose up from the Brits as they shuffled toward the exit and the afternoon's tea. Slowly they began to ascend the steep staircase. Danny didn't want to crowd them, so he hung back until he found himself engulfed by a group of Spanish tourists. Then he began the long climb to daylight.

Halfway up, he heard the tour guide tell her charges to go "*straight* to the coach, if you don't mind."

As Danny climbed, the temperature did, too, until he reached the surface – when the heat of the day washed over him in a wave. After the cool, dripping darkness of the cistern, the Istanbul heat took his breath away even as the light rinsed the world of all its colors.

He stood for a moment, just outside the exit, rubbing his eyes. Then he waited, blinking, for his eyes to adjust and when they did he saw them. Or not really that. He didn't actually *see* them – not in the usual sense, because the world before him had the look of an overexposed photograph, bleached of detail. It was more that he discerned them, the shape and bulk of them, lounging against the side of a parked car. One of them seemed to be eating a gyro, leaning forward so that the sauce wouldn't drip on his lapels.

Danny reacted instinctively, turning on his heel. Before he'd actually thought about what he was doing, he was heading down the stairs, shoving his way past

243

the ascending Spaniards. The stairs were only a few feet wide, and protests exploded all around him.

"Hey!"

"Que hace?"

"Por favor!"

Then he was at the bottom of the stairs, heading for the Medusas, still fighting the current of sightseers. Behind him, someone screamed, and he knew from the cascade of shouts and squeals that Zebek's tag team was in pursuit – in fact, they were almost upon him.

His plan, such as it was, was to get to the other exit, but from the sound of things, his pursuers weren't as gentle as he had been and they were gaining ground. When he reached the Medusas, instinct took over. He slid under the walkway's railing, paused for a moment on the platform – and dove into the ice-cold water. It went through him like an electric shock. But the fear that he felt was even stronger and drove him through the water toward the darkest corner of the cistern.

For the first hundred feet or so, he could make out the columns. They were arranged in rows and he swam between them, making as little commotion as he could. *There's no way out.* Every ten or twenty yards, he swam underwater as far as he could, surfacing for a breath of air. Eventually, he reached a point where he could no longer see where he was going and slowed. Finally, he stopped. His feet found the floor beneath him, and he realized that the water was only about four feet deep. Turning, he glanced in the direction of the illuminated area – which was eerie and spectacular, a sunken palace – and was surprised to see how far he'd come. He was a couple hundred yards from the Medusas, far beyond the reach of the lights. There was still a commotion where he'd gone into the water – a weird cacophony of shouts amplified by the acoustics of the stone surfaces and vaulted ceiling. His dive had disturbed the tranquil surface of the water and the light bounced off it, sloshing and shifting dizzily against the columns and the vaulted ceiling. Nor was he the only one in the water, he realized. He could hear someone slogging toward him, but off to the left.

His teeth chattered and he mashed his lips together. Flashlight beams began to play against the columns, fluttering across the water, then steadying to probe the darkness. A fish slid past, grazing his leg, and he almost screamed.

He couldn't stay in the water much longer. It was just too cold. His jaw was trembling, and his body was quaking. Eventually, the cold would freeze out the tremors that he felt and, in the end, he'd turn to stone. There was a limit to how long he could stick it out.

But for now, he stayed put, watching and listening in the darkness. The ruckus around the Medusa stones was resolving itself into a semblance of guessable behavior. Some officials – guards, he supposed – had become involved, and now they were clearing the cavern of tourists. They were also searching for him in the water, moving along the gangways with their flashlights. Somehow, Danny understood that they feared that he'd drowned.

They'd find him sooner or later. He was sure of that. And then his fate would be in the hands of guards assigned to protect a cistern – a prospect that did not fill him with confidence. They'd probably put him in handcuffs and turn him over to the police – which was fine with Danny. Except that the handover would probably not go smoothly. His pursuers would not have gone away. They'd be standing outside, waiting for him to emerge. And when he did, they'd take him down – hard. Handcuffs would just make it easier.

So he began to swim toward the light.

With all its submerged spotlights, the Wishing Pool – halfway between the exit and the entrance – was the brightest spot in the cavern. When he came near it, Danny crouched in the water behind a pillar and took a look around. Guards still stood off to his left on the walkway in the vicinity of the Medusa heads. Two more were in a small rubber raft, paddling among the columns, probing the darkness with their flashlights.

Most of the crowd was gone. The remainder – maybe twenty people – were being herded up the exit steps by the guards. The steps leading down from the entrance, Danny saw, were empty.

He swam toward the broad platform at the base of the stairs, where tour groups stopped so that people's eyes could adjust to the darkness. When he reached the platform, he clambered out, making more noise than he would have liked. Stiff and clumsy from the cold, his body began to loosen up as he charged the stairs, taking them two at a time.

Vaulting the turnstile at the top, he burst out into the street, where he stood for a moment – dripping, panting, dazzled by the sunlight. Then the Brow came into view, standing sideways about five yards to his left, talking animatedly into his cell phone. There were only two ways out of the cistern. Obviously the Brow was monitoring this one and his pal was at the exit. Turning, the big man had just enough time to register surprise as Danny slammed into him, driving him backward five or six steps. *Ass over teacups,* as Dad would have said.

It was a good hit – especially for a guy who didn't

weigh more than 160 pounds, soaking wet (which he was). He used the Brow's mouth as a starting block and took off in a sprint. The last thing he wanted to do was get into a wrestling match with a guy who seemed to be equal parts gristle and bone.

He needed a crowd and he knew where to find one – at the foot of the Galata Bridge, where the ferryboats were. He turned into an alley, feet squishing as he ran, then into a side street, heading nowhere in particular except downhill. Occasionally he looked over his shoulder to see if anyone was behind him, but no – the Bulky Boys weren't built for speed.

He remembered a map that he'd seen in the in-flight magazine for Turkish Airlines. It showed the routes of the ferryboats, with parabolic arcs from one side of the Bosphorus and Golden Horn to the other. From Eminönü you could get just about anywhere in Istanbul or sail all the way to the Black Sea. Like New York, Istanbul was defined by the waters that lapped its shores.

In the end, it only took him a couple of minutes to reach the docks, which were, as ever, choked with smoke and swarming. Wet enough to draw stares but no longer dripping, he got in line to buy a ticket to wherever the next boat was going.

Üsküdar. Slip Four. Two minutes.

He walked quickly to the ferry, turning once or twice as he went, looking to see if there was anyone on his heels. But there was no one – or no one he recognized, anyway. Just a swarm of lookalike Turks with short black hair and mustaches. Crossing the gangplank that linked the ferry to the shore, he climbed the stairs to the upper deck and sat down on a worn pine seat with his back to the bulkhead, invisible to anyone on the docks. A minute ticked by, the seconds dragging toward eternity. Finally, a horn sounded. The deck trembled. And the ferry slid away from the shore.

A sigh of relief fell from his lips, and the tension drained from his shoulders. He was safe for the moment, but only for the moment. Somehow, they kept finding him. *But how?*

He hadn't used his credit cards, just cash. So it wasn't as if they were tracking him that way, even if they could. And they hadn't found him just once or twice *but three times*. There was the Abruzze Hotel in Rome, which they probably got at by hacking the voice mail on Caleigh's phone. Then they found him in Istanbul at the Asian Shore Guesthouse. But how? He'd only made a single call – to Remy Barzan – and (once bitten, twice stung) he hadn't left a message on the guy's phone. So how did they find him *that* time?

It took Danny a while to figure it out, but two possibilities suggested themselves. The first was Star-69. Someone monitoring Barzan's phone. Did they even *have* that in Turkey? Could you just dial a number to identify the last number that called the phone you were on? Then look up the number in a reverse directory? Did they have reverse directories for Istanbul? Danny had no idea. It was possible, at least. The country was obsessed with modernization.

And there was another possibility. That was the registration card that Danny had filled out at the hotel. The cards were collected each morning by the local police, who checked them against some kind of lookout list. It was the same everywhere. London. Paris. New York. You had to register.

But was Zebek that well connected? And were the

police that efficient? Maybe, Danny decided. *Apparently.*

A rusting containership – the *Kodama Maru* – glided into his field of vision, obliterating the Istanbul skyline.

Then again, Danny thought, how had Zebek even known that he was in Istanbul?

It didn't take a minute to answer that one. *He probably guessed,* Danny decided. It wouldn't have been hard to figure out where he was going. Zebek had the same names Danny did. Because Danny had given them to him. They were names on Chris Terio's phone bill. Barzan in Istanbul and what's-his-name in Oslo. Rolvaag. So maybe Zebek sent one team of knuckledraggers to Turkey and another one to Norway. And just in case Danny went home? A third team there.

That would make sense.

Except . . . it didn't explain how they'd tracked him to the street outside the cistern. Even Danny didn't know where he was going when he left the hotel. So how did the Brow know? Was it luck? *Not really,* he decided. There weren't a lot of ways out of the Cankurtaran neighborhood. It sat on a spit of land, overlooking the Sea of Marmara. Unless you had a canoe, you had to go past the Aya Sofia or the Blue Mosque. Uphill or downhill. And now that he thought about it, who had the Brow been talking to on his cell phone? Zebek? Maybe. Or maybe the Brow and his friend had colleagues. If so, it wouldn't have been hard to find him on the way out of Cankurtaran.

A gaggle of schoolgirls squeezed past, giggling, throwing shy glances Danny's way. He realized he'd been talking to himself, and he could see that the kids had picked up on it. He didn't need to speak Turkish to know what they were thinking: *Look at that guy! He's wet! He's crazy!*

Danny shook his head and laughed to himself. *It's a nightmare,* he decided. *And why is Zebek going to so much trouble, anyway?* Danny didn't know that much – not really – and what he did know he couldn't prove.

Of course, there was no way for Zebek to know that. All Zebek knew was that Danny had copied the files from Terio's computer and that he'd given them to Inzaghi. Whether Danny had bothered to *read* the files was itself an open question. By now, Zebek would have found the floppy in the duffle bag, but even that wouldn't change anything. For the billionaire, hunting down Danny Cray was just a kind of "due diligence." He had the resources. Why not use them?

The vast bulk of the containership slid from Danny's field of vision, and Istanbul reappeared, as if a curtain had been drawn aside. On the far shore, skyscrapers slalomed downhill to the water's edge, their broad white shoulders brilliant in the sunshine.

But what if it wasn't any of that? Danny wondered. *What if it wasn't the answering machine or the registration card? What if it was something else?*

A horrible thought dawned on him. *What if . . . what if I'm wearing a transponder?* A little radio button sewn into the collar of his shirt or hidden in the heel of one of his shoes.

But no, it couldn't be the shirt. The shirt was new. All his clothes were new – he'd bought them in Rome. Except the shoes. The shoes were the same ones he'd been wearing when he went to meet Zebek the day of the Palio. His "good" shoes, his Cole-Haan loafers.

He stared at his feet, feeling like a baby elephant with a tag stapled to his ear. Then he reached down and, one by one, removed his shoes. He tried to waggle the heels back and forth, but they didn't move. They seemed normal. But then, of course, they *would*. Zebek's guys were professionals. Top-of-the-line thugs. They'd probably learned shoemaking in prison.

The bottom line was: There wasn't any way to know how they'd found him. There were too many possibilities. The truth was, there was nowhere to hide, not in the twenty-first century. Between voice mail and Star-69, registration cards and transponders, hackers and enhanced 911, the right to disappear was a thing of the past.

Taking his shoes in hand, he padded to the railing of the ferry and, one by one, dropped the loafers into the green water sliding past the hull. *From now on,* he told himself, *I'll wear flip-flops.*

Behind him, the schoolgirls cackled with glee.

Thirteen

Üsküdar turned out to be a graceful suburb that sat at a remove from the city's more hectic neighborhoods. Leaving the ferry, Danny wandered along a leafy boulevard that ran beside the Bosphorus. Uncertain what to do or where to go, he bought a pair of tennis shoes at the first shoe store that he saw. Soon afterward, he found himself standing outside a barbershop, looking in the window at a signed photograph of a young Turkish soccer star. The kid's head had been shaved so closely that it looked as if a shadow was lying upon it.

Entering the shop, Danny pointed enthusiastically to the picture and then to himself. The barber was only too happy to oblige and, using an electric razor, accomplished the deed in about three minutes. While the barber's assistant swept the American's blond-tipped locks from the floor, Danny stared at himself in the mirror – at once aghast and pleased.

He looked nothing like himself.

Leaving the barbershop, he returned to the port and bought a ticket to Besiktas, which lay across the Bosphorus from Üsküdar. The crossing was spectacular, with the ferry plowing through the waves toward a sort of Versailles, a seaside castle, backed by a forest of condominiums and office buildings. He would have liked to have known the name of the castle, but there was no one to ask, and besides . . .

Debarking, he went in search of a travel agency and soon found one – though no one seemed to speak English. Eventually a young man put a finger into the air and Danny understood that he was to wait. This he did until a much older fellow appeared. Peering at Danny through wire-rimmed glasses, the old Turk said, "And you would like to go to?"

"Uzelyurt," Danny replied.

The man blinked and ran a hand through his gunmetal-gray hair. Then he leaned closer as if to hear better. "Excuse?"

"I'm told it's near Diyarbakir," Danny explained.

Frowning, the man chewed on Danny's pro-nunciation for a while, and then he understood. "Deeyarbakeer!" he exclaimed. "What an interesting place to visit!"

"Is it?"

"Absolutely! From airport to city – one knife fight guaranteed. In the city, who knows?"

If he had to wait in the Istanbul airport, he'd have preferred the nonsmoking restaurant. But he saw at a glance that if he waited there, he'd be the only one doing so, and the last thing he wanted to do was stick out like a sore thumb. Better to disappear in the occluded atmosphere of the restaurant's counterpart, where smoking was not only permitted but enthu-siastically embraced.

Finding a booth, he sat with his back to the wall and his eyes on the entrance. Dressed as he was, bald as he was, he might have passed for a Turk, an impression he encouraged by spreading a copy of an Istanbul daily, *Cumhuriet*, on the table before him.

Unlike those around him, time did not fly. A cup of soup. A cup of coffee. A glass of apple tea. Then a woman's voice came over the public-address system, announcing that the flight to Diyarbakir was delayed until nine forty-five.

It was pitch-dark outside when his flight was finally called. He let another ten minutes pass, hoping to avoid the crowd, then hurried toward the gate indicated on his boarding pass.

He half expected to find Gaetano and the Brow waiting for him, but they were nowhere to be seen. This was a relief, but the fact remained that they kept finding him and he was just guessing about how they were doing it. He didn't *know* that it was a transponder in his shoes. Or someone hacking answering machines. Or tracing hotel registrations. He told himself that unless you believed in the supernatural, it had to be some combination of those factors.

Did Zebek's thugs know that he'd gone to the AFP looking for Remy Barzan? Did they know he was on his way to Uzelyurt? Maybe so. *Probably*. It wouldn't be a big intuitive leap.

The sounds of people speaking Turkish washed around him, making Danny feel isolated. He shuffled forward in line, thinking that even if his moves could be anticipated, what else could he do? It seemed to him that there was still something at stake, that Zebek had something to hide – because people kept getting whacked. Danny had to find out what that something was, and as far as he knew, there were only two paths to that knowledge. One went through Barzan, the other by way of Rolvaag. And while his moves might be predictable, they were the only moves he had.

There were the usual security checks on the way to

the gate. He stepped through the metal detector, expecting to be patted down on the other side, but found instead that it was the women, and especially the ones in traditional dress, who were searched by the glum-faced guards.

At the gate itself, each of the passengers was made to walk past the baggage carts and identify his or her suitcases. As they did, the security guards made a chalk mark on each one. This led to an awkward moment, with Danny pantomiming that he had no suitcases to identify while the guard glared at him as if he was wasting his time. Finally, a woman in a head scarf laughed: "He doesn't know what you are saying. He thinks you're making fun of him." With a chuckle, she turned to the guard and said something in Turkish. With a scowl, he waved Danny along.

The plane was packed – every seat taken. No first class. No business class. Just folks. Danny found a window seat next to an olive-skinned man with a brace of gold teeth. The man smiled at Danny and offered him a handful of pistachio nuts. It was the second act of kindness that he had been shown by a Turk – the first was Hasan's decision to take it on the chin for his guest – and it made Danny feel good about the people around him.

Half an hour into the flight, dinner was served. The container showed a red silhouette of a pig imprinted with a circle, bisected by a diagonal line.

*No pork was used
to prepare this meal.*

A vegetarian, Danny would have preferred a meatless dinner, but this was Turkey and vegetarians were about as common as storks. Popping the little plastic bag that contained an array of ice-cold utensils, he patiently separated the vegetables and rice from the meat, leaving a little mound of chicken in yogurt sauce at the side of his tray.

As he ate the rice and veggies, he thought about what he'd learned from Mamadou's e-mail – which wasn't much. He didn't believe Jason Patel's death was "a gay thing." Not for a second. But the suggestion about industrial espionage had been interesting. Maybe that *was* at the heart of it all.

Zebek had gone to a lot of trouble to locate Terio's computer – so he could destroy the files that were on it. The only reason anyone would do that would be if the files were incriminating. So maybe that was it. Maybe Terio's files consisted of blueprints and plans, or correspondence and reports between Zebek or his agents and scientists at another firm.

Terio hadn't been a scientist, but he'd certainly gotten interested in some very esoteric technology. That was obvious from the books on his shelves. Not the ones on religion – religion was his field. But the other ones, the ones about "protein computers" and stuff.

Danny had no idea what a protein computer was – the term was an oxymoron, like *cold heat*. When he thought about it, the only thing that came to mind was a T-bone steak with a little pick and a tiny banner that read: INTEL INSIDE. Still, it had to be about something way high-tech, because Terio was talking with Jason Patel and Patel was the tech-meister at Very Small Systems. *So . . .*

Danny looked out the window at the reddening sky. *So what?* he thought. It had something to do with technology – but what didn't? He was sitting in a plastic seat at thirty-five thousand feet, eating genetically modified rice that had been cooked in a microwave by a flight attendant who probably had been cloned. *Everything* had to do with technology.

The only thing that was certain, really, was that Zebek was killing people. Inzaghi had been killed because the priest had seen the computer files. That was a fact to which Danny could attest. It seemed reasonable to suppose that Terio had been murdered because of what was on those files, that they reflected knowledge in Terio's possession, knowledge damaging to Zebek. As for Jason Patel, he'd been caught up in the same tar baby. Until Danny told Zebek about Terio's phone calls to Patel, the scientist had been fine. Then he became an obit.

As for Danny himself, his own circumstances were as bleak as the dead men's. He'd had the files in his possession and so might have read them – reason enough, it would seem, to whack him. And then there was the revenge thing: he'd tricked Zebek by copying the files for Inzaghi, which gave the billionaire a second reason for wanting to kill him.

So it was all about information and technology – but *which* information and *what* technology? *You can't imagine what he's up to, this Zebek!* Danny sank back in his seat, frustrated. That was the trouble: Inzaghi was right. He *couldn't* imagine what Zebek was up to because –

The plane dropped like a rock. The dinner service rose up on the seat table in front of him, then slapped down again as the Airbus bottomed out and shuddered. *Air pocket,* Danny thought as the pilot's voice crackled over the intercom, first in Turkish, then in English. Danny didn't understand a word that was said in either language, but no one put his head on his knees or started screaming, so it must be okay. The seat-belt sign popped on as the plane took a second jolt, then shuddered into a wall of clouds in a way that reminded Danny of his father's Volvo surfing over the washboarded road in Maine. Across the aisle, a woman's tray clattered to the floor, and the man beside him cracked a nervous smile and bounced his eyebrows.

To Danny's amazement, none of this bothered him, though he was ordinarily a nervous flier. Somehow, he knew that whatever turbulence they encountered, whatever wind shear might find them, the plane would be safe. Because Zebck was trying to kill him, Danny continued to feel the way he had during that crazy taxi ride into Istanbul. He was immune to the everyday disasters that might befall other people. Their deaths were up for grabs, while his – well, his had been *reserved*.

The airport at Diyarbakir wasn't quite "an armed camp," but it was close. Soldiers were everywhere, walking in pairs with submachine guns cradled in their arms. And what was even more alarming, they didn't have the bored attitude of patrols on routine duty. These guys seemed to be very *alert* and their wary unease contributed a definite tension to the usually tedious process of arrival.

Only passengers were allowed in the Baggage Claim area, causing many to peer through the glass of the automatic doors and wave excitedly at those outside. Danny stood for a moment, waiting out of habit for his bags to tumble onto the carousel, then remembered that he didn't have a suitcase. That made him the first one through the doors, pressing his way through the waiting crowd. At the Turkish Air counter, he asked the clerk if he spoke English.

"Of course."

"I need to get to Uzelyurt," Danny told him. "Is there –"

The man frowned. "What is 'Uzelyurt'?"

Danny wrote the name on a scrap of paper and handed it to the clerk. "It's a city," he said. "Or a town. Small town."

The clerk frowned. Raising his head, he caught the attention of a uniformed young woman, who came to his side with a shy smile. With a glance at the paper, she gave Danny an appraising look and said, "It's near Sivas. You could take a *dolmus* to the bus station and then a bus. Or . . ." She looked him up and down, as if to decide whether or not he could afford it. "You could take a taxi."

"What's a *dolmus*?"

"It's like a van – a minibus. They go everywhere from the airport. One goes to the *otogar* – that's the bus station. Here in Diyarbakir the bus station is all the way on the other side of the city." She hesitated. "Once you get there, you might have to wait some hours for a bus."

"How much would a taxi cost?"

She considered the question, then seesawed her head. "To Uzelyurt? Maybe fifty, sixty dollars."

He was tempted. But he didn't know how much longer his money would last, so . . . no. He'd take his chances with the *otogar*. "I think . . . the bus," he said.

The clerk wrote down the words *Diyarbakir Otogar* on a slip of paper. "Show this to one of the van drivers," she told him. "He'll see that you get where you're going."

Leaving the brightly lit terminal, he found a parade of buses and vans coming and going outside. The night was warm. He showed his slip of paper to a man with an exuberant mustache and was directed to a white minivan that already held a number of travelers. He took his place in the middle seat and, when a man spoke to him, shrugged an apology and said, "American." This actually earned him many smiles.

Those around him, having just arrived from a trip, talked excitedly. He found their enthusiasm engaging – so unlike the frequent fliers he usually saw, glazed, bored, and worn-out, muttering into their cell phones on the Dulles shuttle. Everyone here was friendly – although maybe this was because he didn't speak their language. They treated him with a kindness usually reserved for children. Still, their smiles and encouraging looks made him feel upbeat. And there was another positive thing: no sign of Gaetano or the Bulky Boys.

Five minutes from the airport, the *dolmus* was made to stop at an army checkpoint. The soldiers who came to the van were humorless teenagers in camouflage, carrying what Danny guessed were Uzis or maybe Kalashnikovs. He wasn't up on his automatic weapons, but he did know enough to pay attention to people holding them. Ordering everyone out, the soldiers stood at the side of the road, checking IDs and poking at the baggage. Danny's passport, still damp from the cistern, provoked a certain amount of grumbling and questions he didn't understand.

"Washing machine," he said, and made a gesture with his hands – a gesture that, he had to admit, looked nothing like anything any washing machine had ever done. The guards stared, frowned.

Finally, one of them smiled. "Maytag," he said, and explained the situation to his buddy, who ventured a commiserating look. Returning Danny's passport with a friendly salute, the soldiers waved their weapons at the *dolmus,* indicating that everyone should reboard.

Twenty minutes later, they arrived at the outskirts of Diyarbakir, following what seemed to be a ring road that skirted the old part of the city.

Danny didn't know what he'd been expecting, but Diyarbakir was a surprise. It was modern and sprawling, with vast apartment blocks whose curtained windows were aglow with what Danny had begun to think of as "Third World light" – a late-night mix of fluorescence and CNN. The modernity of Diyarbakir shouldn't have surprised him. Had he imagined that outside Istanbul everyone was living in a yurt?

Not really. In fact, he hadn't imagined anything. That was the point. Until recently, he'd given no more thought to Turkey than he had to Bulgaria or Kyrgzstan. And now, here he was, with these cheerful strangers, not just in Turkey, but headed for a town so remote that even Turks had to look it up.

They arrived at the bus station a little after midnight. Entering the terminal, Danny found a bewildering array of ticket windows, each of which seemed to be run by a different bus line. Not that it mattered: every one of them was closed.

It occurred to Danny that he could head out in search of a hotel or ask a cab driver to take him to one. But there were no cabs outside the terminal – at least nothing that looked like a cab to him – so that was out.

So was the idea of wandering around Diyarbakir at one A.M., looking for a place to crash. With a sigh, he went back into the terminal and, seeing a plastic bench, lay down upon it under the watchful eyes of a photograph of the "founder of modern Turkey," Kemal Atatürk. Soon he was fast asleep.

Dawn arrived at the end of a nightstick, gently prodding him in the ribs. Blinking awake, he found an irritated policeman standing over him, repeating something that sounded like "Uyanmak!"

"Sorry. . . ."

The cop stepped back, confused, abashed. "Amerik?"

Danny sat up, pinched the sleep from his eyes, and got to his feet. "Yeah. Look, I'm sorry –"

"Is good," the policeman said, and, with a crisp nod, turned on his heel.

Danny looked around and saw that the terminal was coming alive. Light streamed in through the grimy windows overhead as passengers filtered in, lugging oversized plastic suitcases and swollen knapsacks. He bought a cup of coffee from a vendor with a rolling cart and thought about how he was going to get from A to B.

Fully half of the ticket windows seemed to be open for business, and he went to each of them in turn, repeating "Uzelyurt?" as if it were a snack that he was selling. But he must not have been pronouncing it right, because all he got in reply was a series of shrugs. Finally, he wrote the name on a slip of paper and showed it to an elderly man in a tattered blue uniform. The old man parsed the name and nodded to himself. Then he took Danny by the elbow and escorted him to a window at the end of the terminal. A brief conversation ensued between the old man and the yawning clerk, after which the clerk nodded his understanding. Pointing to his wristwatch, he described a circle with his index finger, looked back to Danny, and made a V sign. Two hours. The American nodded and bought a ticket.

During the long wait, Danny purchased a kind of Turkish pizza, with vegetables and cheese, and washed it down with a liter of mineral water. Then he wandered outside, thinking about Caleigh.

Even though he'd warned her not to talk to him, there was nothing to prevent *him* from calling her. If nothing else, he'd hear her voice – she'd sense his presence – and if she *did* talk to him, he'd repeat his warning in a way that she'd have to take seriously. So it wasn't as if he was calling her for no reason. Or so, at least, he rationalized.

As for the possibility that Zebek was tracking Caleigh's incoming calls, now that he'd had more time to think about it Danny had come to the conclusion that this was not how they'd traced his whereabouts in Rome or Istanbul. Even if they had a tap on her phone, they couldn't find out where he was calling from – not unless he announced his location or stayed on the line for a lot longer than he intended. He was pretty sure Star-69 would not work on a pay-phone in Turkey. The only other way to find out the origin of a call was from the phone company's own records, but those took time to post and wouldn't be available to anyone, even the phone company, for at least forty-eight hours.

He bought a one-hundred-unit phone card at a news-and-tobacco kiosk in the terminal and went looking for a public phone. He found one across the street, at the edge of a little park. Inserting the card in the slot, he was glad to find that it worked the same way that it did in the States. Then he dialed the number and waited with his heart in his throat as the phone began to ring in America.

Once. Twice. Three times. And then the message began to play. Only it wasn't the message he was used to – it wasn't the one that *he'd* recorded, the one that began, "Hi, you've reached Caleigh and Dan. . . ." It was a new message, this time in Caleigh's voice, and what it said was: "Hey! It's Caleigh. Leave a message, and I'll call you back."

Jesus Christ! he thought. *I've been expunged.*

Fourteen

The landscape beyond Diyarbakir was a mono-chromatic blond – the color of wheat fields, the color of builders' sand, the color of Caleigh's hair. The only variation was in the windbreaks of poplar trees planted in regimental lines and in the occasional vineyard. Unlike vines in America, which clung to trellises, the Turkish vines were left to sprawl against the earth.

Anatolia. The steppes. Rolling prairie, jaundiced sky.

Every fifteen or twenty minutes, the bus wound around a hill into a village or town. Gunesli, Urkelet, Sarioglan. It seemed to Danny that the adult popu-lation of these towns was almost entirely male. There were no women to be seen, or very few. And those who could be seen reminded him of nuns. Their clothing was entirely black or entirely white, and it covered them from head to foot.

At first, it appeared as if all the towns were under construction, with piles of stone everywhere and cranes standing tall against the sky. Sturdy and square, the buildings bristled with double solar panels and hot-water heaters on their roofs. But gradually, as the bus wound deeper into the countryside, the towns grew smaller and farther apart. The landscape became more rural, and he caught glimpses of shepherds standing with flocks of sheep. Farmers worked the earth with primitive plows, relying on animals in the absence of engines.

Then it all began to change again. Suddenly the bus was cruising past wildly improbable conical rock formations. These were the same honey-blond color as the earth and reminded Danny of barnacles clustered on the hull of a boat. The stone was obviously soft, because entire houses had been carved into it. From the back of the *dolmus* it looked as if the windows and doorways were perfectly "true," cut into the rock at ninety-degree angles. Peering out through the window, he saw that some of the caves had satellite dishes bolted to the rock, cars parked out front. Electric lines hung in the air like strokes from a pen.

It was the most foreign place Danny had ever been or seen or imagined. Everything was unfamiliar, and not just unfamiliar – it was strange. As the miles and minutes passed, the likelihood of learning anything he needed to know in a place as remote as this seemed slim to none. For one thing, no one seemed to speak English, and his Turkish was limited to four words: *evet, yok, tuvalet,* and *merhaba.* Danny was glad he'd picked them up, but the ability to say *yes, no, toilet,* and *hello* was unlikely to resolve the issues at hand.

Beyond the few words that he knew, there was a name that he listened for throughout the morning: *Uzelyurt.* He expected to hear it at every stop, but it was a long time coming.

Again the landscape changed. The road ran for miles along the side of a steep gorge, carved by a broad stream that had long ago slaked the thirst of dinosaurs. The road veered off to the south, and the hills softened. The blond earth deepened to a golden color, then seemed to catch fire as the *dolmus* plunged past fields of poppies, quavering in the heat. In the distance, astride a low hill, a Mediterranean villa basked in the sun. Then the bus went round another curve, and the villa was gone, and so were the poppies.

Danny wondered about the occupants of such a house in such a remote place – but not for long. A few miles down the road, the driver killed the bus's engine in a sort of parking lot at the edge of a very small town. A rusting placard announced their whereabouts: UZELYURT. It was just after noon.

Climbing out of the *dolmus*, Danny found half a dozen buses parked beneath a corrugated iron awning, with knots of people either looking bored or jostling to climb aboard. Workmen in long pants and tightly knitted caps idled against a cinder-block wall, smoking cigarettes, their eyes on the American. Then the bus that he'd taken began to pull away, rumbling off in the direction of the sun. Without wanting to, Danny inhaled the diesel fumes as he followed the *dolmus* with his eyes, suppressing an impulse to run after it.

The town consisted of a single paved road, with maybe a dozen side streets acting as tributaries. Each side of the road was fronted by a row of small shops, selling everything from groceries to farm implements. There was a gas station with a single pump, a hardware store that reeked of oil, and a welding shop that snapped, crackled, and popped. The only restaurant that he could see appeared to be closed, but there was a surprisingly nice patisserie in the middle of it all. Danny stopped in for a glass of apple tea, then ordered a second one to wash down a wedge of baklava.

Returning outside, he saw a sign for OTELI HITTITE and set off uphill in the direction of a three-story building. Midway, he stopped at a small store whose entrance was flanked by open burlap bags that brimmed with pistachio nuts, dates, and other fruit. Inside were shelves of Pepsi, beer, and water, cereal, and detergent. A rack of videos stood beside the counter on a rotating wire stand. Danny checked the offerings, which consisted mostly of American films repackaged in Turkish boxes. He recognized *Swordfish*, *Pulp Fiction*, and *The Matrix*.

He bought a toothbrush and a bottle of mineral water, two bottles of Efes Pilsen, and a paper cone filled with dried apricots. The proprietor smiled at him as he made change for a ten-million-lire note.

"Canadian?"

Danny shook his head. "American."

The man's smile expanded. "My son! He was Columbia University. Now he is Morgan-Stanley!" He gestured to a Columbia decal on the back of the cash register, then pointed to a resin replica of the rock formations around the town. "One day – he is caves. Then Ivy Lick. Then . . . I don't know!" A booming laugh.

Danny laughed. "He must be smart. Columbia's tough."

The man nodded and smiled, but Danny could tell that the grocer's English vocabulary wasn't much larger than his own repertoire of Turkish.

"Well," he said. "Catch you later."

"Oh, yes!" the grocer replied. "Later!"

The Oteli Hittite was a no-star affair, which meant that it was very basic. The "lobby" consisted of a small room with high ceilings and a front desk that was actually a desk. The old man behind the desk didn't speak English, but a sign on the wall indicated that single rooms were six million lire – about five bucks – a night.

Danny gave his passport to the old man, who clucked at its condition, then handed it back, along with a hotel registration card. He offered a pen and waited, smiling, while Danny filled out the card. When this had been done, the old man glanced at the card and placed it on top of half a dozen others. Finally, he got to his feet and, flapping his hand, gestured for Danny to follow him. Which Danny did – after grabbing the registration card and jamming it into his pocket.

They went along a dark corridor and outside to a courtyard with plastic tables shaded by large red umbrellas. A riot of flowers grew against concrete walls topped with shards of broken glass. With a tug on Danny's sleeve, the old man put the palm of his hand beneath his chin and pretended to scoop something into his mouth.

Danny smiled. "Got it. A little later, maybe."

With a deferential nod, the clerk handed him a key with the number 7 on it and gestured to a flight of stairs.

His room contained a large cot with a thin mattress, a metal table flanked by mismatched chairs, and a tired wooden dresser. A threadbare kilim lay on the tiled floor beneath a bank of windows overlooking the street. No screens, but heavy shutters, painted blue. Overhead, a single fixture held a compact fluorescent bulb encased in a pleated shade. That was it, except for a can of Raid that stood beside the cot. The insecticide gave him pause, but only for a moment. While the room was down-at-heels, it was scrupulously clean, the cot's snowy sheets crisp to the eye and deeply inviting.

Danny resisted temptation, wrote Barzan's name on the back of the bus ticket, and headed back downstairs.

The eldery desk clerk stared at the name, thought for a moment, and shook his head. Then he looked up and, with a sweet smile, returned the scrap of paper to the American.

Leaving the hotel, Danny walked out into the furnace of mid-afternoon, wincing at the light. The blond stone and treeless landscape. The bleached sky and waves of heat. It took your breath away. A woman of indeterminate age, shrouded in white from head to foot, bared her gold teeth in a silent hello. Across the street, a boy of about ten labored uphill with a dead lamb slung over his shoulder, its white eye staring. It was all so disorienting – like stumbling onto a stage set.

Halfway down the hill, he began to ask about Remy Barzan, showing the scrap of paper to one shopkeeper after another. He made his first inquiry at the grocer's, moved on to a store that sold beer and arrack, then crossed the street to a dusty carpet shop. Just inside, three young men sat near the door, hunched over a backgammon board, laughing and drinking tea. Seeing Danny, the biggest of the three, wearing a new-looking Nike T-shirt, jumped to his feet and greeted him with (literally) open arms. *"Wilkommen! Hereingekommen, bitte!"*

Danny gave him a look that was at once confused and apologetic. "Actually," he said, "I'm American."

The young Turk grinned. "Even better. My German's lousy. Where you from?"

"Washington," Danny replied, astonished to hear his own language.

The Turk's face contorted into a look of pained

commiseration. "Buhhh-ddy, buhhh-ddy," he said, miming a little set shot, "you guys *never* get into the play-offs." Turning to his friends, he translated, and they laughed along with Danny.

"Michael's gonna play," Danny told him. "That ought to help."

"I heard he got hurt," the Turk said. "Maybe no comeback after all."

Danny shrugged. "We can hope," he said. "But anyway, right now –"

"You're looking at rugs?" Before Danny could reply, he added, "You come to the right place, man."

"Listen –"

"I give you best price."

"Thanks, but –"

"Buhhh-ddy, buhhh-ddy – I am no bullshit. Best price!"

Danny shook his head. "Some other time maybe, but right now I'm looking for a person. Not a rug."

The Turk gave him a bemused look.

"A friend," Danny said. "Maybe you know him?" He handed the scrap of paper to the Turk, who glanced at it and showed it to his pals. One of them muttered something that Danny didn't catch. Finally, his *buhhh-ddy* made a soft clicking noise and jerked his head backward.

Danny had seen the gesture before: it was a Turkish way of saying no – as in No *way, never heard of him.*

"I don't think this guy's from anywhere around here," the man said. He looked at his friends. "If he was, we'd know him." Returning to his seat on a pile of rugs, he took a sip of tea and gave up on the conversation.

Suddenly there was no more *buhhh-ddy buhhh-ddy*

271

in the room, and Danny found himself standing awkwardly beside the door. "Well," he said, "thanks anyway." The others nodded without looking up.

No one said it was going to be easy.

Crossing the street to the bus station, he went into the ticket office where a neat little man stood behind a grille, helping customers. There was a short line, and Danny waited until it was his turn. Then he gave the paper to the clerk, who peered at it through a pair of gold spectacles. After a moment, he pushed the paper back to Danny, cocked his head, closed his eyes, and wagged his forefinger back and forth as if it were a windshield wiper. Then he stopped and opened his eyes.

"You know him?" Danny asked.

The clerk went through the same routine a second time, then made a point of looking over the American's shoulder to the next person in line.

He was beginning to get the point.

Leaving the bus station, he found a cabdriver who seemed eager to help, then drove away when it became apparent that the American wasn't interested in a ride. The police station (a concrete cube at the edge of town) was only a block away but turned out to be "closed." *How the hell can a police station be closed?* Danny wondered.

Nearby, a couple of soldiers sat in a Jeep, cradling their M-16s. Approaching them with a smile, Danny showed them the scrap of paper on which he had written Barzan's name, but there was no reaction. A bored glance, a shrug, and they looked away.

That's when he caught a whiff of roasting peppers, garlic, and onions wafting along the street and realized how hungry he was. With his nose as his compass, he traced the smell to an upstairs restaurant whose sign had long ago toppled from its perch above the door. Stepping inside, he found himself in a large dining room, cooled by a pair of industrial fans. Overhead, an acoustic tile ceiling bristled with scores of knotted tubes, compact fluorescents fitted into receptacles meant for what Danny guessed were prohibitively expensive incandescent bulbs.

An elderly waiter welcomed him with a bow, then led him to a refrigerated case that held an array of dishes under glass. The *mezze*, or appetizers. Danny pointed to a mound of deep-green *dolmas* stuffed with rice, a tomato-and-eggplant salad, hummus and *pide*, and a bowl of greens. The waiter nodded his approval, then sent him over to a long grill.

A light-haired man wearing a blue T-shirt presided over pyramids of kebabs, covered with plastic wrap. Danny pointed to one of the smaller piles, and the chef scowled in disapproval, gesturing toward the lamb, chicken, and sausage kebabs.

Danny shook his head. "Just veggies," he explained.

The cook looked surprised. "U.S.?"

Danny nodded.

"Hey, I got a cousin," the chef said.

"No kidding."

"Rehoboth Beach, Delaware. He's got a cleaning business."

"That's not too far from D.C., where I'm from."

"No kidding? Rehoboth – it's good?"

"Yeah," Danny said. "It's great. You know – sun, sand, the ocean." He shrugged. "Really different from here, though."

The man stuck out his hand. "I'm Atilla," he said, flashing a big smile. "Like the Hun."

Danny had to laugh at that. "Danny Cray."

Atilla gestured toward the kebabs. "So just vegetables, huh?"

"That's it."

"Boy, are you in the wrong country!" He turned a knob and flames shot up; he made an adjustment and the flames diminished. "Except for pistachios. We have the best pistachios in the world."

"Your English is great. Where'd you learn it?"

"School."

"You have good schools here?"

Attila picked up a pair of vegetable kebabs, brushed them with oil, and drizzled them with the juice from a lemon. Then he sprinkled them with salt and pepper and laid them on the grill.

"Yeah," he said, "the education system is pretty good. Everybody goes to school until they're twelve. After that, you have to qualify. High school, technical school – university, if you're smart. We've got thirty of them."

"And anyone can go?"

Attila shook his head. "No way. It's hard to get in. You have to take a test. It's very competitive."

Danny pursed his lips in sympathy.

Attila chuckled. "I know what you're thinking – I'm cooking kebabs. But, actually, I did okay. I went to Bogazici. That's a university in Istanbul. Studied economics." He looked up from the grill. " 'The dismal science.' "

"That's what they say. So why'd you study it?"

"Because that's what they gave me. It's not like you get to choose. I wanted to be a veterinarian, but the state decides what it needs. But I don't mind. Because that's where I learn English. Once you get to

274

university, almost everything is in English." He turned the kebabs.

"So . . ."

"What am I doing here?"

Danny nodded.

Attila flashed a wicked smile. "I'm making kebabs for you, my friend, what do you think?" He paused for a moment, and added, "I'm *from* here. This is my father's place, but . . . He can't be here right now. So I'm helping out."

"I see."

"You do? I don't think so."

"Why not?"

"Because he's in prison." Seeing Danny's surprise, he added, "We're Kurds. Everyone here is. Except the army – they're . . . whatever. So there's a lot of trouble, you know?"

"I heard."

"They want to kill the culture, so they go after the language. Until ten years ago, we can't teach it, speak it, broadcast it. I can't even name my kids what I want. I have to give them Turkish names."

"So it's better now?"

He turned the kebabs again. "Not much. Personally? I'm moving to the States, start out with my cousin. Soon as I get a visa. Other people give up. Or join the PKK."

Danny didn't know what the initials meant, and his face must have shown it.

"They're Kurdish separatists," Attila explained. "Very hard-line. Ankara calls them 'terrorists.' "

"And are they?"

Attila smiled. "Yeah. Big-time. Only lately, kind of quiet." He paused and laughed.

"Why is that?"

"Their leader got caught."

"You don't seem all that sorry."

Attila shrugged. "Little towns like this – people get squeezed. The PKK and the army think the same way: you're part of the solution, or you're part of the problem. So you're fucked, no matter what you do."

Danny frowned. "You mean –"

"These guys come in – I'm talking about the PKK – they come in, they want a little help. Food, money, a place to sleep. You don't give them what they want, they fuck you up. Big-time. Then they take what they want. Because they *can*. They've got guns. So, naturally, you give them what they want and, after a while, they move on. Like locusts. Then the army shows up. And they say, 'We hear you're helping the rebels.' *Pow!*" He chuckled bitterly. "That's how guys like my father end up in prison. And that, my friend, is why *I'm* making kebabs." With a grin, he lifted the sizzling skewers from the grill and slid them onto a platter. Then he dished out some rice with a dollop of yogurt sauce and gestured toward the dining room.

Danny carried his plate to a table where the appetizers were waiting.

"What do you like to drink?" Atilla asked. "Lemonade? It's not from a can."

"Yeah, great," Danny said, taking a seat.

Atilla called out to the waiter. Nearby, a quartet of old men sat in the corner playing cards. The waiter hustled back with two lemonades. Atilla pointed to the chair across from Danny. "You don't mind?"

"Not at all." Besides the old guys playing cards, Danny was the only customer.

Atilla sat down, sipped his lemonade. "You're not a tourist," he said.

Danny laughed. "You can tell?"

"Yeah."

"How?"

"Because we don't *have* any tourists. We're ten miles from Syria, twenty miles from Iraq. So what we get is drug dealers. Spies. Carpet buyers. Snakeheads. Once in a while, an academic. Which are you?"

Danny shook his head. "Actually ... I'm a sculptor." The hummus was delicious.

" 'A sculptor,' " Atilla repeated, as if Danny had confessed to being a stork.

"Right," Danny said, "but that's not why I'm here. I'm looking for someone."

"In Uzelyurt?" Atilla looked incredulous.

"Unh-huh."

"Well, that shouldn't be hard. What's his name?"

"Barzan," Danny told him.

The Turk's face went slack.

"Remy Barzan," Danny added.

Atilla nodded thoughtfully, then drained his lemonade and got to his feet. "I better get back."

"Wait a second!" For the second time in an hour, all the goodwill had flown from a room. "You know who I'm talking about, right?"

The Turk shrugged. "Maybe. So what?"

"How do I find him?"

"Ask around." He turned to go, paused, and turned back again. "Though maybe that's not such a good idea."

Danny didn't get it. "Why not?"

"Because I don't think he wants to be found."

The American nodded. "That's what I figured, but –"

Atilla put his hands on the table and leaned toward him. "Look," he said. "This isn't the kind of place you come into and ask a lot of questions. Remy's got a big family, a big clan. The Barzans are related to everybody, and they're involved in a lot of things."

"What kind of things?"

Atilla straightened up with a derisive snort. "There's a civil war – it's been going on for a hundred years. They do what they have to do."

"Like what?"

"Whatever it takes. And they do it for all of us."

Danny didn't know what he was talking about, and it must have shown.

"The old man – the grandfather – has a lot of responsibilities," Atilla explained. "He's an Elder."

Something clicked. "You mean . . . the Yezidis."

It was the cook's turn to be surprised. Finally, he said, "Right."

"Then –"

"Look – you want to find Remy? Maybe you should see Mounir."

"Who's 'Mounir'?"

"The old man. Sheik Mounir. He's Remy's grandfather. I don't think he'll tell you anything, but if you go door-to-door like this . . ." He shook his head. "You could get hurt."

Danny raised his hands up in mock surrender. "So where do I go?"

The cook sighed. "You saw the poppies?"

Danny thought about it. The ride into town on the *dolmus*. The fields ablaze with flowers. "You mean . . . on the way into town?"

Atilla nodded. "And the house? The big house —"
"On the hill? That villa?"

For some reason, the cabdriver wouldn't take him where he wanted to go, so he hitched a ride out of town in an old truck driven by a jovial farmer. The truck was ripe with barnyard smells, but it was only a few miles to the villa. After ten minutes, the truck turned a corner and there it was, bolted to a hill in a sea of poppies.

"This is good," Danny announced, smiling his thanks.

The farmer glanced at the house, rolled his eyes, and swore beneath his breath. Then he stepped on the gas.

"Hey! Hold up! We're here!"

The farmer clicked his tongue and threw his head back. Danny got the message but didn't know what to do. The truck rumbled on for the better part of a mile, with Danny getting up the courage to jerk the keys from the ignition. Then the house and the poppy fields disappeared from view and the farmer brought the truck to a shuddering stop in the middle of the road. Abruptly he leaned across the front seat and threw open the door. *"Ayril!"* he ordered. *"Ayril!"*

So now Danny knew a fifth word in Turkish. *At this rate,* he thought, *I'll be fluent in about a hundred years.*

It was a ten-minute walk back to the Barzan spread, where a country lane arced through the poppy fields toward the house. Walking uphill, Danny saw that the villa stood behind a stone wall whose ramparts glistened with broken glass. It was not the kind of house that one could approach unmolested and, sure enough, he began to sense that he wasn't alone.

Turning, he found two young men walking quietly behind him, about fifty feet away. Each of them was smoking a cigarette and carried an automatic weapon as if it were a lunch pail. Danny smiled nervously and gave a little wave – "Hey" – but the greeting went unacknowledged. His companions continued as they were, their faces impassive, their distance respectful but easy to close.

Soon he arrived at the wall in front of the house. Passing beneath a stone arch whose massive wooden doors were thrown open to the sun, he entered a plain courtyard whose only adornments were a silver Jaguar and a burbling fountain, slick with algae.

By then, the young guns were at his side.

After ascertaining that their visitor spoke no Turkish, the older of the two patted the air with his left hand, indicating that Danny should stay where he was. Then he muttered something to his friend and went into the house.

Minutes crawled by as Danny lounged against the fountain, admiring the house under the unwavering gaze of the young man with the AK – or whatever it was. An enormous villa in the Mediterranean style, it had tall rectangular windows and unpainted stucco walls. Each of the windows, Danny saw, was occluded by a curtain, drawn tight.

Soon the guard who had gone into the house emerged. Gesturing for Danny to raise his hands and spread his legs, he handed his weapon to the second guard and began to pat the American down. This was not the kind of frisking that a man might suffer at the security gate at Heathrow or LaGuardia. It was a slow and meticulous *search*, a massage, almost, that took the better part of a minute. When the search was finally done, the guard retrieved his AK and gestured for Danny to accompany him into the house.

The villa's interior was nothing like Danny had imagined. He had expected to find a page from one of the catalogs that Caleigh was always receiving – French Country Living or something like that. Instead, he found himself in what might have been the lobby of a Four Seasons hotel. Subdued lighting. Air-conditioning. Wood paneling. Expensive and tasteful furniture of no obvious provenance. Classical music played softly in another room, and it seemed to Danny that he might have been anywhere. The only clue to the villa's actual whereabouts was a collection of old prints hanging from the walls in plain gold frames. On inspection, he saw that these were nineteenth-century steel engravings on Ottoman themes: the covered souk in Istanbul, some dhows sailing on the Golden Horn –

"Avete desiderato vederli?"

Danny swung round to the voice and found an elderly man in a dark business suit regarding him through a pair of gold spectacles. Despite the man's age, he had a full head of iron-gray hair and a Vandyke beard of the same steely hue. Though stooped with age and leaning on a cane, he was still as tall as Danny.

"I'm sorry," Danny said, "but –"

"You don't *capiche*." The old man smiled. "My friend, here, thinks that you're Italian."

Relieved to find that the old man spoke English, Danny introduced himself and asked if he was the grandfather of Remy Barzan.

"Yes. I am Sheik Mounir Barzan."

"I was hoping you could help me," Danny told him. "It's important that I find him right away."

The old man frowned. "You are a friend of Remy?"

Danny shook his head. "Not really. I mean, we haven't actually met."

"And yet . . . you've come all this way?"

Danny shrugged. "I was in Rome. It's not so far, and . . . it's important that I see him."

The old man looked skeptical. "I think Remy would prefer to be alone right now."

"I understand that," Danny explained. "But we have a problem, a problem in common. And I thought we might be able to help each other."

The old man walked slowly to the window and gazed out across the courtyard. "I'm afraid I haven't seen Remy in several weeks."

"But you know where he is," Danny guessed.

"Perhaps," he replied.

Danny sighed, uncertain how much he should say. Finally, he said, "Remy's in a lot of trouble."

Mounir Barzan nodded to himself. "I know. That's why he's come home. And what about you, Mr. Cray?"

"I'm in trouble, too."

The old man gave him a look of commiseration. "I'm sorry to hear that. Perhaps *you* should go home, as well."

Danny shook his head. "It's not that easy. I really need to talk to your grandson."

The old man's shoulders rose and fell, as if to say, *I'm sorry, but there's nothing I can do.*

"Look," Danny said. "I don't know how much you know about this –"

"I don't know *anything* about it, Mr. Cray. Remy hasn't confided in me."

"Well, I know it sounds melodramatic, but . . . the point is: There's a man who wants to kill him."

The old man's face twisted into a frown. Then, ever so slowly, it softened. "These things happen. Young men get in trouble. He'll be safe where he is."

Danny gave him a skeptical look. "The man who's looking for him has a lot of resources."

Mounir Barzan bared his teeth in a thin smile. "We're a big family," he said. "If Remy needs help, he knows where to find it."

"Mr. Barzan, I don't think you understand –"

"I think I do. You said that you and Remy have a problem in common. Which means that the man who's looking for Remy is also looking for you. Is that correct?"

Danny nodded.

"Then I'm sure you'll understand: the last thing Remy wants or needs is a visit from a stranger." He paused to let the words sink in, then turned to the young security guard and gave an order. "Yusuf will take you back to your hotel," he said. "When I see Remy, I'll mention your visit. Now, if you don't mind, I'm leaving on a trip tomorrow."

Climbing the stairs to his hotel room, Danny turned on the fan, kicked off his shoes, and dropped into bed, exhausted by the heat and discouraged by his visit to the villa. His intention was to nap for a few minutes, maybe half an hour at the most, but everything conspired against it. The crisp sheets. The breeze from the fan. The artificial twilight conjured by the closed wooden shutters.

Without wanting to, he slept for hours, and when he awoke there was a long moment of deep confusion. The hotel room had a strange, almost surreal cast to it, and he felt as if he'd slept through the night. But no.

He'd fallen asleep in the late afternoon and, since then, the shuttered twilight had given way to a more pervasive darkness. Squinting at his watch, he saw that it was almost ten P.M. Though he wasn't hungry, he knew that he should eat – and anyway, it wasn't as if he could go back to sleep. He might as well go out for a beer.

Then he was walking downhill toward the restaurant and feeling the cold. One thing about the steppes – when night fell, the temperature dropped in a hurry. He supposed this was because there wasn't anything to hold the sun's heat. The landscape was Marilyn blond, the macadam road a characteristic gray. Most of the buildings were the color of cement, the others whitewashed. Nor was the town large enough to create its own microclimate. There were only a few cars and trucks, a streetlight here and there, fluorescent lights in houses – and that was it. So when the heat went, it was *gone*.

Soon he found his way to an outdoor café that he hadn't noticed before. It was in a courtyard on one of the side streets. A charcoal brazier sat in one corner, its embers covered in white ash, while a television glowed on the wall. Grizzled workmen sat at sturdy wooden tables, smoking cigarettes and playing cards. Danny recognized a couple of people – one of the boys from the carpet shop, the waiter from the restaurant, some men he'd buttonholed to ask about Remy Barzan.

With a nod to the locals, he took a table near the hibachi and ordered a bottle of Efes Pilsen. Then he leaned back in his chair and gazed up at the sky, expecting to be blown away by the kind of starscape that you can only see in the distant boondocks. But no.

The night was gauzy with dust, the stars smudged and faded.

Which was more or less the way he felt himself. He'd spent most of the day sticking his head in doorways and making a general nuisance of himself. The visit to the villa had been a washout, and now . . . if Remy Barzan was in Uzelyurt, it was a bigger secret than the Manhattan Project.

Which left him . . . where? On the morning bus to Diyarbakir. From there, it was a short flight to Istanbul. But what was the point? He'd learned nothing in Turkey – except that he was tapped out. Istanbul was no better than Uzelyurt or Washington. He'd try Oslo, sure, but he wasn't optimistic. After that there were no more leads to follow, so the only thing left to do was . . .

Run.

It was all he could do. But how long could that last? Sooner or later – in fact, sooner – he'd run out of money, and Zebek would close in. It wouldn't be all that hard. He'd probably use Fellner Associates. As Danny knew, Fellner was good at finding people who didn't want to be found. He'd worked a couple of the cases himself: an accountant who'd looted his clients' assets, a husband who'd taken the kids to Paraguay. So it wouldn't take long. And Zebek's instructions would be short and sweet: *Let us know where he is, and we'll take it from there.*

I'm a dead man, Danny thought.

In the end, he had three beers rather than one and left the café a few minutes before midnight. Though he wasn't conscious of making any decisions, he found that he had. Forget Oslo. He could hunt down this

Rolvaag guy on the telephone, on the Net – not that he believed it would go anywhere. Rolvaag was probably dead.

Danny's plan was to catch the bus in the morning, fly to Istanbul, and take the first flight to Washington. There, at least he'd be on his home turf. And who knows? If he went to the police and made a lot of noise, maybe Zebek would back off.

He could feel his mood begin to lift. It was the beer, of course, but it was also the prospect of seeing Caleigh again. Passing a ragged little park with stunted pine trees, he suddenly realized how dark it was. Most of the light came from a crescent moon. Working streetlights were few and far between. Most of them seemed to have been vandalized: bouquets of wire fanned out from the tops of the standards, where the fixtures should have been. In all likelihood, that was the municipality's doing. Electricity was expensive in Turkey – you could tell from the prevalence of solar panels, fluorescent bulbs, and . . . darkness.

A tractor rumbled by and then a dump truck with a busted muffler. He passed some teenage kids playing a game that might have been tag. He paused to watch, but they were hard to see, tearing around in the dark, hooting and jeering, giggling.

At the foot of the hill leading up to the hotel, he passed a dry-goods store. Like everything else, it was closed, but it had an open feel, despite that. Its goods were still outside and still on display. Kettles and washboards, colanders and toilet brushes, candles and bicycle tires – and a lot more – were looped together with a length of chain and hung above the doorway.

It's like being in a ghost town, Danny thought, *only I'm the ghost.*

A black Mercedes glided downhill on the other side of the road, the thin light of a street lamp sliding over its hood. As the car passed, it seemed to slow, and Danny hesitated, thinking that he'd been mistaken for a local – and that, in a moment, the window would roll down and the driver would ask him for directions. He was getting ready to shrug an apology when the Mercedes suddenly picked up speed and and he realized he'd made a terrible mistake.

Fifteen

He'd heard it a million times. Everybody had. Whether it was a semi jackknifing on the interstate or a purse snatching on a downtown street, everyone agreed on one thing: *It happened so fast!* That's what they said. And they were right. They were always right.

The Mercedes went from zero to fast in an instant, tires squealing as it swung into a U-turn that ended prematurely as a J-, blocking the street in front of him. There wasn't any time to react. He turned in time to see another car rock to a stop at the curb, just behind him. Doors flew open. Men jumped out. Reflexively he took a step backward and had started to turn when an arm curled around his neck and jerked him off his feet. Dragged toward the Mercedes, he lashed out with his foot, connected with something soft, and drew a yelp of pain. Then he was wrestled into the backseat and shoved to the floor. A knee came down hard against his spine and stayed there.

The car was roaring uphill on its way out of town, accelerating into the darkness. Angry and scared, Danny struggled to his hands and knees, then crashed back down to the carpet when a fist slammed into his ear. A shower of lights shot through his vision. Pain pressed against the back of his eyes.

A voice whispered, "You move, I cut you." He could feel the tip of a knife against the skin under his jaw.

288

There was nothing he could do.

The air went out of him, and he subsided against the carpeting. Someone wrenched his arms behind his back and bound his hands with plastic cuffs. Then, nothing. He lay there on the floor, listening to his heart pound, the carpet's synthetic smell filling his nostrils. He had no idea where they were taking him. To a cave or to one of the gorges that he'd seen on the way into Uzelyurt. Some dark place where they could kill him and dump him without a fuss.

He didn't hear anything for what seemed like a long while – just the whir of the tires and the engine's muffled roar. A lyric from an old Dylan song went round and round in his head, like a roulette ball that wouldn't quit:

> *There must be some way outta here,*
> *Said the Joker to the Priest . . .*

The line might have been funny if he wasn't so scared. But he was – he was *so* scared. And not just of dying. Zebek had a way of killing people that gave dying a bad name.

Suddenly the car swerved to the right, rumbling over a washboarded surface onto a long stretch of gravel. Danny could hear the pebbles pinging off the undercarriage. Then the driver braked, the car slid, and a rush of adrenaline slammed through his heart. *This is it,* he thought. *This is how it ends. At night, in the cold, on the side of the road. Soon I'm going to be garbage.*

A whiff of garlic and his captor's breath, hot against his ear. "Nothing," the man whispered. Danny stayed where he was, crumpled on the floor with the cool blade of a knife pressed against his throat. The seconds crawled by as if they were minutes.

Then the driver's door opened. There was a rush of cold air and a burst of Turkish. The man with the knife grabbed Danny by the shirt collar and pulled him up into a sitting position. There was only enough time for a glance. He saw the back of someone's head, a beam of light through the windshield, shapes. He said, "Wha –" and then someone clapped a strip of duct tape over his mouth and a pillowcase fell over his head. Finally, a cord tightened the hood around his neck, and he was dragged out of the car.

The pillowcase smelled like soap.

An arm went round his shoulders and pulled him close. "Listen to me – *buhhh-ddy*."

Danny stiffened, recognizing the voice. The guy from the carpet shop! He was sure of it.

"Be cool," the man was saying in a soothing voice. "Don't fight it, okay? You fight, and I'm gonna have to give you a shot. I don't want to do that, y'know? With Ketamine, you get sick, you vomit – you could drown. So be cool, okay?"

Danny nodded. Mumbled. Swayed where he was standing.

"We're going to put you in a truck. So maybe it gets a little rough, y'know?"

Danny's stomach folded into a knot.

When he was a kid, his older brothers used to torture him in the good-natured way that siblings do. Once, they put him in a cardboard box, sealed it up, and tumbled him down a steep hill. (He'd gotten a concussion.) Another time, when the family visited a Civil War fort in Maine, his brothers dangled him over the edge of the ramparts, with the ocean foaming onto the rocks below. Kev had one leg, Sean the other, and it cracked them up, pretending they were losing their grip. "Uh-ohhh – almost lost him that time."

In their defense, they never let anyone else pick on him. On the contrary. But their persecution taught him a lesson: Giving in never gets you anywhere. Giving in just makes it easier for someone to mess with you. That's why he hit Kevin with a roll of quarters that night, came up behind him and hit him so hard it was scary, hit him even though he knew he'd get pounded. You had to make it hard on people who wanted to hurt you. You had to make them think twice.

He kept his brothers in mind as the Buddy/Buddy Guy talked about how important it was to stay calm. But the way Danny saw it, it wasn't important at all. He was as good as dead. Whether he drowned in his own vomit or was beaten to death in the boondocks was six of one and half a dozen of the other. So he didn't have anything to lose when he locked in on Buddy/Buddy's voice and, taking a step forward, drove his forehead down into what he hoped was the bridge of the other man's nose.

There was a satisfying crack, a bark of pain, and . . . a cherry bomb went off in his brain. He saw the flash, felt his head explode, found the darkness.

When he came to, a minute or an hour or a day later, he couldn't figure out where he was – or even where he *could* be. Somewhere hot. He was soaked with sweat. And there was a kind of rushing noise that seemed to be coming from inside his head. His hands were bound behind his back, and he couldn't see anything. The pillowcase was still in place, as was the duct tape. Still, he could tell that he was in an enclosure of some kind. A box or . . .

Then it hit him, and a geyser of terror sparked through his chest. His body arched, and he flailed like a fish on the deck of a boat, flopping this way and that in a seizure of pure fear. *I'm buried alive.*

Only he wasn't. He couldn't be. The noise. It wasn't coming from his head. It was coming from an engine. It was road noise, and, wherever he was, he was moving. He was in a car, then, or a truck. In the trunk or under the chassis.

Slowly he began to calm down. And as he did, his other senses started to function. He could smell hot metal, oil, diesel exhaust. Once in a while, a pebble pinged against the metal underneath him. Less often, when the driver braked or turned, Danny's body rolled or slid, sent this way and that at the mercy of Newtonian forces that he could neither anticipate nor resist. A couple of times the truck – it had to be a truck – hit a bump and sent his body careening against the sides of his container. In this way, he was able to work out the dimensions of the thing that held him. It was, he figured, about the size of a coffin.

But it wasn't a coffin, he told himself. For one thing, it was made of metal. And it seemed to be suspended from the undercarriage of a truck. Whatever the container was, it was stifling inside – so much so that it took all of Danny's willpower to suppress the panic in his heart. *I can't breathe. There isn't enough air.*

He gnawed at the duct tape over his mouth, hoping to bite through it to the air, but the task was impossible. The taste in his mouth was a rubbery, chemical mess. Nauseated and breathing through his nose, Danny felt his consciousness begin to flicker. The darkness intensified, and then . . .

The truck came to a stop. Or maybe it was already

stopped. He couldn't tell. He couldn't be sure if he'd experienced the truck slowing to a halt or if he'd woken to find that the prison in which he found himself was suddenly at rest. In either case, he felt the silence as a kind of free fall, as if the ground had fallen away from beneath him. The engine's roar had been his only reference point and context. Now, he was alone and *at rest*.

His heart stumbled.

Then he heard the doors of the truck open. Voices. The engine ticking as it cooled. At first, he thought that they'd arrived at their destination, that they'd be coming to get him at any moment, but then he understood (although he wasn't sure how) that the truck was at a checkpoint. He tried shouting, but the noise stayed in his head. He rolled against the sides of the container, but there wasn't enough room, really, to make any noise. Then the engine roared to life as suddenly as it had stopped. Gears ground, and they were moving again.

He felt sick. Entrained by the engine, his body trembled uncontrollably. His head was pounding, and his stomach heaved. Panic came at him in waves. He worried that there wasn't enough air and then that he'd throw up and drown – just as his buddy from the carpet shop had warned. *He should have listened.* Sweat rolled off his temples and stung his eyes. He was completely dehydrated. He was soaking wet.

It occurred to him that he would probably die before his captors could kill him.

Sooner or later, he thought, *they have to let me out – so they can kill me. So that's when I'll make my move,* he decided. *When they pull me out of the truck, I'll make my move.*

He rocked on for a while, holding that thought. Then asked himself: *So what's my "move"? I'm handcuffed and blindfolded. The most I can do is throw up and fall down – which doesn't really count as a "move." So, maybe my move is, I'm all outta moves.*

He thought about where they might be going and why they hadn't killed him already. It didn't make sense – unless they had something "special" in mind. *Don't go there,* he told himself. *Don't even think about it. Think about . . . Washington. Your friends and colleagues.*

He could imagine the scene at the gallery, with Ian in rapt conversation with the Earring Lady. What was her name? She always wore huge dangling earrings. It irritated him unreasonably that he couldn't remember her name. He could imagine the Earring Lady asking about him: *Whatever happened to Danny Cray? Such a nice boy!*

And Ian, looking pained: *You didn't hear? They found him – migod, he was skinned alive. In Turkey or some such place! His girlfriend was devastated – of course! I mean, you can imagine. But she's moved on.*

He giggled. Sobbed. Lost track of what he'd been thinking. In the roaring darkness of the container, Danny's lucidity came and went, as if there were a loose connection in his brain. Time passed – in clumps – until a torrent of gravel flew up against the truck's undercarriage, creating a thunderous racket. Danny felt the driver brake and the truck crunch to a stop.

This is it!

He heard a chain dragged through the shackle of a lock, then stiffened as someone's hands grasped him under the arms and dragged him into the cool night air. Where he stood, swaying blindly from side to side. It

294

was definitely time for his move, but he was having trouble staying on his feet. He lost the battle, his legs buckled, and he sank to his knees like a priest at prayer.

He was thinking, *I won't hear the shot. I won't even feel it.* He imagined the exit wound, the tumbling cartridge blowing out his eye. Then someone took him by the arm and jerked him to his feet. Stumbling over the rough ground, he went where he was led. A door creaked open on its hinges, and he was guided to a straight-backed chair. Someone cut the plastic cuffs from his wrists, then used a roll of duct tape to lash his arms to the sides of the chair. A second person tied his ankles to the chair's legs, using the same material.

Then the hood was jerked from his head and the tape was stripped from his mouth. The cold oxygen-rich air sent a charge of euphoria through him. But it didn't last. As uncomfortable as the hood had been, it had served a purpose that might be construed as benign. So long as his captors took precautions against being seen, there was at least some hope that he might be released.

No more.

Reluctantly he raised his head. There were two men in the room with him. One was, as he'd expected, his old pal from the carpet shop – the Buddy/Buddy Guy. With a bruised cheek. He touched it, his face expressionless, as Danny looked at him.

The other man was thirty or so and the taller of the two. Clean-shaven and handsome, he wore a knitted skullcap, a faded-to-pink Chicago Bulls T-shirt, khakis, and a pair of running shoes. When the man turned his back, Danny was surprised to see that the name on the shirt was Kukoc, not Jordan.

The room was small, with a concrete floor and cinder-block walls. There was a bare cot, a couple of mismatched chairs, and a dilapidated kilim on the far wall. Overhead, a fluorescent coil simmered and popped. That was it, except for a tool bench in the corner and strips of fly paper, peppered with insects.

"Tough ride, huh?"

It was the guy in the Chicago Bulls shirt. A smile played on his lips in a way that didn't seem friendly.

When Danny didn't respond, "Kukoc" became expansive. "We don't usually move people like that. It's for ... *goods*, you know? For people, there's a special truck – got a toilet and everything. Only right now, it's in Bucharest." He shrugged. "You use what you got, y'know?"

It was a rhetorical question, and Danny ignored it. He was trying to find out if there was any wiggle room in the tapes that bound him to the chair. There wasn't.

Kukoc leaned in. "Hey! Home-of-the-Brave – wake up." He had fathomless brown eyes. "I ask, you answer. That way, everybody gets along!" When Danny didn't reply, Kukoc shook his head in disbelief. "You fuck with me?"

Danny sighed. No matter what he said, he was going to get hit. (At best.) It was just a matter of time. So he gave in – not to Kukoc, but to that part of himself that was forever in junior high school. When someone got in your face, you stepped up. That's just the way it worked. That's what you did if you didn't want to run and hide forever. So he said, "I don't know. Why don't you suck my dick –" He was about to add "and we'll find out," but he never got that far. He heard the Buddy/Buddy Guy snort in disbelief. Then Kukoc swung for the bleachers, landing a punch that drove

Danny's front teeth straight through his lip.

The next thing he knew, he was lying on the floor, still lashed to the chair, his mouth salty with the taste of blood. Kukoc and the Buddy/Buddy Guy picked him up and righted the chair.

Then they *lifted* the chair off the ground, tilted it forward, and dropped him on his face. It was "only" a four-foot drop, but he hit the floor like a pancake and one of his front teeth snapped off at the gum. The pain was indescribable, the sound sickening.

So much for the Turkish sense of humor.

They left him where he lay, stunned and drooling blood, and went off by themselves for a cigarette. Leaning against the tool bench, they talked quietly in Turkish while Danny stared at their feet. Asics and Tevas, with Kukoc a big pronator.

The floor was dusty and gave off a whiff of urine – not, to Danny's way of thinking, a good sign. Obviously, he wasn't the first person to be questioned in the little room.

A minute went by, and his chair was righted. The Buddy/Buddy Guy leaned into Danny's face and shook his head in a way that was almost admiring. "That was so funny," he said. "I had to laugh. But now you gotta get serious, okay? I forgive you for this." He put a finger to his cheek. "I don't blame you – you're cornered, like an animal. But come on, man. Be smart. You piss off my friend, you're gonna lose more than your tooth."

Danny couldn't help himself. He had a problem with authority, with people telling him what to do. Anyone with older brothers would understand. If you backed down too easily – if you showed them your throat – they'd go for your neck. So he sighed and braced himself and said, "Fuck you." Because of the missing tooth, it came out, "Fuh-dju."

Up went the chair – higher this time – and *down*. Once again, the fall was broken by his face. Once again, they righted him. His problem with authority was beginning to resolve itself.

"Buhhh-ddy, buhhh-ddy, don't do this to yourself. It's like, 'Once a philosopher, twice a pervert.' " He chuckled. "I mean, Jesus, man! We haven't even gotten to the questions. At this point, we're just *socializing*!"

Danny bit the inside of his cheek to stop from trembling. His vision was blurred with tears, and he knew that he couldn't handle this – not for long. He was a sculptor, not a commando. And, anyway, what was the point? Zebek would kill him no matter what he said or didn't say.

"So," Kukoc asked, assuming a formal tone, "how was your ride? Did you like it?"

Danny shook his head. "No."

"Much better." Kukoc paused, and Danny could almost hear the gears shift in his head. "So what were you doing in Uzelyurt?"

Danny couldn't believe it. *What did they* think *he was doing in Uzelyurt?!* It wasn't exactly a secret. He'd gone door-to-door, asking for Remy Barzan. But he sensed (from the blood, the pain, and the swelling) that a sarcastic reply would not help his cause. So he said, "I was looking for Remy Barzan." As he spoke, his noticed that his jaw made a kind of clicking sound. *Not good,* he thought.

"Excellent," Kukoc told him. "I give you simple questions, you give me simple answers. Now: why were you looking for him?"

Danny shook his head. "It's a long story," he said.

The Buddy/Buddy Guy waved his finger back and forth, as if it were a pendulum.

"We've got time," Kukoc said.

Danny noticed that his accent was almost perfect, though he hadn't really mastered the "vee" sound. *Give* was *gif*, *have* was *haf*, *we've* was *weef*. Danny repressed a crazy impulse to correct the guy and started talking: "About three weeks ago, a man named Belzer got in touch with me. Jude Belzer. That's what he said."

"Then what?" Kukoc asked.

"We met."

"Where?"

"At the airport."

"In Istanbul?"

Danny shook his head. "Washington."

"And what did he want?"

"He wanted to hire me," Danny said.

"To find Remy?" Kukoc suggested.

"No. He said someone was smearing him in the press."

Kukoc and the Buddy/Buddy Guy exchanged a couple of words in Turkish. "You mean, making up lies?" Kukoc asked.

"Yeah. Like that. And putting them in the paper."

Kukoc cocked his head to one side and then the other, looking skeptical. "And he comes to you because . . . you're some big spook, right?"

"No."

"You CIA? You MacGyver, my man?"

Danny wasn't sure what he meant. Finally, he said, "No."

"Final answer?" Kukoc demanded.

Danny got the joke but didn't see the humor. "Who's 'MacGyver'?" he asked.

The Buddy/Buddy Guy laughed. "We get a lot of reruns," he explained.

"Oh," Danny said. "You mean TV."

Kukoc nodded.

"I'm an artist," Danny told him. "Sometimes, I do investigative work. For law firms and stuff. Part-time. Mostly, I go to the courthouse. Look for records. Like that. But . . . look, you know all this stuff, so –"

Kukoc shook his head. "I don't know any of it."

"Well, Zebek does. He knows all about it."

Kukoc and the Buddy/Buddy Guy snapped into focus. " 'Zebek'?"

"Yeah," Danny replied, puzzled by the change in his questioners' demeanor.

"*Zerevan* Zebek?"

"Right."

"What do you know about Zerevan Zebek?" Kukoc demanded.

"I was working for him. That's why I'm here!"

Kukoc flushed and swore beneath his breath. Then his anger spilled over, and he clapped his hands against Danny's ears – hard. It shouldn't have hurt so much, but it took him completely by surprise, and, once again, Danny's eyes welled up with tears.

"You fuck with me?" Kukoc shouted.

"No!"

"You said you're working for this . . . Jew – this Belzer guy!"

"No," Danny replied. "He's not Jewish. I mean, how would I know –"

"You *said* he was Jew!" Kukoc insisted, his voice rising.

"No. I *said* he was 'Jude.' It's different."

"Jew? Jewed? I ask you again: You fuck with me?"

"No!"

"Okay." Kukoc took a deep breath, as if to emphasize that he was doing his level best to get control of his anger. "So," he said. "This Jew? *He* hired you?"

"Yes, but –" Danny replied.

"Or was it Zebek?"

"That's right! It *was* Zebek, but –"

Bam!

He never saw what hit him. Suddenly his jaw snapped shut on his tongue, something flared behind his eyes – and he was out. For how long he couldn't tell. A few seconds. A minute. Half an hour. He had no way of knowing.

When he came to, he was lying facedown with his head at the end of the cot, watching a fly dervishing on the concrete floor. *Death spiral,* he thought. *Spinout.* Nearby he heard a hiss of air, followed by the unmistakable sound of a match being struck. Then nothing. Kukoc cursed. Danny turned his head to see what they were up to, and what he saw drained the color right out of his face.

Kukoc and the Buddy/Buddy Guy were standing at the tool bench, trying to light a propane torch. Danny heard himself say, "Hey," his tone identical to Rodney King's in the aftermath of the LA riots. *Can't we just get along?*

Then a second match, and a third, with Kukoc becoming angrier and angrier. The torch was out of gas. *Thank you, Jesus!* Swearing, Kukoc tossed the canister onto the bench and said something to the Buddy/Buddy Guy. Coming to Danny's side, Buddy/

Buddy shook his head in disbelief and said, "This must be your lucky day. Propane's a bitch." Then he pulled Danny's shoes and socks from his feet and bound his ankles with tape. The air was cool and luxuriant on the soles of his feet.

"Wha . . . what are you doing?" Danny asked.

Kukoc came to the foot of the cot, holding a length of rusted pipe in his hands. "No more bullshit, my man. I told you: First I ask a question, then you give an answer."

"But –"

Crouching at Danny's side, Kukoc adopted a friendly and confidential tone. "Look – my friend – I'll be honest with you. After this, I got nothing left."

"This"? What "this"?

"After this, it's an acetone bath and we dump you on the road with a note in your mouth. So help me out. . . ."

"I will! I want to!" *"Acetone bath"? What's acetone?*

Kukoc got to his feet, and the Buddy/Buddy Guy locked on Danny's ankles, hard. In the long moment of silence that passed between them, Danny heard Kukoc take a deep breath. *A solvent,* Danny thought. *Like nail-polish remover. It dissolves things.* Then the length of pipe slammed into the soles of his feet, crushing the nerves. Danny's mouth flew open in a gasp that was so far gone it couldn't become a scream. Then Kukoc hit him again and again, pounding the arches and turning the nerves in his feet to pulp.

"Falakka," the Buddy/Buddy Guy explained, as if he were a tour guide. "That's what it's called."

"Who is the Jew?" Kukoc shouted.

It was insane. And as soon as it stopped, they were going to dissolve him.

Pain is its own jagged landscape, laced with crevices in which the victim seeks shelter, believing from one moment to the next that he has escaped, that the ordeal is over, that it must be over, that the body can't handle any more. But it does. The body endures, and so does the pain.

For what it was worth – nothing, as it turned out – the Buddy/Buddy Guy wasn't really into it. Danny caught a glimpse of his face and saw in an instant that the violence scared him. His lips were drawn back in a grimace, and he looked ready to puke. Which frightened Danny even more, because he was the one being beaten.

It took a while, but he got the story out. Everything from the Admirals Club to the chase through the cistern, Terio's suicide, and Father Inzaghi's defenestration. The information poured from him in bursts and cries and screams, the sequences mixed up by the non sequiturs that found their way into Kukoc's questions. How much of what Danny said was intelligible he had no idea – probably less than half. But after he had repeated the story half a dozen times, Kukoc finally got the point. "Jude Belzer" was an alias that Zebek had used in his dealings with Danny – and Danny had fled Zebek a few days earlier to warn Remy Barzan in the hopes of saving both their lives.

Danny faded out of consciousness and when he faded back in heard Kukoc and the Buddy/Buddy Guy arguing briefly in Turkish – or maybe it was Kurdish, Danny couldn't tell. "Ohhhhhhhh . . ." Kukoc said in response to some point Buddy/Buddy made, his voice a

303

realization siren tinged with regret. "No shit. . . . You think?"

Danny heard the pipe clatter against the concrete. Then his torturers left, and he was alone in the room, lying on the cot with his drool strings and pain.

Through it all, an amusing thought occurred to him. It was that there must be something *to* reflexology, because the pain that he felt was everywhere. It wasn't just his feet. It moved through his body like an old vaudeville tune, tap-dancing up and down his spine, tenderizing every nerve it touched. He could feel his feet swelling like overripe tomatoes, skin cracking, fluids seeping. His mouth felt as if he'd been chewing razors, and his heart pounded in bursts, racing from one freeze-frame to the next.

Looking up, he saw a rectangle of light behind the kilim on the wall. For a moment he thought he was hallucinating, then realized that the kilim must be hanging over a window. Morning, then. And he'd been beaten stupid.

Eventually, the pain gave way to numbness, which opened up the emotional space he needed to be truly frightened. Finished with the debriefing, his captors had gone off to set up the acetone bath they'd promised to give him. Find a vat, mix the chemicals . . .

That it had been a *debriefing* (rather than an interrogation) was apparent. Obviously, Zebek wanted to know how much Danny knew – after which Danny became a disposal case.

Galvanized by the prospect, he struggled with the bonds that held him and finally succeeded in freeing his hands. Breathless, he sat up on the cot and stripped the tape from his ankles. Time to go. With a deep breath, he swung his feet to the floor, and –

!!!

Jesus Christ! His feet were the size of pillows, the texture of jelly. Even the lightest touch was agonizing. With a gasp, he jerked his feet from the floor – fell back on the cot and thought, *That's it. I'm dead. There's no way out.*

He must have fallen asleep – or maybe he just lost consciousness – because the next thing he knew, the Buddy/Buddy Guy was crouching beside him, holding a little plastic bucket. Danny eyed the bucket, wondering what it held. Acid? Acetone? His body tensed, then relaxed as Buddy/Buddy dipped a sponge into the bucket and squeezed it. He wasn't wearing gloves or goggles.

"Buhhh-ddy, *Buhhh-ddy,*" he crooned, "you should be more careful." Gently he cleaned the blood from Danny's face, then washed his feet, running the cloth between each of the toes. It was tender and painful, all it once, and made Danny wonder if this was some kind of preburial ritual practiced by the Kurds.

Finally, the Buddy/Buddy Guy rolled Danny's socks onto his feet and tried to put on his shoes. No way. He disappeared, returned with a big pair of rubber sandals. He slid these onto Danny's feet, then buckled them up as a parent might for a toddler. Then he helped Danny up and, with an encouraging smile, guided him to the door. It was slow going, with Danny mincing along like a Chinese woman with bound feet.

The door opened onto a blazing sun. When his eyes adjusted, he saw that he'd been held in a stone shed beside an enclosure for farm animals. The Buddy/Buddy Guy led him around to the side of the building and gestured toward the passenger seat of a bright green John Deere Gator. Despite the pain he was in, Danny chuckled with surprise. The Gator was the identical twin of the little utility truck that Caleigh's parents used on their ranch in South Dakota. Seeing Danny's expression, Buddy/Buddy grinned, and it occurred to Danny that maybe they weren't going to kill him, after all.

The Gator navigated a gravel drive, bordered on either side by rows of pollarded willow trees. A slight breeze ruffled the silvery leaves, turning them inside out so that they seemed to glitter in the sunlight. As lovely as it was, every rut in the road drew a wince of pain from Danny, who kept his feet crossed at the ankles and rolled on their sides. The Buddy/Buddy Guy shot him a sympathetic look but never actually slowed down.

The little road ascended a hill to an arched entryway in a long stone wall topped with the usual shards of broken glass. A guard leaned out the window of a small gatehouse, exchanged greetings with Buddy/Buddy, and disappeared. Moments later, an electronically controlled gate slid open and the Gator moved slowly forward, passing through the archway into an expansive courtyard planted with flowers and trees. Amid the trees was a stately villa of honey-colored stone.

Danny saw at a glance that it was a two-story affair, with the main residence sitting atop an arcade of what looked like utility rooms – kitchen, laundry, servants' quarters, and so on. With the Buddy/Buddy Guy's help, Danny climbed from the Gator and mounted a flight of stairs to the second floor. There his escort tapped a keypad on the wall and a pair of antique wooden doors swung open on silent hinges. Even as his eyes adjusted to the change in light, Danny heard first a piano playing and then a low growl that froze him in his tracks. Standing as he was, stock-still, he soon picked out a second growl – a somehow wetter noise, maybe three or four inches from his balls. Lowering his eyes, he found himself caught in the ferocious gaze of a muscular Rhodesian Ridgeback and its snarling twin.

The Buddy/Buddy Guy chuckled to himself, then cooed the dogs' names. "Castor . . . Pollux . . ." Instantly the snarls turned to yawns. One of the dogs padded away. The other lay down and began licking himself.

Accompanied by his former torturer, Danny moved deeper into the house and soon found himself in the most spectacular private room he'd ever seen. It was a huge space, with a barrel-vaulted ceiling at least twenty feet high. Two of the walls and the ceiling were carved from massive blocks of honey-colored stone. The third and fourth walls were glass. One looked out upon the garden, the other upon a lush atrium at the center of the house. Oriental rugs glowed like jewels on the marble floor. The Goldberg Variations danced in the air.

One of the walls was traversed by a stone bench whose hard surface was cushioned with kilim-covered pillows. Above the bench were paintings and drawings by German Expressionists. At a glance, Danny recognized works by Otto Dix, Emile Nolde, and Oskar Kokoschka.

A third wall was given over to a long slab of hand-rubbed chestnut that held a computer, a Bose stereo system, and a quartet of flat-panel monitors set into the wall. Seated in an Aeron chair before the monitors, a man tapped away at Microsoft's idea of an ergonomic keyboard. Jammed into the waistband at his back was a decidedly unergonomic forty-five-caliber handgun. The Buddy/Buddy Guy touched Danny on the shoulder and gestured for him to wait. Then he approached the man at the computer.

Danny squinted at the bank of closed-circuit monitors, which showed various gates and doors, the road leading up to the villa, and the interior of the shed in which he'd been beaten. With a shudder, he turned his attention to the paintings and, in particular, to one that was very different from the others. This was an Impressionist work, one of the blue-and-green palm-leaf cut-outs that Matisse had made during his travels in Morocco. Perfectly placed, it mirrored the vibrant colors to be seen through the window overlooking the atrium. Danny was so taken aback to find a Matisse in such an improbable place that he didn't notice that the man at the computer had come to his side.

Too played out to jump, the most that Danny could manage was a slow double take.

The man beside him was a few years older than himself and about the same size. He had jet-black hair that needed cutting and a shadow of beard on his cheeks. As he reached out to shake hands, a gold Rolex glittered on his wrist. "Remy Barzan," he said, then gestured to the kilim-covered divan. "Can I get you something?"

Danny didn't reply at first, just took the seat that he'd been offered. He was trying to understand how someone who owned a Matisse could sit in front of a television monitor and watch another person being tortured. With the Goldberg Variations playing softly in the background. It took a minute for Danny to get his bearings, and when he did, he said, "Yeah. A shot of Novocain would be nice. And a champagne chaser."

His host looked surprised. "Champagne?"

"I'm celebrating," Danny explained.

"*Are* you?! And why is that?"

"For a while, I thought I was getting an acetone bath."

Barzan looked embarrassed and regretful. Then he sighed and said, "Well, the night's young."

Sixteen

There wasn't any Novocain available, but Barzan came up with the next best thing – oil of cloves. Danny dribbled the extract onto a wad of cotton and gingerly pressed it against the ragged edge of his tooth. The gum began to sting, but, to his surprise, the pain receded almost immediately.

"I'm sorry about what happened," Barzan told him.

"No problem," Danny mumbled, although he didn't mean it. Barzan's generic apology hardly made up for what had happened to him. But for now, he'd learned his lesson about questioning authority from a position of weakness. This guy was his host. He could hardly walk. Better to wait and see.

"I didn't know about Chris, you know," Barzan said. "Although I suspected something had happened to him."

"He was your friend?"

"Yes." Barzan ran a hand back through his hair. "Look. Why don't you rest for a while? I'll see that you get some clothes, and we can talk later."

It wasn't a suggestion, really, and anyway, Danny wasn't in the mood to talk – not just then. Whenever he spoke, something went off in his left ear and a shooting pain bolted through his jaw. One of Barzan's retainers was sent for and returned pushing an antique wheelchair. Danny would have preferred to walk, but his feet were swollen and throbbing. Like overripe tomatoes, they felt and looked as if they might split open at any second. With a ragged sigh, he eased himself into the chair and fell back against it.

"Till dinner, then," Barzan said.

He fell asleep in a leather easy chair beside a window in a bedroom overlooking the courtyard, his feet soaking in a numbing bath of ice-cold water. It was a deep and dreamless sleep that went on for hours, then ended in a myoclonic jerk that sat him bolt upright, uncertain of his whereabouts. And scared.

Then he remembered.

Beyond the window, the sun was a suggestion of pink behind the courtyard's walls. The water at his feet was tepid. Billie Holiday's voice floated down the hallway.

Slowly he got to his feet and hobbled across the stone floor to the bathroom. There he opened the taps to the tub and adjusted the temperature of the water. Then he went to the sink and leaned on it, feeling woozy, bruised, and nauseous. Warily he turned his eyes to the mirror and, seeing himself, groaned. The front of his shirt was flecked with blood, as if he'd been sprayed with muddy water. His lower lip was torn, his cheek bruised, his right eye swollen shut. Grimacing, he was startled to see the gap where a tooth should have been.

The bath restored him – though not to the point of feeling *well*. That was a condition jump-started with the Percocet that came to his room on a silver tray, accompanied by a cold bottle of St. Pauli Girl. He washed down two of the pills and put on the change of clothes that Barzan had arranged for him. Dark linen slacks, a white shirt, and leather sandals. Big leather sandals. Wondering when the pills would kick in, he limped along behind a servant, following him to a sitting room, where Remy Barzan was seated in a chair beside a crackling fire.

A servant delivered a second round of beers. Barzan held his up, a kind of toast. "Cheers," he said. "Now, tell me about you and Zebek."

It was difficult to talk, at first, but as the Percocet came on and the pain receded Danny became almost garrulous. It took him nearly an hour, but he covered most of the bases – from the meeting in the Admirals Club to the quest for Terio's computer, Inzaghi's murder, and his own flight to Istanbul. Barzan listened hard, as a good journalist would, asking only a couple of questions. At some point, a servant came in with steaming bowls of garlic soup and a platter of bread and cheese. Danny wolfed it down, surprised to find how hungry he was. When the story was done, Barzan took Danny back through it a second time, eliciting details that he had omitted – Terio's calls to Patel, the way Zebek kept tracking him, the loss of the backup floppy that Danny had made.

"So you gave him the names of the people Chris called," Barzan said.

Danny nodded.

"How many names?" Barzan asked.

"Just a couple," Danny replied. "Well, three."

"This man, Patel –"

"– a guy named Rolvaag –"

"The Norwegian," Barzan said, almost to himself. "So that was his name."

"Ole Gunnar Rolvaag."

Barzan nodded. "So there were three names on the

list, then." He counted them off on his fingers. "Patel, Rolvaag, and – ?"

"You," Danny admitted.

Barzan thought about it. "And that's how Zebek knew about me and Chris. That we were in touch."

"I guess. I mean: yes. That's absolutely how."

The Kurd shook his head and sighed.

"I didn't know this would happen," Danny told him. "Getting the toll calls was like routine. It's what a PI *does*."

"Well, in this case it got some people killed, didn't it?"

"I know."

Barzan looked regretful. "Patel and then . . ." His hand came to his face, a pained gesture. "My housekeeper – she just wanted to borrow the car, that was all."

"They told me about her – in Istanbul. Donata – at your office – she mentioned the car bomb. I'm sorry."

"The police said it must have been a kilo of C-4," Barzan went on. "Rigged to the ignition. When it went off, it was like the whole street exploded. There was glass everywhere. Body parts."

"So you came here," Danny said.

Barzan nodded and changed the subject – sort of. "You have any idea what Zebek was looking for?"

"When?" Danny asked.

"In Italy."

Danny thought about it. "You mean, on the computer . . . ? No. He never said. I didn't ask." A pause. "Industrial secrets?" Another pause. "Do *you* know?"

To Danny's surprise, his host nodded almost imperceptibly. "I think so. . . ."

313

Danny waited for Barzan to elaborate and, when he didn't, nearly exploded. "Well!? *What* then?"

"Tree rings."

Danny thought he'd misheard. "Excuse me?"

"I think he was looking for tree rings. JPEG files, showing tree rings."

It must be the Percocet. . . . "No," Danny said. And then: "What do you mean, tree rings?"

Barzan didn't answer. "That's the reason Chris was on the phone to Rolvaag in Norway. Have you tried to get in touch with him by the way?"

"Not yet."

"Maybe it's time. Do you know what city he's in?"

"Oslo – the Oslo Institute."

"If it's not too late, we could warn him," Barzan said in a neutral voice. A thought brightened his face. "And perhaps get the report!"

"What report?"

But the face had clouded again. "I don't like Rolvaag's chances." Barzan stood up and walked over to an antique desk that held a very modern-looking telephone. He sat down and began making calls, trying to get the number from Information in Norway. It wasn't easy. Danny was feeling the effect of the drugs and stared at the flickering fire. He'd nearly fallen asleep when he heard the amplified sound of a phone ringing: two-burst rings. Barzan had switched the telephone to speakerphone.

A machine answered, the recorded female voice rattling away in Norwegian.

"Of course," Barzan said. "It's nighttime in Norway – what am I thinking? The place is closed." Barzan had leaned over and was about to hang up when someone picked up the phone.

"Hallo! Vaersa snill." This had happened to most of the people on the planet. Clearly she meant for the caller to hang on until the message finished. Barzan did so. It took about twenty seconds.

"Hallo," the woman said again. *"Taak."*

Barzan picked up the receiver, but the phone still broadcast into the room. "You speak English?" Barzan asked.

"Oh, yes," she said.

"I'm trying to reach Ole, Ole Rolvaag."

"Ole?" she said in a surprised voice. "I'm sorry, it's not possible."

"Can I leave a message?"

"I'm sorry, that's not possible."

"But –"

She rushed on. "I mean – he's . . . died?" The way she said it, it sounded like a question. "He's – August eleventh – he's killed."

"I see," Barzan said. There was a staticky hum on the wire, then both of them spoke at the same time.

"I –"

"He –"

"Please," Barzan said.

"It's an accident?" the woman said. "Ole is leaving work on his bike and a car – what do you call – run and hits him."

"Hit-and-run," Barzan said in a flat tone.

"Yes – this. He's killed on the spot. They don't find this car."

Barzan cleared his throat. "Mr. Rolvaag –"

"Dr. Rolvaag, yes?"

"He was doing some work for a friend of mine, a Christian Terio."

"Oh, yes?"

315

"An analysis of an artifact. Is there someone I could speak to about obtaining a copy of that report?"

"You can speak to me," she said, in a kind of Scandinavian singsong. "They all are going into the database, you see. All reports are available for paying the fee."

Barzan spouted information: Terio's name, the approximate date of submission, but the woman stopped him.

"We catalog by requester name, alphabetical. That is the first criterion. Spell the name, please."

Barzan did.

"Ohhhhkay. I take a look."

They could hear the clacking of the computer keyboard. A minute's worth or so. "No?" she said. "I'm not finding this? But recently we have trouble with the computer system. Perhaps I take a look in the physical files, which are kept with the artifacts. Do you like to wait? Or calling back?"

"No, I'll wait," Barzan said. "I'll wait." Danny didn't know why this "tree ring" stuff was so important, but he could tell from Barzan's impatient and anxious body language that it *was*.

At last the woman picked up the telephone again. "Sorry," she said. "I don't find anything – this file is missing! *Even the artifact* is not here – although I see it was here. I see even the Plexiglas sample container. And no one is signing *anything* out." Her outrage was clear. "This does not happen at the Oslo Institute. There are procedures. . . ." Her voice trailed away.

"Well," Barzan started.

"Perhaps I ask some question tomorrow," she suggested, "and you will call back?"

"That would be great," Barzan said in a dejected tone. "Thank you."

"Okay. You are . . . ?"

"Remy Barzan."

She asked him to spell it, wrote it down. "Okay," she said. "I will leave message for you?"

"Thank you."

"*Ha det*," she said brightly. "Good-bye then."

Barzan hung up.

"What's this report? What *artifact*? What's she talking about?" Danny asked, although it sounded, even to him, as if he was half-asleep.

Barzan cocked his head, looked at him. Then he glanced at his watch and got to his feet. "We can talk about this tomorrow. I've got to make some calls, and you're going to need a dentist. You should get some sleep."

In the morning, Danny's lip was stitched together by a shy young woman who might or might not have been Barzan's girlfriend. When she was done, she led him outside to where a Jeep waited. Seated in the Jeep, reading a comic, was a big kid with an M-16 at his side. Seeing Danny, he smiled and tossed the comic into the backseat. They drove in silence to a small town about thirty miles distant, finally stopping at a storefront whose business was hinted at by a large sign above the front door. Depicting a giant bicuspid from which little lines of joy radiated, the sign reminded Danny of a British pub – the Happy Tooth or something. The prospect of dentistry in such a place gave Danny pause, but Dr. Cirlik was both painless and efficient. Within an hour, Danny was fitted with a stainless-steel cap and sent on his way with a blister pack of antibiotics. The dentist held up a hand mirror so Danny could take a look. To his eye, the gleaming metal cap on his tooth looked almost as bad as the gap.

Back at the villa, he found Barzan sitting at a long wooden table in the courtyard, reading a newspaper. Like beige parentheses, the Ridgebacks lay on either side of him, snoozing on the ground. Barzan gestured to a chair across from him and Danny eased into it.

"Your house has a nice feel."

Barzan smiled. "It's not mine." Seeing Danny's surprise, he added, "It belongs to a friend in Ankara. He's in parliament. If I'd stayed at one of my family's houses, Zebek would have found me in a day or two. This way, it will take a little longer."

"Hnnh," Danny said.

"And at the moment, he has a bonus. He finds me, he finds you also."

"So maybe I should –"

Barzan interrupted before Danny could finish the sentence. "You're quite free to go."

But of course the truth was that Danny had nowhere to go and no place to hide. He reminded himself that Danny Cray was a starred item on Zebek's to-do list, just like Remy Barzan. Barzan hadn't exactly tracked him down and kidnapped him. No. He'd been brought to this villa because his intentions had been misunderstood, but he was the one who had traveled to Uzelyurt *searching* for the man across from him. Because Remy Barzan had been one of his two remaining leads. Ole Gunnar Rolvaag had been the other.

"Maybe he won't find us at all," Danny suggested.

Barzan shook his head. "Oh, he'll find us," he said.

318

"He's a Yezidi. Even with half of the guys at the checkpoints reporting to *me* . . . it's just a question of when."

"So, what you're saying is: we're fucked."

Barzan smiled. "Maybe not. Maybe we'll move on before he finds us. Maybe we'll sort it out before *he* sorts us out. Let's hope so."

Despite the fact that the man had watched him being tortured, Danny couldn't help liking Barzan. He liked the guy's droll sense of humor and self-effacing manner. He found that he was curious to know more about his host.

"What's your family like?" Danny asked.

"Big," Barzan said. "Six sons, three daughters, four uncles, five aunts, twenty cousins, grandparents. I've got two brothers in the military – one in the army, hunting the other in the PKK. Two in business – one legal, one not. The others – one in politics, one not. That's me. I have a vineyard near Cappadocia with a line of interesting wines coming along, and then I've carved out something of a niche for myself in the French press, reporting on Kurdish affairs. I'm the family dilettante." He laughed and poured each of them a tumbler of single-malt scotch, no ice. "You?"

Danny shrugged. "Not such a big family. Two brothers and me. No generals or senators."

"You're better off," his host joked.

When the espressos arrived, accompanied by a plate of pistachio baklava, Danny asked about the tree rings.

Barzan pursed his lips. "We'll get into that later. Tell me – how much do you know about us?"

"Which 'us'?"

"The Yezidis," Barzan replied. "Or the Kurds, for that matter."

319

Danny remembered the conversation that he'd had with Father Inzaghi. "Inzaghi talked about it," he said, "but . . . I was pretty focused on the computer." He paused and tried to recall. "I remember, he said they worship the devil – the Yezidis, I mean."

Barzan chuckled. "Most people remember that," he said, "but there's a lot more to it."

The Kurds, he explained, were a people without a country – as the Jews were before Israel. The Kurds' homeland encompassed the region historians know as Mesopotamia, consisting of bits and pieces – and whole swathes – of Turkey, Iraq, Syria, Iran, and Azerbaijan. "There are thirty million of us," Barzan told him, "in an area the size of Texas. If we had our own country – if there *was* a Kurdistan – it would have more people than any nation in the Arab League except Egypt. Which is why it will never happen."

Though they had their own language and customs, Barzan thought it unlikely that the Kurds would ever live in a sovereign state of their own – no matter how hard they fought for it. Tribalism had torn them apart, and the realpolitik of the region conspired to keep them that way.

The Yezidis were one of several Kurdish subethnic groups. Some Kurds were Christians, some were Muslims, some were Zoroastrians, some were Yezidis, and some were simply unclassifiable. But they all had a long history of participating in insurgencies against the governments that ruled them. Not surprisingly, this had led to counterinsurgencies of surpassing violence, with whole villages being razed and the Kurdish language and culture suppressed. In Iraq, the Kurds had been attacked with chemical and biological weapons. In Turkey, they'd been fighting a guerrilla war for decades. It was still going on, but at a lower intensity.

Danny winced. "Sounds rough."

Barzan shrugged. "I was lucky," he said. "It was harder for Zebek – a lot harder."

"How so?"

"When his parents were killed, he was taken to the underground city –"

"There's an 'underground city'?"

"There are lots of them," Barzan replied. "The whole of eastern Anatolia is honeycombed with them. There must be a dozen in Cappadocia alone. Tourists line up to go into them." He shrugged. "Not so many this far east, although there are some famous ones in Syria."

"But when you say they're 'cities' –"

"They're more like ant farms. The rock is tufa, so it's easy to work. And they are ancient. Archaeologists think they go back to 9,000 B.C. – almost as old as the Sphinx."

"And they're big?" Danny asked. "As big as the cistern in Istanbul?"

"Oh, much bigger. The one outside Uzelyurt – Nevazir – is a kilometer across and seven stories deep. It's got its own ventilation system, trapdoors, and storage areas for food and water," Barzan told him. "Thousands of people could live in it for weeks."

"But why? What's it for? What were *any* of them for?"

"No one knows, really. They were likely places of refuge, you understand, ancient fallout shelters, places to hide when the various conquerors swept through. Anyway, that's where Zebek was taken after his parents were killed – to Nevazir, underground. It seemed like the safest place to hide him, and in some ways it was. But it didn't work out the way it was supposed to. The people who left him there were killed the next day."

"So . . . ?"

"So he was alone. He was six years old. The candle burned out – and there he was, in the darkness, thirty meters underground."

"Jesus – how long was he there?" Danny asked.

Barzan shrugged. "A few days. Maybe four or five."

"Christ!"

"They said he was pretty disturbed when he came out."

"Yeah, well, that'll happen," Danny remarked, his voice heavy with sarcasm.

"It got better for him."

"How could it not?"

"Some Kurds are simply slaughtered in these periodic . . . repressions. But if your family has money, they can close up the houses and leave. Wait it out, until the situation changes. My parents took me to Paris when I was five. Zebek's relatives took him to Rome about the same time. I didn't come back until five or six years ago."

"So your whole family left?"

Barzan shook his head. "Almost. My grandfather stayed to look after things."

"You're talking about Sheik Mounir?"

Barzan nodded.

"It doesn't surprise you that I know who he is?" Danny asked.

"Of course not. How do you think you got here?"

"I don't know," Danny mumbled. "I thought maybe

the guy with the Kukoc shirt or the one who's always going, 'Buddy, Buddy.' "

"Well, of course," Barzan told him. "They *brought* you, but –"

"They work for Mounir?" Danny suggested.

Barzan frowned. "Not 'work,' exactly. They're more like . . . constituents. They do what he asks, but they also act in his behalf. Sometimes without his knowledge."

"So Mounir's like, what? The mayor?"

Barzan laughed. "He's one of the Elders."

By the way that he said it, Danny could tell that the *E* was capitalized, and he wondered about it.

Seeing the look on his face, Barzan said, "You've been honored." Then he went on to explain that the Yezidis were led by an Imam, who was chosen for life by a council of nine Elders from different geographic regions.

"Like the pope," Danny suggested.

"More or less."

"So if your grandfather is a Yezidi, then you must be one, too."

Barzan nodded. "The Yezidis – they're an ancient people, you know. One of the earliest flood myths – the one later considered to be the flood of Noah – this is first known in the myths of the Yezidis of Kurdistan."

Danny frowned. "So you're a Yezidi. You worship the devil?" Barzan didn't look the type.

Barzan smiled. "I'm not religious."

"So what does that make you – 'a lapsed Yezidi' or something?"

"Exactly."

"And Sheik Mounir?" Danny asked.

"Ah, well, that's a different story. My grandfather is very old-school."

"Which means –"

"That he worships the Peacock Angel, Malak Tawus. 'Lucifer' to you."

Danny blinked.

"Call it devil worship if you want," Barzan told him, "but that misses the point. What the Yezidis believe is that the Tawus was the most powerful, the most wonderful, of all the angels. God's favorite."

"Same as Lucifer," Danny remarked.

"But in the Yezidi tradition," Barzan explained, "there's no fall from grace, no struggle for men's souls. The *Black Writing* tells us that God created the earth in six days and rested on the seventh. And then, on the eighth day, he lost interest. His attention turned to other things, and the Tawus became his overseer. One day, we're told, the Tawus will walk among us on the earth. And then the world will belong to the Yezidis – because we will have been his only followers."

Danny didn't see how any of it was relevant to what had happened to him, to Terio, to Patel. So he maneuvered the conversation back to its point of origin. Or tried to. "Last night, you said Terio was sending you some files."

"E-mail attachments. They never arrived."

"You said they had to do with tree rings," Danny reminded him.

Barzan nodded. "I met Chris when he was doing research in Istanbul. We hit it off, and I was able to help him with some contacts in Diyarbakir. He was there when the Imam was assassinated." Seeing Danny's surprise, Barzan went on to explain that the Imam was the Yezidis' spiritual leader, or Guide. At eighty-seven, he'd held the position for nearly fifty years.

"How did it happen?"

Barzan waved the question aside. "Two men on a motorcycle. One drove. The other shot."

"And they got away?"

Barzan nodded.

"But why?" Danny asked. "If the guy was eighty-seven years old –"

"What you mean is: who?" Barzan paused. "The police blamed it on the Kurdish Workers Party."

"And *you*?"

"I *know* who did it: Zebek."

"But if this Imam guy was eighty-seven, why –"

Barzan patted the air with his right hand, as if to say, *Patience.* "After it happened, Chris came to Uzelyurt. He wanted to write about the Yezidi succession. Said it was 'a once-in-a-lifetime opportunity.' And, of course, he wanted to see the Sanjak. He *had* to see the Sanjak."

It was obvious the word meant nothing to Danny.

"It's a religious statue," Barzan explained. "There are a dozen Yezidi tribes, and each of them has its own Sanjak – and some of them have a couple. We keep ours in Nevazir, the underground city I told you about." At Barzan's side, one of the dogs lifted his head. His ears trembled to attention, and his muzzle swiveled 180 degrees. *Woooooof.* It was a low, ruminative bark, as if the animal was wondering, *What's that?* Barzan scratched the dog behind his ears and resumed. "Chris was fascinated by the underground cities. He *said* they were the only example in the world of 'collective entombment.' "

"And there's a statue down there?"

"The Sanjak."

"Must be kind of hard to see. I mean, what do you use – a flashlight? Candles?"

Barzan chuckled. "Actually, no one saw it at all for nearly fifty years. And I was . . . well . . . violating the rules to let Chris see it. But –" He shrugged. "As I said, I'm not religious. To me, it's a cultural artifact."

"Why is that? That no one saw it for fifty years?"

"For one thing, it would have been destroyed if it hadn't been hidden." Seeing the puzzled look on Danny's face, Barzan went on to explain that "even after Atatürk, this country is still an Islamic society. And you probably know that in Islam it's forbidden to make images of anything that has a soul. This is why the frescoes in the ancient churches are defaced and why the Muslims plastered over the mosaics in the Aya Sofia. Whenever the Sunnis find pictures, or statues of saints, they destroy them – like the Taliban did with the Buddhas in Afghanistan." For the first time, Barzan's English failed him. "What do you call them – the people who break these pictures?"

"Iconoclasts," Danny suggested, surprising himself.

"Exactly!" Barzan exclaimed. "Everywhere in Turkey, paintings and murals are defaced. The faces are scratched out, the images destroyed. Animals, too. Even before Islam became dominant, there were Christian iconoclasts – back around A.D. 800 or so. For centuries, it was open season on any work of art depicting a face. So the Sanjak was hidden! Even in Nevazir, the statue is always covered, except when the Elders meet to choose a new Imam. Then the statue is revealed so it can observe the proceedings – and perhaps influence them."

" 'Influence' them?"

Barzan shrugged. "Maybe it gives a sign. To me? It's

326

all ritual without meaning. The Sanjak is a statue, no more. To my grandfather, it's all infused with meaning and the statue is a sacred object."

Interesting, Danny thought, but he didn't see how any of this was going to save his life. He was about to remind Barzan about the tree rings, when the dogs scrambled to their feet and, barking madly, dashed around to the side of the house. Suddenly, Barzan's cell phone tootled and he flipped it open. After a few words, he stood up and said, "I'll be just a minute."

"Problem?" Danny asked.

Barzan shook his head. "Some soldiers from the checkpoint up the road. They look in on me every couple of days."

While his host met with the soldiers, Danny tried to make sense of what he'd been told. But none of it hung together, really. If Barzan was right, the Yezidis' spiritual leader had been assassinated by Zebek – but why? And what was the connection with a religious statue in an underground city?

When Barzan returned a few minutes later, the dogs padding silently in his wake, Danny reminded him about the tree rings. "You said that's what this is all about."

"It *is,*" Barzan agreed. "But you need to know about the Sanjak – or none of it will make sense. Chris wanted to see it. In fact, he wanted a picture of it – and I agreed to help." He paused. "Would you like to see it? The picture?"

"Absolutely."

Barzan got up and went into the house. Moments later, he returned with a snapshot in his hand and a faint smile on his lips. "I'll be interested to know what

327

you think," he said, handing the photo to Danny.

At a glance, he saw that the picture had been taken with a flash. A harsh white light suffused a cavelike chapel carved from the honey-colored tufa. At the center of the photo, resting on an altar, was a beautifully carved wooden bust – of Zerevan Zebek.

Danny gaped. There was very little hair on the back of his neck, but what was there stood up. It was creepy. "You're kidding me." The likeness was perfect.

"Chris had the same reaction."

Danny couldn't believe it. The heavily lidded eyes and high cheekbones, the cleft chin and widow's peak. Whatever was going on was no accident. The Sanjak was Zebek. "How did Terio know who it was?"

"He didn't. All he knew was that he'd seen the same face in Diyarbakir. A man getting out of a Bentley."

"And he *remembered* that?"

Barzan nodded. "You don't see a lot of Bentleys this far from Ankara. And if you do see one, it's natural to check out the guy getting out of the back."

Danny recalled his luncheon with Inzaghi and the priest joking, *You'd think the devil would have a Rolls* . . . Remembered, also, his meeting with "Belzer" in the Admirals Club. *They say he's in bed with the Mafia* . . . *They say he's the devil incarnate*. The phrase did a little somersault in Danny's head. "So what are we supposed to think?" he asked. "That Zebek is the Tawus?"

Before Barzan could reply, his cell phone went off for the second time and he answered it with a sigh of impatience. After a brief conversation in a language that Danny didn't understand, his host closed the phone and got to his feet. "We'll have to finish this later," he said. "I've got a car waiting."

"A car?"

"I have to see my grandfather."

"Mounir? But when will you be back?" Danny asked.

"A day. Maybe two. The old man's going to Diyarbakir in the morning – and then to Zurich after that. I can't let him go without talking to him."

"And what if you're seen?"

"I won't be."

"But what if the soldiers come?" Danny asked. "What do I do?"

"Layla can handle it. She's the one who fixed your lip. Just stay out of sight and everything will be fine."

Danny spent the night in the villa's library, soaking his feet in Epsom salts and his brain in Percocet. Finding a crimping tool and a spool of nine-gauge copper wire on the desk, he idled away the time before dinner making a mask of Zerevan Zebek. Finally satisfied with the image he'd created, he crushed the wire into a ball and dropped it in the wastebasket.

The crimping tool was cool, Danny thought. You could make interesting things with it. Maybe he'd make something for Barzan – a sort of thank-you-for-not-killing-me gift.

The villa's owner had eclectic tastes, with a great collection of jazz and a wall of art books that Danny had never seen before. He was paging through a catalog raisonné of Caillebot's works, listening to a Lisa Ekdahl CD, when a servant brought him dinner on a copper tray. Hummus and bread, tabbouleh, rice, and vegetable kebabs. A cold bottle of white wine.

It was perfect, in its way. All he needed, really, was Caleigh. But he resisted the temptation to call her –

she'd probably hang up on him anyway, and if not he didn't know what to say.

In the morning, his feet were almost back to their normal size – 10s, instead of 12s. He could get his shoes on, although he didn't *leave* them on. After breakfast in the courtyard, he retrieved the crimping tool from the library and began to play with it, sitting beneath an apricot tree. An hour passed, and then a second. The woman who'd sewn up his lip came by and, seeing the little objects he'd made, giggled brightly and clapped her hands.

"For shish, I think – yes?"

Danny nodded. "For shish," he agreed. *What the hell is shish?*

"This one," she asked, holding the biggest of the pieces up to the sun, "is kink?"

He wasn't sure what to say. Then it hit him. He'd made a chess set – or the beginnings of one, at least. "Right!" he exclaimed. "That's the king – and this one's the rook. And the bishop."

"So good!" she told him. "Maybe . . . yes, I think . . . he is artist!"

"Thank you," Danny said. It was the nicest compliment he'd had in a long while. By now, his hands were tired and his fingers ached. Setting the crimping tool aside, he went into the library and sat down at the desk in front of the computer. While the machine went through its boot routine, he gazed at the bank of TV monitors on the wall behind the desk. One of them was dedicated to the front gate, where the dogs snoozed on the ground like twin Sphinxes. A second monitor changed pictures every few seconds, shifting from the living room to the kitchen to the hall. A third monitor showed the countryside beyond the gate, while a fourth was trained on the room in which Danny had been beaten. *How much of that,* he wondered, *did Barzan watch?*

He wanted to check his e-mail, but as he began to type in his name he changed his mind. With Zebek's resources, Danny would not have been surprised if the billionaire had bribed his way into the servers at AOL and Yahoo. And Danny knew it was possible to trace a message all the way back to the computer – not just the Internet service provider but the actual computer – from which an e-mail had been sent.

So he abandoned the computer and checked out the bookcase. He found an English edition of Orhan Pamuk's *The White Castle,* stretched out on the couch beside the window, and began to read.

The next thing he knew, Layla was waking him. "Now is eating," she told him. "Is night, okay?" With a smile, she snapped on the light behind the couch and gestured to a tray beside the computer. "Good," she promised, waving shyly as she left the room.

Swinging his feet from the couch, Danny checked out the tray: a steaming bowl of lentil soup, a plate of grape leaves stuffed with rice, pita, a cold bottle of beer. All of it was delicious, and he dove into it while watching a soccer game on television. Galatasaray versus Fenerbahce. Good game. Nice night. He could feel his body healing.

Barzan returned late the following night – too late to talk, as it happened. But he was eager to meet with Danny in the morning, waking him at seven for coffee in the library. Coffee poured, they sat down, but before they began talking a loud thump from the direction of the wall of windows claimed their attention. They both jumped and turned toward the verdant green of the atrium. Barzan strode toward the glass and peered down. "A bird," he said. "They see the reflection of the trees in the glass and fly right into it." He shook his head. "They lose a few every month, the grounds-keeper tells me. The atrium is not so much a sanctuary – which is the way the architect saw it – as a death trap."

Danny peered down and spotted the bird on the ground, next to a flowering bush. "Maybe it's just stunned." Surreptitiously he tapped his head three times, some kind of little spell he'd learned from his Aunt Martha. Dead birds were bad luck.

Barzan stirred sugar into his coffee. "I tried to get Mounir to postpone the meeting, but he refused." He shook his head.

"What meeting?"

"The Elders. And Zebek. They meet in Zurich," Barzan told him. "A week from tomorrow. At the Baur au Lac in Zurich."

"With Zebek? But the guy's a psycho," Danny objected.

Barzan gave a bemused shrug. "It's very hard to keep my grandfather out of Zurich."

"And why's that?"

Barzan rolled his eyes. "Well, as a matter of fact, Granddad's got a . . . what should I say? A Swiss miss?"

"A what?"

"There's an escort service," Barzan explained. "He goes to it every year."

"You mean – hookers?"

Barzan nodded.

"But he must be eighty years old!" Danny exclaimed.

"Closer to seventy-five, but it isn't just Heidi that takes him to Zurich. It's business, as well as pleasure. All of the *ulema* will be there. It's a *shura* – happens every year, same time, same place. But this year, it's even more important."

Danny wasn't sure what Barzan was talking about – *ulema*? *shura*? – and it must have shown on his face, because the journalist explained.

"The *ulema* are the Elders," he said. "When they get together, it's a *shura*. It's like an intertribal council, but in this case, it's actually a board-of-directors meeting for Tawus Holdings."

Danny gave a little shake of his head. "I'm missing something," he said.

"Remember what I said about the Sanjak?" Barzan asked.

Danny nodded.

"Well," Barzan said, "I don't know who Zebek got to carve it, but –"

"You think it's a fake? That he replaced the original?"

"Of course," Barzan replied.

"But why?"

"So he'd be named the new Imam. When the Elders meet to discuss succession, the ritual is that the Sanjak is brought out. To *oversee* the proceedings, if you will. In this case, the old Imam was elected when he was only forty and he lived to be a very old man. So no one had seen the thing in almost fifty years. Once it was uncovered –"

"I get it."

"What happens is that when the Imam dies, the

Elders stay in the underground city, in Nevazir, until they're able to agree on a successor. They deliberate in a room with the Sanjak. It can take days – even weeks. It's like electing a pope. There's a lot at stake."

"And how long did it take them to pick Zebek?"

"My guess is about a minute," Barzan answered. "Once the statue was uncovered, it was seen as a sign."

Danny shook his head. "But how did they know who it *was*? If Zebek moved to Italy as a kid . . ."

Barzan nodded. "There's a Turkish television show – like *60 Minutes*. Very popular. Profiles, investigations, consumer pieces – you know the kind of thing." Barzan's hand opened, as if he were releasing a moth that he'd caught. "Most of the people they profile are celebrities or politicians. But every once in a while, they'll do a story about a Turkish artist or an entrepreneur who's making it big in London or New York. The idea being to remind people that Turkey is a Western democracy, a modern state that's ready for NATO."

"And Zebek was on the show?" Danny asked.

"A couple of months before the Imam was killed."

Danny thought about it. "So what you're saying is: First, he was profiled on the show –"

Barzan shook his head. "No. *First,* he had the statue carved. Then he switched it. *Then* he went on the show."

"Some of the Elders saw it –"

"*Everyone* saw it. It's the most popular news program in the country," Barzan corrected.

"Okay, so everyone saw it, and . . . what did they think?"

Barzan shrugged. "They couldn't believe it! The last time a Kurd was profiled, I wouldn't want to guess.

334

And here you had this slick and charming businessman
– did you know he'd gone to M.I.T.?"

"Yes." Danny paused, trying to make sense of it all.
"So what you're saying is, the TV people made a big
deal about him being a Kurd –"

"No," Barzan replied. "That's not what I'm saying.
It's much subtler than that. The 'TV people' didn't
have to make a big deal out of it. In Turkey, 'Zerevan
Zebek' is like 'Menachem Goldberg.' You hear the
name, you don't have to ask his religion or ethnic
background – you just know. In fact, if he lived here,
he'd probably have adopted an alternate name, a
Turkish one – although that is finally beginning to
change."

"So the Elders see the show –"

"And they remember it," Barzan said. "It's no big
deal, but they remember. *I* remembered."

"And the Imam –"

"Is fine. But not for long. A month goes by, another
– and he's murdered in Diyarbakir. There's a *shura*,
two days later in Nevazir. The Sanjak is revealed and
. . . it hits them. They remember."

"Zebek becomes the Imam."

Barzan nodded.

"Have you told your grandfather about this?"
Danny demanded.

"Of course."

"*And?*"

" 'And' nothing. He can't act without proof.
He can't even bring an accusation. You must understand –" He leaned toward Danny. "Many of the
Elders believe that Zebek *is* the fulfilment of the
prophecy in the Writing. That he is the Tawus
returned. That they will now inherit the earth." He

335

shook his head. "Not only are they not inclined to question him – they think he's a deity, the living god. That's why Rolvaag's report was so important."

Danny sighed. "The tree rings, right? What's that all about? I don't understand the connection."

Barzan steepled his fingers and rested his chin on the apex for a moment. "When Chris saw the picture of the Sanjak, he remembered the man he'd seen a few days before getting out of the Bentley."

"And he knew it was Zebek?"

Barzan shook his head. "No. All he knew was that the man in the Bentley was a dead ringer for the Sanjak. But *I* knew who it was. I'd seen him on television – like everyone else."

"And you told Terio?"

"Of course. The thing is, Chris was more outraged about it than I was. He was incensed about what he considered a perversion of an ancient tradition. He was determined that Zebek was not going to get away with it."

"So then what?" Danny asked. "What did you *do*?"

"The idea was to prove that the Sanjak was a fake," Barzan said. "That Zebek had switched one statue for another to engineer his election as Imam."

"And how did you expect to prove that?" Danny asked.

"Tree rings. It was Chris's idea. You can date wooden objects – the masts of ships, the logs in a building – by comparing the grain in the wood to cross sections of trees whose age is known – so long as they come from the same area. What makes the comparison possible is the way rainfall varies in different parts of the world in different years."

"And Terio knew how to do this?"

Barzan shook his head. "Chris was a scholar. Religious historians, you know, often work hand in hand with archaeologists. And archaeologists work with dendrochronologists all the time – these are the guys who do tree ring studies. Anyway, the technique is used to date wooden artifacts and sometimes those are connected to religious chronologies. So Chris knew about this and he got in touch with Rolvaag in Norway."

"Rolvaag was a dendrochronologist?"

"Right. And there's a huge database relevant to this area because – well, because we're in Mesopotamia. Archaeologists have been digging around here for a couple of hundred years. They've dated everything. They have a bunch of different time lines – but the big ones are ceramics and tree rings."

Danny thought about it. "So the idea was . . . what? To date the head?"

Barzan nodded. "It should be about eight, nine hundred years old. Sheik Adi was supposed to have carved it himself."

Danny looked confused. "But how –"

"We made a second trip to Nevazir and bribed the caretaker to leave us alone with the Sanjak. Then we shaved a section from the base – like a piece of veneer – and sent it to the man in Norway."

Danny groaned. "Rolvaag."

"Yes. By the way, I called the young lady in Oslo again," Barzan said, "to see if she turned up the report. Or the sample." He made a thumbs-down gesture.

"But," Danny began.

"What?" Barzan asked.

"We could do it again. We could take another sample of the statue –"

Barzan was shaking his head. "No."

"Why not? You did it before!"

"I'm sure it's long gone. No reason for anyone to look at it now until the next *shura*. In other words not until Zebek dies. Besides, the man who let us into Nevazir had an accident," Barzan explained. "One of Zebek's men took his place. The way the statue's guarded now, it's impossible to get in without permission."

"Then let's get permission. Your grandfather –"

Barzan shook his head. "Only the Imam can grant it – or the Elders. *All* the Elders."

"And they won't do it?"

"What do you think? They think Zebek is the living god."

The two men said nothing for what seemed like a long while. Finally, Danny broke the silence. "Here's what I don't get," he said. "Why? What's in it for Zebek? Why bother? He's already the next best thing to God. A billionaire. He's a master of the universe!"

Barzan chuckled.

"I'm not kidding," Danny insisted. "He's got his own jet –"

"It's for the money," Barzan said. "He needs the money."

"What money?"

"The tribe's money." Barzan smiled. Weakly. "There's quite a lot of it."

"There *is*?" Danny asked, unable to hide his doubt.

"I know what you're thinking. I know what it looks like," Barzan said. "Tourists come to the area around Uzelyurt, the few who do, and they see shepherds, farmers planting apricots, women weaving kilims. They see the dusty towns and one-room stores with

338

cheap fluorescent lights. They look inside – and there's nothing there, really. So they think the Yezidis are poor, but we are not. It's enough to drive you crazy."

"What do you mean?" Danny asked.

"I mean at first I was glad to see the old Imam go. There are villages that don't even have a reliable water supply. Towns that don't have a way to get produce to market. The Imam could have done something about that, but he didn't. For forty-seven years, the only checks he ever wrote were for 'Kurdistan' – which is to say, for C-4, guns, and Semtex. Mostly to the PKK, in other words. What the people need is an on-ramp to the twenty-first century. And the money is there."

Danny gave him a puzzled look. "So where does it come from?"

"Guano."

It was a word Danny hadn't heard before. "What's 'guano'?" he asked.

"Bat shit," Barzan told him. "At least, the money used to come from that. Now, it's generated by investments. But it wasn't so long ago that Yezidi caravans came and went from Uzelyurt, traveling the Silk Road to China. Some of the traders returned by sea. And on one of those trips, a Yezidi named Derai exchanged a kilo of saffron for some uninhabited islands in the Sulu Sea."

"Saffron," Danny repeated.

Barzan nodded. "The islands were honeycombed with caves, and the caves were thick with bats. So the guano had been piling up for centuries, drying in the dark. It was better than a gold mine. This was the richest fertilizer in the world. It was lightweight, easy to mine, and simple to transport. And these islands were practically choking on it."

"And the guy who discovered it –"

"Derai –"

"– got rich?" Danny asked.

"No," Barzan said. "He got cholera. Died on the way home. So the islands became the property of the tribe and produced for nearly a hundred years. Eventually, they played out, and anyway, chemical fertilizers came along. By then, of course, we'd diversified."

"Through the holding company," Danny suggested. "Tawus Holdings."

"Right."

Layla came in with fresh espressos on a silver tray, and Danny saw that she was indeed Barzan's girl. The Kurd put his arm around her and drew her close. She blushed, then scurried away with a secret smile.

"Nice girl," Danny said.

Barzan grinned. "The best. And a huge heart."

Danny sipped his perfect espresso.

"At first I thought what you thought," Barzan said.

"What do you mean?"

"Zebek, he's already a master-of-the-universe! He's got his own Boeing. What does he need *our* money for?"

Danny shrugged. "Exactly. Doesn't make sense."

"Well . . . he needs it." Barzan stood up, stretched, and rocked back on his heels. "Needs it big-time. Whatever he's doing at VSS – and they don't even have a product yet – it's terrifically expensive. I talked to a friend at Morgan-Stanley. Said I was thinking of throwing some venture capital that way. Two days later, he calls me. Says VSS is three hundred million in debt, has twenty million in cash, and is spending about four million a month."

"When was this?"

"Couple of months ago."

"So he's going under," Danny suggested.

"He *was*. He *would*. But once he gets his hands on Tawus Holdings – once the Elders give him control – he'll be fine."

"There's that much money?"

"Yes," Barzan said.

Danny nodded. And frowned. *So that's what this is all about? The Tech Wreck?* He was vaguely disappointed. And he didn't believe it, really. It didn't feel right. He could understand how someone might kill for money, but what Zebek had done went way beyond that. There was real venom in the murders he'd committed. "You don't bury someone alive," Danny mused, "just to get a credit facility." And as he said this, he realized that his suspicion about what had happened in the basement of Terio's farmhouse had hardened into certainty: Chris Terio had not committed suicide.

"But what made Zebek go after Terio?" Danny asked. "I mean, how did he find out Terio had any interest in him?"

"Remember how you got my name? From the phone records?"

"The ones I turned over to Zebek."

"Yes. Well, Chris and I didn't talk regularly. Not at all. My name showed up on that short list because Chris called with big news. He was excited, even elated. He'd heard from Norway. The tests had been completed, he told me, and we were right. Of course we were right! Chris was waiting for the written report, but Rolvaag told him over the telephone that the sample of wood we sliced off the Sanjak was no

341

more than one hundred years old, probably less, and that it came from Yemen. So this was proof: the Sanjak was a fake. Chris told me he'd fired off a letter to the Elders, in care of Tawus Holdings, formally questioning the statue's authenticity. I suspect that's what got him killed."

"But why?"

"Because Tawus only *has* a single employee – a woman named 'Pastorini.' She's new, and you can bet she works for Zebek."

Danny groaned.

Barzan frowned. "You know her?"

"We met." Danny eyes wandered up to the bank of TV monitors. "Your friends are here," he remarked.

Barzan looked up from the computer to the bluish screens on the wall. Most of them showed no activity, but at the gatehouse two men in uniform were getting out of a Jeep. One of the men adjusted his beret, then rapped on the gatehouse door. In the courtyard, the dogs began to bark.

Barzan pushed his chair back from the desk. "Excellent," he said. "I want to talk to them. See if anyone's been asking about us."

It was then, just as Barzan got to his feet, that they heard it – a single shot and then two more, like a cap pistol going off in the distance. Turning back to the monitors, they saw the soldiers standing side by side under the camera, guns drawn.

Barzan swore as he yanked the forty-five from his belt and ran to the door, working the slide. "Stay down!" he ordered, and burst from the room.

Stunned, Danny couldn't take his eyes off the monitors. The dogs were going crazy now, throwing themselves against the gate, bouncing back, and jumping up again. Layla dashed through the courtyard on one monitor while Barzan crashed out the front door on another. The kid who'd taken Danny to the dentist ran past the fountain with a submachine gun in his hands. Then the gate sprung open. The dogs leapt. All hell broke loose.

Seventeen

Danny's eyes flicked from monitor to monitor as gunshots crackled in the courtyard. On one screen, a soldier fell to his knees beside the fountain, a black stain on his chest and a look of wonder on his face. On a second monitor, an open truck rocked uphill toward the house, trailing a cloud of dust. In the back of the truck, half a dozen soldiers sat with their rifles pointing at the sky. Other monitors seemed to blink as people and dogs ran past the cameras, flashing in and out of sight in different parts of the house and garden.

He knew he should be doing something besides looking at the monitors. His mind was screaming, but he couldn't seem to move, couldn't seem to take his eyes off what was happening on the screens. It was a massacre in soft focus, the underwater blue of the monitors rendering it all as a blur. Shouts and screams cut through the afternoon, seeming to rise and fall independently of the little television screens, while rifles and handguns banged away at one another. Danny saw a soldier buckle and collapse to the ground as one of the Ridgebacks took him by the throat. In an instant, the second dog was on him, burying his muzzle in the man's groin. Another soldier came running to help the first, firing wildly. Then his head exploded as the kid with the M-16 strode into view, shooting from the hip.

Now Barzan was back at Danny's side. "Come on," he said, shoving a gun like his own into Danny's hands. He stared at it for a moment, feeling helpless, while on the monitors two trucks jerked to a stop at the front of the house. Soldiers jumped to the ground. Getting to his feet, Danny saw Layla dashing into the room on the other side of the atrium. For an instant, their eyes locked – then a burst of gunfire hit her in mid-stride. Like a dancer who has lost her balance, she swam through the air and dropped. Then a second burst of gunfire turned the atrium window into a waterfall of glass.

Danny hobbled after Barzan as best he could, watching the Kurd's yellow sweater dwindle down the hallway and around a corner. *How many are there?* Danny wondered. *Two trucks plus. Maybe a dozen soldiers, probably more.* And him with his damaged feet and a gun he didn't know how to shoot. *More Dumbo than Rambo.*

Suddenly Barzan reappeared, walking backward, hands in the air, talking quietly to someone Danny couldn't see. Danny was fizzing with adrenaline now, raising his gun with both hands, the way they do on television. He was waiting for whoever it was that had Barzan in his sights to turn the corner.

But no one did. They just opened fire with some kind of automatic weapon, ripping Barzan up from the pit of his stomach to the top of his chest. He backpedaled into a table, sent a vase full of roses flying, and reeled to the floor. Then the soldier who'd shot him hove into view and with a look of surprise saw Danny.

Danny caught a wave of beginner's luck – the first shot blew out the side of the soldier's head. The second

345

and third shots shattered the window overlooking the atrium.

Danny ran to Barzan's side, slipped in a pool of blood, caught himself against the wall, and took a deep breath. His friend was dead. He could see it in the eyes, which, open and unmoving, had the bright, stony look of marbles. He could still hear shooting in the courtyard, but not as much as before, and now he also heard the sound of soldiers going room to room, kicking in the doors.

There was nowhere to run, really. Nowhere to go. They were coming down the hall from both directions, heading toward him in a sort of pincer movement. Once either contingent turned the corner . . .

Instinctively he grabbed a kilim-covered cushion from the bench along the wall and crossed to the window he'd shot out only moments before. Using the cushion to protect his hands, he brushed away the larger pieces of glass that clung to the sash and looked down.

It was a ten-foot drop – painful under the best of circumstances, but with his feet the way they were . . . He draped the cushion over the jagged glass at the bottom of the window and tried to summon the gumption he needed, or maybe just wait for the gumption to find him.

He heard soldiers running down the hallway. He glanced at Barzan lying in a pool of blood, climbed through the broken window, crouched on the ledge – and vaulted to the ground.

He hit the ground flat-footed, and for an instant he could have sworn he'd landed on a bed of nails. Pain geysered up from the soles of his feet, exploding behind his eyes like a barrage of Roman candles. Instinctively he clenched his fists and gritted his teeth in a silent cry, then staggered across the atrium to the surrounding arcade.

The arcade was a series of arches, supporting the second floor of the house – its living quarters – and was itself a chain of utility rooms that alternated with passageways into the courtyard. A bank of washing machines lined a wall to Danny's right, where a fat woman in a white dress and head scarf stood quaking beside a tub of laundry. Behind her, he saw plastic drying racks, festooned with bed linen, and a tub of bottles, waiting to be recycled.

Putting a finger to his lips, Danny stepped past the woman and edged closer to the courtyard. Bodies everywhere. Four soldiers. A woman he didn't recognize. The kid who'd driven him to the dentist. One of the dogs. And behind the bodies, the wall of honey-colored stone that surrounded the villa and its grounds.

The top of the wall glittered with shards of broken glass. There was no door that he could see. The only way out was up and over, or through the gate at the other side of the house – a gate he felt sure was crawling with soldiers. A calico cat drowsed in the sun near the drying bedsheets, rolling onto its back as he approached.

The wall was six feet tall, with the broken glass adding an extra inch or two. *It's do-able,* Danny told himself. A high jumper in high school, he'd cleared six-one in the regionals. But that was then. It had taken him three tries, and he'd never done it before or since. So it wasn't really do-able – not by him, anyway. Not without leaving his back in ribbons. Danny turned away from the wall just as a gunshot broke the stillness in the house.

For a moment, he thought that he'd been seen – that someone was shooting at him and that others would soon come running. But no. The first shot was followed by a long pause. Then a second shot and a second pause. Then a third. The cat spooked and slunk off toward the wall, low to the ground. This didn't sound like a gunfight. It was more like someone taking target practice. Then it hit him. Someone was going from body to body, delivering a coup de grâce, making certain everyone was dead.

I'm outta here, Danny told himself. Crossing the courtyard to the wall, he tried jumping up to see what lay on the other side, but with his feet the way they were, his vertical leap was practically nil. The best he could do was a half-assed hop. (So much for his fantasies of clearing the wall with the Fosbury Flop.) All he could see was the twilit sky and, off to the right, the plumed tops of the willow trees that lined the gravel drive.

Returning to the laundry room, he jerked the mattress off the cot, eliciting a mewl of protest from the woman in the head scarf. Was this where she slept? The little sound was enough to break his heart. "C'mon," he said, and beckoned for her to follow. But no. That was not going to happen. There was no way this terrified woman was going over the wall with him.

"They'll kill you," he told her.

She shook her head violently, uncomprehendingly.

By way of explanation, he drew a finger across his throat and pointed toward the house. This terrified her even more, so that she squeezed her face shut against him, as if to make him disappear. There was nothing he could do.

So he grabbed a straight-backed chair and strode

into the courtyard, dragging the mattress behind him. His back tingled with anticipation. He could imagine a bullet slamming into his spine, sending splinters of bone through his chest, the slug tumbling through his lungs. He could imagine . . .

Shut . . . up.

He pushed the chair against the wall, stepped up on it, and took a look.

The gravel drive was to his right. Although he didn't see the military truck (it must have proceeded through the gate after the guard was gunned down), a Jeep idled outside the guardhouse, which was maybe thirty yards away. Close enough so he could hear the staticky noise of its radio. One soldier sat in the driver's seat, a walkie-talkie clapped to his ear. Two more leaned against the guardhouse, smoking, indifferent to the body at their feet.

Off to the left, Danny could see the little shed in which he'd been beaten. Beyond it were other sheds, corrals, and animal pens. Maybe he could get to one.

He laid the mattress over the glass, stepped up on the chair, and threw his leg over the top of the wall. Rolling off the mattress, he dropped to the ground as quietly as he could, this time landing on his toes. Then he pushed the mattress back over the wall behind him, left it where it lay, and took off, running in a crouch.

Instinctively he headed for the shed where he'd been held – then remembered that it was hooked up to a closed-circuit camera. Veering right, he slogged through a sheep pen, spongy with dried manure. On the other side of the pen was a small barn with a sliding door that was half-ajar.

The first thing he noticed as he entered the barn was the smell – a fruity odor that seemed entirely out of place. Standing in the darkness, he listened to his heart pound while his eyes adjusted to the light. Soon a neat array of shovels and rakes came into focus, leaning against the wall. A box of rags, a tiller, an empty trough, and a stack of plastic jerry cans. On each of the cans, written in neat block letters, was the word ACETONE.

Danny leaned against the wall and slowly slid to the floor. *This is not where I want to be found,* he thought. *Not here. If they find me in an open field – it's over in a second. A shot to the head, and . . . that's it. I'm gone. Not good, but not . . . protracted. They find me here, they see the acetone – maybe they'll think,* Let's have some fun.

Time to go.

Struggling to his feet, he stepped to the door and, looking out, saw a car winding up the drive toward the house. *Big car,* Danny thought, and then went cold when he realized what kind of car it was: a Bentley. Drawing closer to the house, the big black car came to a stop.

A soldier ran down the drive from the direction of the house, rifle thumping against his side. Halting beside the car he placed a hand on the roof, leaned over, and waited for the backseat window to roll down. A brief conversation ensued, with the soldier laughing and gesturing toward the house. Then he stepped back from the Bentley and executed a crisp salute.

The car stayed where it was, idling quietly. After a moment, the back door opened and Zerevan Zebek stepped out. With a glance to his left and a glance to his right, he unzipped his fly and began to pee in Danny's direction. For a moment Danny was sure he'd been found, the gesture meant as an insult. But no. His mission accomplished, Zebek rezipped, got back in the car, and continued on his way toward the villa.

Which was when Danny saw the soldiers moving through the fields with their eyes on the ground, rifles at the ready. Looking for someone, anyone, *him*.

Turning, he cast a frantic eye around the barn, looking for a place to hide. Seeing a crudely made ladder leaning against an overhang, he crabbed his way up to a loft, where bales of hay were piled. As he pulled the ladder up after him, he saw in the corner of his eye something skitter, vanishing into the hay. A mouse, he hoped, but from the way it moved, a snake.

Danny didn't like snakes.

Seated where he was, well back from the edge of the loft, he noticed for the first time that his leg was wet. The nice linen pants that Barzan had loaned him were plastered against his skin, just below the right knee. Reaching down, he pulled the pant leg up by the cuff and saw that his calf was covered with blood. Reaching for a handful of straw, he wiped the blood away, revealing a deep gash.

When did that *happen?* he wondered. *On the wall, maybe, or maybe not.* It didn't matter. The important thing was to close the wound and stop the bleeding. Removing the braided leather belt that he wore around his waist, he wound it around his calf, just above the cut, and pulled tight. The bleeding stopped.

He lay there for nearly ten minutes, fearful of the soldiers, worried about the snake, terrified of Zebek. Every so often, he released the pressure of the tourniquet he'd made, then pulled it tight again. It occurred to him that he must have cut himself when he climbed through the atrium window. Or maybe on the wall. Either way, he'd been bleeding for quite a while, really. There was probably blood on the ground, blood on the wall – a *trail* of blood.

With a moan of unhappiness, he rolled over and looked at the floor below the loft. Unlike the barn itself, the floor was concrete, and, sure enough, he could see splotches of blood from the door to where the ladder had been. He might as well have left a sign with an arrow pointing to the loft.

By now, his eyes were adapted to the twilight of the barn. Leaning over the edge of the loft, he searched the building with his eyes, looking for a source of water. Spotting a length of coiled hose attached to a spigot on the side of the barn, he lowered the ladder and climbed to the ground. Then he went to the spigot and turned it on. The water emerged with such force that the end of the hose bucked and slapped at the concrete.

He lowered the pressure with a twist of his wrist and sluiced away the blood. Had anyone heard him? How could they not? The hose was like a tin drum. And now that he thought about it – too late – what would the soldiers make of the wet floor, if they came in?

I'm not cut out for this shit, Danny thought, turning off the water and re-coiling the hose. Then he clambered up the ladder, pulling it after him when he reached the top. *As soon as it's dark,* he promised himself, *I'm out of here.*

Something skittered along the wall.

Time slowed down, sauntering past as if it were window-shopping. To say that he was uncomfortable did not come close to the truth. He was hungry, hurt, and scared. The smell of the acetone – laced with hay, laced with manure – was oppressive. Flies dived at his face. No-see-ums sucked his blood. He couldn't remember what he'd done with the gun and he cursed himself for somehow losing it. With a gun, he might have a chance. . . .

The acetone made him think of Caleigh, who painted her nails with clear fingernail polish, a practice he'd thought of as very South Dakota – until she showed him around the club scene in Pierre, where the prevalent look seemed to be a rhinestone cowgirl version of Vampira.

The thought of Caleigh brought him even lower, plunging him into a pool of longing and self-pity. *How to win her back?* he asked himself. First step: don't get killed.

But how? Wait until dark. Steal a car or hitch a ride to . . . the border. That's what they did in movies. They crossed the border, and they were safe – the good guys were always safe. But what good would it do to drive to the border, even if he had a car, even if he knew which way to go? His passport and wallet were in the house – with all the dead people. And the soldiers.

One of whom he'd just killed.

He didn't want to think about that, but he couldn't keep the images out of his head. Barzan, gunshot and reeling, crashing into the table. The vase and the roses tossed into the air. The soldier looming into view, the look of surprise on his face, the quick swerve of his eyes toward the gun the instant before Danny fired it. And then the soldier's head flying apart, the spew of gore and blood.

So driving to the border wasn't what you'd call a brilliant idea. Because he'd never get through a single checkpoint and, even if he did, he'd never get into Syria or Iraq without so much as a driver's license. They had visas for that kind of thing, and it was Danny's impression that Customs officials were pretty strict about it.

Which left the embassy. In Ankara. Same problem, but no borders to cross. Just eight hundred miles of mountains and steppes. If he was lucky –

The fat brown snake with an ugly head slid through the straw toward Danny's leg, its little tongue fluttering at the smell of blood. Seeing it first in his peripheral vision and then square on, Danny went rigid, white and cold. The snake paused, its beady eyes locked on the space between Danny's sandal and the blood-soaked cuff of his pant leg.

It was – he could read its mind, no question – thinking about entering that attractive hole, even as Danny was thinking of throwing himself out of the loft to the floor below. So what if he broke his neck? At least –

The soldiers came in on tiptoe, eyes darting left and right, Uzis or AKs (or whatever they were) at the ready.

Danny's heart threw a rod.

The soldiers spoke quietly to each other as they moved slowly through the little barn, looking for someone or something – probably Danny. So, too, the snake, which raised its head and swung it, first to the left and then to the right and down. Almost idly, it inched closer to his foot, and, as it did, something rose in Danny's throat.

At first he didn't know what it was, and then he did. It was a scream.

Which he swallowed.

But then another one was coming – straight from the heart – and it was by no means certain that he'd suppress this one as he had the first. He could feel it, a high-pitched sizzle of neuronic dread so intense that he

354

was sure the soldiers could sense it as easily as the snake sensed his blood.

Then the snake turned away and, a moment later, one of the soldiers said something that made the other laugh. And they tromped out.

Jesus wept.

Danny, too.

Eighteen

He came awake in the dark all at once, the reek of acetone reminding him where he was. It amazed him that he'd been able to sleep, the result, he supposed, of the blood he'd lost and the adrenaline he'd burned. Groping in the darkness for the ladder and finally finding it, he lowered it to the ground and climbed down. Shuffling through the pitch-black quiet of the barn, he moved with his hands in front of him – like a just-made Frankenstein's monster taking his first steps in the laboratory.

Outside, the moon was an opalescent smear behind a dome of scudding clouds. Standing just inside the door to the barn, he listened for whatever there was to hear. He heard the thin chatter of a radio or maybe a television off in the distance. Otherwise, nothing. No voices. No tramping boots. No traffic. He tried to think – which way to go? Which way was the road?

He had no idea.

Then the moon slid away from the clouds and he saw the tops of the willow trees, their leaves glinting silver in the moonlight. The trees were at the edge of the gravel drive, an allée of sorts. He remembered them from his ride to the dentist. The ride he took with the kid. The big kid – who was now the dead kid.

He set off toward the willows, found the drive, and began to walk along its shoulder, on the packed dirt beside the gravel. Lit by the moon, the drive was easy enough to follow. He'd have run if he'd been able – but he couldn't.

The end of the drive was marked by stone pillars with rounded balls at the top. When he first caught sight of them, he froze, thinking they were sentries. The way the light came through the trees, the pillars seemed to move – to sway. When he realized that it was just a trick of light, he hurried toward the road at the foot of the drive.

But which way to go? The unlined asphalt veered left and right, disappearing into the darkness. Turning his eyes to the vault of night, he found the Big Dipper and remembered that the handle pointed north.

Or was it south? Or maybe it was east or west.

He went left.

The noise of traffic carried a long way, but he heard nothing as he trudged along on the side of the road. When he finally heard a car – he guessed it was a mile away, the whine of its engine rising and falling as it worked its way through the hilly terrain – he panicked. What if it was the army? What if it was Zebek? Leaving the road, he crouched behind a wall of brush and listened to the car as it closed the distance between them. And then, when it was almost on top of him, he changed his mind and charged down the hillside, waving like a lunatic.

Too late – he cursed himself as a BMW shot past, headlights tunneling through the darkness. He was angry with himself. Because it wasn't as if he had any choice. He couldn't *walk* to Ankara. He needed a ride, and there was no way that he could size up every vehicle that came down the pike. He had to take a chance.

Then again . . . he'd killed a soldier. Killed him in self-defense but killed him nevertheless. Danny didn't know much about the Turkish judicial system – just what he'd seen in *Midnight Express*. He didn't want to go there – especially with Zebek on his case.

On the other hand . . . he couldn't be sure that the men at the villa were actually soldiers. Sure, they were wearing uniforms, but that didn't prove anything. Not really. And now that he thought about it, it occurred to him that his presence at the villa might have been unknown to the men who'd attacked it. Clearly they were looking for Barzan. He was the one they wanted to hit, and he was the one they'd expected to find. As for Danny Cray, well . . . only a couple of people knew he was there, and as far as Danny could tell, they were loyal to Barzan. Or dead.

The more he thought about this scenario – and the longer he walked without anyone coming after him – the more likely it seemed. The confusion at the villa had been so great, with Barzan and the kid shooting back, people running everywhere . . . Danny's presence probably didn't register. If it had, he thought, they'd be looking for him. And as near as he could tell, they weren't. Of course, it was only a matter of time until they found his passport – that would get their attention.

An hour went by, or two (who knew?), before he heard another vehicle. It was a long way off, a truck by the sound of it, and underpowered for the terrain, laboring up and down the hills. He stood and stared, waiting for it to come into view. When it finally did, he saw that it had only a single headlight – and this gave him hope that it was not a military truck. Stepping into the road, he raised his arms, palms out, and prayed.

The truck rattled to a stop about ten yards in front of him, although the driver did not turn off the engine. Whiny Turkish music blared from the radio. Danny stood in the headlight's glare, heart rocking in his chest. A sweet smell drifted toward him . . . *cantaloupe*. The truck's open bed, its sides enclosed by sheets of plywood, was heaped with the fruit. The man who stepped down from the truck's cab was in his late twenties, early thirties. He wore jeans, a T-shirt, and a baseball cap, backward, which he now took off to reveal a thatch of dark hair. He kept his distance, shouted something in Turkish.

"Little help?" Danny yelled, affecting a hapless grin. "Got a big *problemo*!"

The man looked him up and down, frowned, and twisted his hat around. "What the fuck?"

"I'm in trouble," Danny said, concentrating on getting the right tone of supplication into his words. "I need –" And then it struck him that the man spoke English. Struck him dumb. He stood there swaying on his wrecked feet, staring.

"How'd you get out here, man? Where's your car? You crash it?"

"You speak English," Danny said, sounding stunned.

"Yeah. German, too. What happened to you?"

Danny laughed and approached the truck. "Talk about the lucka the Irish!"

"Don't you know it's dangerous out here? How did you get here, anyway?" The man glanced around for a car, a bike.

"I –" Headlights swung round a hill in the distance, coming from the direction of the villa. "It's okay to get in the truck?"

He held his breath until it became clear that the car had gone the other way. At least, there were no lights behind them. The sky was brightening into a predawn gray as Danny finished a cock-and-bull story about how he'd come to be in the middle of nowhere with blood on his sandals and no ID. It was, in essence, a story that he'd read in a Lonely Planet guidebook: A young guy, traveling by train, meets some friendly strangers. They hit it off and have a beer together in the dining car. Two days later, he wakes up by the side of the road. No wallet, no passport, no luggage, no hope.

The driver, Salim, nodded sagely. "I have heard this story many times," he said. " 'The Turkish knockout.' But, mostly, it is women they go after – and they're raped." He glanced at Danny. "You weren't raped?"

"No," he replied. "I'm fucked, but I wasn't raped."

Salim laughed. "Sometimes, they are using gas. Very bad. You're lucky to be alive."

Danny nodded. He didn't like lying to the guy, but what was he supposed to say? That he'd just killed a soldier in the middle of a massacre?

"This place," Salim went on, nodding at the countryside, "is not so good to visit these days. Until last year it's not even permitted to tourists. Even now, no one is coming. Too dangerous." He pronounced the word as if its last syllable rhymed with *moose*. "This part of Turkey – it's not recommended." He looked at Danny with a scolding expression.

"Tell me about it."

Salim gave him a puzzled look. "I am."

Danny smiled. "It's an expression. '*Tell* me about it.' "

The driver's puzzlement turned to a frown.

"It's like this," Danny explained. "A man is hanging off a cliff – I mean, he's clinging by his fingernails, okay? And this other guy passes by. 'You're in a tough spot,' the guy says. And the first guy, the one who's hanging off the cliff, says –"

" – 'tell me about it!' " Salim's face exploded in a smile. He laughed, then repeated the phrase as if it were a linguistic treasure, nodding his head with satisfaction. Then he turned serious. "So – they took your passport? Money?"

"Everything."

"Bummer."

Danny nodded in agreement. "I figure the embassy will help. It's in Ankara, right?"

"Yes, you are correct."

"And these melons – they're going to Ankara?"

Salim laughed. "No. These melons are going to Dogubeyazit."

"What?"

"When there were tourists," Salim explained, "they call this place 'Doggie Biscuit'. It's on the plain below Ararat. Near the border with Iran."

"Iran?"

"Yes, certainly. I'm living there – this is my town. But I will try to find a ride for you to Ankara."

Danny brightened. "You think you can do that?"

Salim shrugged. "Maybe."

"I . . ." Danny didn't know what to say, how to express his gratitude. He thought of promising to send money but sensed that Salim would be offended by the offer. "I will thank you forever."

"One day, my turn will come to need help," Salim said.

They bounced along in an envelope of road noise,

the truck's cab dense with the fragrance of ripe cantaloupe. Danny struggled to stay awake as Salim told his own sad story. He'd once been a tour guide, leading groups of climbers up Mount Ararat, but business had fallen off with the "troubles" – the PKK insurrection – when tourists and hikers kept away from eastern Turkey. More recently, he'd lost a bundle in the currency crisis, and his cell-phone distributorship had gone belly up. He was married, had two kids, and now he was driving trucks for his father-in-law while waiting for the economy to improve.

"Well, that sucks," Danny told him.

Salim shrugged and flashed a smile. "Tell me about it." He chuckled and adjusted his baseball cap. "I think it gets better, someday. Then we will see what the opportunities may be."

Dawn arrived and with it the amazing sight of Mount Ararat, a perfect snowcapped conical mountain that looked like Japanese prints of Mount Fuji. But it was huge. The biggest mountain Danny had ever seen. He couldn't believe the size of it. Salim explained that it was more than five thousand meters high but seemed even higher because there were no foothills – it rose straight up out of the plain. Danny did the math: seventeen thousand feet.

They passed through two military checkpoints before reaching Dogubeyazit. In both instances, Salim cautioned him to pretend to be asleep. He tensed, listening to the unintelligible conversations between Salim and the guards, but no one bothered to speak to him.

In the brightening dawn, Salim skillfully maneuvered the truck into a warehouse loading bay and left it to a team of hardworking men who in rapid order unloaded the cantaloupes into huge baskets. He followed Salim to a cramped office, where the Turk signed some papers. Then the two of them walked a few blocks and stood on a corner until the *dolmus* arrived.

Salim lived in a one-bedroom apartment in a small concrete apartment block on the outskirts of town. The apartment was on the top floor, and the windows were heavily draped to keep out the heat – which was, even at seven A.M., eighty degrees and rising. Salim's shy, pretty wife greeted her husband, bowed to Danny, and made them each a glass of apple tea. Danny sipped his while the two of them held a rapid-fire discussion that turned out to be about the blood on his pant leg.

"Ayala says you need to tend this wound," Salim informed him. "And she is right."

Ayala fetched a pair of scissors, a basin of water, and a white washcloth. First she soaked the fabric of the pant leg in water, then pried it away from his skin. Then she wiped away the dried blood with the washcloth.

It wasn't so bad, really – a clean slice, about three inches long. Going into the bathroom, Ayala returned with a bottle of what turned out to be hydrogen peroxide. "That's okay," Danny said. "I don't need –"

She swung her forefinger like a pendulum in front of his eyes, then opened the bottle and slowly poured about half its contents into the cut. The wound foamed, and Danny felt as if his leg had been cauterized with a blowtorch. It was all he could do not to scream.

Salim chuckled. "Tell me about it," he said.

When Ayala was finished and the wound bandaged, she made some more tea and retired to the bedroom.

While he and Salim sipped their drinks, Danny could hear her voice murmuring to a crying baby and now and then the high, piping voice of a child. After a few minutes she reappeared with the two children – who had obviously just woken from their naps. Salim played a complicated game of patty-cake with the older child while Ayala jounced the baby on her hip, watching her husband with undisguised pleasure. The little boy opened his mouth and tugged one of his teeth. He spoke animatedly to his father, pointed at Danny.

"He wants to know about your silver tooth." A complicated look came across Salim's face, but then he shrugged.

Danny was embarrassed. Obviously his host was finding it difficult to believe a Turkish knockout, *plus* some other calamity.

"My cap fell off," he said, remembering when this calamity had happened to his mother. "You know, I had a porcelain one, but it was cracked or something. This is temporary." He winced. "Looks great, huh?"

"My son admires it," Salim said. "He thinks it's an extra-strong tooth. Supertooth."

Danny smiled wildly, flashing his tooth, and the little boy hooted with laughter. And then Ayala gathered the kids up, said something in Turkish, and blew a kiss to Salim.

"They go to her parents," Salim said, "so I can sleep. Also, it's air-conditioning there. You would perhaps like to bathe? Ayala says this would be good for you."

Ten minutes later, Danny was in the tiny bathroom, standing before a steaming tub. Everything stung as he lowered himself into the water, the various abrasions obliterating for a moment the pain in his feet, jaw, and shoulder. He didn't like looking at his feet, which were only now beginning to fade from the eggplant color they'd turned.

It was the exact shade of one of Caleigh's favorite jackets, a realization that made him wonder what Caleigh was thinking – right then. It was midnight in the States, so she was probably asleep, but . . . she was probably dreaming of him. In bed with Paulina.

He launched a little plastic boat on the surface of the bath water and watched it bob beside his discolored feet. By moving his hands in a swirling motion he could set up enough centrifugal force to send the boat rocking around the perimeter of the tub. It was a nice way to spend the morning.

"You want to sleep now?"

Danny came out of the bath, wearing the clothes that Salim had set out for him. A pair of khakis that didn't quite reach his ankles, and a T-shirt that had the words I'M WITH STUPID printed across the front.

"That would be great," Danny told him.

The Turk gestured toward a makeshift bed that he'd set up on one of the kilim-covered benches. Then he excused himself and went into the bedroom.

Danny lay down on the bench, closed his eyes, and slowly drifted off, listening to the domestic sounds around him. Muffled voices and Arab music. The rumble of traffic. Distant car horns. And, every so often, the opening notes of the *William Tell* Overture, signaling Salim that he had a call on his cell phone.

"Are you awake?"

Danny opened his eyes, blinked, and sat up. Salim was standing in the doorway to the kitchen, smiling broadly. It was evening. And still hot. "That was good," Danny told him. "I really needed that."

"Good," Salim replied. "Now, let's see who's going to Ankara."

The Turk had a rapid, efficient walk and Danny struggled to keep up. He worked out a kind of rolling gait that depended on turning his ankles so that in effect he was walking on the outside edges of his feet. After a half mile or so, they entered a café crowded with men sipping tea, playing cards, reading newspapers, talking. Christiane Amanpour spoke from a television screen on the wall. No one paid her any attention.

With Danny at his side, Salim went from table to table, where he laughed and joked with various men – occasionally nodding to Danny, who smiled awkwardly and shrugged a lot.

"I . . . ah . . . jeez," Danny said as he followed Salim toward yet another table. "You're probably sorry you stopped for me."

The Turk looked offended. "But it's my opportunity to help you," he said. "The Prophet puts you in my path for a reason."

Finally, they sat down at a table with some other men and accepted glasses of apple tea. Everyone was friendly and smiling, but the result was always the same. Salim would give a sad shake of his head and turn the palms of his hands toward the ceiling. Meaning: *He's broke. No money at all.*

It seemed hopeless, and Danny was more or less resigned to the prospect of hitchhiking. But Salim urged patience, and after a second round of apple tea they got lucky. An elderly man came to the table and had a word with Salim – who brightened. "We have to go," he announced, jumping up from his chair. Leading Danny to a café on the next street, he explained that "Hakan Gultepe has to travel west this very night! Pistachios. I am asking his boss to gives you a ride."

Once inside, Salim made a beeline for a table in the back and had a short, pleading conversation with a skeptical-looking man, who seemed to dismiss every argument Salim could muster. But, in the end, the matter was settled with smiles and hand-shaking.

"You have a ride," Salim announced, "but we have to hurry."

They walked double-time to the market where Salim had delivered his cantaloupes, and Danny was introduced to Hakan Gultepe. He was a big guy in his thirties with a thick black mustache and a mouthful of gold teeth. Hakan tapped Danny on the arm with a reassuring pat, as if he were a horse or a dog.

"He doesn't speak English," Salim said. "But he's taking you to Bingöl. From there, I'm giving you enough money – no no, this is something I'm doing – enough money to get to Ankara. Don't worry – it's not much. But don't get lost. Hakan leaves you at the *otogar* in Bingöl, then you take a bus to Kayseri. In Kayseri, you change for Ankara." He wrote this down on the back of his business card and handed it to Danny with a ten-million-lire note.

Danny didn't know what to say. "I'll pay you back."

Salim shrugged. "Whatever. It is one of the pillars of Islam," he said. "To give alms to the poor . . . is a duty. But I want you to remember that, yes, bad things can happen in Turkey – but good things, too."

"Salim –"

"I gave you my card," Salim said. "When you get back, I want an e-mail, okay?"

"Yeah. Okay. You got it."

An *abrazo* – "Ciao!" – and Salim strode off in the direction of the village center. Danny watched him go as the *William Tell* Overture sounded yet again: *Dah-dunt! Dah-dunt! Dah-dunt-dunt-dunt-dunt* . . . Then he climbed into the passenger seat of a truck that appeared to be the twin of Salim's own, except that this one was piled high with burlap bags of pistachios. Hakan Gultepe bared his teeth in a gilt-edged smile as the engine coughed, and the truck lurched off into the night to the sound of a sappy Arab tune on the radio.

Nineteen

It was a long walk from the Ankara *otogar* to the U.S. Embassy on Atatürk Boulevard, but there was no other way for Danny to get there. He had about a million lire left from Salim's bounty – enough to buy a gyro but not enough to hail a cab. So he ate as he walked, nearly choking on a piece of green pepper when the amplified ululations of the muezzin cut loose at midday.

It was an hour later that Danny saw it, hanging limply in the pulverizing heat. The flag. Or as he thought of it: *the flaaag*! His heart did a little jig. His Adam's apple seemed to swell. And, for a moment at least, he was as good as home.

But not really.

He had always been under the impression that one of the main responsibilities of the American embassy – *any* American embassy – was to help Americans. Fellow citizens who had hit a rough patch in a foreign land.

But no.

The foreign service officer he spoke with was a young man of about his own age. But there the resemblance ended. Where Danny was dressed in borrowed khakis and a dopey T-shirt, the FSO wore a dark-blue suit, immaculately pressed, and a crisp white shirt with a russet-colored tie. On his desk was a copy of the Princeton *Tory*.

Which brought a snicker to Danny's lips, exposing his remarkable tooth. It was sour grapes, of course. He knew it was wrong to blame the consular official for the fact that he himself was dressed in borrowed clothes, had blood on his sandals, and looked like a madman. Still . . . the Princeton *Tory*?

Leaning back in his chair, the FSO swiveled from side to side, listening to Danny's story with the air of a much older man, his attitude a mix of impatient boredom and naked contempt. Finally, he sighed and said, "Surely you've read the guidebooks. Surfed the Internet or something. I mean, why would *anyone* go to the area around Lake Van, for God's sake?"

"Well –"

"It's *asking* for trouble."

"Right," Danny told him. "That's the point. I'm *in* trouble."

"I can see that," the FSO replied, and, chuckling, shook his head. "But I'm not sure what you expect *me* to do about it."

The remark came as a shock, and for a moment Danny wasn't sure what to say. After a bit, he explained, "I kind of thought you might be able to help. I mean, that's why you're here, isn't it? To help Americans?"

Another sigh. "As a matter of fact," the FSO remarked, "that's probably the least important thing that I do."

"*Is* it?!"

"Yes. Actually, it is."

Danny wanted to smack him, but like the twit in front of him, he, too, had a more important mission – and that was to get home. Preferably without his hands cuffed to his belt. So he swallowed his pride and said,

"Well, I'm sorry about that, but ... what do you suggest I do? How do I get home?" It occurred to him to add, *So I can pay your salary* – but, to Danny's credit, he refrained.

The Princeton man gave him an exasperated look and unscrewed the cap from a Mont Blanc fountain pen. "You said you lost your passport –"

"I said it was stolen."

"Exactly. It was 'stolen.' When?"

"Three days ago."

"And where did this happen?

"Dog Biscuit," Danny replied.

"*Where?*"

"Sounds like 'Dog Biscuit.' I don't know how to spell it."

The FSO, spitting out each syllable, properly enuciated the name of the town, wrote for a bit, then looked up. "What about your luggage?"

"My luggage?"

"Yes. Your clothes and things. Suitcases."

"There was just a backpack," Danny told him. "I don't know what happened to it."

"What about money?" the FSO asked.

Danny shook his head. "They got my wallet, too."

"So you don't even have a driver's license."

Danny nodded. "Right. No clothes. No money or ID. Nothing. I'm a tabula rasa."

A chuckle of contempt. "What did the police say?"

"What police?" Danny asked.

"When you reported the assault."

"But I didn't."

"Why *not*?"

Danny shrugged. "I was pretty confused."

The FSO laid his pen down and sat back in his chair.

371

Folding his hands in his lap, he regarded Danny with a gimlet eye, certain now that something was . . . up. Then he glanced at the clock on the wall – twelve twenty-six – sighed, and pushed a form across his desk. "Fill this out," he said. "We'll make some verifying calls – at your expense – and issue a temporary passport. I'll arrange a one-way ticket to Washington –"

"Thank you."

The FSO snorted. "Don't thank me. It's going to be fucking expensive. I'm not your travel agent and, anyway, there is no advance purchase. You get what you get. And you'll have to reimburse us within thirty days. If you don't, you'll be taken to court and your wages will be garnished." A poisonous smile as a thought occurred to him. "Do you even have a job?"

Danny returned the smile in the same spirit. "No," he said. "I'm an *artiste*."

Three hours later, he had a spanking new passport and a small envelope containing four twenty-dollar bills and a one-way ticket to Dulles. He signed a paper agreeing to repay the United States Treasurer $1,751.40. In his passport photo, behind the iridescent display of eagles and arrows, he looked wasted, like a model in one of those Calvin Klein ads that were popular in the heyday of junkie chic.

He rode out the night in the Hotel Spar, which cost him $8.25. Basic, if clean, it was a kind of purgatory – neither heaven nor hell but somewhere in between. Flat on his back on its hard, thin bed, he lay in the darkness with his eyes on the ceiling, thinking of the bloodshed of the day before. Or was it the day before that? Without newspapers or television – or any responsibilities (other than the need to survive) – time was beginning to get away from him. And he himself was changing, getting older in certain ways. He could feel it.

Layla and Barzan. The washerwoman. The dogs. The soldier's head disintegrating in the air. He remembered something – about the gun. He had very deliberately placed it next to Remy Barzan's body, as if he'd been returning a borrowed book.

Eventually, he fell asleep.

In the morning, he caught a taxi to the airport, where he spent half an hour answering questions at the security gate. It didn't surprise him. He had a one-way ticket, paid for in cash, and no luggage. The clothes he wore were obviously not his own, the pants too short, the shirt too . . . Turkish. His hair was at a peculiar stage, too short to comb, too long to brush back. And then there were the scrapes and bruises. The tooth.

If he'd been a cop, he'd have arrested himself.

Still, it's an ill wind that blows no one any good. Though there were plenty of seats on board, the embassy hadn't bothered to secure him a place on the aisle or next to a window – so he found himself wedged into a middle seat beside an eight-year-old boy and a matron with a head scarf. No sooner was he seated than the woman pressed the call button. A hasty conference with the flight attendant ensued, and Danny soon found that he had three seats to himself.

Which left him with his thoughts – not Barzan, this time, but Caleigh. What should he do? What *could* he do? It occurred to him that he could just show up at her door, looking wounded and pathetic – but no. Pathos wouldn't get the job done, and neither would flowers. Winning Caleigh back was going to take a campaign.

He'd have to lay siege to her and, even then, the outcome was . . . dim.

Until he'd arrived at the embassy in Ankara, there was no way for Zebek to know where he was (though he might have guessed that he was still in Turkey). How wide a net did Zebek cast? Could he access Customs and immigration records? Maybe, maybe not. But sooner or later, Zebek would know that Danny was back in the States – and sooner was probably closer to the truth.

And what was Danny going to do about that? He couldn't run forever. He wasn't cut out for it. No one was. Among other things, he couldn't imagine disappearing from the life of his parents and friends. Not to mention Caleigh. So there wasn't any decision to make. Not really. He had to expose Zebek. As a murderer and a fraud.

That's all. Only . . . how?

The Atlantic slid by under the belly of the plane. The Tanqueray and tonics that the flight attendant gave him were just the thing. Before long, he drifted into an exhausted stupor that was more like a coma than real sleep. When the flight attendant woke him up, it was dark, and the plane was beginning its descent toward the gauzy sprawl of light that was Washington.

His parents still lived in the house where Danny had grown up, across the Potomac in the Rosemont section of Alexandria, a leafy neighborhood only fifteen minutes from National Airport. Their house, a turn-of-the-century colonial on a quarter-acre lot, was as familiar to him as his own heartbeat – which more or less came to a full stop when he knelt beside the planter to feel for the key to the front door and a barrage of

374

security lights flared. He froze in a cone of brightness that would have sufficed to stop a breakout from Attica.

Jesus! When did they put that in?

He shook his head and waited for the tumult in his chest to subside. Since retirement, Dad had gone on a do-it-yourself bender. Restrained for years by lack of time, he had become the Fix-up King, always in the middle of one project or another. Danny fit the key into the dead bolt and let himself in, grateful that the old man had yet to get around to an alarm system.

Standing in the kitchen, he cranked up the air conditioning and grabbed a beer from the refrigerator. Padding silently through the house, he went to the bathroom on the second floor and stripped off his clothes. Then he took a long, hot shower, letting the water pound on his back and shoulders, his face to the ceiling, eyes closed. If he didn't know better, he'd have thought: *Life is good.*

When the hot water threatened to run cold, he wrapped a thick towel around his waist and headed for his old room on the third floor. As befitted the youngest son, this was the smallest bedroom in the house – an attic space with sloping walls and lots of dormers.

Between two of the dormers was a dresser with clothes that he hadn't worn for years but which his mom kept washed and ready – apparently, for days like this. Letting the towel fall, he picked out a pair of jeans and a red sweatshirt, fresh underwear, and socks, and dressed, luxuriating in the feel of his own clean clothes.

The room was pretty much as he'd left it: clunky wooden furniture and muted plaids. A Phish poster on

375

one wall, an "early Cray" on another. In the corner, on a small bookshelf, was a tacky collection of dusty soccer trophies and a plaque commemorating his second-place finish in the eight hundred at the Woodbridge Invitational.

A little pile of mail was stacked on the desk – non-urgent stuff that still came to his parents' address. His mom held it for him, and every couple of weeks, when he dropped by to see them, he went through it. And it was always the same: alumni appeals from T.C. Williams and William & Mary ("the College of Knowledge"); some art-supply catalogs, and credit-card offers – the usual junk, in other words, except this time there was one envelope of real interest. And he didn't have to open it to know what it was: its stiffness and weight, coupled with the printed injunction that it should not be forwarded, marked it as a credit card.

A Platinum Visa card, as it turned out – with a William & Mary embossure. It was probably the first account he'd ever had, and given the interest rate it charged, he'd intended to cancel it. But now the renewal had gone through on its own, and he was glad. It had a 2004 expiration date and a ten-thousand-dollar limit – which made it a gift from the gods.

The paper folder that held the card noted that it was necessary to activate it from your home telephone number – in this case, obviously, the phone at his parents' house. So he shuffled down the hall to Kev's old room and punched in the numbers. Then he went through the rest of the mail while he waited on hold. A clutch of postcards from galleries (they never seemed to update their mailing lists), including one from Neon. The front bore a photo of *Forest and Threes*. The back announced:

The announcement looked great – Lavinia had done well by him. But Jesus! The opening! How was he going to mount it? And with what?

Finally, a real person came on the line and he activated the card. After shaking off a pitch for "credit insurance," he hung up the phone, nicked the tape from the back of the card, and peeled it off. Then he went to his room, because finding the credit card reminded him of money, and money reminded him of –

The closet in his room. This was one of those 1920s creations, suitable for someone who owned three shirts, two pairs of pants, a belt, a tie, and a jacket. Recognizing the need for more storage space, Danny's father had undertaken one of his first home improvement projects. This was a box at the back of the closet, measuring thirty inches on each side. It had served during Danny's childhood as the repository of successive ruling passions. At one time or another, it had held Star Wars toys, Nintendo games, hockey pads, a Fender Stratocaster and a Sidekick amp, a wet suit and flippers. But that was just the *top* of the box. Danny had long ago undertaken his own "home improvement" project, creating a false bottom that was about an inch deep. It was in this hiding place, under the Nintendo games and hockey pads, that he'd kept his copies of *Playboy* and *Penthouse*, packages of Marlboros, Zig-Zag papers, and the occasional plastic sandwich bag stuffed with marijuana.

But Danny's stash was not just a repository for

passing vices. It also contained what his brother Kev called "the cache." This was a secret savings account to which each of the brothers had contributed, squirreling away whatever spare change they happened to find at the end of the day. The goal: to buy a racehorse – specifically, an Arabian. And not just any Arabian – it had to be a stallion. And not just any stallion – it had to be . . . black.

Kevin, famous for his passionate enthusiasms, was behind it, but that didn't matter. The dream had been pursued by the three of them for months on end. In its earliest days, as much as fifteen dollars a week – money earned by mowing lawns or, legend had it, by searching the couch and the car seats for lost change – had been secretly deposited. The limited dimensions of the cache made it necessary for the change to be regularly converted into dollar bills, which Danny did each week. And then, every other week. And then – once a month . . . or every other month. He'd take the coins in a Tupperware container to the local Safeway, where a machine counted the change in return for a cut.

Eventually, Kev did the math and revealed that it would take about three hundred years for them to save enough money to buy (he'd already named it) Yankee Pasha. And so the money remained where it was, abiding the moment when they might all agree on how it should be spent. Which they never did.

Getting down on his knees, Danny reached into the storage box that his father had built and removed the false panel at the bottom. Reaching inside, he rooted about until he came up with a fistful of hard cash in each hand. Taking the money to the bed, he sat down and separated the currency by denomination. This done, he found that he had two stacks of bills, containing 126 notes. When counted, the total came to $182.

As "walking-around money," the bankroll was at best an awkward asset, so thick that it would not allow him to fold his wallet. Going down to the kitchen, he found a rubber band in the "junk drawer" next to the stove and trussed the money into a thick cylinder. Pocketing the cash, he saw with a groan that, on inspection, the bankroll made him look like a pervert.

But there was nothing he could do about that. Wandering through the house, he thought about sleeping downstairs on the big bed in his parents' room, but when he got there it didn't seem right. Though his own bed was short and the space cramped, the little room at the top of the stairs had been a refuge throughout his childhood and adolescence. It was no different now.

The birds woke him at six. His mother fed them and even paid one of the neighbor kids to "keep them going" while she was gone. The holly tree outside his window sounded like a bird ghetto. He went downstairs and made himself a cup of coffee, then sat by the window overlooking the garden, doodling on one of his father's yellow legal pads.

He wanted to call someone – Caleigh most of all – but *someone* in any case. His brothers. His parents. But no. That would only put them in harm's way, and there was nothing to be gained from it – except solace. And he wasn't that selfish. Besides, he wasn't ready to face that cold High Plains look that Caleigh got when she was mad or feeling victimized. Better – *safer* – to let Zebek think that they were through (which, in the absence of a miracle, they were).

By now, the yellow-lined paper was covered with radiant lines and constellations of dots. Danny thought for a moment, then scribbled:

1) Dew
2) Patel case

Then he reached for the phone and dialed a number he knew by heart: Fellner Associates. At the prompt, he tapped in the code for Mamadou's extension.

A soft voice answered distractedly, "Boisseau."

"Dew? It's –"

Click.

He stared at the phone, baffled. Dialed it a second time. Got the voice-mail recording. *Maybe someone's in his office,* Danny thought, and made a second cup of coffee. He'd try Dew later, at his apartment.

Except he didn't have to because, a few minutes later, the phone rang and when he picked it up it was Mamadou at the other end, sounding out of breath and outside. Danny could hear the surf of traffic in the background.

"What the fuck were you thinking?" Dew exploded. "Were you outta your mind?"

"I don't think so," Danny replied. "What are you talkin' about?"

"First you cut out the firm on work for one of its biggest accounts. So Fellner's pissed, but that's not so bad, 'cause the client came to you – right?"

"Right."

"Only then you ask *me* – your poor African-American friend – to put together a dossier on the guy, which makes me, like, an *accessory.*"

"To what?" Danny asked.

"What do you think?"

"I don't know. I don't know what we're talking about."

"Industrial espionage!" Dew barked.

"What?!"

"That's what they call it. That's the kind of case they're building," Dew explained. "You take a job with the guy, walk off with all kinds of proprietary intelligence –"

"Oh, bullshit –"

"Lemme ask you a question," Dew suggested.

"Okay," Danny replied, feeling increasingly uncomfortable.

"Did you pick up a computer for someone? In Italy?"

"Yeah."

"And you claimed to be a cop, right?"

"Well –"

"Jesus Christ, man! You're going to the joint!"

"Dew –"

"This ain't no bullshit – this guy Zebek, he's hired the firm to find you!"

"Calm down," Danny told him. "It's not like that."

"I'm telling you: you're our biggest case! I am now talking on the telephone to our biggest case!"

Hmnnn . . . Danny took a deep breath and hoped that Mamadou would take the opportunity to do the same. "Whose case is it?"

"Pisarcik."

Ooof. Until the year before, Pisarcik had headed up the CIA's operations directorate.

"If it was me," Dew said, "I'd stay away from known haunts. In fact, if it was me, I'd think about . . . Yokohama. Or the Bering Strait, or something."

"You mean –"

"I mean your apartment's under twenty-four-hour surveillance." He let that sink in. "You know how much that costs? Three two-man teams, giving twenty-four/seven coverage?"

Danny groaned. "Where else?"

"*Every*where else! Pisarcik's got a wall map with pins in it: the gallery, your studio, your folks' place, Caleigh's office –"

"My folks' place, huh?"

"I told you – everywhere. Pisarcik even hired a local to keep an eye on your parents place in Maine. So forget about that too. But the Adam's Morgan apartment is the only place that's twenty-four/seven. Everywhere else, it's mobile. Guys making the rounds, going from one place to the other."

A thought occurred to Danny. "So how did *you* know where I was?"

"Rocket science! I got Caller ID."

Danny sighed. He could hear the traffic rocking past his friend. Finally, he said, "Well, I owe you one."

"There's more!"

"About what?" Danny asked.

"Zebek's firm."

"Sistema –"

"Not that one," Dew insisted. "The one on the Coast! VSS."

"What about it?"

"It's a nanotech firm."

"Which is what?" Danny asked.

" 'The next big thing.' Get it?"

"No."

"Nanotech. Very Small Systems! 'Big thing'?"

"I don't know what you're talking about."

"It's like . . . one of those just-around-the-corner things. Gonna change everything."

"*Is* it —"

"Unh-huh."

"And how's it gonna do that?" Danny wondered.

"I don't know. But the whole thing is: It's *small*. *Very small*, get it? A way of building things from the ground up – like nature. Except we're talking robots – the size of molecules. These particular bots, they're like . . . proteins. And that's what this guy, Zebek, is into. Technically, VSS is a subsidiary of the Italian company, but trust me, it's the tail wagging the dog, you know what I'm saying?"

Danny was about to say *Unh-huh* when the doorbell went off in his head like a cluster bomb – and his heart dove for cover. "Someone's at the door," he whispered.

"Well, don't answer it."

Danny checked the sight lines. From where he was sitting, he couldn't be seen. And there were no lights on in the house. It was morning, and the kitchen was the brightest room.

With the phone pressed to his ear, he went into the dining room, where the windows were shuttered against the street. Through a slit in the shutters, he saw two men in suits standing at the front door. The doorbell rang a second time.

"Guys in suits," Danny whispered.

"You recognize them?"

"No."

"Then they're probably subs."

Subcontractors. "Probably," Danny agreed.

One of the men pressed his nose to the sidelight next to the door, shaded his right eye, and peered into the house. After a moment, he said something to the second man, and they returned to their car, a gray Camry, parked across the street in front of the Lanmans'. Danny waited for them to drive away, but . . . they didn't. "They're just sitting there," he said.

"Where?"

"In the car."

"So wait 'em out," Dew advised. "They got a whole checklist of places. Half an hour, they'll be gone."

"Then what?"

Dew chuckled. "Flaps up – head down. Learn a foreign language."

He found an old L.L. Bean backpack in the mudroom, picked out a change of clothes from the chest of drawers in his room, added some extra T-shirts and boxers, a toothbrush, a razor. That done, he made sure that he had his passport, the new credit card, and the Yankee Pasha bankroll. Then he sat down with a copy of *Harper's* and waited.

Dew obviously knew what he was talking about. After twenty-five minutes, the Camry roared to life and pulled away from the curb. Danny gave it another ten minutes, in case they came back, then let himself out through an old garage door whose existence was concealed by a vast and overgrown camellia bush. Pushing out through the screen of heavy foliage, he remembered the many times he sneaked out that way when he was a kid. He felt a little stupid and theatrical as he cut through the Whitestones' yard. Until he remembered Remy Barzan. Inzaghi. Chris Terio.

The King Street Metro was only a few blocks away. When he got to the station, he fed a couple of dollar bills into the fare-card machine, caught the blue line train, and rode it to Rosslyn, a clusterfuck of high-rises opposite Georgetown on the Virginia side of the Potomac.

He was thinking about nanotech. What little he knew owed more to a half-forgotten NPR program than to anything that Dew had said. The program was the *Diane Rehm Show,* and he'd listened to it in the car, riding out toward Harpers Ferry with Caleigh.

Mamadou had it right: the basic idea was to create machines capable of working at the atomic level. That way, you could make things from the bottom up. Instead of tunneling into rock to extract diamonds from a mine, you'd fabricate them one atom at a time – just as nature does. In theory, then, you could make almost anything – diamond wire or a perfect rose – from materials as common as seawater, air, and sand. And it wasn't just what the machines could *make* that gave nanotech so much promise: it was what they might someday be able to *do*. Working at the atomic level, they'd be able to restore the ozone layer, identify and eliminate individual contaminants from the water supply, and a lot more.

The train rolled along: Crystal City, Pentagon City, Pentagon. Danny thought about Chris Terio's house and in particular the bookcase in his study. He had all those books on religion, of course, but there were other books that didn't seem to belong. Danny didn't remember the titles, but one of them was about "protein computers" and another one – at *least* another one – had *nanotech* in the title.

So Terio was onto it, knew enough to reach out to Patel. And who was Patel? The main tech guy at Very Small Systems. And what was VSS? According to

Remy Barzan, it was Zebek's baby. And it was burning through cash like there was no tomorrow.

Georgetown itself doesn't have a Metro stop. When the subway was being built, the neighborhood's upscale residents balked at the prospect, worried about "the kind of people" who use mass transit.

Danny rode the escalator to ground level in Rosslyn, emerging in the heat of the day, surrounded by twenty- and thirty-story buildings. Rosslyn always struck him as strange. Beyond the purview of the District's height restrictions, it seemed to happen all at once, rising up out of nowhere, the architectural equivalent of Ayer's Rock. Gannett's silver towers gleamed in the sun as Danny walked across the Key Bridge into Georgetown.

At a safe remove from the city's commercial heart, Georgetown University's campus was organized around an old-fashioned quad. Entering the university library, Danny relished the arctic air that enveloped him.

Working for Fellner, he'd long ago learned that most universities were generous with their resources. While you needed a card to check out books, no one seemed to pay much attention to who was using the computers or reference materials. The assumption was that you were a student or faculty member.

Taking a seat at the end of a long table, he logged onto the Lexis/Nexis database and searched for newspaper and magazine articles that mentioned Jason Patel.

Unlike Chris Terio's "suicide," Patel's death was a brutal and unsolved murder, a high-profile case with lots of media coverage. It only took a minute or so to come up with 126 hits – everything from MSNBC transcripts to newspaper reports and obits in the *San Jose Mercury* and other, smaller papers.

Basically he was looking for names. Friends, relatives, coworkers – anyone who knew Patel and who might be willing to talk about him. He printed out a selection of stories and clicked on the NEW SEARCH button.

He wanted to see how much there was on the Net about "Very Small Systems or VSS or V.S.S." Not much, as it turned out: only twenty-seven hits – which was nothing when you considered that Nexis included even the most obscure technical and business journals.

Danny looked at each of the citations and found that most of them stemmed from a single conference on protein engineering, held three years earlier in Philadelphia. VSS had hosted a hospitality suite, and the organizers of the conference had mentioned the fact in a press release.

A search for "Zerevan Zebek" turned up next to nothing. Danny wondered how someone with so much money could keep a profile that low.

Finally, he left Nexis and moved to a different computer, surfing the Web for articles about nanotech. Using the Google search engine, he punched in "nanotechnology" and was immediately rewarded with nearly half a million hits. He went from one to another for more than an hour, finally printing out a dozen articles on the subject.

Then he tapped his accumulated take into a tidy stack and went out for something to eat. Stopping at the Staples on M Street, he bought a Kraft-colored accordion file to hold the printouts. Then he crossed the street to a pizza place and took a table in the corner, away from the windows. While he waited for his food, he took a second look at some of the pages he'd printed out.

An hour later, the pizza was history, he was on his second cup of coffee, and he knew quite a bit more about Jason Patel and his murder. The official obituary was in the *Cupertino Courier*. It noted that Patel was a graduate of UC Berkeley and Caltech, with advanced degrees in computer science and molecular biology. He'd done postdoctoral work at M.I.T., published widely, and received the Sidran Prize for research on micro-electro-mechanical systems (MEMS). He was forty-two years old at the time of his death. Survivors included a sister, Indira, of Delhi, and a "life partner," Glenn Unger, of Cupertino.

The earliest stories about the death hinted that foul play was suspected. By the second day, however, it was murder, and it was page one. Vague statements from police spokesmen about "substantive leads" and allusions to the murder as a suspected "crime of passion" were buried in the gruesome details, most of them provided by shaken members of the Interior Department team that had stumbled upon Patel's corpse in the desert.

There was an interesting interview with an archaeologist who theorized that the manner in which Patel was left exposed perfectly mimicked the ancient burial practices of certain Amerindian tribes. It was called excarnation – bodies left so that birds would take the flesh. The professor spieled on about how very old the practice was, about how it was still followed by sects in parts of the Middle East, about its connection to the Prometheus myth. In the Patel murder, there were also, the professor opined, resonances with the central event of the Christian faith. The tribes and sects practicing excarnation used it as a ritual after death, building burial grounds or platforms where bodies were left to the birds. Patel, however, had been alive when his body was pierced by dozens of cholla spines, alive when he was strung up on the cross-shaped Joshua tree.

Crucified.

Twenty

Back in the library, Danny clicked through cyberspace, looking for cheap flights to San Francisco. He had to get out of D.C. anyway, and California beckoned because the more he learned, the clearer it became that Very Small Systems was the key to everything.

Not that he was planning to ask for a tour of the facilities. The idea was to start by doorstepping Patel's friend, Glenn Unger.

A pop-up ad from Hertz launched an unhappy thought. You pretty much *had* to have wheels in California, and Danny had been intending to rent a car at the airport. But as the yellow Hertz logo blinked on his screen, he realized that there was a problem. He didn't have a driver's license.

Could he take a taxi to Glenn Unger's doorstep? Where *was* Cupertino from the airport anyway? What about San Jose? Could he fly there? By the time he got the answer from MapQuest, he decided a car was essential. He'd have to hit the DMV and replace his license.

But he only had an hour to book the great fare he'd found on Hotwire, so he might as well do that first. Halfway through the process, he changed his mind. He didn't want to use his card for the flight if he could help it. Zebek might not have access to credit card transactions, but then again, Danny wouldn't bet on it.

There was no reason to advertise his itinerary if he could avoid it. The Yankee Pasha bankroll wasn't going to take him very far, but he could use the platinum card to get a cash advance at a bank.

Before logging off the library's computer, he checked the Virginia DMV Web site. He'd kept his Virginia license and registered the Olds at his parents' address. The insurance was cheaper. The Web site listed a branch in Rosslyn, right across the river. He left the library, walked through a wall of heat to the Riggs bank on Wisconsin and M, and came out the door a few minutes later with twenty-five hundred dollars, his cash advance limit.

After a twenty-minute walk to the DMV, he stood in line to get a number. Waiting his turn, he tried to guess the languages he was hearing – Spanish, of course, but Arabic, too. German and Chinese. Vietnamese or Thai – he couldn't tell the difference. Something else. Russian or Czech.

What a country. . . .

Finally, his number was called. He explained to the woman at the counter that he'd lost his wallet sailing.

"How did you do that?" she asked.

"I was hiking out."

" 'Hiking out'?" She made a face. "I thought you said *sailing*."

"It's when you hang out over the side of the boat," he explained, "so the boat can go faster."

"Then why don't you just get a *motor*?" she wondered with a little smile.

"Because *then*," he replied, "it wouldn't be sailing."

She gave a good-natured shake of the head, tapped something into her computer, and sent him on his way. He soon found himself seated on a stool in front of a

391

walleyed woman with talonlike fingernails. "Say 'queso'!" she ordered.

He smiled weakly.

She waited, one eye on him, the other on the next guy in line.

Ten seconds later, he said, "Queso."

She smiled, and the camera went nova.

Finally, he was summoned to the front counter, where a laminated driver's license awaited him. He didn't want to look, but . . . *Jesus*! It was even worse than the picture in the passport shot. He had that crazy-wasted-and-stunned look that you see in police photos – eyes neither open nor closed but caught in mid-blink, his mouth frozen on the brink of a smile. It was enough of a smile to reveal the gleam of the stainless steel cap, and this added a demented edge to his overall appearance. All this against a bright blue background.

But hey – at least his hair was back (kind of).

The flight was direct via Salt Lake City. He had the middle seat near the back of the plane, wedged between a pair of elderly golfing buddies returning from a tour of the Scottish Highlands. No sooner were they airborne than one of them obtained a couple of plastic glasses from the flight attendant and began pouring shots of single-malt whiskey, decanting the golden liquid from a silver-plated hip flask.

"You golf?" someone asked.

Danny shook his head. "No, I –"

"Well, you'll get around to it," a second man said. "Everyone does, sooner or later."

They told stories about their trip, Danny's head moving back and forth as if he were watching a tennis match. Eventually the golfers drank themselves to sleep, leaving Danny free to read the articles that he'd printed out at Georgetown.

It was not a rational selection. He'd just clicked on entries that sounded interesting, with the result that he had a mish-mosh. Some of the material was impossibly technical, while other articles were so moony and gaga about *The Future* that they were useless. Still, by the time the plane crossed the Continental Divide, he'd read enough to know what nanotech was and what it promised.

The grandfather of the field was a guy named Eric Drexler, who'd written a book in the eighties called *Engines of Creation*. An M.I.T. research fellow, Drexler was considered a clear-eyed visionary by some and a delusional dreamer by others. The former declared that Drexler had found the key to the Promised Land, while the latter insisted that he'd hypothesized a science that couldn't possibly work.

As Danny understood it, the basic idea was to manufacture things by rearranging matter with atomic precision. This would be accomplished by protein engineers (!) working with computer scientists to program and create self-replicating robots no larger than molecules. By arranging individual atoms these bots or "assemblers" could carry out an array of tasks, manufacturing everything from micron-thin diamond coatings to submicroscopic sprays capable of healing wounds in an instant. Within the body, other tiny bots would target cancer cells, destroying them one at a time, or might scrub arterial walls of plaque. As above, so below – as within, so without. The assemblers could be programmed to dismantle pollutants, to purify the air and water – *all* of it – constantly, globally.

393

Eventually, enormous efficiencies would result, creating a world of absolute abundance. Poverty would become a thing of the past. The environment would be healed, and life prolonged.

Bots, Danny thought. Like robots, only *not* robots – because they'd be made of DNA. Which meant they'd be alive. Tiny Frankensteins, then.

His two seatmates lurched off at the stop in Salt Lake, but Danny stayed put. He read a description of a hypothetical something called "utility fog." This was a primordial *stuff*, a network of assemblers capable of being – literally – all things to all people. Engineered to assume the shape and characteristics of a house, utility fog could be programmed to change not only its texture and color but also its very state – and to do this on command. That is, it could be solid as a brick one moment and porous as air the next. With a wave of the hand, the occupant of such a house could walk through walls and extrude furniture from the floor, as needed, in whatever shape and material he desired.

In short, nanotechnology promised (or threatened) to devise a world so deeply embedded with possibilities – so flexible – that even the most ordinary activities would be indistinguishable from magic.

Once in the air again, Danny sipped a gin-and-tonic and resumed reading. But not without an effort. Some of the articles he'd downloaded were more than fifty pages long and, to him, incomprehensible. At some point or other, they lost him with references to things like "petaflops," "extropians," and "Knuth's arrow notation." The truth was, he didn't have the background to understand a lot of what he was reading.

Still, by the time they began their descent into San Francisco he understood enough about nanotechnology to know that it was important, controversial – and, for the most part, still theoretical. The promise was so great that a ton of money was going into the field and it was being spent by some big names. Hewlett-Packard, IBM, companies like that. The government gave the field a big push during the Clinton administration, doubling its investment in nanotech to half a billion dollars.

A quote from the National Science and Technology Council in support of the increased funding put it this way:

> Nanotechnology could impact the production of virtually every human-made object – everything from automobiles, tires, and computer circuits to advanced medicines and tissue replacements – and lead to the invention of objects yet to be imagined. . . . As the twenty-first century unfolds, nanotechnology's impact on the health, wealth, and security of the world's people is expected to be at least as significant as the combined influences in this century of antibiotics, the integrated circuit, and human-made polymers.

Which was saying something. The consensus seemed to be that most applications were at least a decade away. Certain innovations (creating vaccines, et cetera) might be closer, and there'd been a recent breakthrough in building a nanotransistor. This promised to transform microelectronics, allowing the manufacture of integrated circuits on an unimaginably tiny scale, stuff that would work at room temperature, that would not be as sensitive to dust and contamination as silicon and other materials.

To date, however, the most important advances seemed like parlor tricks. One scientist had built a nanoguitar; another had fashioned a pair of tweezers small enough to pick up single molecules. A molecular switch had been constructed, and a "quantum corral." These modest achievements had required enormous efforts by teams of geniuses. Many scientists continued to believe that the technical problems of producing assemblers with workable "arms," capable of manipulating matter at an atomic level, were insurmountable.

This was the crux of the anti-Drexlerian position: the devices required to make nanotech work were stipulated by computer scientists (for the most part), but the actual task of creating them would fall to biochemists, microbiologists, and molecular engineers – who, as often as not, did not have a clue as to how to make them.

For instance, the prevailing wisdom was that for raw material the assemblers would use air, water, and dirt. These materials would be deconstructed at the molecular level and reassembled according to specifications. But how would the assemblers be fueled? By the sun? Perhaps. But even if solar energy could be used, the process of taking apart and putting together molecules was certain to generate heat – and probably lots of it. What was to be done with it?

Moreover, while visionaries drew up cute cartoons of critters with nanotube arms capable of sundering and fusing molecular bonds, skeptics wondered how one created tools small enough to manipulate individual atoms. And what about the "arms" on the assemblers? How would they "hold" individual atoms so that they could be assembled according to plan? To the suggestion that chemical bonds might be used to cause the fragments to "stick," skeptics replied that such bonds were often quite strong. How could the assemblers be made to release the atoms or fragments that they held?

Some of these questions would be answered. Perhaps all of them would. But it was going to take a while – probably quite a while. *So why,* Danny wondered, *why are people dying now?*

It was a little after eight P.M. when his flight touched down at San Francisco Airport. A shuttle bus took him to the Alamo facility a couple of miles up the road, where a white Prism waited for him. He wanted to pay in cash, but because of insurance regulations, Alamo wouldn't rent the car without putting the card number on the agreement. He told himself it was a *car,* after all, a moving target. Besides, although the card was being checked for authorization, there was no actual transaction yet. With luck, nothing would post up to his account until he returned the car. He signed on the dotted line.

He got lost for about an hour, heading off in the wrong direction, and by the time he recovered, driving to Cupertino that night seemed like a bad idea. So did showing up at Glenn Unger's door at eleven or eleven-thirty. Passing a Doubletree Motel in Burlingame, he said the hell with it, cut a U-turn, and pulled in. Half an hour later, he was sound asleep, too tired to turn out the light on the nightstand beside the bed.

He'd expected to wake up early because by now his body had no idea what time zone it was in, but he slept for fourteen hours straight. He took his time over breakfast, anyway. Waiting for his Belgian waffle, he read a story in a magazine he'd taken from the plane.

He'd found it in the seat pocket during a break from his long session with the nanotechnology documents, an issue of the *National Geographic Traveler*. Leafing through, he'd spotted an article about Easter Island. And that's why he took it. For the first time, looking at the photographs, he saw the monumental heads not just as remnants of a mysterious civilization but as *sculpture*. And as sculpture, they interested him.

Turned out, Easter Island was a cautionary tale. The original Polynesian travelers had stumbled into paradise. The island was bountiful, so full of natural resources – water, timber, fish, vast flocks of birds – that the population increased rapidly. As evidenced by the complex hieroglyphic writing and hundreds of massive stone figures left behind, the islanders developed a sophisticated civilization. Experts considered that quarrying, transporting, and erecting the huge stone figures would be difficult even today. The techniques used to accomplish the feat by "primitive" islanders were still in dispute.

After a thousand years, the bounty of the land had run out and Easter Island was an ecological disaster. The forests were completely gone, leaving the islanders without a means of building boats, either for escape or for offshore fishing (not big planners, Danny thought). The ground cover was history, too, probably eaten. With no trees to generate moisture, the springs dried up; the vast flocks of birds – with no place to roost and nothing to eat or drink – flew off and did not return. Warring factions developed around 1600. By the time the Dutch explorer who gave the place its name "discovered" the island on Easter Sunday in the year 1720, the islanders were literally eating their young. Cannibalism had become the major source of protein. Women and children were considered the most tasty, fingers and toes the choicest bits. *Nice*, Danny thought, glad he was a vegetarian.

It was close to noon when he got a second cup of coffee for the road and headed south toward Cupertino.

A few miles down the road, he started to get an idea about an installation for the Neon. *Talking Heads*, he'd call it. He'd construct some big Easter Island–like heads out of papier-mâché, but they'd be . . . media figures. Dan Rather, Mike Wallace, Oprah. Present-day icons. Most of the heads on Easter Island were built on platforms called *anu*, in which the islanders had placed ritual objects. In the installation maybe he'd build open platforms – wooden frameworks – and put the heads on top. Inside the frameworks, he'd put . . . television sets. Television sets that would be turned on . . . to news programs or talk shows or MSNBC.

The idea had a kind of fuzzy logic to it that he liked. He wasn't sure what it *meant*, but that was okay. He turned on the radio and let it all slosh around in his head as he drove on toward Cupertino.

Patel's house – which now belonged to Glenn Unger – was an immaculately restored bungalow that, given the neighborhood, was probably worth at least a million.

The beautiful door, flanked by diamond-mullioned sidelights, had been stripped back to its natural oak – which set off the black wreath at its center. Danny had never seen a mourning wreath before, and it creeped him out. The thing was actually made of *feathers*, black and curling feathers, so shiny as to be almost iridescent. With a grimace, he reached for the brass knocker encircled by the wreath.

The instant his hand touched metal, the door flew open, as if it were being yanked away from his fingertips – which, in fact, it was. The effect was startling, almost like an electric shock, and it made him jump.

"*Yes?*"

The man in the doorway was forty-something and in great shape, as was made clear by the fact that he wore only a pair of running shorts. That was it in terms of clothing, except for a pair of reading glasses and flip-flops. "Can I help you?"

"Doorstepping" people was not something that Danny liked to do. No one did, really. But it was something every investigator had to do from time to time – because some people refused to answer their phones. Or if they answered their phones, they might not then be willing to take the next step of inviting the investigator to meet with them. The first time Danny had been told to doorstep a reluctant "source," he'd complained. *What am I supposed to say? I don't even know the guy!*

So? Pretend you're trick-or-treating, his boss told him. *Give him a copy of the* Watchtower! *I don't care. Just do it.* And so he had. As it happened, he was pretty good at it.

"Mr. Unger?"

The man narrowed his eyes. "Yesss?"

"My name's Danny Cray, and . . . I was hoping we could talk about your friend. Mr. Patel."

An exasperated sigh. "Ohh, for God's sake," Unger

whined. "What are you? Some kind of . . . alternative newspaper reporter?"

"No –"

"Because I'm not interested in publicity."

"I understand that, but –"

"Good. Then you'll understand why I'm closing the door. Bye!" The last word was sung and, somehow, came out as two syllables rather than one. *Bye-eee*.

Danny had never actually "stuck his foot in the door" – not literally. But this time, he did. "I've come a really long way," he said.

Unger glanced at the intrusive foot, then looked up. "Do you mind?"

"Like . . . thousands of miles."

"Aren't you embarrassed to do that?"

Danny shrugged but left his foot where it was. "I think I can tell you why Mr. Patel was killed."

Unger frowned and cocked his head and gave Danny the once-over. "Is that supposed to be news? Everyone knows why Jason was killed."

It was Danny's turn to be surprised. "They *do*?"

"Of course."

Danny blinked.

"He was murdered by some gay-bashing, homophobic nut. Or nuts. It still happens. Now, if you have information –"

"I don't think so."

Unger gave him a skeptical look. "Pardon me?"

"I don't think it had anything to do with sexual preference."

The man in front of him hesitated, the indecision easy to read on his face. "If this is bullshit . . ."

"It isn't," Danny told him.

With a sigh, Unger stepped back and held the door open wide. "All right," he said, "you might as well come in."

The interior of the bungalow was like an antique shop devoted exclusively to Craftsman style. Everything was of the period, every picture frame, every *objet*. Danny almost expected to see price tags attached to the furniture. Unger ushered him straight through the rooms, through the "vestibule" to the "parlor" to a period kitchen and, finally, to a little patio in the rear.

This was as perfect as the house itself, with a small fountain burbling in the corner. Set out on a wrought-iron table was a pitcher of iced tea and a plate of micro-thin ginger cookies. Unger gestured to a chair, and the two men sat down opposite each other. Using a swizzle stick in the form of a giraffe with a very long neck, Unger stirred the pitcher and looked up. "Iced tea?"

Danny nodded. "Thanks." The hardest part – getting through the door – was over. It was now up to Danny to convince Unger, in his grief, to confide in a stranger. The only way Danny knew to accomplish that was to establish his own bona fides with a confession. So he cleared his throat. "I think I may have been responsible – indirectly – for Mr. Patel's death."

A sharp intake of breath across the table, and a look of alarm.

"I was hired by a man named Zerevan Zebek," Danny explained, "to find out who another man – a professor named Terio – was talking to." He took a sip of tea. "Zebek said he was being smeared in the press," Danny went on, "and that Terio was behind it – Terio and some other people."

Unger folded his arms and sat back, a look of wary impatience on his face.

"He wanted me to find out who Terio was talking to," Danny said. "And I did. I got a copy of his telephone records –"

"You can do that?"

Danny nodded. "There are information brokers who sell that sort of thing."

Unger's voice became droll. "And that didn't strike you as an invasion of Jason's privacy?"

Danny made a hapless gesture. "Yeah, I suppose it did, but – working as an investigator, it's . . . well, one of the things you do."

Unger was not impressed. "Well," he said, "it's one of the things *you* do."

Danny took the point. "Right," he admitted.

"Go on."

"Anyway, I found out Terio was talking to your friend – and two other men. A scientist in Oslo. And a journalist in Istanbul."

Unger's skepticism manifested itself in a snort. "Jason's never been to either of those places."

"That's not the point," Danny said.

"Then what *is*?"

"They're all dead," Danny told him.

"Who arc?"

"Terio. The scientist in Oslo. The Turkish journalist. Patel."

Unger took a sip of tea. After a bit, he leaned forward and said, "Bull-dooky."

The expression caught Danny by surprise, but he kept a straight face and shrugged. "It's not."

"You're suggesting Zebek had Jason killed –"

"That's right."

"But Zebek *owns* VSS."

"That's right," Danny agreed. "He does."

"And you're suggesting he had Jason killed after *stealing* him from Protein Dynamics? After *luring* him with bonuses and options?"

"Yes."

"Well, it doesn't make sense," Unger insisted. "Jason wasn't just a worker bee over there. He was like a guru. VSS will never replace him. His loss is a disaster. Everyone says so. He was brilliant!"

"I'm sure he was," Danny replied. "But something happened."

"You mean this, this *nonsense* about smearing the company?"

"No, that was just a pretext –"

"Then what?" Unger asked.

Danny sighed. "I don't know. I was hoping you could tell me."

They went over it again, with Danny taking it from the top. As he talked, he watched the skeptical expression on Glenn Unger's handsome face evaporate. A bewildered look set in and, finally, a distressed one.

"I could go on," Danny said. "But that's . . . the major stuff."

"Have you told the police about this?" Unger asked.

Danny shook his head. "I don't think the local police could get their heads around it. We're talking about, what, five murders in four countries? Plus the 'collateral damage' in Turkey. And the only thing I can prove, really, is that the people who were killed knew the same guy – Terio."

Unger nodded, his forehead tunneling into a frown. "Jay *was* worried about something – something at work. And he *did* know this Terio person. They talked on the phone, once or twice. There may have been e-mails, and I think they may have met at a conference somewhere." He looked up, trying to remember, then shook his head. "But . . ." He laid his hand over his face, covering his features. For a long moment he stayed as he was, and then he drew his hand up and over his forehead, until it perched atop the crown of his head. He sat like that for what seemed like a long time, pressing his fingers into his skull. Then he let his arm drop and shook his head. "I don't know," he said. "I just don't know."

The guy had tears in his eyes. "You okay?" Danny asked.

Unger nodded. "What you're saying about Zebek – if it's true." A pause. "It doesn't bring Jason back – nothing can. But it restores him to me, in a way. Because the police . . . everyone assumes we're promiscuous . . . that we're constantly cruising, out of control. But the truth is: I work so fucking hard – I'm an architect. And as for Jason, well, don't get me started on Jason! I had to *drag* him home from work. But the police . . . they seem to think it's normal for someone like Jason to be killed that way. To them, it's some kind of 'gay thing' and that's all." He paused, drew in a long breath, then exhaled. "So . . . I guess I owe you."

"No, you don't –"

"Just tell me what I can do."

Danny thought about it. "You could show me his computer."

Unger tilted his head from side to side, as if to say, *Yes and no.* Then he got to his feet and gestured for Danny to follow. Together they walked into an alcove off the dining room, where a flat-screen Silicon Graphics monitor sat on a vintage oak desk. Unger seated himself in a matching swivel chair, reached under the desk, and turned on the computer.

"Is that it?" Danny asked. It looked like a Dell, and he was expecting something snazzier – though what he couldn't say.

"This one's mine," Unger told him. "Jay had a laptop that he used and another one at the office. And a Palm."

"Which are where?"

"The police have them," Unger said, sitting back in his chair.

The Microsoft Desktop swam into view with a fanfare from the speakers. The wallpaper was a picture of Unger and another man, hanging over the railing of a cruise ship. The second man was short, dark, and handsome. "Is that Jay?" Danny asked.

Unger nodded.

"What about his e-mail?" Danny asked. "Can you get it?"

"I don't think so," Unger replied. "I'm a Yahoo person, and Jay got his mail at work. They've got firewalls and everything."

"Do you know his password?"

Unger made a scoffing sound. "It wasn't a word. It was a jumble of letters and numbers and God knows what else! I think there were a dozen of them and, anyway, the security people made them change it every month, so . . . no."

Danny thought for a moment. "What about VSS?" he asked. "Do you think you could get me in?"

" 'In'?"

"Yeah. So I can talk to someone on the inside. Find

out what's going on. Find out what they're doing –"

Unger turned his palms to the ceiling and shook his head. "It's impossible," he said. "I mean, I can drive you there, but you won't get past Reception. It's a fortress."

"Huh."

"But *I* can tell you what they're *doing*," Unger said. "They're curing cancer."

It was Danny's turn to be skeptical. "Are they?" *Funny,* he thought, *Zebek didn't seem to be the kind of guy* . . .

"Yes, as a matter of fact, they *are*. They're going after breast cancer first – then other kinds of tumors." He made an expansive gesture. "It's going to be huge."

"Breast cancer," Danny repeated.

"That's why Jason left Protein Dynamics. It was a chance to *do* something. It wasn't just . . . widgets! And it wasn't just theory. Jay's mother died of breast cancer, so that was part of it. And, of course, there was going to be *a lot* of money. Eventually. But that wasn't it. They were doing important science. I can even tell you how it works – sort of. They were building these tumor bombs, some kind of nanoshell that would enter breast cancer cells, and only breast cancer cells – and destroy them. And of course, down the road, the technology will be adapted to other cancers."

Danny frowned. The more he learned, the less he knew. "Earlier, you said Jason was worried about something. Something at work."

Unger nodded. "Gray goo."

Danny blinked. "What?"

"For a long time, Jay thought the whole gray goo business was some kind of Luddite fantasy – that's what he called it. But lately . . . he was worried about it."

Danny raised his hands and patted the air before him. "What are you talking about?"

Unger looked surprised. "The gray goo problem."

"Which is what?"

"You don't know?"

Danny shook his head.

Unger sighed. Thought for a moment. Said: "Well, it's . . . the end of the world. *At least*."

Twenty-one

Danny didn't say anything for a long while. Finally, he said, "Mr. Unger –"

Some quick *tsks* and: "It's *Glenn* – please. My *father* is Mr. Unger."

"Right. Glenn. So . . . What are we talking about here? I mean: the end of the world, that's . . . a pretty big deal, isn't it?"

Unger laughed. "Well . . ."

"I mean, what's up with that?" Danny asked. "Did I step through the looking glass –"

Unger shook the question off. "How much do you know about nanotechnology?"

Danny thought for a moment, sighed.

"I know what it *is*."

"But you don't know about gray goo?"

Danny shook his head.

Unger opened his mouth, as if he were about to explain, then shut it. Tight. Finally, he said, "I think you ought to talk to Harry. I'm an architect, not a scientist."

"Yeah, but –"

Unger jumped up, interrupted. "It'll be fine. Particularly if I buy him dinner." He cocked his head, considered the idea, approved it. "But he might get a little squirrely if I call him and it's like a *plan*."

"Who are we talking about?" Danny asked.

"Harry Manziger. He's a protein engineer at VSS. Very spur-of-the-moment. I think the best thing would be to just drop by . . ."

Unger asked Danny to move the Prism, then opened the garage door to reveal a cobalt-blue vintage T-Bird, the model with the little round window. He backed it out, then changed his mind and returned it to the garage. "If we do go to dinner, Harry won't fit. Maybe we'd better take *your* car."

A light rain was beginning to fall. The streets were slick, the traffic heavy. Danny made the turns, following Unger's directions, thinking, *I don't know where I'm going – not in* any *sense.*

Before long, they pulled up in front of a bungalow that shared the same lines as Unger's. But that was where the resemblance ended. Instead of the carefully landscaped front yard, Manziger's house was buried behind overgrown foundation plantings. The yard in front of the plantings was bare and weedy, the overstuffed garage open to reveal a small warehouse of boxes, toys, tools, bikes, rakes, skis, cans of paints, and old computers, monitors, and TVs. A fat teenager in black clothing opened the front door, his dead-white skin lit up with acne.

"Is Harry home?"

"Dad?! You got company!"

"Who is it?" a voice yelled back.

"Publishers Clearing House!" the kid replied.

"*Jordan!*"

The kid held the door open for them as they walked inside. An elderly poodle, one eye milky from a cataract, began a frenzy of yipping.

From the basement, a voice shouted, "I'll be right up!"

The kid turned to the poodle. "Turing!" he growled. "Will you shut the fuck up?" The dog looked hurt as the kid grabbed a ring of keys from a hook beside the door. "Tell Dad I took the car, wouldja?"

Unger rolled his eyes.

To say that the place was a mess was an understatement. The two of them stood on a bloodred shag carpet embedded with pet hair and bits of dessicated food. A coffee table piled with newspapers and magazines stood in front of a shabby green sofa. Abandoned objects and discarded clothing lay everywhere. Empty soda cans. Someone's sweatshirt. A couple of Pete's Wicked Ale bottles rested on the coffee table beside a pair of plastic TV dinner trays. Except for crimson smears of cranberry sauce, the trays looked as if they'd been licked clean.

"Harry's probably going to be a little nervous at first," Unger warned. "Anxious type."

Footsteps thudded up from the basement and Harry Manziger emerged through the doorway to the kitchen. He carried a pink laundry basket jammed with unfolded clothing. And he was big. Six feet and change, carrying maybe three hundred pounds. He wore a pair of chinos with a rolled waistband slung beneath his belly and a shirt so tight, it defined his rolls of fat. In his left ear was a diamond earring.

"Glenn," he said, his chubby face immediately assuming a worried look. "What's up?" He glanced at Danny, then looked away. As he turned his head, Danny saw that he had a jack-o'-lantern tattoo on the side of his neck.

"This is Dan Cray," Unger said. "I was hoping you

could explain a few things to him. Mind if we sit down for a sec?" Without waiting for a reply, he strolled into the living room, tossed aside some clothing, and planted himself on the arm of a wing chair that seemed to be molting. Danny followed, although only a major excavation would have provided a surface he could actually sit on. Manziger crabbed his way toward them.

"Explain what?"

"Oh . . . like the gray goo problem and whatever it was that Jay was worried about at VSS."

The fat man clutched the laundry basket to his chest as if it could protect him. "And why would I want to do that?"

"Because you were Jay's friend. And because Dan thinks his murder had something to do with VSS."

Manziger's blue eyes shot around the room as if he were looking for a way to escape. "The police have a different theory," he said.

Unger's exasperation exploded in a little puff of air. "The 'police' – *please*!"

Danny saw that Manziger actually wore a pocket protector. It was doing its job, too, the white plastic revealing a blue haze that, upon a closer look, revealed itself as a network of threadlike lines of ink. The big man shifted from foot to foot, eyes on the floor. "I don't know," he said.

"Harry? Just do it for Jason. It's not about anything proprietary. Just tell Dan about the goo – and maybe we can stop there."

"I guess I could," the big man started, then wagged his head. "I don't know."

"Well, while you're trying to decide, *I'm* going into shock. I mean it! I'm hypoglycemic!"

412

"I could make you an English muffin," Harry suggested.

"Why don't we just go out? We can talk over dinner – my treat."

The idea of free food seemed to put Manziger over the top. He put the laundry basket on the coffee table and excused himself to "freshen up." A minute later, he returned with his hair combed, reeking of Old Spice. "Okay," he said, as they headed out the door toward the Prism, "but I'm not going to talk about the project itself. Not in any detail. That's *verboten*."

They ended up at a place called the Blue Potato, Unger apologizing in advance in the event that it should be a bust. "It's new, so I don't know if it's any good, but so many of the places around here . . ." He shrugged, and added, "Memories . . ."

A pale waif, who seemed as new to the earth as she was to restaurant work, gave them menus and took their orders for drinks. The three of them sat in silence, studying the menu. Most dishes, Danny saw, had a potato component.

Finally, the waif returned, walking the short distance from the bar with the fierce concentration of a toddler. Pinot Grigio for Unger, a Bombay Sapphire martini for Manziger, and a Sierra Nevada for Danny. Then they ordered, with the waif taking pains to draw each of the words on her little pad, a task that was made more difficult by the fact that she gripped her Bic in a sort of monkey fist.

When she'd gone, Unger turned to Manziger. "You were saying?"

"Right right right," Manziger replied, fishing the olive from his drink and popping it into his mouth.

"Well, it's all about exponential curves. And restrictive environments." His voice trailed away. There didn't seem to be any follow-up.

"That's it?" Danny said.

Manziger squirmed in his seat and heaved a sigh. "Look, for practically his entire career – *forget* the last month – Jason dismissed the gray goo issue as the worst kind of hysteria. And I'm still in that camp. The only real problem at VSS is cash flow. No one's getting paid, and nothing's getting done. Though I guess that's about to change. We got a memo from the top –"

"From Zebek?" Danny asked.

"We got a memo *from the top*," Manziger repeated. "There's a major cash infusion on the way, so we're full steam ahead in September. But as for the rest of it . . ." He shook his head.

"You weren't worried?" Unger asked. "Not at all?"

"Nah," Manziger said. He held up his thumb and forefinger, pinched an eighth of an inch of air. "About that much. I thought Jay was having . . . some kinda midlife crisis. Turning into a pussy in his old age." Manziger chuckled.

"Please," Unger said. "My female friends find that metaphor offensive."

Manziger rolled his eyes and took a long sip of his martini. "I didn't know you *had* any 'female friends.' "

A shocked *tsk* from Unger.

Manziger smirked. "All right! I apologize."

Unger looked away.

"You were saying?" Danny asked. "About the goo?" He was losing his patience.

Manziger nodded, took a second sip of his martini. "Different people have different opinions. Personally,

I'm not worried about it. And I think I know what I'm talking about. Nanotech promises an end to hunger, disease, illness – maybe even to death. It promises an end to scarcity and a disruption of every hierarchy in the world – but only if we let the tech play out. And right now there are people who use the gray goo issue as an excuse to place restrictions on something that needs to evolve without a lot of hindrances."

"What do you mean when you say nanotech is going to disrupt all the hierarchies?" Danny asked.

Manziger shrugged. "Stands to reason," he said. "If you can make just about anything out of raw materials that are basically free . . . some people aren't going to be happy. I mean, if you can *make* oil, diamonds, gold . . . what happens to Exxon, De Beers, and Homestake? You think they're going to be grateful?"

"I see what you mean," Danny said.

"Talk about a redistribution of wealth!" Manziger enthused. "Nanotech is it! That's why it's so important to let the thing develop on its own – like the Web. Yes, the Web is chaotic, but if it hadn't developed in the unrestricted, organic way that it did, it wouldn't exist at all. Or if it did exist it would be useless to most of us, restricted in ways we can't imagine."

"I'm down with that," Danny told him, "but I don't see what it's got to do with this goo thing."

"I think Harry's just laying the groundwork," Unger observed.

"That's right. I am! I'm layin' the groundwork." He was obviously warming to his subject, but before he caught fire, the waif tiptoed to their table, laden with plates of calamari and a "potato haystack" for Danny. She set the plates down in slow motion, so slowly, in fact, that it was like watching a performance artist.

Unger dipped a ring of calamari into marinara sauce, chewed, swallowed, and pronounced it "surprisingly good."

Manziger said, "Yeah?" and dove into his plate.

Danny pulled his hand through his hair, sighed, and waited as Manziger attacked his squid. Finally, the engineer tapped his mouth with his napkin. "You understand how nanotechnology works," he declared.

Danny shrugged. "Pretty much."

"Good," Manziger announced. "Essentially, it's all about assemblers. . . ." It was interesting how all of Manziger's social clumsiness evaporated as he talked about his field. He was one of those men who would have made a good teacher. "Protein-engineered robots building molecules to spec. You name it, they can make it. You could build houses out of diamonds if you wanted to.

"But every job is different. Every task requires an AI program and specialized assemblers. Lots of them! You need billions of the little guys to do anything!" He paused to devour a few more rings of calamari.

"I read about that," Danny told him.

"Bear with me. Now, building the first assembler is a bitch. At VSS, we've been working, maybe six years, on an assembler designed to build nanodevices targeting breast cancer. And there's no way that anyone will ever be able to manufacture enough assemblers to do anything! It would take forever, and it would cost a fortune! So what you have to do is make them self-replicating."

"In other words," Unger interjected, "you make the first one, and you program it to make copies of itself."

"Exactly. And that's what gets people worried. Although, when you think of it . . . why should it?" He

416

pointed a thumb at himself. "*I'm* self-replicating – and so are you – at least, we are in tandem with someone else." He pointed to the cloud of shredded tuber on Danny's plate. "Your spuds are self-replicating. So what's the big deal?"

Danny shook his head and forked a tangle of potato into his mouth.

"The big deal," Manziger continued, "is that *we're* making these guys, not Mother Nature, so no one trusts that they'll stop making copies of themselves – even though there's a jillion ways to program that in."

"Like what?" Danny asked.

Manziger ran the tines of his fork through the smear of marinara sauce on his plate and licked it off. "You could make it so they only reproduce at certain temperatures – minus ninety Celsius, say – or in atmospheres you just don't find in nature. There's lots of ways."

Danny nodded. "And the gray goo . . . ?"

"Almost there." He paused and nodded at Danny's potato. "You gonna finish that?"

Danny shook his head.

"You don't mind?" Manziger asked.

"No. Go right ahead."

Manziger nodded briskly, switching plates with Danny. "Anyway, after a huge investment of man-hours at some place like VSS, you finally get your first assembler up and running. It probably took about ten years to make the goddamn thing, but now that it's rolling, it only takes the assembler maybe ten minutes to copy itself. So now you have two. Ten years for the first one, ten minutes for the second. And so it goes. . . ." With a smile, he leaned toward Danny, moist eyes bearing down. "How far did you get in math?"

"Long division," Danny replied.

"Seriously!?"

Danny shook his head. "Just kidding . . . what's the point?"

Manziger looked relieved. "You know what an exponential curve is?"

"Not exactly," Danny told him.

"Yeah, you do – you just don't know what it's called." He dipped his finger in his martini and drew a sort of hockey stick on the table.

"What people don't understand," Manziger explained, "is that in the early stages of an exponential progression, the rate of acceleration is practically invisible." He pointed to the beginning of the curve, where the blade met the shaft of the stick. "It's almost horizontal. But as you can see" – his finger followed the curve up the shaft – "once things get rolling, the line veers toward the vertical."

"Okay, but –"

Manziger held out a hand. "Hear me out. And don't worry, because I've got a great fable for you."

Danny drained his beer and raised his empty glass to the waif. *How,* he wondered, *did I get here? To this exact point? Sitting in the Blue Potato, listening to this admittedly intelligent slob talk about exponential curves as a way of explicating something about gray goo. And now a "fable." What happened to my life? What's wrong with this picture?*

Something of this must have shown on his face, because Unger frowned at him from beneath his peaked eyebrows. "Are you all right, Dan?"

Danny shrugged. "Yeah," he said, "I'm fine. I'm just not sure where this is going."

"Trust me," Manziger said. "You need to hear this

fable. And then everything will be clear. If it's just numbers, you won't understand it."

Danny said nothing.

"Go ahead, Harry," Unger insisted, giving him an encouraging look and throwing a sort of buck-up nod in Danny's direction.

"Okay," Manziger said, pressing his chubby hands together. "Here's how it goes." He paused. "You play chess?" he asked.

"Almost never," Danny told him. He thought, for a moment, of his time back in Barzan's hideout and the things he'd been making with the crimping tool. And Layla. He thought of her and felt this pressure in his chest. Sadness. *This one,* she'd said, holding the biggest of the pieces up to the sun, *is kink?*

"Well, this is about chess."

"The *invention* of chess. Which was a Chinese thing. And the Chinese emperor is so delighted by the game that he wants to reward its inventor. One of the court mathematicians. So the emperor tells the inventor he can have anything he wants. 'You name it,' he says. And the inventor, a real smart-ass, points to the chessboard. The only thing he wants is a grain of rice on the first square, then two grains on the second . . . and so on, doubling the number of grains on every subsequent square."

Manziger was animated, completely in his element, his face alive with storytelling. While Danny sat in his chair, half listening, sinking into depression.

"So the emperor's thrilled," Manziger continued. "He's gettin' off cheap!"

Danny was thinking, *I'm probably wanted for murder in Turkey. . . .*

"And, at first, that's the way it looks. Because the

progression starts slowly. One, two, four, eight . . . they're counting the grains from a teaspoon of rice."

My girlfriend hates me. . . .

"But *then*, they need a tablespoon, a cup, a bowl, a barrel. And it keeps going." Manziger looked at him. "You with me?"

Danny nodded.

Manziger rolled his hand through the air. "By this time, the emperor sees he's in trouble. They're only halfway across the board, and already they need an oxcart! Two or three more squares, and they're gonna need a silo!" Manziger laughed and fell back in his chair with a look of contentment.

"But what happened to the inventor?" Unger asked.

"They cut his head off," Manziger answered. "What else were they going to do? The guy was asking for something like eighteen million trillion grains of rice! That's . . . that's –"

"– more than all the rice in China," Danny suggested.

Manziger exploded in a nasal *hee-hee-hee*. "Exactly! More, in fact, than all the rice fields on earth could produce. That's why the emperor killed the little smart-ass."

"What does this have to do with gray goo?" Danny asked.

"The assemblers would replicate exponentially, just like the rice," Unger said. "You start with one. . . ."

Manziger snapped his finger at Unger. "Bingo! And you wouldn't even see it happen. Not at first. After twenty minutes or so, you've got two assemblers. Another twenty minutes, and you've got eight. Four hours later, you've got something like one hundred and twenty-eight thousand – but you still can't see 'em!

420

You need a scanning, tunneling microscope to get a look at them. But, after ten hours or so, you've got about sixty-eight billion assemblers! *Now* you can see 'em! That's a lot of biomass. And then – and only then – it goes turbo! It's only the first day and already you're onto the vertical part of the curve I was talking about." He licked the tip of his finger and redrew the hockey stick. "Right there," he said, pointing to a spot just above the blade.

Danny stared at the little smear.

"After two days," Manziger went on, "if you can't stop the replication of assemblers, they'll outweigh the earth. Four more hours, and they'll exceed the mass of the sun and the planets. Four *more* hours and . . . well, if they can find the fuel and material, they go for the stars." He drained his martini and set it down so hard that a diner at the next table turned to stare. "That's the gray goo problem," he said. "In a nutshell."

"So why do they call it that?" Danny insisted, his mind coming to grips with the implications. *Is this real?* he wondered. *Or some kind of exercise?*

Manziger held up a finger, gestured toward Unger's remaining calamari, raised an eyebrow. Unger nodded, and the engineer dipped a ring of squid into the marinara sauce, popped it into his mouth, and chewed.

"I asked Jay the same thing," Unger told Danny.

"Yeah?"

"He said it was 'geek humor.' "

Danny nodded. *What's that supposed to mean?*

"Gray goo," Manziger said. "No shape, no color. No nothing. See? It's just . . . boring glop!"

"So . . . ?"

"So that's the point!" Manziger continued. "Theoretically, the assemblers could eat the entire universe in three days – and yet nothing *interesting* would have happened." He rubbed his hands together. "I mean, they could have been making toilet paper or soccer balls – and that would be it! *Armageddon.* The universe swallowed by . . . goo."

Manziger was still chuckling when the waif approached them with their entrées, tottering toward them in a slow-mo ballet. Danny's plate held a pile of vegetables heaped into a pyramid whose instability caused the waif problems. Danny almost applauded when she succeeded in setting it down intact. Unger peered suspiciously at the dish in front of him, a construction of sweet potatoes and shrimp. Manziger attacked his steak *frites* with gusto. Obviously, the prospect of Armageddon had no effect on his appetite.

"So," Danny asked, "could this actually happen?"

"What? The end of the world?"

Danny nodded.

Manziger gave a dismissive shrug. "Theoretically? Yes. The assemblers are alive and they're programmed to replicate. But in reality?" He shook his head no. "Look at it this way: You got a monster. But it does a lot of work. So what do you do? Do you kill it? No. You keep it in a cage. A *strong* cage." He sawed away at his steak, reducing it to bite-sized pieces, which he prodded into a square. "Anything else and you're throwing the baby out with the bathwater. Jay used to talk about it all the time." Out of nowhere, Manziger's voice rose in what Danny guessed was an imitation of Jason Patel's Indian accent. " 'It is not enough for nervous nellies to say, "Well, this might happen." I'm a scientist. Show me the evidence. Give me a scenario! Otherwise . . .' " Unger shrugged and forked a piece of steak into his mouth. Grinned.

"So what kind of cage are we talking about?" Danny asked. "How do you keep the assemblers in lockdown?"

"Lots of ways," Manziger replied.

"Like what?"

Manziger patted his fleshy lips, scratched at his tattoo. "Well, the first thing you'd do is, you'd program them to stop reproducing at a certain point – when you had enough of them. That's how the system *works*. You program them to replicate and perform a particular task, and you program them to self-destruct when the job's done."

Danny thought about it. "So it's like a software program."

Manziger nodded.

"Like Windows," Danny suggested.

Manziger nodded again.

Danny threw his hands up. "Well, I don't know about *your* computer," he said, "but mine crashes two or three times a week. I wouldn't want to bet the planet on the nanotech equivalent of Windows 98."

Manziger chuckled. "Good point. But you wouldn't put all your eggs in the same basket. If you don't trust the programmers to get it right – and we *don't* – there are other precautions you can take to make it fail-safe."

"Such as what?"

"Well, you can set it up so that the only way the assemblers can replicate is in a really weird environment. Something that doesn't occur in nature."

"Like what?" Danny asked.

Manziger didn't hesitate. "A deep-freeze would be one way. Program the assemblers so they're only capable of replicating in a certain temperature range. A lot of viruses work like that. As long as they're within a couple of degrees of ninety-eight-point-six, they're fine. The host gets a fever? They're kaput. So, if you limit replication to environments colder than, say, twenty below zero – and your factory's here in the Valley – that ought to take care of it then and there."

"I get it."

"Another way is you could restrict the kind of raw material the assemblers use. I mean, you'd want them to use something cheap and plentiful – seawater or something – but you'd also want to throw in something extra. Something rare. Osmium, maybe, or even xenon. So if we get a cold snap and the assemblers go nuts, the little bastards still won't work!"

Danny started to say something, but Manziger wasn't finished.

"Another way," the engineer said, "is you could program them to shut down if there were too many of them in the neighborhood. That's the way bacteria work. They're self-limiting." The big man shoveled a clutch of fries into his mouth and chewed noisily.

"One way or another, it's all Mother Nature," Unger sighed.

Manziger agreed. Said: "Yup."

Danny wasn't so sure. "The thing I don't understand," he said, "is why your friend changed his mind. I mean, for years, he wasn't worried about it – and then all of a sudden he was. What happened?"

Unger bounced his eyebrows. "He was worried about shortcuts at the plant. That's what he told *me*. There was a lot of pressure to cut corners."

" 'Pressure'?" Manziger repeated. "We're talking about curing cancer! Breast cancer, anyway. Do you know how many lives we'd save? Or what your options would be worth?" The idea made him snort. "Jay got cold feet over something so unlikely . . ." He shook his big head.

"And what *was* that?" Danny asked.

Manziger seemed to ignore the question. "The thing is," he said, "it's such a long process *anyway*. You want FDA approval, you have to jump through *hoops*. The safeguards Jason was talking about would have set us back a couple of *years* – and VSS doesn't have the money for that. Not in this economy." The idea was so upsetting, Manziger had begun to spray bits of french fry as he talked. "So we erred on the side of *science*, rather than . . . I don't know what. Fear! Is that so bad?"

"So what changed Jason Patel's mind?" Danny asked.

The waitress arrived to ask about dessert. Danny and Glenn Unger declined, while Manziger took a quick look. "I'll have a crème brûlée and a decaf cap. And, uh . . . how about a Slippery Nipple?" The waitress glided away and Manziger turned back to Danny. "Jason was worried about mutation," he said.

"Mutation?"

"Yeah. Something happened. In the lab. One of his nucleotide sequences changed from one generation to the next."

"Jay freaked!" Unger remarked. "I've never seen him so upset."

Manziger nodded. "It could have been anything. It's a lab, you know? But Jay thought it was a mutation. And maybe it was. I mean, the assemblers – they're alive. So theoretically, it could happen."

"And that would be bad," Danny suggested.

Manziger looked uncomfortable. "Oh, yeah." He rolled his eyes. "The nightmare scenario is – okay, suppose you program the bot so it can only replicate in the presence of rhodium or something?" He flapped his fingers dismissively. "Doesn't matter what – but *some* restriction."

"Whatever," Danny said.

The waif brought dessert and Manziger fell silent until the treats were laid before him. Then he picked up where he'd left off. "Jay thought the assemblers might be like roaches – or bacteria or viral organisms. Maybe they'd develop a resistance. Maybe they'd *adapt*. Not all of them, of course. But that's the point. You'd only need one."

"And then the monster would be out of his cage," Danny said.

Manziger gobbled his crème brûlée. "Right. Exactly."

Danny sat back and exchanged glances with Unger.

"I always wondered," Unger said, his voice a little hesitant, "why that doesn't worry *you*, Harry?"

The big man shrugged. "Because I don't believe there was a mutation. I think Jason fucked up. In his programming protocol, probably."

"But that's not what *he* thought," Danny suggested.

"No. He swore it happened, but he couldn't prove it. The original samples – the nucleotide sequences he started with – were destroyed. And that's how paranoid he was. He thought –"

"Harry!" Unger protested.

Manziger regarded him blankly. "*What?*"

"Jason isn't here to defend himself," Unger replied.

Manziger managed to look contrite, even as he shrugged – even as he finished the crème brûlée. "Jay claimed the samples were deliberately destroyed. Which was ridiculous." Manziger ran his spoon around the ramekin, digging into the grooves for little bits of pudding that he'd missed.

"Ridiculous?" Danny asked.

"Of course," Manziger shot back.

"Why?"

Manziger's eyes widened. "Because no one would do that," he said. "No way."

Danny gave him a skeptical look. "You said yourself, there's a lot of money at stake."

Manziger scoffed. "Money? If Jay was right . . . we're *fucked*. Nanobots can't mutate. They must be entirely stable. It doesn't matter about the particular mutation he saw. It's the *fact* of mutation – *any* mutation. It would shut down the field – overnight." Manziger lowered his head, spooned foam off the top of his cappuccino, and slurped it.

"Because it would mean . . . ?"

"Goo!" Manziger actually shouted the word, so that several diners wheeled toward their table. He made a gesture, then smiled an apologetic smile. "But Jay wasn't right. He couldn't have been."

"How can you be so sure?" Unger asked.

"Because we have artifacts of all our code – trials, everything. We have an archival system, right? We have to. You program a sequence, it works or it doesn't. If it doesn't work, you make a note and change it. In order to know what to modify, you've got to know what went before. Right?"

Danny and Unger were silent.

"That's just the way it *is*. So you tell me, how likely is it that the *one sequence of code* that Jay was talking about – the one sequence – was eradicated from the archive?" When neither Danny nor Unger replied, Manziger asked, "Who would *do* a thing like that?

"Anyone at VSS," Danny suggested. "It's going to make you all rich, right? I mean, unless it goes under."

Manziger shook his head. "You don't get it, do you? This isn't some arthritis pill. I'm not talking about fudging clinical trials so the product looks better than it is. If these assemblers *mutate*, it means they'll adapt. Not today, not tomorrow, but eventually. And the limitations we've embedded in them won't work."

"You couldn't stop them then?" Unger asked.

"Maybe the program controlling replication would still kick in. If not, you'd have about twelve hours," Manziger replied. "Possibly you could nuke it. Otherwise . . . welcome to the Slime Planet."

"So what you're saying," Danny suggested, "is that if you knew these things could mutate and you still went ahead, you'd have to be crazy."

Big snort from Manziger, who drained his cappuccino in a gulp, leaving a fleck of foam on his upper lip. " 'Crazy'?" he repeated. " 'Crazy' doesn't cut it. You'd have to be evil." He thought about it for a moment. "More than evil," he said. "You'd have to be . . . the devil incarnate."

Twenty-two

Danny could feel it on the back of his neck, the spider crawl of apprehension. "Someone walked on my grave," Grandma C. used to say with a shiver. And that's exactly what he felt, a cold lick of menace, the whispered threat of his own mortality.

The devil incarnate.

Inzaghi had used the same phrase and so, for that matter, had "Belzer." How had he put it describing the slurs against Zebek? *They say he's in bed with the Mafia – that he's an arms dealer . . . a polluter, and a cheat.* They say *he's the devil incarnate.*

And so they did. He was "the Peacock Angel," strutting along the balconies of Sistema di Pavone, roosting atop Tawus Holdings, surveying the dead at the villa near Lake Van. He was the same man Terio saw getting out of a Bentley in Diyarbakir.

But he was *not* the devil. Danny was spooked, yes, but nothing supernatural was involved. He was sure of that, though he wasn't sure that it mattered. Zebek was crazy-evil, no matter how you sliced it.

And Danny couldn't do a thing to stop him. Not really. The air in the restaurant seemed to close around him. His mood collapsed. The Elders would have their directors meeting in Zurich, where they would cede control of the Yezidi assets to Zebek – who would use them to launch the First Assembler. Within a year, there might be a cure for breast cancer. Within a year, there might be a cure for life.

Danny paid the bill, thanked Manziger and Unger for their help, and drove them home. Then he headed north to the airport in South San Francisco, hoping to catch a red-eye back to Washington. Dusk faded into night, a night full of mist. His headlights tunneled into it. Every few moments his wipers slapped back and forth across the damp windshield. He turned the radio on, flicked through the channels, then switched it off. What had he been thinking? What kind of music could possibly be appropriate for the way he felt?

A dirge. He shook his head at that and allowed himself a bitter smile. Because after all, he'd done it. He'd investigated the hell out of this case. He'd solved the puzzle, learned Zebek's motive for murdering Terio, Patel, Barzan, Inzaghi, Rolvaag. The dead were sacrifices to Zebek's greed and ambition, eliminated so that the billionaire would not be exposed – as an impostor defrauding his people, as a madman willing to roll the dice on the future of the universe. Zebek was willing to mow down anyone who stood in his way, anyone who threatened his access to the Yezidi fortune – the money he needed to bankroll his project at VSS. And Danny had helped him identify his human obstacles. He might as well have set them up as targets. And now? Now there was nothing Danny could do to stop him. The game was over. And he'd lost.

By the time he returned the car to Alamo and took the shuttle bus to the terminal, it was a little after eight-thirty. The red-eye turned out to be an eleven forty-five United flight that got into Dulles at eight forty-five in the morning. There were plenty of seats and no lines.

Which left him with some time to kill. He drank a bottle of Sam Adams in the Lindbergh Pub, where half a dozen solitary travelers watched a preseason football game on television. Briefly, he considered getting drunk – at least he'd be able to sleep on the flight – but decided against it. He wasn't much of a drinker, really. And, besides, he didn't want to make it easy for them. If he was going down (and he was pretty sure that he was), it wasn't going to be with a hangover. So he walked out of the bar and wandered through the terminal, searching for a newsstand.

What he found instead was a place called *Hook Me Up!*, which rented "data pods" with Internet connections, phones, and faxes. For thirty dollars an hour, Danny could have his own little office, where he could check his e-mail, surf the Net, and call around – not that there was anyone in particular that he wanted to speak to (or, more accurately, there wasn't anyone he wanted to speak to who was still speaking to him).

A young guy in black jeans and a Ben Folds Five T-shirt directed him to a cubicle, where he was left to his own devices. He sat for a minute, staring at the Dell logo on the monitor, wondering about the point of it all. It really was the end. Everyone who knew anything about Zebek was dead. Except Danny – and, as the joke went, *he wasn't feeling so good himself*.

Still, he might as well put it down on paper. Make a record of what had happened and spread it around. A copy to Caleigh (in case he didn't get to her before Zebek got to him); a copy to his brothers, Kev and Sean; another copy to Mounir (he could probably reach the Elder through Poste Restante, Uzelyurt); and a copy to the local cops investigating Patel's murder. It probably wouldn't do any good. But what the hell.

431

So he moved the cursor onto the Word icon, clicked with the mouse, and began to write a sort of "after-action" report that began: *In the event of my death, you should know* . . .

An hour later, he had a five-page document, memorializing everything that had happened, beginning with the call from Zebek summoning him to a meeting at National Airport. In his report, Danny explained about the list of toll calls that he'd obtained and recounted his search for Terio's computer as part of an effort to neutralize the supposed "smear campaign" against Zebek. He put down everything that he could recall about the events in Italy, including his escape from Siena to Rome, where he left Father Inzaghi lying dead in the street. He wrote about his search for Remy Barzan in Istanbul and "Kurdistan" but left out the story of his own kidnapping. (*I found Barzan through a circuitous route* was the way that he put it.) With this established, he repeated what Barzan had said about Zebek's ascendancy among the Yezidis – the way the faltering financier replaced the sacred Sanjak with a forgery carved in his own image, then engineered a timely appearance on Turkish television, knowing that the Imam would soon be assassinated and a successor chosen.

It was a complicated tale, and Danny's account was anything but elegant. In fact, it was barely coherent. He found himself writing about the dendrochronologist's role (and the unhappy fate that the Norwegian shared with so many others) when he realized that he had not yet mentioned Tawus Holdings. At another point in the letter, he realized that he had neglected to spell out Zebek's objective – which was, of course, to take control of the Yezidis' assets so that the First

432

Assembler could be put to work at Very Small Systems, Inc. And oh, yeah – it would probably mean the end of the world.

Even so, as slapdash as it was, the document was still a useful one that might someday cause Zebek a bit of trouble. Danny added a few sentences about the First Assembler and referred the reader to Glenn Unger and Harry Manziger for further details. Then he printed out half a dozen copies, adding the *Wall Street Journal* and the U.S. Office of Technology Assessment to his list of recipients.

In truth, he had little hope that anything would come of the rambling missive rolling out of the Deskjet at his side, but getting it all down on paper was the only thing that he could think of to do. *Make a record. Put it out there. What's to lose?*

When the printing was done, he collated the reports and bought some stamps and envelopes from the Hook Me Up! guy. Returning to his cubicle, he went on-line to find the addresses that he didn't know, then took the envelopes to a mailbox across the hall and sent them on their way. Finally, he decided to see if he had any e-mail.

He did. In fact, he had sixty-seven messages, most of which were jokes, spam, or pitches for *hot chixxx!*, penis enlargement(s), and art supplies. After he deleted the junk, including fourteen jokes from his brother and twelve from Jake, three messages of interest remained. One from Lavinia Trevor.

Danny boy! Where are you? Working hard, *I hope*! We take down the September show Oct. 1 & 2. It should all clear by the 3d, at which point you should begin to install. The opening is set for First Friday, Oct. 5, at 7 P.M. Hate to bother you, but *do* get in touch. I'm a little anxious.

He fired off a reply: *No problem – all set – can't wait – cheers!* What the hell? If he lived long enough, he'd mount some kind of show (though God knows what he'd put in it). He was warming up to the idea of the *Talking Heads*. The practical end of it – the construction – wouldn't take a lot of time, and the installation would be a snap. Getting *Babel On II* set up would be more of a challenge, that and organizing display plinths for everything else. Still, it was do-able. If he was still on the planet.

Next was a message from the folks. They were back in Maine, and where was he? They'd spoken to Caleigh – *What happened!!!? Mom's worried – call home!* He hit REPLY and sent them a note that was meant to be soothing, if short on detail. *Welcome home! See ya soon. Not to worry. I'm working on the Caleigh thing. Love ya much, Danny*

The third message was a whine-o-gram from Ian, announcing that Danny had been fired. In a burst of improbable maturity, Danny resisted the temptation to fire off a smart-ass reply and apologized for his unexpectedly long absence. He'd explain when he got back.

He thought about e-mailing Caleigh but decided against it. Writing to her would be a waste of time. Any communiqué from him would be deleted with about as much thought as he'd given to the proffers of hot chixxx and penis enlargements.

He did send a message to Salim, his benefactor in Dogubeyazit, thanking him all over again and wishing him and his family well. Someday he'd do something for the guy, pay him back somehow.

So he had about an hour to kill and nothing in particular to do. In two days, Zebek would meet with the Yezidi Elders in Zurich – and that would be that. Mounir and the others would get Danny's "after-action report," or whatever it was, but not until after the meeting. Nothing would come of it anyway. He was sure of that. Because it was too little, too late – a gesture when what was needed was proof. His rambling missive up against what most of the Elders thought was the Tawus incarnate, a living god. Was there any chance? Nah. He didn't think so.

He had no doubt that the proof was out there. Some-where. Terio and Barzan had gone to great lengths to obtain a sample of the Sanjak in the underground city. The tree guy had almost certainly documented the forgery, but the tree guy was dead and so was his report. Dead or missing. Either way . . .

It's probably sitting in a filing cabinet, Danny thought, *somewhere in Norway. Or on the guy's computer.* But no. That was a base Zebek would have covered. Like Terio's house, Rolvaag's had probably gone up in flames.

The Ben Folds Five guy ducked his head in the cubicle. "You need anything, man?"

"No, I'm good," Danny said in a distracted voice. Distracted because an idea had occurred to him.

"You want anything – holler."

Danny sat back in his chair, swiveling from one side to another. He was thinking about something Remy Barzan had said. Barzan and Terio had been waiting for Rolvaag's written report, dating the sample taken from the Sanjak. At some point, Terio had spoken by phone with Rolvaag, who must have outlined his findings. Because Terio had then written his letter to Tawus Holdings, asking for a meeting to discuss the Sanjak's authenticity. Arriving on Paulina's desk, the letter had been given to Zebek – who promptly arranged for Terio to be killed.

But did Rolvaag know about Terio's murder? Danny wondered. Probably not. Terio had been entombed for weeks before his body was discovered. Meanwhile, Rolvaag had presumably gone ahead with what he was doing and finalized the report. At some point, he would have mailed it to his client or sent the report as an attachment to an e-mail. Or both.

Danny threw back his head and swiveled in a circle, coming to a stop in the same place that he'd started. *Mail didn't stop coming to you when you died. And neither did e-mail.* AOL would cut you off if the credit card your account billed to was rejected – but not until. And as for free accounts with companies like Yahoo and Angelfire, well, for all Danny knew they'd remain operational forever. University accounts might be different, but Danny suspected that they, too, would linger on. It wasn't as if they *cost* anything – not really. In all likelihood, their status would be reviewed once a year – if then.

Which meant that Rolvaag's report – and the proof that Danny needed – was probably sitting on a server somewhere.

It only took him five minutes to locate Terio's e-mail account at George Mason University. He'd logged onto Mason's Web site, clicked through to the Department of Philosophy and Religious Studies, and quickly found the faculty listings. Terio was there all right – in the form of a photo, c.v., list of publications, and the two courses he'd been scheduled to teach in the fall. His e-mail address was listed as c.terio@gmu.edu.

Danny knew that most universities had a multitier

server system, accessed through Telnet. He called a number on the Web site for information about on-line registration and was soon connected to the "Webmistress," a polite young woman. She accepted his pretext about writing a freelance piece about Web servers and told him what he needed to know about GMU's servers. There were four ("so far, but we're growing!"), and they were named after various patriots: Madison, Jefferson, Adams, and Hale.

He logged onto Telnet and tried each of the patriots' names until he finally connected to the Terio account in "Adams." It was then that the system requested a password.

The cursor – a gray square on black background – blinked patiently.

He knew – from conversations with techies at Fellner Associates – that the most common password, the one used by something like ninety percent of the people who owned computers, was *password*. With nothing better to do until his flight was called, he tried it:

password
login incorrect

Okay, Danny thought. *So Terio wasn't a part of the thundering herd. He was some kinda password wildman.* Which meant that he probably used the name of one of his pets. Or children. Or wives. That's what ninety percent of the remaining ten percent did (according to Fellner's very own IT expert, Bob LaBrasca). Only in Terio's case, the professor was unmarried, childless, and without pets (to the best of Danny's knowledge).

Danny glanced at the professor's curriculum vitae,
looking for clues. Seeing his birthday, he plugged it in:

10-14-60
login incorrect

He tried the college where Terio had done his undergraduate work:

georgetown
login incorrect

He tried a number of variations, including johns-
hopkins, then moved on to names and words that might
have held a special place in Terio's lexicon: *mani,
zoroaster, sheikadi, shaykadi, yezidi, peacock, sanjak,
mesopotamia, avatar* . . . It was hopeless, Danny
decided. Even if he happened upon the right word,
Terio might have spelled it backward – or added a 1 to
it. The truth was, Danny didn't know enough about the
guy. Maybe he was obsessed with film directors:

louismalle
login incorrect

or physics particles:

neutrino
login incorrect
neutrino1
login incorrect

It could be anything! It could even be one of those
really secure kinds of passwords that mean nothing to

anyone and which no one in his right mind could ever remember:

ljq3%7tf0'5

for instance. The cursor blinked at him.

Any password could be cracked, of course. LaBrasca laughed at them and said they were useless. All you needed was a decent computer and the right software program – and, eventually, you'd get in. But not the way Danny was doing it. Doing it Danny's way – guessing words and typing them in – could take a hundred thousand years. It was like that fairy tale. Guess the little guy's name. Rumpelstiltskin. The chick in the fairy tale never would have guessed it. Danny didn't remember exactly how she came up with it, some kind of insider knowledge.

With a dispirited sigh, he leaned back in his chair, spun once to the right and once to the left, his eyes on the ceiling's acoustical tile. He was stymied, and there was no way out. Sheik Mounir, according to his dead grandson, was not the kind of guy who'd change his mind on the basis of *a story*. He required proof.

Closing his eyes, Danny searched his memory. What else did he know about Terio?

fertilecrescent
login incorrect

He thought back to his conversation with Father Inzaghi, Terio's one good friend in the world.

inzaghi
login incorrect

439

The priest had talked about how surprised he'd been to learn of Terio's "suicide," how Terio had been a man in love with life, a man who liked to laugh.

unfertilecrescent
login incorrect
larry
login incorrect
moe
login incorrect
curly
login incorrect

Stop it, Danny told himself. *You're wasting money, sitting here. So what if he had a sense of humor?*

shemp
login incorrect

There was something about "a reminder question." Some corny joke that Terio liked. A pun. What was it? Danny thought back. Like Rumpelstiltskin, it had something to do with a nursery rhyme. Then he remembered:

Heigh-ho the terio
login incorrect

He tried it without the hyphen and got the same result. Danny ran a hand through his hair (it was long enough now that he could do that) and stared at the words. The terio part was wrong, of course. That's where the pun came in. That's what made it *funny. (As*

440

if . . .) The way the nursery rhyme actually went was *Heigh-ho the derio.* Which had something to do with a farmer.

Danny sat in front of the monitor, his eyes on the blinking cursor, and it came to him. He hummed the tune:

> *The farmer's in the dell,*
> *The farmer's in the dell,*
> *Heigh-ho the derio,*
> *The farmer's in the dell.*

Farmer. Dell. What dell? What's a dell? A glen. A glade. A computer! *The farmer's in the Dell. In the Dell – not the dell.*

And, in fact, the word was right in front of him, emblazoned on the monitor: *Dell.* That's what the farmer was in. He was in the computer.

> *farmer*
> *login incorrect*
> *thefarmer*
> *login incorrect*
> *farmer'sinthedell*

Instantly a long list of e-mails spilled onto the screen, scrolling down. Danny's heart did a flip, and he saw at a glance that the unread e-mails went back nearly two months.

He scanned what was there. In orderly columns headed *Sender, Date, Size,* and *Subject* he saw that the professor had more than a hundred messages that he hadn't read and perhaps a thousand others that he had read but failed to delete. As Danny did with Yahoo,

Terio had used the university's server as an on-line filing cabinet.

From the headers Danny could see that most of the messages were irrelevant – interdepartmental notes or queries from students and the like. But it didn't take long to spot what he was looking for:

Sender	Date	Size	Subject
O. Rolvaag	7-22-01	7k	Nevazir Artifact

He clicked on it.

Dear Mr. Terio –

The AMS carbon results are back from Alpha Analytics. These results, coupled with the tree-ring comparison arrays that we've done in our own laboratory, establish that the tested artifact is no more than 111 years old.

Indeed, the 100-gram (cedar) sample is probably younger than that. If you would like, we can do further testing and perhaps establish its age more precisely. Such tests, however, would be time-consuming and relatively expensive. In light of the fact that your interest is confined to a single question – is the sample at least 800 years old – we have suspended our efforts, pending further instructions.

The public-address system crackled, and Danny heard his flight called. Ignoring it, he returned his attention to the monitor.

The artifact appears to have been carved from a tree that stopped growing between 1890 and 1920 C.E.

442

Initial array comparisons indicate that the tree was probably native to the Yemen.

Accompanying this e-mail are several attachments, including: 1) a JPEG file, showing the compiled index cluster of comparison rings, the results of a computerized correlation scan, and a description of our methodology; 2) the digitized photo-analysis sheet, with explanatory notes suitable for a layman; 3) the Alpha Analytics report, which includes calendar calibration information, pretreatment methods, a statement outlining analytical procedures (in this case the AMS technique), and the lab's conclusions.

A full invoice will be sent to your office by conventional mail.

While radiometric testing might further refine the date of the sample, the fact that tree-ring comparisons and AMS testing concur on a relatively recent range of dates rules out the possibility that the sample is as old as claimed. Accordingly, there would seem to be no reason to proceed with further testing unless litigation is involved. (Where antiquities and litigation are concerned, more experts and tests are always better!)

Nevertheless, if you would like us to undertake such tests, we remain at your service. (NB: In such an eventuality, the sample would be tested to destruction. Please advise on this point if further testing is in order.)

*Finally, with respect to litigation, it has been my
experience that false claims about the antiquity of
objects sometimes provoke legal action. In this
connection, you may be interested to know that
Alpha Analytics can provide an expert witness,
experienced in testifying about carbon-dating
techniques. If similar testimony about tree-ring
analysis is needed, I, too, am available as an
expert witness (at 1,400 USD per day, plus
expenses).*

*When you so instruct me, I will forward a hard copy
of this report, accompanied by the 100-gram sample,
to your office.*

"United Flight One-sixty-one for Washington's
Dulles Airport, now boarding at Gate Twenty-three.
United Flight One-sixty-one . . ."

*Do let me know if you wish to utilize your own
account number (or that of your institution) for the
courier's payment.*

*Best to you,
Ole Rolvaag, Ph.D.*

Danny took a deep breath, blew it out, and fell back
in his chair, at once galvanized and paralyzed. The
proof of Zebek's treachery was on the monitor in front
of him. *Gotcha,* he thought. And added a second
thought: *Now what?*

He downloaded the e-mail and its attachments to a
floppy disk, then printed out a hard copy to read on the
flight to Washington. Each page, he saw, was slugged

across the top with the words: *Oslo Institute – Mesopotamian Dendrochronology Project. "Nevazir Artifact."* The pages themselves appeared to explicate the carbon-dating procedure and included a three-page explanation of how C-14 dating results were tied to a calendar year using known dendrocalibrations of tree rings.

It seemed solid enough. It would have been better, of course, if the report had said that the sample was taken from a tree that was exactly 82 years old (or something like that). But the point was, whatever else the artifact might be, it had not been taken from an object carved by Sheik Adi. Danny didn't remember when the old boy lived, but he thought it was something like 1200 C.E.

The public-address system sizzled, and Danny's flight was called for the third time. Scrambling to his feet, he collated and stapled the various reports, then went out to settle up with the Ben Folds Five guy.

The kid eyed Danny's stack of paper as he made change. "Hey – you want one of these?" he asked. He offered Danny a Tyvek envelope printed with the logo of a winged desk. Danny thanked him for it, slid the documents inside, and loped off in the direction of Gate Twenty-three.

It only took him a minute, and when he arrived at the gate, out of breath, the ticket agent gave him a smile that reminded him so much of Caleigh that he felt as if he'd been punched in the heart. Then her smile turned to a scolding look as she took his boarding pass and slid it through a machine atop the little podium in front of her. "You're it," she said. "The last passenger. I've been waiting for you." The ticket popped out and she handed it to him. "Do you always cut it so close?" she asked, rolling her hand toward the jetway.

"Yeah," he said, in a dazed voice. "I do. As a matter of fact I think I do."

Twenty-three

As the 747 soared toward the Continental Divide, Danny sat beside the window with a glass of red wine, staring out at the dark expanse of America. It was after midnight, but lights persisted in the inky darkness, occasionally flaring into galaxies when a town or city slid beneath the wings.

The flight was nearly empty. He had a whole row to himself, as, indeed, did most of the people on the plane. He was trying to remember what Barzan had said about the Elders and the meeting in Zurich. It was a board of directors meeting for Tawus Holdings, but since all the directors were Yezidi Elders, it had a different name too. A *shura*. And Barzan said it would be *a week from tomorrow*. At the Boar O'Lack.

Somehow Danny knew the Boar O'Lack was a hotel. But how long had it been since Barzan said the meeting would be "a week from tomorrow?" Six days, seven? Five? It was important. Obviously, there wouldn't be any point in going to Zurich – and he *had* to go to Zurich, now that he had Rolvaag's report and the JPEG files – if the meeting had already taken place.

So he sipped his wine and tried to remember.

It was practically the last thing Barzan had said to him before the shooting started. There was to be a meeting of the Elders in Zurich scheduled for *a week from tomorrow*.

447

Barzan's "tomorrow" began with the night ride to Salim's village. This was followed by a second truck ride, followed by a bus to Ankara. There was the night at the Hotel Spar in Ankara and a flight out to Washington the next day (which would have been day three of Barzan's seven). After that, Danny had spent the night at his parents' house (still day three) and flown to California the following afternoon. How many days was that? Four, counting the night in the Doubletree outside San Francisco. And then today, talking with Unger and Manziger. That was five (though, strictly speaking, "today" was now yesterday because it was just after one A.M.).

So this is day six, Danny thought, the beginning of day six. *And the meeting is . . . tomorrow.* In Zurich, it was day six also, but it was already breakfast time. Still, even with the time change, he ought to be able to make it. He'd get into Dulles around nine. By two or three in the afternoon, he'd be on his way across the Atlantic. He'd land in Zurich in the early morning of the seventh day, the day of the meeting.

With a reassuring nod to himself, he finished the glass of wine and set it down on a tray two seats away. He shut off the overhead light, pulled a blanket up to his chest, and lay back with his head against the edge of the window, thinking, *Did I do that right?*

The information desk in the Zurich airport was easy to find, marked as it was with a giant exclamation point. Danny learned from a smiling brunette whose proficiency in English outpaced his own that the best way ("by far!") to get into town was by train. "Take the escalator down. Trains depart every twelve minutes for the Hauptbahnhof. That's the main railway station." She looked at a schedule. "There is one at 9:04, platform five, another at 9:16, platform three. Once you arrive at the railway station, you will find a taxi just outside. Or, if you don't have too much luggage, it's possible to walk. May I ask where you are stopping for the evening?"

"The Boar O'Lack."

He caught the slight knitting of brows as her dark eyes took in his sweatshirt and jeans. His tooth. "Very nice," she remarked. "Did you send them arrival information?" she asked. "Because this hotel usually provides transport for the guests."

"No," Danny told her. "I was in such a hurry . . ." He shrugged.

She looked at him with an inquiring expression. Finally, she said, "Well, it's just off the Bahnhofstrasse, about a kilometer." She unfolded a tourist map, reversed it on the desk so that Danny could read it, and drew circles around the Hauptbahnhof and – now he saw the proper spelling – the Hotel Baur au Lac.

He caught the 9:04, sat upstairs in the second-class carriage, and watched the burbs roll by. It wasn't the Switzerland of his imagination. There were no cows that he could see, no Alps, no skiers or blondes with braided hair. The train swept past sturdy stucco houses with tidy vegetable gardens in the rear. Closer to the city, apartment blocks took over, with perimeter walls displaying lots of graffiti. It was a different style than he was used to seeing in the States, with lots of representational images and a vivid palette.

Nor was it the cool Swiss climate of his imagination. He walked out of the big station into the humid swelter of what might have been a summer afternoon on the

Gulf coast. The air was tremulous, dense and gray, as if the sky were about to explode.

The Bahnhofstrasse turned out to be a busy avenue crammed with expensive shops, private banks, and zipping trams. Danny followed the street's gentle curve, covering a dozen short blocks in as many minutes, arriving finally at Borsen-Strasse. In the near distance, a passenger ferry steamed across Lake Zurich against a backdrop of spruce-clad hills.

Turning right on Borsen-Strasse, he suddenly found himself in a hushed and luxurious Eden. The Baur au Lac was a stately white stone building set in its own parkland, a block from the lake. Three flags flew above the central peak of the roof, the middle one – a red field with a white cross in the center – as familiar as a Swiss Army knife.

A uniformed man stood sentry at the entrance drive. They exchanged smiles, and Danny headed toward the front door, then veered off at the last second to enter the patio café. He stood there, apparently taking in the scene, in fact catching his breath. In the back of his head he could hear the voice of his old high school coach, Nilthon Alvarado, urging him to take it easy. *Tranquilo, tran-QUIL-o,* he used to say, patting the air in front of him with his open palms.

A scatter of well-dressed and expensively coiffed patrons – many of them Asian – sat at tables under white umbrellas. The whole patio was shaded by two enormous trees of a kind he didn't recognize. Three extremely well tailored golfers – their golf bags occupying neighboring seats – sat nearby, cursing the weather.

"Buckets," one man announced in an aristocratic British accent. "It's going to come down *buckets.*"

In the garden beyond the patio burbled a fountain in the shape of a lyre, its "strings" formed by wire-thin streams of water. A waiter with a white napkin draped over his arm came to attention in front of Danny and executed a crisp theatrical bow. "May I help you, sir?"

Is it so obvious I'm American? "No, that's okay," Danny said. "I'm just passing through." With a smile, he turned toward the lobby, thinking, *Here goes*.

At the desk, a middle-aged woman, expertly made up and wearing a lacy white blouse, watched him from above a pair of half glasses. To each of his questions came a crisp answer.

The Tawus Holdings meeting was scheduled for four P.M. In the Winterthur Room. Third floor. And yes, Herr Barzan was indeed registered, but – she rang his room – the gentleman was not available at the moment. "Would you care to leave a message?"

"Yes."

She smiled and presented him with a heavy piece of cream-colored stationery embossed with the hotel's name and crest, along with a matching envelope and a white pen. She gestured toward the lobby, where a fleet of easy chairs floated on a sea of tiles. Ignoring the chairs, Danny stood at an antique escritoire with a burgundy leather inset and began to write.

What do you call a sheik? Danny wondered. *What's the salutation?*

Mr. Barzan –

he wrote, then paused, trying to think of the most powerful way to put his case.

I have urgent information for you, information that you must have before the Tawus Holdings meeting.

He looked up into the room, trying to decide how much detail to include.

By now you have been told that your grandson – who came to be my friend in the few days that I knew him – has been killed. At four o'clock this afternoon, you will be meeting with the man who ordered his murder.

Before Remy died, he confided in me about his efforts to prove the Sanjak is a fake. He told me of your need for proof.

He paused again. How was Mounir going to contact him? He didn't have a hotel or even a cell phone. Best, then, to suggest a time when Danny might call *him*. He glanced at his watch, but it was still on D.C. time. Which made it five hours earlier. Or was it six? Uncertain, he turned toward the desk, looking for a clock – and saw her standing there. The beautiful Paulina, her limpid brown eyes fastened on him with all the affection of a raptor.

The two of them stayed where they were for a long mo-ment, ferociously dumbfounded. Then Paulina broke into a hurried walk, click-clacking across the tiled lobby toward the elevators where, Danny now saw, the Brow loomed with his back to the lobby.

Danny went the other way. He accelerated through the patio, hustling past startled men and women, and hit the grass running. He passed the lyre fountain, burst through the trees and plantings, and found himself at the edge of a canal. He turned left. Emerging on Tal-Strasse, he zigzagged between onrushing trams, crossing the street to a little park where vendors sold *rosti* and apertifs. With a nervous glance over his shoulder, he saw the Brow standing maybe fifty yards away on the Bahnhofstrasse, looking left and right.

Danny wanted to run, to leave his bag where it was and *sprint* for the busy plaza on the other side of the Limmat River. If he could cross the bridge without being noticed, it wouldn't be hard to get lost in the crowd. But that meant walking.

Joining a queue to buy Italian ices, Danny stripped off his sweatshirt and stuffed it in the pocket of his carry-on bag. Paulina and her friends would be scanning the crowd for a red top, not the white T-shirt he now wore. Looking up, he saw that the Brow had been joined by a second man. The two of them were on their toes outside a camera store, looking in opposite directions, up and down the Bahnhofstrasse. A few feet away, Paulina whispered into a cell phone.

Danny took a deep breath, then turned on his heel and walked slowly in the direction of the crowded plaza. To his right was Lake Zurich, to his left the Limmat River. If he had to, he could vault the railing, make a splash among the swans.

The short walk across the bridge seemed to take forever. As in Rome, the challenge was to keep his back to those who were searching for him. This meant not looking back, and *that* meant not knowing where *they* were. He was pretty sure, though, that if he was spotted, one of them would shout to the others – and Danny would hear that. In which case, he'd drop his bag and run.

But what if he was wrong? What if the Brow saw

him walking across the bridge and didn't say a thing? What if he just . . . came on? In that case, death would come as a surprise. A knife in the ribs. A bullet behind the ear. An arm around his neck, a quick twist.

I'm racewalking, Danny thought, and, gritting his teeth, slowed his pace. He could feel their eyes on his back, a kind of visual gravity pushing gently against his shoulder blades.

Then he was across the bridge and picked up his pace. He followed the path of least resistance, zigzagging between cars and pedestrians, heart hammering. Soon the plaza was behind him and he found himself in a warren of ancient streets, too narrow for cars and trucks. The streets were lined with expensive shops and restaurants, with tiny alleys spoking off in every direction. He followed a long flight of steps to a small park overlooking the river. In the center of the park was a circular fountain fed by three lions, spouting arcs of water from their maws. A girl with long blond hair stood by the fountain, washing a thermos. Suddenly she frowned, and for a moment Danny thought it was the way he looked, ragged and out of breath.

But no.

It was raining. You could see it on the stippled surface of the fountain. The first few drops were so big and slow, it seemed to Danny that he could walk between them. Then the pace of the shower picked up and he couldn't. Moments later, it was pouring, raining so hard that it *stung.* Everywhere people massed in doorways and under overhangs, seeking shelter from the deluge.

He ducked into an unoccupied doorway and pressed himself against the wall. The rain was a torrent, flooding the gutters. Four inches in front of his face, a curtain of water sheeted off the overhang into the street.

He needed a hotel – a place to make phone calls. The message he'd been writing to Mounir was crumpled in his pocket, incomplete and unaddressed. He'd have to call the Old Man and try to meet him.

So . . . A hotel, then. But which one? Danny squinted into the gray downpour. *Not here,* he thought. *I need something in a different part of town.* The warren of streets that had worked in his favor a few minutes earlier could just as easily work against him a few minutes from now. This part of Zurich, the old part, was a maze of byways and alleys – the kind of place where you'd be likely to "bump into" someone you knew.

Danny did not want to bump into anyone he knew.

When the rain stopped, the cobblestones streamed and he followed the streams downhill. Soon he turned a corner and emerged into a wide and busy street where people stood with umbrellas, waiting at a tram stop. A sleek trolley with the number 23 on it was just pulling in, and he ran for it, hopping onto the back car through a pair of accordion doors. It was crowded – which was good. And no one seemed to pay. The driver drove. There was no conductor.

All of the seats were occupied, as was most of the standing space. Pools of water trembled on the floor. Windows ran with condensation. Soon they were at a complicated intersection where a lot of the lines seemed to converge. An electronic voice announced: "Bellevueplatz." Through the open door Danny could see a huge Ferris wheel standing beside the lake. On an impulse, he joined the exodus, crossing the tracks with

455

a crowd, then boarding another tram. The number four. He took a look this time, squinting through the fogged windows at the crowd, looking for Paulina and her friends. As the train pulled away from the plaza, he thought he saw the Brow, soaked and walking by himself beside the river. But maybe not.

Danny got out of the tram a little while later, finding himself in a more residential area. The sign on the corner identified the street as Seefeldstrasse. The shops along it were not the sort built for the tourist trade but the kind that served city residents. He passed a hardware store, a hole-in-the-wall selling small appliances, a health-food store, a hairdresser's, a travel bureau, and two or three shops selling secondhand designer clothing. He passed what looked like a gun shop, its window bristling with crossbows, guns, and knives. A mannequin in camouflage gear aiming a rifle at a stuffed boar.

And so it went. A podriatrist's office. A hairdresser's. A Feng Shui shop. He'd gone three long blocks and was beginning to think he'd have to get back on the tram when he arrived at the Hotel Seefeld.

The desk clerk was a gorgeous blonde wearing white lipstick and long silver earrings. He asked if the hotel had a room and was told crisply: "Of course." As she tapped the computer keyboard, they talked about the weather. "A real heat wave," she said. "So un-Swiss." She slid the key card across the brushed chrome surface of the counter and gave him a rueful smile. "And I can tell you're not one of those Americans who expects air-conditioning everywhere he goes, are you?"

Danny shook his head. Of course he didn't.

His room was an ultramodern cockpit on the third floor, all burled wood and chrome, black, white, and charcoal. And hot as hell. He drew the drapes to the side as a prelude to opening a set of French doors leading out to a tiny balcony overlooking Seefeldstrasse. But it wasn't as easy as that. The doors were operated by a mechanism as complex as a Swiss watch. Crouching before it like a safecracker, he played with the mechanism for five long minutes, beads of sweat rolling down his temples. Finally, the doors sprang open and a gush of damp air flooded the room.

He picked up the phone and asked the operator to connect him with the Baur au Lac. Soon the phone was ringing in Mounir Barzan's room. After the sixth ring, a recording asked if he'd like to leave a message for the guest. He thought about it. And hung up.

With a heavy sigh, he stripped to his boxers and stretched out on the crisp white bedspread to think.

The way he saw it, he'd only been in Zurich a couple of hours and, already, everything had changed. Now that Paulina had seen him, getting into the Tawus Holdings meeting was going to be next to impossible. Zebek would have someone in the lobby, someone at the door, someone waiting somewhere else. So much for the element of surprise. *(Way to go, Slick. . . .)*

Still, Zebek had no way of knowing how much Danny knew. As far as the Yezidis' brand-new Imam was concerned, Danny had been running so hard that he hadn't had time to think. Zebek wouldn't know how much Remy Barzan had told him – or, depending on whether the search of Barzan's borrowed villa had turned up Danny's passport, even that he'd found Barzan. Zebek would not know anything about what Manziger had told Danny. Neither would he know about Danny's success in cracking Terio's e-mail and acquiring Rolvaag's report.

Not that it mattered, really. Zebek would kill him anyway, just to watch him die. He didn't actually have to *know* anything.

On a table next to the bed, a digital clock blinked 12:18. He needed to get to Mounir – before the meeting. But how? He closed his eyes and remembered something Remy had said, about his grandfather, that talk of "a Swiss miss."

Danny sat up, grabbed the yellow pages – and saw that it was in German. Or Swiss German. Whatever it was, he couldn't read it. For a moment, he thought he was going to have to ask the blonde at the front desk for help. But then he saw that, like *golf* and *disco*, *escort service* did not require translation.

There were about thirty of them, and the idea of calling every one of them was depressing. But it wasn't as if he had anything else to do, so he started in on the list. It turned out that his worries about language problems had been misplaced. It wasn't the locals who needed "escorts." It was foreign business-men who had a night or two in Zurich. After a few calls, he had the feeling that the women he spoke to could have fielded questions in Japanese, Spanish, Russian, or whatever. Every one of them was fluent in English.

He made up a story about how he was the personal assistant to Mounir Barzan. It was essential that he talk to him, a matter of great urgency. The women were pleasant but uniformly unhelpful. He'd been through about a dozen services when a throaty-voiced madam told him he was wasting his time.

The rebuke surprised him. "Excuse me?"

She laughed, a musical trill. "First of all," she said, "if you were actually this fellow's personal assistant, wouldn't you have been the one to organize this activity?"

"Well, yeah, but –"

"Secondly," she said in an amused voice, "do you think you can just call up and ask for people? Do you think someone's going to answer the phone and say, 'Hang on, pet, I think he's just finishing up with Helena'? Not likely."

"You're right," he admitted. "No question, but . . . I really have to find this guy. He's in serious trouble."

"You mean, you are."

Danny started to object, then sighed and said, "Is it that obvious?"

"Let me ask you something," she said.

"What?"

"The gentleman you're looking for? Is he an Arab, or African or . . ."

"What's that got to do with anything?" Danny asked.

"Well, certain services *specialize*."

"Oh. I didn't know that. He's . . . Kurdish, actually."

"Kurdish, I don't know. But I think Thai Centerfolds is popular with clients from the Middle East. And Little Black Book. But just leave the message. Don't dress it up. It's an emergency and the man should call you."

It was good advice, and Danny thanked her for it.

"You're welcome," she said. "And who knows? You might get lucky."

He did and he didn't. By one-fifteen, he'd called every whorehouse in the phone book. And no one seemed to recognize Mounir's name. He was yawning with jet lag but didn't want to fall asleep. He tried the desk to see if they had room service. No dice. He splashed cold water on his face, which helped for a couple of minutes, but between the stifling air in the room and his lack of sleep he soon found himself beginning to nod off again. He didn't want to fall asleep. He *couldn't* fall asleep. He had to think of something, some way to reach Mounir. He had two hours and change to figure something out. He willed himself to focus, conjuring up Inzaghi's crumpled body, the massacre of Remy Barzan, summoning up Manziger's gray goo scenario, to fight off his fatigue. But the truth was, his brain was so fogged that he couldn't come up with a single idea about what he might do or how he could get to Mounir. Then, minutes later, he just couldn't stop yawning. He needed coffee, *at least* coffee.

He took the phone of the hook, reasoning that if Mounir Barzan got a busy signal he'd call back. He sprinted to the café at the end of the block. They had no drip coffee, only espresso drinks. Just the cooler air of the street and the smell of coffee helped revive him. He ordered a triple-shot latte to go and speed-walked back to the hotel with the paper cup burning his hand.

He couldn't have been gone for more than five minutes, but as soon as he replaced the receiver the little red light on the phone blinked at him. Swearing, he punched the button to retrieve the message, then listened to Mounir's heavy voice, with its formal intonations. "Mounir Barzan is speaking. I return this message, but you are not here. I am staying at the Hotel Baur au Lac. I am occupied all this day with meeting. For emergency, you can reach me this evening." The message logged off with a time tag, in English: twelve forty-five. He realized from this that Mounir had called while he was still phoning escort services. The hotel's phone system did not include call waiting, and it must take a while for a message to post into voice mail. His relief that his coffee run was not the reason he'd missed Mounir's call lasted a split second and then he succumbed to a frustrated rage.

"Sonofabitch!" He slammed the phone down in its cradle and looked wildly around the room. Then he crossed the room to the balcony (it was only two steps away), went outside, and growled, *"Come on!"*

He was losing it.

He dropped onto the bed and lay there, staring at the immaculate white ceiling, feeling as if he'd been clubbed. *Now what?* A tram hurtled past beneath his balcony, its iron wheels slicing through the dull wash of traffic noise. Women came and went in the hall, speaking a language he couldn't even identify. One of them laughed, and her delight was so genuine, it made him feel all the worse. And so it went – nowhere – for ten, fifteen, twenty minutes.

Eventually, he found the gumption to try the Baur au Lac again. But "Herr Barzan" was not in his room. He sat with his head in his hands on the side of the bed, thinking about his options and sinking deeper into despair – when it hit him. He remembered that gun shop he'd passed on the way to the hotel, the mannequin in camouflage. *Why not? In for a penny, in for a pound. What the fuck? I'm a dead man anyway.*

For one semester in the tenth grade, encouraged by the thought of spending serious time on a bus with sweet Holly Saxton, he'd joined the Debate Club – of which she was a star. A cynical but not unintelligent ploy, it might have worked if Danny had been any

461

good at debating. But he wasn't, and so found himself left off the teams that actually traveled to tournaments.

Until now, the Debate Club had been a symbol of failure, but suddenly it paid its dividend. While he never got within two bus seats of Holly Saxton, Danny knew more than a little about Swiss gun laws.

In a debate about gun control, Danny had been assigned to defend what amounted to the National Rifle Association's position: *Resolved, that restrictive gun-control laws have little or no impact on crime.* In this argument, his big gun (heh-heh) was Switzerland. Because here was a country with *lots* of guns, few regulations, and hardly any violent crime. The murder rate in Switzerland was lower than it was in countries – such as England, Canada, and Japan – that had some of the world's most stringent gun-control laws.

Like the Americans, the Swiss had won their independence in a revolutionary war fought by an armed citizenry. And they were still packing, discouraging potential invaders with a policy of heavily armed neutrality.

Switzerland had universal military conscription for males. Accordingly, every adult male was required by law to keep a gun in the house – and not just any gun. It had to be an assault weapon!

The only firearms that required a special permit were handguns and automatic weapons – and even in those cases, permits were easily obtained. Shotguns, on the other hand, were completely off the books. Buying a twelve-gauge was like buying a toaster. The same for semiautomatic rifles. And although its European neighbors had pressured Switzerland about it, attempts to pass laws regulating gun sales to foreigners had been repeatedly shot down by the Swiss equivalent of the NRA. So, as strange as it seemed, Danny knew for a fact that he could walk down the block to that gun shop and buy a fucking cannon if he wanted.

The problem was that he wouldn't know what to do with it. Despite the fact that he'd just shot a guy less than a week ago, that gun had been handed to him, loaded and ready to go. It was like a cap gun; all he'd had to do was pull the trigger. He wouldn't know what to do with a rifle, let alone a semiautomatic weapon.

There were no hunters in the family. Not a single one, even among his cousins. He realized, of course, how unusual this was. Every American family had at least one crazed loner uncle who took his nephews shooting and stopped by each Thanksgiving with neatly wrapped packages of venison for the family freezer. But not the Crays. There was no one. And even if there had been, Danny was a *vegetarian*.

Now Caleigh – Caleigh was a whole other story. She could shoot the lights off a rhinestone cowboy. While Danny was practicing step-over drills with a No. 4 soccer ball in the backyard, *she* was in the Black Hills shooting rattlesnakes – and getting good at it. But that was Caleigh. He was him.

Still, he thought. *I'm a guy. How hard can it be? Just point and shoot. Or not.* And, anyway, what about that guy he shot? And hit. So, maybe he was a natural. Like that Woody Harrelson character in the Oliver Stone film.

But somehow, he didn't think so.

Not that it mattered what he thought. The gun idea was the only idea he had. It was like the bluesman said, *If I didn't have the gun idea I wouldn't have no idea at all. . . .*

He tried the Baur au Lac one last time. No Mounir.

With an effort, he got to his feet and bounced on his toes, revving up a sense of energy that he didn't really feel. Then he closed the door behind him and took the stairs, two at a time, down to the lobby. Two minutes later, he was standing inside the William Tell *Speicher des Jagers*.

The man behind the counter was fifty, with piercing blue eyes and a florid face. In his left ear was a single earring in the shape of an edelweiss flower. He inclined his head. *"Bitte?"*

"I'm looking for a gun," Danny said, restraining an inclination to roll his eyes.

The man raised an eyebrow, offered a little smile. "As you can see . . . you're in the right place. What sort of gun? "

An impressive one, he thought. *Something I can wave around.* "What about that one?" he asked, nodding toward a black, boxy-looking thing. Whatever it was, it looked lethal, the kind of gun Schwarzenegger might carry into a bikers' bar in San Berdoo. The idea that some nut could walk in off the street and buy it off the shelf – as he was about to do – was terrifying.

"The Uzi?"

"Yeah. Right."

The man closed his eyes and nodded in approval. "An excellent piece of equipment if you are wanting an assault rifle that's lightweight – and very reliable. And the folding stock makes it even more compact for easy transport." By way of demonstration, he picked up the gun and folded the stock against the barrel.

"Excellent," Danny remarked.

"But let me ask you something."

Here it comes, Danny thought, expecting a fusillade

of questions, expecting, in fact, to learn that he was wrong, that you could not just waltz into a gun shop in Zurich and buy a cannon. There was a waiting period, a background check.

"You're from where?" the man asked. "The U.S.?"

Danny nodded. "Uh-hunh."

"I ask because your ATF has recently forbidden the importation of certain features available for the Uzi."

"Oh," Danny said, feigning disappointment. *It's got "features"?*

"For example, you will not be permitted to take it home with the bayonet mount or the grenade launcher."

Danny made a *tsking* sound, as if to say, *What a bummer.*

The man turned to the case behind him and brought out another gun. He laid it down on the counter beside the first weapon. The two were very similar. "This one creates no problems with your ATF. Even with the large-capacity military magazine. Happily, that's still permitted."

"Large-capacity, huh?"

"A hundred rounds. It's standard-issue, IMI."

"That should be plenty," Danny remarked. "More than enough." Then: "What's IMI?"

The man looked surprised. "Israeli Military Industries."

Danny shrugged, tried a smile. "Great."

"Nine pounds – quite portable." He hefted it. Tossed it from one hand to the other. "Pistol grip. And, of course, the clip is inserted at the base of the butt – which is perfect for night work."

"Why?" Danny asked.

"Because you can reload without looking. All in all,

it's a nice, compact assault rifle." He laid it down upon the counter.

"How much is it?"

The man reached for his reading glasses, which hung from a cord around his neck, and settled them on the bridge of his nose. "U.S.?" he asked.

Danny nodded.

The gun dealer turned to a computer that rested on a small desk behind the counter. He tapped at the keyboard for a few moments and waited. Finally, he turned back to Danny and said, "Two thousand, seven hundred, and eighty-one dollars. There's no VAT. We're Swiss." He smiled.

"Well," Danny said, hesitating. It often took him days to decide whether or not to buy a particular sweater. The idea of splurging on an Uzi –

"Of course, it's used," the dealer said. "In fact, a retired law enforcement weapon." He made a little facial shrug. "Well cared for, in other words."

Danny took a deep breath. "You take Visa?"

Twenty-four

The clerk wrapped the Uzi in plastic foam and eased it into a cardboard box fitted with stiff cubes of polystyrene. Then he wrapped the box and the ammunition clip in brown paper and tied up the parcel with white string.

It could have been someone's laundry.

On the way back to his hotel, Danny thought hard about how he was going to get into the Tawus Holdings meeting. He supposed he could take a cab to the Baur au Lac with the Uzi wrapped up, just as it was, then rip the package open in the men's room and storm the meeting.

Except he'd never get that far. Knowing that Danny was in Zurich, Zebek would have his people staked out all over the Baur au Lac's grounds. So, if he was going to get in, he'd need a cover of some kind. Or a disguise.

Arriving at the Seefeld, he took the stairs two at a time to his room and called the Baur au Lac, asking for Mounir's room. By now, he knew the number by heart. If he could just get through to the old man, he might be able to meet him somewhere else. Give him the floppy with Rolvaag's report and catch the next flight out. But no. That would be too easy. The telephone rang and rang, its unanswered double bursts as mournful as a foghorn.

So . . . no miracle. It was up to him – just him and his friend, the tightly wrapped Mister Uzi.

Which meant that he'd need a disguise. Something to get him into the lobby. (The gun would get him into the meeting.) Thinking about disguises, he remembered the way Remy Barzan had reacted – or, more accurately, how he'd *not* reacted – to "the soldiers' " arrival. It wasn't until they'd started shooting that Barzan realized they were there to kill him.

The truth was, people saw the uniform – not the person wearing it. Unfortunately, there weren't any uniforms walking around the Baur au Lac. Only the doorman, and Danny couldn't get that close. The only people *he'd* seen were businessmen and golfers.

The image of the golfers sitting on the patio went off in his head like a cartoon lightbulb. The thing about golfers was: they carried golf bags. And golf bags were more or less ideal for taking an automatic weapon through the lobby of a world-class hotel. Danny thought back to the golfers on the patio. They'd been wearing little hats – which was good – and sunglasses would not have been out of place.

He glanced at the clock: 2:43. Tucking the Uzi box under his arm, he made sure that he had the floppy disk with the dendrochronologist's report. Then he ran downstairs to ask the blonde where he could buy some golf equipment.

"Very nice, sir! And if I may say so, sir, it's gratifying to see a young man, such as yourself, embracing the game with such enthusiasm." The dark-haired salesman took a step back and sighed contentedly.

For his part, Danny was aghast, gawking at himself in a three-way mirror in the Sporting! section of the

Jelmoli department store on the Bahnhofstrasse. Golf clothes were about as far from his natural style as one could get. And yet here he was: Golfman, decked out in fawn-colored knickerbockers, argyle knee socks, and black-and-white saddle shoes. Above the waist, a gold polo shirt with a moiré pattern lay open at the throat, hooked by one of the stems of Danny's new Ray Bans. Completing the ensemble were a Scottish driving cap, which concealed Danny's buzz cut from public view, and a suede golf glove stuffed insouciantly in his rear pocket.

"Will there be anything else, sir? Rain suit? Umbrella?"

"No, this ought to do it."

With his hunter-green Gore-Tex golf-bag trimmed in premium cowhide, the outfit was at once convincing – "Hey, Mabel, get a loada this guy!" – and outrageously expensive. The bag held a minimal collection of Jelmoli's least expensive clubs, the woods shielded from harm by knitted covers. Danny had selected the bag for one feature: the inner framework holding the clubs separate from one another lifted out so that the interior of the bag could be cleaned. Danny intended to scrap that framework to make room for the Uzi.

"I think I'll wear it out," Danny said. "I'm teeing off in an hour."

"Of course. May I wrap up your other clothing for you?" The salesman took Danny's Visa card and carefully folded his blue jeans and sweatshirt, depositing them in a box that looked as if it cost more than they did.

Danny thought about dealing with the Uzi then and there – just going into the dressing room, unwrapping it, and putting it into the golf bag. But he decided against it. There were undoubtedly surveillance cameras in the store, and he couldn't afford a hassle with Jelmoli's security people. So he just signed the credit-card slip and took off.

The Baur au Lac was only a short walk up the Bahnhofstrasse, but he felt like a stork, dressed as he was and carrying a golf bag. Better to arrive by taxi. He found a rank of cabs on a side street. The driver popped the trunk, put the golf bag inside, and laid the box with the Uzi beside it. Then he held open the rear passenger door.

Danny spotted the first of Zebek's sentries at the end of the hotel's drive. Gaetano, looking worried and very focused. He peered into the taxi as it passed but didn't give Danny – in sunglasses and golf cap – a second look.

Nor did anyone else. Stepping out of the cab at the entry to the lobby, he tipped the driver, recovered his golf bag and package, and sauntered past a bulky Italian man loitering near the door.

On his way past the front desk, Danny noticed a gilt-framed placard on a standing easel:

Novartis Pharma A.G.
Jungfrau Room – L 1
2:15 P.M.
Tawus Holdings
Winterthur Room – L 2
4 P.M.

Continuing past the desk to a polished oak door with a brass plaque marked HERREN, Danny went into the men's room and closeted himself in a stall. Leaning the golf clubs against the door, he sat down

470

with the box from the gun shop and stripped away the paper. Lifting the Uzi from its foam compartments, he clapped the ammo clip into the grip, just behind the trigger. It made a satisfying *thunk*, just as it did in the movies. Then he pulled the clubs from the golf bag and propped them up against the door to the stall. Next came the bag's interior cage, which he removed and placed on the back of the toilet, along with the box containing his old clothes. Finally, he lowered the gun into the bag, rearranged the clubs, and flushed.

Re-emerging in the lobby, he suffered a surge of adrenaline that made him want to bolt. But he didn't. He walked calmly to the elevator, repeating the soccer mantra of his youth: *Tranquilo, tran-QUIL-o* . . . A swarthy man in a black business suit joined him in what seemed like an interminable wait for the elevator. Danny punched the elevator button again and again, glancing around for an indicator that might show which floor it was on. But there was none. Finally, the doors swept open with a soft chime and a bellhop emerged, wheeling a gold cart piled high with Tumi luggage.

The journey from the lobby to level one, where the businessman got out, was a joke. It seemed to take about a minute – which isn't very long, really, unless you're holding your breath. Which Danny was, however inadvertently. The elevator chimed. The businessman exited. The doors slid shut. Danny took a deep breath.

Tranquilo.

His plan (if you could call it a plan) was pretty straightforward. Get off at the second floor. Dump the clubs and crash the meeting – locked and loaded (whatever that meant.) Tell everyone to *shut the fuck up and freeze*!

That's what Bruce Willis would do.

A soft chime announced his arrival on level two. The doors slid open. Sitting in a chair next to the closed double doors of the Winterthur Room, directly across from the elevator, was the muscular rectangle that Danny thought of as the Brow.

They saw each other in the same instant, but it took the Brow *one, two, three* seconds to grasp the fact that the Beau Brummel who stood before him was, in fact, the punk artist he was supposed to kill. The first second was consumed by a check-it-out glance that ended in bemused dismissal – followed, a second later, by a bloom of shocked cognition. The third second ended with the Brow levitating in his chair – just as the doors to the elevator closed.

Danny had no idea which button he'd pushed, but when the doors opened again, he saw from the numbers outside the rooms that he was on Level Three. He stuck a foot into the door and leaned out, looking up and down the corridor. At either end of the hallway was a stairwell, marked by a lighted green sign showing a stick figure running down an outline of white stairs.

Dumping the golf clubs onto the floor of the elevator, he pulled the Uzi out and tossed the golf bag aside. The gun felt cold and dense in his hands. It gave off an oily, metallic smell. And even though it was *his* gun, the unfamiliar way it looked and felt and smelled sent a little zigzag of alarm through his heart.

He stepped back. *Tranquilo.*

The doors whooshed shut, and a wave of claustrophobia crashed against his gut. *What am I doing!?* He couldn't believe it. The gun. The clothes. The situation. He shook his head, trying to throw off the trapped sensation that he felt, but it didn't work. The air was thick, the elevator tiny, the gun in his hands ever so heavy. *What am I doing what am I doing?* There was a sizzling noise in his head, as if he had a fuse running from ear to ear. *What if something goes wrong? It's a machine gun. What if there's a massacre? What if I kill 'em all?* Panic zoomed around the inside of his skull like a roach trying to escape a smoldering pan.

Ding! The little chime went off in his head like a hand grenade.

When the doors opened, the Brow was standing outside the Winterthur Room, talking urgently into a cell phone. Seeing the Uzi even before he noticed who was holding it, he paused. Said, *"Ciao."* Let the phone drop and put his hands in the air.

In his peripheral vision, Danny caught the motion of men running toward him from either end of the corridor, where they must have been manning the stairways. But their pace slowed all at once, then stopped entirely when they saw what he was holding. "Stay," he said, as if ordering a not-so-obedient Labrador to wait at the corner. Then, using the Uzi as a pointer, he motioned the Brow to precede him into the Winterthur Room.

Zebek sat at the head of a long wooden table, its polished surface gleaming in the afternoon light. Around the table were nine elderly men, dressed as Zebek was, in dark business suits. In the center of the table, lying on its side, was a curved knife with a jeweled haft. "Sorry about this," Danny said, shoving the Brow away from him.

Each of the men had a glass of water on the table

before him, along with a closed blue folder and an expensive-looking pen. The folders were embossed in gold with the words TAWUS HOLDINGS. These, then, were the Yezidi Elders, and Danny saw that three of them, including Sheik Mounir, had laptop computers in front of them.

"Sheik Mounir," Danny said, "I need to speak with you." His voice sounded hollow, as if he were speaking in a room without echoes.

"Call security," Zebek ordered, nodding toward the beautiful Paulina. She reached for her cell phone.

"I'll blow your arm off," Danny told her.

She put down the phone.

"And if you go for the gun in your purse," he added, "I'll blow your head off."

Now she looked hurt. Folded her hands in her lap. Pouted.

One of the Elders asked a question of Mounir in Turkish. Mounir shook his head. Turning to Danny, he asked. "Do I know you?"

"I came to your house – in Uzelyurt, remember? A couple of weeks ago." In the corner of his eye Danny saw the Brow inching closer. "Don't," he ordered, and swung the Uzi in an arc that ended at the big man's chest.

The Brow froze.

Danny turned back to Mounir and removed his cap. "You had me kidnapped," he told him. "The guy with the basketball shirt – and the other guy. They took me to your grandson. To Remy. I'm sure he told you."

Mounir peered out at him from within the nest of wrinkles around his eyes. Danny could see the wheels turning. The old man was remembering Danny's visit and what had happened afterward: the kidnapping and interrogation, followed by Remy's acceptance of him. "Ohhhh, yes, of course," the old man muttered, talking as much to himself as to anyone else. "But, Remy –"

"I know," Danny said.

Zebek chuckled. Turning to Paulina and the Brow, he said something in Italian. Paulina did a double take, giggled, and swiveled in her seat to look up at Danny. The Brow swore and, to Danny's surprise, stepped toward him, ignoring the Uzi that was pointed at his chest. Before Danny could warn him off, the big Italian reached back, as if he were going to throw a baseball, then pivoted into a roundhouse slap that sent the American crashing into the wall.

It seemed like the room lights dimmed and flared as Danny staggered and fell. Seeing the Brow jerk a handgun out from under his jacket, Danny warned him once – "Don't!" – then pulled the trigger on the Uzi.

Click!

Paulina giggled.

Click click click!

Zebek laughed. Even the Brow smiled as he reached down and took the Uzi from the American's hands. "It won't shoot with the safety on," Zebek explained.

"My bad," Danny acknowledged, and, getting slowly to his feet, launched himself at Zebek. The move took everyone by surprise, including Danny, who hit Zebek three times in the face, sending him sprawling out of his chair. Dropping a knee into his chest, Danny was about to hit him again when the Brow dragged him away by the collar of his polo shirt.

"Get him out of here!" Zebek gasped. "He's a lunatic!"

The Brow began to pull Danny toward the door

when Mounir's voice rose above the jabber of the other Elders. "I will hear him," he announced.

Still on the floor, Zebek couldn't believe his ears. "What!?" Clambering to his feet, he pounded on the table and began to argue in a language Danny didn't understand.

"I said, 'I will hear him.' "

Zebek spoke again, his words as unintelligible as their meaning was obvious. He was warning Mounir against something.

The old man nodded. "You're the Imam," he acknowledged. "And I am the Chairman. Since this is a *business* meeting, the young man will be heard." He turned to Danny. "How did my grandson die?"

"He *killed* him!" Zebek insisted.

"Is that true?" Mounir asked.

"No," Danny replied. "It's not true at all."

"Then tell me what happened," Mounir ordered.

While one of the Elders quietly translated for those of his colleagues who did not speak English, Danny explained that Remy Barzan had been hiding from Zebek – even as Danny fled from the same man.

Twice Zebek attempted to interrupt him, but on each occasion he was silenced by Mounir.

"Remy had some arrangement with the soldiers at a checkpoint up the road," Danny reported. "They came to the house, once or twice a week. I don't know if they were looking in on *Remy* or if they were watching the house for someone else, but . . . Remy was used to them. Then – I don't know if they were soldiers or some guys *dressed* as soldiers, but they showed up at the house one day and . . . Remy saw them on the security monitor. He wasn't worried about them. He

476

went out to talk to them! Then they started killing everyone."

Zebek scoffed.

"And you?" Mounir asked, his eyes locked with Danny's.

"I ran. I hid."

"And you don't know who they were?"

"Yeah, I do! They were Zebek's!" Danny exclaimed.

Before Zebek could deny it, Mounir patted the air with his right hand. "How do you know?" he asked.

"Because I saw him."

"Don't be stupid!" Zebek warned.

"He was riding in a Bentley."

Mounir held Danny's eyes for a long moment, then took a deep breath and turned to Zebek with a questioning look.

Zebek thought for a moment, rubbing his jaw where Danny had hit him. Finally, he cleared his throat and spoke. "You said it yourself, Mounir: this is a business meeting. What happened – or didn't happen – between Remy and me . . . has nothing to do with why we're here. I'd suggest we get on with our business and leave these other matters for another time."

Mounir turned to Danny. "Is it true what he says? What happened to Remy has nothing to do with why we're here?"

Danny shook his head. "It has everything to do with why you're here."

"And how is that?" Mounir asked.

Danny took a deep breath. "I sent you a report," he told him. "You'll get it in a few days – in the mail. Meanwhile . . ." Reaching into his pocket, he pulled out the floppy disk on which he'd copied Rolvaag's report, replete with the JPEG files. Sliding the floppy

477

down the table to Mounir, he said, "It's all on that."

Mounir gave the floppy to an older man who was seated beside him. The older man slipped it into a laptop and called up one of the files. Mounir glanced at the monitor, which showed a comparison array of tree rings from different times and places. "What is this?" Mounir asked, a look of bafflement on his face.

Zebek leaned back in his chair, the better to see the monitor. A puzzled expression flickered on his face and then hardened into something else as his eyes widened in recognition of the image on the screen.

"Let me tell it from the beginning," Danny suggested. "Or it won't make sense."

Mounir gave him a go-ahead nod.

"This guy called me about a month ago," he began, with a gesture at Zebek. "Said his name was Belzer and would I meet him at the airport . . . ?"

It took him a long time to get the story out. He kept forgetting details and so had to loop back to make sense of things. Once or twice, the translator asked him to stop, so that he could catch up. But in the end, it all came out. "The point being that our friend here substituted a fake for the Sanjak that Sheik Adi carved – because that was the only way he could get the money he needed for his business. Chris Terio and Remy Barzan found out about it and had the wood tested by Dr. Rolvaag. You can read Rolvaag's report, but the conclusion is obvious. Mr. Zebek is . . ." Danny thought about it. "A menace."

The room was airless and still, the loudest noise an occasional click on one of the keyboards. Then Zebek started to applaud, clapping his hands in slow sarcasm. When he had the attention of everyone in the room, he put his fingers together in a prayerful way and began to speak in a matter-of-fact voice. "He invades our meeting, armed with a submachine gun. He attacks your Imam with his fists. And still you listen to him?" He paused. "Isn't it obvious," Zebek asked, "that this man and the others – this Terio fellow and Remy Barzan – isn't it obvious they have their own agenda?"

"What agenda?" Danny asked.

Zebek didn't even look at him. "He works for a business espionage firm called 'Fellner Associates.' They're trying to destroy my company to get at its patents."

"Bullshit!" Danny exclaimed.

Mounir patted the air with his right hand, then pointed at the monitor in front of him. "And this?"

"What about it?" Zebek asked.

"Are you saying these files are a lie?" Mounir asked.

Zebek frowned. "You mean this report from the – what is it? The Oslo Institute? The dendro-chronologist's report?"

Mounir nodded. All the Elders fixed Zebek with their gaze.

He made a little moue and said, "No, I don't think the report is inaccurate. I'm sure it's quite correct." He paused to let the words sink in.

"Then . . ." Mounir began.

"I'm sure the wood is just what this scientist says – fifty years old! One hundred years old! In any case, much too young to have come from the Sanjak." He paused again. "But what does that prove?" he asked. "That the Sanjak is a fake? Hardly. The only thing it *proves* is that Terio and Barzan gave this man, Rolvaag, a piece of wood that came from something other than the Sanjak."

479

"Like what?" Danny asked.

Zebek shrugged. "A cigar box, perhaps." Then he shook his head. "I can't believe we're still listening to this," he said.

The Elders burst into argument among themselves. Unable to understand a word, Danny turned to Zebek. "You're a seriously fucked-up man, y'know that?"

Zebek looked away.

After a bit, Mounir raised a hand, and the room fell silent. "We need to resolve this before any further business can be conducted."

"I quite agree," Zebek told him. "You need to decide who to believe. Your Imam – or this . . . this maniac from America."

Even Mounir smiled at the characterization. "Then it's settled," he said, rising slowly to his feet. "Your plane is at the airport?"

"My plane?" Zebek repeated.

"I was told you have a private plane."

"Well, yes," Zebek said, "but –"

"Then I think we should go."

"But where?" Zebek demanded. "Where do you want to go?"

Mounir ignored the question, turning instead to the other Elders. He spoke to them briefly. Then, one by one, they got to their feet and followed him out of the room.

The plane took off a little after seven P.M., flying to the southeast with its fuel tanks fully loaded. The pilots had been told they were going to Athens, but that turned out to be a ploy. An hour into the flight, Mounir went to the cockpit and announced a new destination: Diyarbakir.

Though he tried not to show it, the change seemed to unsettle Zebek, who fell strangely silent. Danny was quiet as well. It was his first trip in a private jet, and he would rather have been almost anywhere else. For one thing, there was no cabin service, which meant no food. For another, and as he'd tried to explain to Mounir, there was no reason, really, for him to go *anywhere* – except home. He'd given the Elders Rolvaag's report, and he'd told them everything he knew. Why should he have to accompany them to Diyarbakir?

"Because one of you is lying," Mounir replied.

It was a long flight, the European equivalent of New York to Denver. Somewhere over the Caucasus, Zebek got up and walked back to where Danny was sitting and sat down beside him.

"You could have written your own ticket," Zebek whispered.

Danny glanced at him, then looked away into the darkness beyond the window.

"You still can," Zebek announced.

Danny turned to him. "Aren't you worried I'll hit you again?"

Zebek shrugged. "I said you still can."

Danny looked around for another seat, but they were all taken.

"This is about dreams," Zebek murmured. "Not some *salary*. I'm talking about all the money you could ever want, all the money you could ever spend."

Danny shifted in his seat.

"It isn't just the money, it's the time," Zebek continued. "The time an artist needs to find his way. Think of it as Paris . . . with Paulina, if you like –"

Danny turned to him. "What are you so afraid of?"

481

The question made Zebek jump, a little hitch in his shoulders, as if a static charge had run through him. "I'm not afraid of anything. But you should be. I think Mounir is taking us to Uzelyurt –"

"What for?" Danny asked.

Zebek shrugged. "There's going to be a grand assembly – a sort of town meeting – to decide which of us is telling the truth. Frankly, I don't see how it can possibly go well for you."

Neither did Danny. Zebek was the Imam, fluent in the local dialect. Danny was . . . a foreign sculptor in golf clothes with high hopes for his first show.

"So what are we talking about?" he asked. "What do you want me to do?"

"Tell them you lied," Zebek replied. "I can fix the problem with your girlfriend – persuade her that the video was a bad joke. I can fix everything – including the problems you're about to have with the Yezidis. But you have to tell Mounir that you lied. And you have to tell him soon. Trust me –"

Danny thought about it. Said: "Nah."

They landed in Diyarbakir a little after two A.M. While the pilots took care of the Customs formalities, Mounir led everyone else out to the parking lot, where a line of black Mercedes stood idling at the curb. To Danny's surprise, Kukoc and the Buddy/ Buddy Guy emerged from the terminal. At Mounir's direction, they ushered Zebek into the backseat of the first car, where they bookended him, one on each side.

Danny was directed into the second car, where he was soon joined by Mounir and two of the other Elders. They sat where they were for a minute or so, and then the caravan of Mercedes pulled away from the curb.

"When is the meeting?" Danny asked, suppressing a yawn. "I hope it's in the afternoon, because –"

"There isn't any 'meeting,' " Mounir announced.

Danny got a cold feeling at the base of his spine. "But . . . I thought there was going to be some kind of town meeting in Uzelyurt. Zebek –"

"– is mistaken," Mounir told him. "We aren't going to Uzelyurt."

Danny frowned. *Then where? Where else was there?*

Mounir seemed to read his mind. "We're going to Nevazir," he said.

"The underground city?" Danny didn't get it. He was stupid with jet lag, wrung out with worry, and physically exhausted. Putting two and two together was almost more than he could manage. "But why?" he asked. "What's there?"

Mounir lit a cigarette, inhaled deeply, and blew the smoke out in a long, thin stream. Gazing out the passenger window, he shook his head and said, "I don't know. Maybe nothing."

It was a two-hour drive that wound through the hills and into the mountains, the blond earth now gray with moonlight. Eventually, the caravan turned off the main road, slowing to a crawl on a dirt track that ended in a clearing bordered by cypress trees. One by one, the Mercedes' engines died and the Elders got out.

Wedged between Kukoc and the Buddy/Buddy Guy, Zebek was practically growling with what sounded like a mixture of anger and fear. While Danny didn't understand a word of the Yezidi dialect, Zebek's tone made it apparent that he felt betrayed. Clearly, he hadn't expected to come here.

They were standing about twenty yards from a doorway that gave entrance to the hill itself. A massive pair of antique iron doors were flung open upon a black cavern. Beside the doorway, a young man stood with a box of Maglites, handing them out to each of the Elders as they entered.

Danny hurried to Mounir's side. "What's in there?" he asked.

The old man shrugged. "Nevazir."

"Yeah, well, if it's okay with you, I'll just wait out here," Danny told him.

Mounir grinned, then shook his head. Taking Danny by the arm, he gave him a flashlight and led him into what turned out to be a long, low tunnel that twisted and turned through a series of cavelike rooms, heading ever downward. The underground city was, as Danny had been told, a gigantic ant farm, with tunnels running off in every direction.

The flashlights' beams sliced through the darkness, splashing against the rock walls. "Where are we going?" Danny asked, breathing through his nose in an effort not to hyperventilate. It was like being in a mine, but a mine with a hundred passageways. *What if we get lost?* Danny wondered. *What if the flashlights give out? What if . . . ?* His jet lag had vanished, consumed by an overwhelming sense of claustrophobia.

"What's that?" Danny asked, pausing next to a massive round stone that rested precariously on a crude plinth in a sort of alcove adjacent to the passageway. As near as Danny could tell, the only thing holding it in place was a much smaller stone, wedged into the space where the plinth and the stone met.

"It was used to block the tunnel," Mounir explained. "If the people's enemies followed them into the city, they could seal off the passages behind them. Eventually, their enemies would give up."

"And then what? They'd roll the rock back?"

Mounir shook his head. "Impossible. They'd have to dig a new passage."

They'd been walking for fifteen minutes or more. The pace was slow, given the physical state of some of the Elders and Zebek's clubfoot. Maybe it was way more than fifteen minutes. Danny couldn't be sure. There was nothing in the underground city to mark the passage of time. No sense of depth or direction. "Where are we?" he asked.

"About twenty meters underground," Mounir told him. "It isn't far now."

It wasn't. They continued walking for another few minutes until the passageway opened upon a cavern with high ceilings and a vaulted recess in one wall. A gold curtain hung limply in the darkness from an iron bar, concealing what lay behind it.

Zebek was standing in the middle of the room, flanked by Kukoc and Buddy/Buddy, fulminating amid the Elders. The flashlights' beams trembled in the moldering air. Danny had a bad feeling.

"So here we are!" Zebek declared with an expansive gesture. "And for what? Why? What is *this* supposed to prove?" His voice seemed higher-pitched than it usually was and stoked with bravado.

Mounir cleared his throat. "I was thinking that you might be right," he said. "That this young man and Remy – and the other man, Terio – conspired against you."

"Exactly!" Zebek shouted. "And why not? Not one

485

of them was a believer! Why would anyone believe him, this American boy, instead of me? We – the true Yezidis, the faithful – we've been schemed against for a thousand years!"

Mounir nodded, as if agreeing. "I asked myself," he said, "how are we to know if the Sanjak is a fake – or if it is the report instead that is a fraud? Did the scientist in Norway test a slice of wood that came from the Sanjak – or was it, perhaps, a piece of driftwood that someone found on the shores of Lake Van? In either case it is a serious matter. If the true Sanjak, our most sacred object, fashioned by Sheik Adi himself, was replaced by a fake, then it is a question of the deepest sacrilege."

The old man paused and cleared his throat. "On the other hand," he continued, "it is possible that parties exist who for their own political or personal reasons do not approve the Imam duly selected by the Eders. It is possible that such parties sought to seed doubt and confusion upon that selection by launching a false report, questioning the legitimacy of the new guide. A play for time, perhaps, while they planned an assassination." The old man looked at Danny, who felt suddenly restless and claustrophobic. *Tranquilo*, he told himself, working to keep his eyes from sliding away from Mounir's calm glance. "A fake report," the old man continued, "would be equally a sacrilege, an attempt to interfere in the will of the Tawus and in the prophecies of the *Black Writing*." Mounir broke off, looked from Danny to Zebek, shook his head. "But how to determine?"

Zebek started saying something, but Mounir held up a restraining hand and the billionaire grew still.

"It occurred to me," Mounir said, "that if the Sanjak

486

we Elders saw while deliberating the selection of the new Imam was a fake, then whoever created it would destroy it as soon as the statue had outlived its purpose. The Sanjak is never on display. It is exposed to view only during the election procedure. The new Imam is young. He should easily outlive every Elder. It is even possible that the genuine Sanjak would have been returned to its rightful place, but of course in such an instance we would know at once upon seeing it that it was a *different* Sanjak, not the one to preside over our proceedings."

Danny's eyes darted from Zebek to the alcove and back again. The bankrupt billionaire was like a deer staring at a lighthouse.

"But if the *report* was a fraud," Mounir went on, "any piece of wood would have served as a sample for testing. And in this case the Sanjak would be here still, exactly as we remember." The old man sighed. "So which is it?" he asked, looking from Danny to Zebek.

"I think I've had about enough of this," Zebek blustered, and turned to leave.

Buddy/Buddy stepped in his path. "Buhhh-ddy," he cajoled. "*Buhhh*-ddy . . ."

Mounir walked slowly across the room to the recess in the wall. As he reached for the curtain, Zebek lunged at him, only to be restrained by Kukoc and his sidekick.

"It's forbidden!" Zebek declared. "It's not to be seen –"

The old man drew the curtain aside, and the Elders drew their breath as one. Behind the curtain was a pedestal of black marble on which a small square of velvet rested – and nothing else. One of the Elders stepped toward Zebek with a flick-knife in his hand.

Zebek sidestepped him, then dove for the passageway out – only to find Kukoc barring the way.

"What did you do with it then, Zerevan?" Mounir asked in a soft voice. "Where is the true Sanjak?"

Zebek seemed to have diminished in size, shrunk into himself. "If I tell you," he wheedled, "will you release me?"

Mounir issued a little snort and shook his head. "Ali and Suha can persuade you," he said, indicating Kukoc and Buddy/Buddy, "or you can save yourself the misery."

"I'm not responsible," Zebek blustered. "I don't know anything about it."

That was Zebek's last, feeble protest. Danny's two old adversaries advanced on him and Danny steeled himself. He wasn't sure he could just stand by and watch what was euphemistically termed a hostile interrogation. In the end, the threat alone sufficed, or maybe Zebek was smart enough to know that resistance would simply prolong the agony. He caved in without so much as a blow being struck.

The word dribbled out of his mouth. "Sotheby's," he said.

Mounir was so stunned, he could barely get the words out. "You *sold* it?"

"Not yet," Zebek said dispassionately. "There's an antiquities auction next month."

Mounir's face went hard and he stood up straight, then executed a small, formal bow. "We leave you," he said, then barked an order that Danny didn't understand. One by one, the Elders filed slowly from the room. Zebek began ranting in Kurdish, his meaning betrayed by his tone: *Don't! Please! For God's sake! I'll kill you!*

It was something like that, Danny thought, a mixture of threats and pleas. As they began to leave the room, Mounir put a hand on Danny's sleeve. "Give him your flashlight," he ordered. "Later, we'll put him out on the platform, for the birds. It's the old way."

The birds? What? Danny remembered something about birds, but he couldn't think about it now. What he could think about was that he couldn't get out of here fast enough. He turned and stepped quickly back into the room. "Here," he said, and thrust the flashlight into Zebek's hands. The disgraced Imam stared at the light for a long moment, then raised his eyes to Danny's. Tears of terror glittered on his cheeks. "Please," he said. "Not this."

Tell it to Chris Terio, Danny thought, but kept the message to himself. "*Ciao,*" he muttered, and, turning, moved quickly out of the room. Re-joining Mounir and the Elders, he watched as Kukoc wielded an iron pry bar, stabbing time and again at the rock that pinned the massive stone to its place in the alcove. Suddenly the rock shifted, its tremendous weight heaving forward. Danny threw a wild glance at Zebek, who was standing where he'd left him with the flashlight in his hand, pointed at the floor, his mouth widening in a silent scream.

Then everyone jumped back as the rock tumbled into place across the passageway, confining Zebek in the pitch-black tomb of his childhood.

Epilogue

The hardest thing wasn't getting ready for the show. It was getting ready for Caleigh.

He'd put together the *Talking Heads* installation for about a hundred bucks, using coat hangers and old sheets to create the frameworks. The papier-mâché that covered the frames was made with newspapers from the recycling center, fifty pounds of bulk flour, and gallons of water boiled on the stove in his mother's kitchen.

Now the heads were more or less done.

There were seven of them, and it was just a matter of pasting on more and more layers of paper until they were sturdy enough to survive the trip to the gallery. For now, they stood in the basement of his parents' house, soggy and surreal, drying amid a forest of borrowed fans and dehumidifiers.

The more he thought about the heads, the more he liked them. Stranded in their suburban setting, they were almost as mysterious as their Easter Island counterparts. Soon he'd cover them with collages of newspaper headlines and photographs of anchormen and talk-show hosts. Mike Wallace and Oprah. Dan Rather and Barbara Walters. Once finished, the installation would say something about the way America elevates celebrity to a kind of gnosis.

That was the idea, anyway.

When he wasn't working on the heads, he was working the phones, getting a nursery to donate enough sod to cover the floor of the gallery and borrowing TV sets to install in the painted plywood plinths that his father had agreed to build for the heads. He was so busy he still hadn't gotten around to getting his tooth fixed. Not that he could afford it, but his mother – who winced every time he smiled – kept after him. "Daniel, I'll pay for it. Call it a late birthday present. You look like a derelict. *Please*."

But there was so much to do. He'd lined up a U-Haul to transport paintings and sculptures – including *Babel On II* – to the Neon Gallery. His father would help him partition that sculpture, color-coding each of the segments so that they could put them together again. Then they'd shrink-wrap the parts, using materials Dad ordered from a company called Mr. Shrinky. His father had already watched the instructional video. "All you need is a roll of polyethylene and a heat gun," he said, psyched with the idea. "You wrap it, you zap it, and the whole thing comes out solid as a rock. You know you can shrink-wrap a boat? You can shrink-wrap anything!"

It wasn't easy – it was a lot of work – but Danny could tell the show was going to be good. In fact, it was going to be great. And the buzz was building. According to Lavinia, *Culturekiosque* wanted to do an on-line interview with him and the *Post* was going to feature him in a Sunday piece about "three Washington artists on the way up."

If only his love life was half so promising.

But Caleigh wouldn't even talk to him. He'd thought about ways to win her back, but all of them were corny or expensive and sometimes both: A billboard or,

491

better yet, a skywriter. In either case, saying the same thing: *Danny* ♥ *Caleigh*. Baskets of daisies (her favorite) delivered to her office. An opera singer beneath her window. A puppy.

It didn't matter if the ideas were corny, actually. He could *do* corny. It was just that he knew they wouldn't work. What he'd done was unforgivable in Caleigh's eyes, and those were the only eyes that mattered. *You blew it,* he told himself. *It's as simple as that.*

Only it wasn't. He was sitting on the couch in his parents' living room, watching *Forrest Gump*, when the idea came to him. If Gump could dance with Elvis and shake hands with JFK – then there was hope for Danny, too. It wasn't exactly ethical, this idea that he had, but it did have one virtue that his other schemes lacked. It just might work.

"Last I talked to her," Caleigh's father said, "she didn't want nothing more to do with you, mister."

The *mister* hit him like a cruise missile, and he faltered. Over the years, Danny and Caleigh's father had come close to something like genuine friendship. They kidded around when they were together and genuinely liked each other's company. And now Danny was "mister." He sighed. He didn't know what to say.

"Mom and I, we just don't know what to make of this."

Mom and I. That was missile number two. Caleigh's parents called each other Mom and Dad. They were the linchpins of a big, hearty family that radiated generosity and good humor. They lived on a ranch in a place that was so wide open that you couldn't see a

492

single artificial light at night – except maybe a plane, and then it would be so high up you couldn't tell it from a star. Ultimate Frisbee with the tribe, shooting the breeze on the porch gliders, pinochle games. Without Caleigh, he'd be losing all that, too.

"Always thought you and Cay would get married one day," Clint told him. "Give us a bunch of artsy-fartsy grandkids." He chuckled.

"I *want* to marry her," Danny swore. "But I can't get close enough to ask her. She won't . . . she won't even talk to me."

There was so much to say that neither of them said anything for a long while. Finally, Clint asked, "So how'd you get on her shit list?" Before Danny could reply, Clint added, "Never mind. I oughta know better."

"It was . . . really stupid," Danny told him.

Clint sighed. A long prairie sigh. "Let me guess. Another dame."

A dame. Danny almost laughed. But what he said was: "It was in another country, and . . . I was drunk."

"That's exactly what *I* said when I hit Ralph Tanner's dog," Clint remarked. "Except it wasn't in another country and, besides – the dog was still dead, you know?"

"Yeah," Danny replied. "I know."

"Thing about Cay is, she don't have what you'd call 'a forgiving spirit.' "

"I know."

"Not at all."

"Not at all at all," Danny added. It was an Evans family expression, and Clint chuckled when Danny used it.

"You got that right," he said.

493

"Listen, Clint . . . I got an idea. Maybe a way of getting her back."

"Oh?"

"Yeah. But I need a video."

"What kind of 'video'?" Clint asked.

"Anything with Caleigh. Just a couple of minutes. A birthday party or . . . didn't you have something with her playing lacrosse?"

"What do you want it for?"

Danny hesitated. "It's kind of hard to explain."

"Why?" The guy didn't back off at all. Not at all at all.

"I don't know. I just thought . . . I thought if I made a film – and she liked it – it might help me to get my foot in the door."

Clint grunted – a grudging sound – and Danny could hear that he wasn't sure he believed him. Finally, he said, "I guess I could help you out."

"Great!" Danny heaved a sigh of relief.

"I just hope you get through to her," Clint told him. "I never thought I'd say this, because the first time she brings you out here, I was skeptical. A vegetarian *artist*? Hoo, boy. But I think you're the one for our Cay."

Jake helped him. They took the video to a place called Technicality and had it digitized. Then they downloaded the trial module of Simulacra software from Sistema's Beta site, loading it onto Jake's IMac. Danny was glad the Web site was still up, though Jake told him you could find similar software on other sites. There were half a dozen companies working on the technology.

Finding a useful rock-climbing video was harder.

Though Google generated 109,000 hits, only a few of the sites made clips available for downloading, and of these, almost all of them were of men. So it took a while, but after an hour he found what he was looking for: a young woman free-climbing a vertical rock face in Australia's Blue Mountains.

"And now," Jake said, "for the Vulcan mind merge."

The machine whirred as the Simulacra program executed. Two hours later, they had a fifty-three-second video that showed Caleigh in close-up, hanging off the side of one of the Three Sisters, her legs splayed as she searched for her next handhold. Then the camera drew back even more to show her from a distance. She was navigating an overhang suitable only for a fly when she missed her hold and fell, plummeting – not to her death, as it turned out, but thirty or forty feet before the rope caught. The camera zoomed in on the little figure, twirling above the abyss at the end of her brightly colored rope. Her eyebrows were raised, and there was a smile on her lips that seemed to say, *Thank you, Jesus!* – but which in reality was the reaction of a child seeing a birthday cake.

It was Caleigh to the core and, except for the fact that the climber was only nine years old and dressed not in rock-climbing gear but in jeans, cowboy boots, and a yellow sweater with pandas on the back, the video was entirely realistic.

"That's unbelievable!" Jake exclaimed.

"Isn't it!?" Danny said.

"I mean – whoa – it's a little scary."

"You think?"

They watched it again. And again.

"Caleigh's knuckles will turn white just looking at it!" Jake announced. "It's unbelievable – and you *will* make your point."

Danny nodded, feeling a little subdued and uneasy. This was the only way he could think of to get her back, but he was a little superstitious about it. Maybe it wasn't a good idea to use Zebek's software to trick the woman he loved into forgiving him. It could be bad karma. *Then again,* he thought, *it could be "poetic justice." And if there was ever a case of the means justifying the end, this was it because the end was love, and love is all you need. John Lennon said so. Or was it Paul?* He vowed to the god of Second Chances that he would be worthy of an answered prayer. Anyway, he'd tell her the truth, someday, he really –

"Earth to Danny! Hello?"

"What?" He looked up from the IMac.

"I said, you *will* make your point!"

"My 'point . . . '?"

"*You* know: that you can't believe your eyes."

He waited until the day of the opening, when everything was done – so he still had something to look forward to in case the video didn't work out. He bought an armload of daisies from three different flower shops and, to his relief, found that Caleigh hadn't bothered to change the locks at the apartment. So at least he didn't have to break in.

Being in the apartment was weird – and not just because of all the daisies he strewed around. Caleigh had boxed up all his belongings and stacked them in a corner. It was like visiting a place where someone had died. Especially with the flowers.

He was in the apartment for twenty minutes before he heard her on the stairs, and when she came in he was sitting on the couch with a flower in his teeth and his heart in his mouth. She did not look happy to see him.

"Cute," she said, hanging her handbag on the coatrack next to the door. "Very romantic. Now, get out."

He let the flower drop. "Before I go –"

"Out."

"Hang on – just gimme a second. Remember that e-mail I sent? Where I told you not to believe your eyes? Remember?"

She looked away. "No. Maybe. I don't know. The only e-mail I remember is your little video." She paused. "Do you mind? I'd like to take a bath."

"No. I mean, look – I didn't send that thing. Swear to God."

She peered at him. "Then who did?" Before he could answer, she threw up her hands and said, "And it doesn't matter, anyway. It doesn't matter who sent it!"

"But it does. It matters more than anything – because it wasn't real. Let me show you." He held up the video that he and Jake had made.

"No thanks," she told him, looking bored and angry, all at once.

"Caleigh. I want you to marry me."

Her face flushed. "*Marry* you?!"

"Yeah!"

Her eyes fell to the cassette. "And what's that? Part Two?"

"No. It's actually . . . you."

"Right."

"I mean it," Danny told her. "It's only about a minute long. And after you look at it, if you still want me to leave . . . I will."

"Deal," she growled. Plucking the video from his hands, she slid it into the VCR and waited for the cassette to load. With her arms crossed and her lower lip sticking out. Finally, she pressed PLAY.

He couldn't see her face, actually. She was looking at the TV with her back to him, but when he heard her gasp he knew that he had a shot. She was terrified of heights and anyway, there was no way it was real.

When she turned to look at him, her face was a study in bewilderment. "So the e-mail attachment you sent —"

"I didn't send it." He gestured toward the computer screen where, even now, the virtual Caleigh dangled from a rope. "It's a trick," he told her. "A software trick."

"Well, I know one thing," she said, her voice cool. "I know that's not me." There was something in her eyes, a skeptical glint that sent a shaft of dread through him. He felt shaky, almost dizzy, certain that somehow she recognized the video as the desperate ploy that it was. *Same brain,* he thought, and at that instant her gaze sharpened, almost as if he'd spoken.

She studied him for a long moment. He hoped that she might accept the video as a bridge to the future, a construct that would allow them to get past this. He hoped that she guessed the truth, but that even so she would find it in her heart to forgive him.

Finally, she took a couple of steps toward him, twirling a daisy between two fingers. She began picking petals off the flower. "He loves me, he loves me not, he loves me, he loves me not. . . ." He watched the petals float to the floor and the way they looked when they settled on it, like white teardrops. It didn't seem like a good sign.

"I love you so much," he said. He'd been holding his breath and the words came out in a high-pitched gasp, as if he'd been holding a toke of marijuana in his lungs and was speaking over it. "I love you so much," he tried again, aiming for a heartfelt tone. This time it came out in a kind of dense Darth Vader whisper.

And he did. He loved her so much. He loved her so much he could hardly stand it. He loved her so much he couldn't talk. He needed her for survival, like air or water.

"Dew called," she said, as if she hadn't heard a word he'd said. Half the daisy's petals had been torn off. She stopped removing them and twirled the flower back and forth between her thumb and forefinger. "I was really worried about you," she continued in the same matter-of-fact voice.

"You were?"

"But I'm not sure . . . I'm really not sure about marrying you," she told him, "if that was actually a proposal."

What did *that* mean? *It means she's not going for it,* he thought. He felt cold, frozen, immobilized. He prepared himself for the knockout blow. *Fuck you.* Or maybe just *Good-bye, Danny.* Finally, he managed to speak. "Why not?" This time, his words came out way too loud.

"Well," she said, "that new tooth, for one thing." She frowned and shook her head, but a little smile wrecked her attempt at a deadpan delivery. "It's not a good look for you."

His hand flew up to his mouth even as relief surged through him.

Then she leaned forward and smiled and tucked the flower behind his ear. "There," she said, "that's better."

If you've enjoyed The Eighth Day, *you'll be just as thrilled by the John Case novels available now in* Arrow Books

THE GENESIS CODE

Italy: a dying doctor makes a chilling confession to the priest in a remote hillside village.

Washington DC: a mother and her young son are savagely murdered. Their house is then burned down.

Joe Lassiter, the woman's brother, discovers a chain of similar killings around the world.

What is the link? Who are the shadowy, merciless killers? And what is the Genesis Code, the secret so unthinkable that powerful men do anything to make sure it remains in the grave?

'Impeccable in plot, immaculate in story resolution, moves with high skill from locale to locale and from suspense to suspense'
Norman Mailer

THE FIRST HORSEMAN

In the Book of Revelations, the Four Horsemen herald the arrival of the Apocalypse. When the First Horseman thunders forth, pestilence will spread throughout the land.

For the First Horseman is Plague.

Why is a disease-ravaged village in North Korea razed to the ground, its inhabitants massacred by the army?

Who are the shadowy terrorists willing to unleash epidemic and death on an unsuspecting world?

What is the deadly treasure that has been ransacked from eighty-year-old tombs in the Arctic Circle before an American scientific expedition can investigate their secrets?

For reporter Frank Daly this is the story of a lifetime. Yet the more he uncovers, the more dangerous the stakes become. Until at last he comes face to face with a shocking secret, pitching him into a harrowing race to prevent nothing less than . . . apocalypse.

'Expertly researched and chillingly related . . . terrifying . . . the sort of thriller which defies you to look again'
Express on Sunday

TRANCE STATE

Don't let them inside your head . . . Don't let them play mind games with you . . . They're merciless. And they'll kill to win . . .

The Institute of Global Studies in Zurich seems like the kind of philanthropic organisation any idealistic young scientist would want to work for. But when Lew McBride gets involved with them, his life takes a horrific turn . . .

Adrienne Cope's sister Nikki has just died in mysterious circumstances and the police suspect suicide. The only clues are locked away in the files of Nikki's psychiatrist, Jeff Duran. But when Adrienne begins to investigate, she discovers that Jeff Duran died years before and there is no official record of a psychiatrist by this name . . .

What are the powerful secrets that link Lew McBride, Adrienne Cope, Jeff Duran and the Institute? What is it that takes Adrienne and Jeff on a terrifying chase across the United States and Europe with violent killers on their trail? And why should the CIA be interested?

'*Trance State* is full of the kind of ripples that distinguish a good paranoid thriller, and doesn't stint on the enjoyable process of winding up its characters and watching them go'
Guardian

THE FAMILY

Mario Puzo

The last novel by the author of The Godfather

'We are a family,' Alexander told his children. 'And the loyalty of the family must come before everything and everyone else. We must learn from each other, protect each other, and be bound first and foremost to each other. For if we honour that commitment, we will never be vanquished – but if we falter in that loyalty, we will all be condemned . . .'

What is a family? Mario Puzo first answered that question, unforgettably, in his landmark bestseller, *The Godfather*; with the creation of the Corlenes he forever redefined the concept of blood loyalty. Now, thirty years later, comes Puzo's ultimate vision of the subject, in a novel that crowns his remarkable career: the story of the greatest crime family in Italian history – the Borgias.

'Head-long entertainment, bubbling over with corruption, betrayal, assassinations, Richter-scale romance, and, of course, family values'
Time

'Pure Puzo'
New York Daily Times

Buy Arrow

Order further Arrow titles from your
local bookshop, or have them delivered direct
to your door by Bookpost

☐	The Genesis Code	0 09 918412 5	£6.99
☐	The First Horseman	0 09 918402 8	£5.99
☐	Trance State	0 09 941648 4	£5.99
☐	The Godfather	0 09 942928 4	£6.99
☐	Omerta	0 09 929680 2	£6.99
☐	The Family	0 09 946474 8	£6.99
☐	The Fortunate Pilgrim	0 09 941799 5	£5.99
☐	Fools Die	0 09 941835 5	£6.99

FREE POST AND PACKING
Overseas customers allow £2 per paperback

PHONE: 01624 677237

POST: Random House Books
c/o Bookpost, PO Box 29, Douglas
Isle of Man, IM99 1BQ

FAX: 01624 670923

EMAIL: bookshop@enterprise.net

Cheques (payable to Bookpost)
and credit cards accepted

Prices and availability subject to change without notice
Allow 28 days for delivery
When placing your order, please state if you do not wish to
receive any additional information

www.randomhouse.co.uk